BOILER BEACH

Peter Tiernan

DEEPWOODS BOOKS

Published by Deepwoods Books.

ISBN 978-1-7325717-1-6

To all my great friends at Bruce Beach,
and to my wife Michelle, who has
always supported my writing,
and, who all will attest,
makes a mean potato salad
for our annual beach get-together

In memory of:
Dave MacLennan (1958-1988)
Sue Moulden (1960-2019)

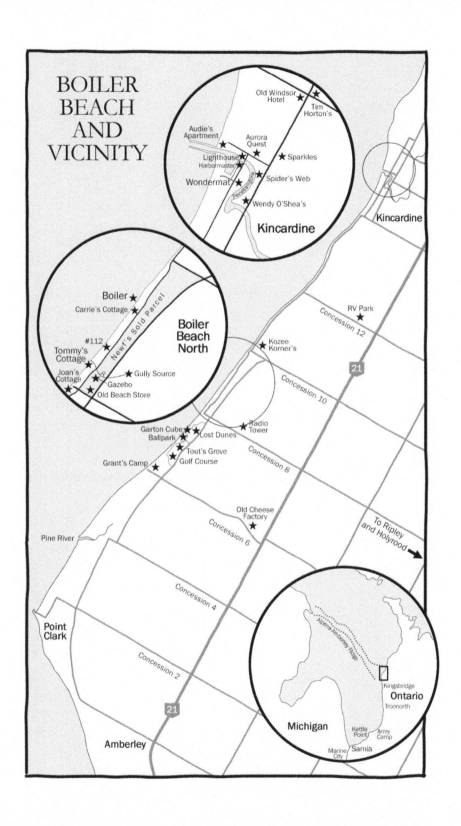

BOILER
BEACH
AND
VICINITY

Kincardine

Old Windsor Hotel
Tim Horton's
Audie's Apartment
Aurora Quest
Sparkles
Lighthouse
Harbormaster
Spider's Web
Wondermat
Wendy O'Shea's

Kincardine

Boiler
Carrie's Cottage
#112
Tommy's Cottage
Joan's Cottage
Gazebo
Old Beach Store
Gully Source

Newf's Sold Parcel

Boiler Beach North

RV Park
Concession 12
Kozee Korner's
Concession 10
21
Concession 8
Garton Cube
Ballpark
Lost Dunes
Radio Tower
Tout's Grove
Golf Course
Grant's Camp

Old Cheese Factory
Concession 6
Pine River
Concession 4
Point Clark
Concession 2
21
Amberley

To Ripley and Holyrood

Alpena-Amberley Ridge
Kingsbridge
Ontario
Troonorth
Kettle Point
Army Camp
Michigan
Marine City
Sarnia

CHARACTERS

Tommy McTavish – *Narrator*
    Frank McTavish – *Tommy's father*
    Kate Snyder – *Tommy's ex-wife*
    Cam McTavish – *Tommy's son*
Grant Rose – *Tommy's teenage friend, youth minister*
Gordon "Newf" Newfield – *Tommy's first beach friend, Holyrood farmer*
    Graham Newfield – *Newf's father*
    Walt Newfield – *Newf's great grandfather*
    Chloe Newfield – *Newf's daughter*
    Bethany Springer – *Newf's Mennonite neighbor*
    Rachel Springer – *Bethany's daughter*
Rob Garton – *Tommy's teenage friend, real estate developer*
    Mike Garton – *Rob's father*
    Les Garton – *Rob's grandfather*
    Bud Garton – *Rob's great grandfather*
    Leigh Garton – *Rob's aunt, Mike's sister*
    Jerry Sharp – *Leigh's husband*
    Bo "Bogue" Garton – *Rob's brother, Tommy's neighbor across the gully*
    Marc Garton – *Bo's son*
Sharon Beam-Garton – *Tommy's first love, Rob's wife*
    Jim Beam – *Sharon's father, last beach store owner*
Audie Bell – *Tommy's teenage friend, artist and shut-in*
    Aaron Bell – *Audie's father*
    Ashley Bell – *Audie's mother*
    Allie Bell – *Audie's sister*
    Andy Bell – *Audie's brother*
Joan Duncan – *Tommy's teenage friend, musician*
    Bryan Jones – *Joan's husband*
    Bruce Duncan – *Joan's son*
Carrie Sinclair – *Tommy's teenage friend, Canadian golf legend*
    Carl Sinclair – *Carrie's father, renowned golf course designer*
    Kaitlyn Sinclair – *Carrie's mother*
Wendy O'Shea – *Tommy's friend, Kincardine bar owner*
Jay Goodwin – *Wendy's ex-boyfriend*
Blair Henry – *OPP officer*
Paul Ackert – *Farmer and tractor collector*
Larry Moore – *Beach President and porta-potty installer*
Molly Moore – *Member of Grant's youth ministry*
Barb Bowen – *Tommy's old doctoral advisor*
Hugh MacLean – *Spider's Web bar owner*
Paul Magnuson – *Handyman*
Derek – *Friend of Chloe Newfield*
Doug – *Friend of Marc Garton*
Cecil George – *Grant's friend at the Army Camp*
Moe Norman – *Famous Canadian golfer*

I'll be damned if I'm going to let that gully overflow and slap up against my cottage. I don't care how many people yell at me for polluting the lake. I'm digging it out. They know what's at stake. Everyone who's accosted me has seen how the banks are eroding away. Just eyeball that side of my cottage. Every year, closer to the edge. Wasn't it enough that my shed toppled into the gully last summer?

What do they expect me to do? This cottage is all I have. I'm not like the Gartons and all the other Boiler Beach elites. I don't have piles of money to buy up old cottages, knock them down, and build monstrosities that ruin everyone's view of the lake. I have this rickety 100-year-old cabin, and if I lose it, I have nothing. The roof is coated in moss. The wood siding is rotting, and the yellow paint is chipping away. The plumbing's bad. The furnace is ancient. I have ants, bees, bats, and the occasional squirrel rumbling around in my rafters. It used to be a cottage other beachers envied. Today, it's considered a blight on these idyllic shores.

That's why I get no sympathy from these people. Six of the seven cottages south of me and two north, across the gully, are the legacy of Bud Garton, the patriarch who discovered Boiler Beach in 1914. Plundered is more like it. Locals knew about these shores well before Bud. Heck, it's just three miles south of Kincardine. And all the Mennonites east of Ripley used to park their buggies at the top of the hill, wend their way through the woods, and congregate on the beach by what's now Concession 8 Road. There's an old picture in town of a group of them, standing in the lake, fully clothed, performing a baptism. Of course, well before the townies and farmers, Indians roamed these shores—"indigenous people," as Canadians say. Whatever they're called—Chippewa, Ojibwe, Stony Point First Nation—you won't see them anywhere near this beach now. They've been pushed all the way south of Grand Bend, where some live in the abandoned Canadian Army Camp, selling hand-rolled cigarettes and bags of weed to the caravan of American vacationers driving north from Port Huron.

When I say Bud Garton discovered the beach, I mean he was the first to stake a claim here, cut a road through the woods, clear a lot, and put up a cabin. Actually, he and Walt Newfield were first. Newfield was the area's biggest cattle farmer. Garton owned a farm equipment company outside of Cleveland. He'd sold Newfield his first steam-powered tractor, and the two had become good friends, so much so that Garton convinced Newfield to help sell the new innovation to his neighbors. For a cut, of course. So, they were business partners, too. That's really the spirit that drove the whole cottage building venture to begin with. The two saw a way to make money off this beach.

You could argue that Walt Newfield is the rightful father of Boiler Beach. He's the one who brought Garton down from his fields on top of the bluff that looms over the Lake Huron shoreline. He's the one who mentioned you could buy the land for a song because no one could live there through the harsh winters. Yes, it was Garton who wondered whether a cluster of summer cabins might lure rich families from Detroit and Toronto. And he put more money into the idea, got dibs on the stretch of beach he wanted, and broke ground first. But if old Walt hadn't walked him down the hill, across the dunes, and into Lake Huron, Bud wouldn't have even known this paradise existed.

And maybe my neighbors wouldn't be such jerks. You see, I'm smack dab in the middle of Garton land. Sure, nearly all my neighbors are distant relatives. But that doesn't stop them from lording it over me. Never mind that they rent their places for a couple months a summer, while I own mine outright and live here year-round. To them, I'll always be the interloper. It has nothing to do with whether I dig out the gully or play my boombox too loud or get drunk and scare their kids. What sticks in their craw is the simple fact of my existence, the sheer travesty that someone other than a Garton should claim their hallowed sands. I see the way they look at me, that *you-don't-belong-here* sneer. They'll never stop hating me for stealing this cottage out from under them. Never mind that it was my dad, and I wouldn't exactly call it stealing.

Here's what happened: when Bud died, he gave all his cottages from 90 to 99 to his only child Les, who dutifully passed them on to his son Mike and daughter Leigh. The only one they didn't own was 96, right next to me, not across the gully, but to the south. It's the original Newfield cottage, and their son Gordie—better known as Newf—still owns it. He never comes around anymore, though. Anyway, when Mike died in 1990, he split his cottages between sons Bo and Rob. Bo got the two north of the gully and Rob got the six from 90 to 95. Mike's sister Leigh still had 97, the original Garton cottage that I'm in today. Then, in 1992, she passed away and willed it to her husband Jerry Sharp.

That's when the trouble began. Jerry was fishing buddies with my dad, Frank McTavish. A better description of it is they were drinking buddies who used fishing as an excuse to get the hell away from Boiler Beach. My dad and Jerry never did anything more ambitious than cast off the Kincardine pier and pay half-attention to their lines while they passed a fifth back and forth.

The beach suffocated Frank and Jerry, but not in the same way. For my dad, this cottage community was a microcosm of everything he wanted to escape at home. He was an advertising exec, and we lived in Bloomfield Hills, outside Detroit. My dad couldn't stand the snooty pretension that went along with living in such a ritzy suburb. He always told people we were from Pontiac, the blue-collar, largely black town north of us. The last thing he wanted in a vacation was to get thrown into another circle of status seekers. Don't get me wrong: not all Boiler Beachers are like that, but there's definitely a snobby faction—and it's getting worse.

My dad was perfectly content with the shack we rented 15 places north of where I am now, where the shore is rockier and there's hardly any sandbar. My mom was happy too, at least before I hit my teens. Then the discontent started, first in the form of wishes and hints—"Wouldn't it be nice not to fight through the rocks to get in the water?" or "Cottage 82 just went up for sale; the one with the big deck and the ankle-deep sandbar"—then as complaints and protests—"I'm ashamed to invite anyone over;" "Why do we stay here when we can afford something better?" My dad always shut my mom down when I was around, but I heard the late-night arguments. They were the first sign for me that there was trouble between them. There were a lot more after that. Then it went beyond signs to threats, and, finally, decisions. They divorced after I got out of high school.

As for Jerry, he suffered a different sort of suffocation. My dad called him the most hen-pecked man in the world. Jerry was nothing like the Garton men. They were loud, back-slapping bears, like Bud. Jerry was rail thin, slump-shouldered, and soft-spoken to the point of muttering. Leigh had apparently suffered enough as the only woman among overbearing men and picked Jerry for his docile nature. Then she proceeded to take on the role of bully she'd escaped. Maybe it was because she had the money in the relationship and owned the cottage. Whatever the case, Leigh made Jerry's life one long, agonizing stream of orders. "Jerry, do this;" "Jerry, don't forget that;" "Jerry, how many times do I have to ask you?"

No wonder the poor guy drank. Sometimes, in the afternoon, he'd sneak off to our cabin and play Jarts with my dad. If you don't know what Jarts are, imagine playing horseshoes with winged railroad spikes. You threw them underhanded, and their feathered ends would twirl through the air until the spike planted into the sandy soil, hopefully within a basketball hoop-sized ring. My dad tossed them like a flat softball pitch. Jerry lofted them high, as if they could catch wind and take flight. He never stayed long, an hour or so, and he'd check his watch the whole time. Still, he'd polish off three or four beers. Then, before climbing into his car, he'd tap out a handful of Tic-Tacs, chew them up, and hurry home.

I got the sense, even as a kid, that those Jart games were the only freedom Jerry could scratch out of his day. And it wasn't all because of Leigh's badgering. He didn't get much love from the rest of the Gartons either. Rob and Bo never warmed to him. They were at least civil, though. Most were downright hostile. The situation got worse after Leigh passed away, and everyone was shocked to learn she'd given the cottage to Jerry instead of Rob or Bo, the way Mike would've wanted. Knowing what a sore point his inheritance of 97 was, Jerry assured the Garton brothers he'd give the cottage back to them when he died, and even went so far as to show them the clause in his will that spelled out the arrangement.

It wasn't even a year after Leigh died that Jerry got sick. It started as a chest cold but got so bad he could barely get from the bedroom to the kitchen without running out of breath. He thought he should go to the hospital and get checked out. But he couldn't get anyone to take him. Bo said he was too busy at the Aurora Quest, the restaurant he ran in town. Rob asked if Jerry was sure it wasn't just a cold, and could he hang on for a day? Jerry didn't think he should wait. He called my dad. Frank took him right away. Good thing, too, because the doctors discovered pneumonia. He was in the hospital for a week and got intubated twice. During Jerry's stay, my dad visited every day, morning and night. Not another soul visited him. Not Rob. Not Bo. Nobody.

Jerry left for home right after he got released from the hospital. Two months later, he died. My dad didn't learn that Jerry had changed his will and left him the cottage until he showed up at the funeral. Bo accosted him as he was getting out of his car and accused Frank of taking advantage of a feeble drunk, tricking him into changing his will. Bo said they'd be taking him to court, and even if he managed to hang on to 97, they'd make his life such hell, he'd be begging to sell off. Rob pulled Bo away before things got really nasty. And Rob's wife Sharon, bless her soul, was kind enough to escort my dad into the church and sit beside him, even as the rest of the Gartons cleared out around them.

That's Sharon for you. I've known her since I was 16, and she's never been anything other than who she was the moment I first met her, running the register at her parents' beach store at the top of the hill. Kind-hearted and warm. Generous and pure. An old soul, as they say. Is it any wonder I fell for her right there and then, standing in line to pay for snacks, speechless and dazed by her sunny presence?

That first summer my dad owned the cottage was every bit as bad as Bo had threatened. He put up a wall of railroad ties on his side of the gully that shoved the creek closer to our foundation. Our outdoor water spicket got turned on in the middle of the night. The cottage was broken into. Furniture got taken, booze went missing, and most of the food in Frank's fridge was thrown on the floor. Mean shit, just as Bo promised.

A couple years after my dad got the cottage, I wondered aloud whether it had been more of a curse than a blessing to stick by a friend like Jerry. That's when my dad gave me his only valuable piece of advice. "The best thing that can be said about you is that you're a good friend. Most people think I'm an asshole. But the people who are my friends know I'd stick by them, no matter what. That's the thing I'm proudest of. It's the only thing I have that's worth passing on. So, don't ever dismiss it."

That winter, 1994, they found Francis T. McTavish, huddled in his car on the snowy shoulder of a lonely road in the Upper Peninsula, clutching a bottle of Jack Daniels, dead from exposure. He'd just completed his will that week—and he passed on to me one other thing besides his sense of loyalty. The cottage that had tormented him so much was mine. I was 28 years old.

Be a good friend. I've never forgotten that advice. Too bad it was about 10 years too late, long after I lost my closest friends. Some of them are people I've already mentioned. Rob shuns me. Sharon pities me as if I'm already dead. And Newf, my best friend, the guy whose cottage I practically lived at my whole summer childhood, doesn't even want to be in my sight. He hasn't been to cottage 96 since the problem between my son and his daughter a couple years back.

I get why Bo despises me. (Incidentally, everyone calls him "Bogue." As a teen, he was a heavy partaker of the sweet leaf, and his buddies gave him that tag. It went so well with his last name. Bogue Garton. Bogarting. As in a joint. Get it? Maybe you're too young.) Anyway, Bogue and I were never friends to begin with. But Newf and Rob, we were so tight we made a pact to be friends forever. And Sharon…well…how can things go so wrong that your first love, the most good-natured person there is, finds it unbearable to be around you?

That's a rhetorical question; I know the answer. One mistake 34 years ago. After it happened, when I woke up in the hospital, I remember thinking, *I'll have to live with this for the rest of my life.* I was right. I just didn't know how heavy the burden would get, how raw the pain would feel, and how unforgiving it would be. I'm being mysterious. I don't mean to be. I wasn't even going to get into that.

Forget I mentioned it. I'm more preoccupied with the rickety state of this cottage. And not all my old friends have abandoned me, either. Take today. I didn't get up at six a.m., before the sunlight angled over the eastern bluff onto the beach, because I was paying penance for that night in 1984. I did it so no one would give me shit about emptying out the gully. I'd dealt with my fill of that last summer, and I figured I might as well establish a new routine right off the bat this year, on the second weekend of June, when most cottagers started opening their places for the season.

And it's not like Grant Rose tried to sneak past me when he walked by on the beach. Truth is, he's the one old friend *I* would've avoided had I not had my back turned and head down digging. It's nothing personal. I'm not the only one who thinks Grant is a bit much these days. Ask around.

Honestly, I have no interest in running into anyone when I'm digging out the gully. I just want to be left alone. There's something therapeutic about stomping on the shovel and cutting a channel to the sloping shore, watching that dark thwarted water filling every scoop I make, following me with perfect patience until I free it into the rushing waves to join the vastness of Lake Huron. Then the water from the gully starts flowing, and that thin furrow I gouged out gets wider and deeper, until it becomes its own stream. Sometimes, I imagine I'm as small as the tadpoles that go drifting by, and the ditch I've dug is a canyon. Yesterday, I imagined the current was inside me, and my digging was a kind of extraction, a cleansing of pent-up malignancies. I do make a game of it. So, I wouldn't be surprised if I was muttering while I played.

"Getting the right answers?" Grant jolted me out of my trance. Who knows how long he'd been there? "What do you mean?"

"You were having a pretty spirited debate with someone." Grant gave me that strange, beatific smile of his, that loopy grin he's never lost, even with everything that's happened. To look at the guy, you wouldn't know he was a former drug addict and an ordained minister, entrusted with the spiritual well-being of the beach youth. No one up here wore the kind of clothes Grant did. He looked like some extra from the Coke "Teach the World to Sing" commercial. He shambled around in his flowing tie-dyed poncho, with tight red paisley pants and sandals. And his hair was down to his shoulders, still thick with just a touch of grey. Then there were those eyes, clear and wide, like he just woke to some wonder. And, of course, that goofy, gawping grin. Was he really as happy as he looked? Given his past, he didn't deserve it.

"Why are you doing this again, Tommy?" Grant patted my shoulder, that touchy-feely habit he had, his face scrunched up with Godly concern. After 35 years, I was used to the hand-patting part. The God thing, not so much.

"Doing what?"

"This." He pointed down at my little stream. "Are you really going to put yourself through all this grief for another summer?"

"Would you rather I let my cottage fall into the gully?" Grant waggled his head, considering the possibility. "Then I could pitch a tent in the dunes and get all kumbaya with you."

"Maybe you should."

"And when it got cold, we could drive south, commune with the Indians, and sell weed." I wasn't kidding about that either. That's exactly what Grant used to do before Rob let him stay in his bunkhouse. He'd spend his winters with the Stony Point First Nation tribe near Ipperwash National Park, or whatever they call the land now that they got it back from the Ontario government.

Grant's face went red. I'd gone too far. "That was their sacred land, you know," he reminded me.

"I know."

"Someone got shot defending their burial ground."

"Alright, Grant. I was just kidding."

"And they aren't Indians. This isn't some American western. They're indigenous people. I tell you that every time."

"I'm sorry."

Grant went quiet and gazed over the gully, up at the bluff. "There really is quite a lot of algae down this way," he said, practically whispering it. He knew it would set me off.

"Here we go."

"I'm just saying. I walk the beach every morning, and there's more algae along this stretch than anywhere else."

"So, I'm to blame for digging out this puny gully."

"There's less beach grass and willows too."

"How many times do I have to tell you? I don't pull the grass. You want to complain about that, go talk to Rob."

"You realize it's not good for the beach, eh?" he went on lecturing. "The grasses help catch the sand and protect the dune."

"Did you even hear what I said? I know the rules. I get the whole environmental thing. You got a problem with the plant clearing, take it up with the Gartons. But you aren't going to do that, are you? Because they're beach royalty. And I'm nobody."

Grant looked like he was going to cry. "That's hurtful."

"Sorry. It's just…I was hoping we wouldn't have to go through all this crap this summer."

"It's not like I haven't talked to Rob," Grant said. "But if you won't stop digging your gully, he won't stop yanking the weeds."

"So now it's *my* gully. Great."

I didn't mean it to be funny, but Grant laughed anyway. He patted me on the shoulder again, hopped across the stream I'd dug, and started north. But he didn't get more than half a dozen steps before he stopped and gazed back up at the bluff. "Funny, I've walked past every one of the gullies to the south. And all of them are nearly bone dry. Why do you have so much water?"

"Who the hell knows? Maybe Bogue set up a hose back in the woods and turned it on. I wouldn't put it past him."

"Are you and Newf still having troubles?" Grant asked delicately, like the mere mention of Newf might trigger an explosion.

"What does he have to do with this?"

"Well," he started with an exaggerated cock of his head, like he was explaining some complex adult issue to a kid. "Whatever water you're getting is coming off the bluff, and that's his land up there."

"Newf isn't that vindictive."

"So…you guys are good then."

"I didn't say that." I slung the shovel up onto my shoulder like a rifle. "Are you just being nosey now?"

Grant shook his head so hard his rock-star hair lost its hold. "No-no-no! It's just—we're all still friends, right? Can't friends care about each other?"

"Have you talked to Newf lately?"

"No."

"Neither have I. So much for friends."

Grant hung his head. Then he opened his mouth and held up a finger. He had one more thing to say. I knew exactly what it was. "Forget it, Grant."

"Just ask Audie. One more time. It's been 34 years."

"I ask her every year. You know the answer."

"You've told her I've changed, right? That I'm born again?"

"I did. But that probably hurt your case more than anything."

"You know I could just show up there. I know where she lives. Right down from the lighthouse. Sharon told me."

"Think that's a good idea, Grant? Think she'd react well to a surprise like that?"

He flapped his wide lips. "Just—just give it another try. Please? It there's anyone who can change her mind, it's you."

"Alright," I agreed just to end the argument. "I'll try again."

Grant pointed back at the bluff. "And I'm going to look into what's going on up there. This much runoff, it isn't right."

"Do what you have to do. Meanwhile, I'm going to keep digging this out."

That seemed to make him sadder than all the talk about Audie. "Will you at least try to see the bigger picture? There's a law at play here—the law of unintended consequences—and I'd hate to see you on the wrong end of it."

Call me paranoid; it sounded like a threat. "You know something I don't, Grant?"

"No. It's just—something's weird, and I know how these sorts of things go." He flashed me that goofy grin of his and continued on his way north.

I stood watching the gully drain until the stream was no more than a gritty trickle. Then I retreated to the cottage, congratulating myself; not a single run-in—if you don't count Grant.

I was putting the shovel away in the old, gutted outhouse that substituted for the shed I lost in last year's flood, when I heard footsteps on the bridge that crosses the gully. There was Sharon, bopping along the path behind the cottages. She was humming to herself, but as she crossed the walkway near my back door, she went quiet, slowed her pace, and tiptoed past.

"Hey, you."

She jolted, threw her arms up, and dropped a stack of papers she'd been clutching against herself. They blanketed the path.

"You scared me!" Sharon pounded a hand against her chest.

"I have that affect." Who could blame her? Put yourself in her shoes; seven in the morning, you're humming a happy tune, then a guy's standing in an outhouse doorway. "This isn't operational," I felt compelled to point out.

"I wouldn't think so," Sharon said. She went to scoop up the fallen papers. I bent down to help.

"That's okay." She warded me off with one hand.

"It's no trouble." I turned over one of the papers and realized why she wanted to keep me away. " 'You're invited,' " I read aloud. " 'Come celebrate the unveiling of the Carrie Sinclair memorial statue at the Garton cottage, June 29.' " I handed the invite over to Sharon. Her face was red. "I'm guessing this isn't for me."

Poor Sharon. I shouldn't have put her on the spot. "I'm sorry, Tommy. I tried. I told Rob you'd be on your best behavior. For this, of all occasions. But after that Labor Day episode..."

"No need to apologize."

Her eyes flittered away and stuck in their corners, staring at the morning sky. If you didn't know Sharon, if you hadn't seen that look before, you'd think she was putting on a face, flirting with you. God, she was pretty. Still. But this wasn't a look. This was sad Sharon. Thinking Sharon. "I wish—" She stopped abruptly.

"You wish…"

It rushed out of her then. "I wish we could all just put it behind us. Go back to how we were. That's what I tell Rob. There's nothing we can do about it. Forgive and forget, right?"

Her eyes locked on mine. "Right." Who were we kidding? No one will ever forget what happened to Carrie Sinclair, least of all me. That's what I don't get about people. For as much anger and sorrow as they may feel, do they think I feel it less? Can they not imagine what it must be like to walk around with this burden? I don't want to go into it. There's no point. But forgive and forget? Not going to happen.

"Let's make this a happy summer." Sharon tried another tack. "Don't—don't be a stranger. Come see us."

I laughed, and Sharon laughed along. But if she knew why I was laughing, she probably wouldn't be. Who did she mean by "us"? Her and Rob? In their new beach palace a mile south? With its four glassed-in stories and the elevator that took them to their wrap-around infinity porch? Was that where I could come see them? Or was it to the annual barbecue—that I annually got strong-armed out of? Or the Labor Day costume party I never got invited to…until I crashed it and made a drunken fool of myself?

"I'll be down with my floatie in an hour." I made a joke of it.

She forced a smile and started retreating. "You always could make me laugh." It came out as a lament.

I let her get past Newf's cottage and over on the far side of his property before I called out, "No invite for Newf, eh?"

Sharon turned slowly. "Rob's talking to Newf." That told me all I needed to know.

"So…he gets to go."

"It's business, Tommy."

"I get it." I walked back toward the lake and onto my mossy deck. Of course, I didn't get it. Weren't we both to blame? Maybe not equally. But still. That was the advantage of power around here. I had a dingy shack on the verge of collapsing, and Newf had acres of farmland looming over Rob's prime real estate, not to mention an indisputable claim to a cottage smack-dab in the middle of those properties. Newf was a force to contend with. I was nobody.

The waves were already kicking up, this early in the day. Swinging around from the north, too. Things were going to get rough.

W ARMED TOMMY SNOT!
Hilarious.

Here we go again. Every summer I have to deal with this crap. I own a laundromat across from the harbor in Kincardine. I'm kitty-corner from the lighthouse on the opposite end of the bridge that goes over the harbor channel. The store's name is "Tommy's Wondermat!" I've got this portable sign out front. It's about the size of a mattress flipped on its edge, with a black, flashing arrow on top. You've seen these kinds of signs in front of mom-and-pop shops. There are rows of tracks on the white plastic front to slide in eight-inch tall sheets of lettering. A few years back, someone started mucking with those letters. It happens about 20 times a summer. I drive in to open up and discover a new business venture: RANDOM TOMMY STEW! MR TOM'S WET DYNAMO! And my personal favorite so far: NEW! SODOMY MART TM. Trademarked; like I was worried about brand infringement.

Today may have topped that, though: WARMED TOMMY SNOT! Maybe the change will improve business. God knows, Tommy's Wondermat isn't killing it. Strangers walk in expecting to see shiny, space-age washers, see-through dryers, or some automated operation. Anything to warrant "wonder." But nope. It's just eight rusty washers, half of which work at one any time, and four clunky dryers. Truth be told, the laundromat up on Queen Street, Sparkles, is a lot better; newer, quicker, more reliable.

But they don't have a room jam-packed with musty old paperbacks. That's where the "wonder" comes in. The building I'm in is a Fifties prefab that managed to survive all the renovation going on around it as the neighborhood evolved from lifelong Kincardinites to well-heeled retirees. If it's more than 800 square feet, I'd be shocked. Anyway, after I fit in all the laundry equipment, there were a couple leftover rooms off to the side. I made the one with the sink my office—and threw a cot in there in case I got over-served in town and needed to sleep it off.

Then there was the big room in back. For the first year after I got divorced and bought the place, I used it as storage. I was still teaching English at the University of Michigan, and my grand plan was to open the laundromat for the summer and make a little extra cash while I wrote research papers. It didn't turn out that way. My drinking caught up with me, the head of the department learned that I'd been having an affair with a grad student, and she suggested I resign. It was a diplomatic way of telling me I was fired. So I moved away from Ann Arbor and became a Canadian business immigrant.

It was a hasty retreat. I had boxes of crap I didn't know what to do with. So, I put them all in there and packed the room to the gills. Being a professor—okay, an associate—I had tons of books. At least 20 back-breaking boxes full, the accumulation of two decades of reading for my job, reading for pleasure, and buying what I thought a clued-in prof should read. And those were just *my* books. My dad was a voracious reader himself, and a hoarder to boot, so I had boxes and boxes of lousy westerns and mysteries to clear out of the cottage.

When I got them all into the back room of the laundromat, I thought, I'm never going to lug these boxes anywhere else in my life. That's when the idea of a used bookstore dawned on me. I had a ready market. Vacationers were always looking for summer reading, but most didn't have room to clutter their cottages with trashy novels. Plus, there were all the boaters who came across from the harbor to wash their clothes and stock up on books before they sailed off. I make it sound like a thriving business. It isn't. Not by a longshot. In a good tourist season, I'll sell 3,000 books, but come October, I'll be lucky to sell three books a day. In my best year, I barely cleared 10 grand. And I'm not getting much more from the washers and dryers. Factor in mortgage and taxes, and this is not exactly a going concern. Still, it puts a little money in my pocket, gives me something to do, and takes my mind off my worries. I could do more with the place. But the simple fact is, I don't want to. Tommy's Wondermat is unambitious by design.

That's why this morning put me in such a foul mood. First, there was the whole warmed Tommy snot thing. But I was used to that. I switched the letters back, scanned the harbor to see if there were any boats I recognized—my latest theory is that the culprit's a seasonal sailor—then went about my routine. Checked that the washers were working. Checked the dryers and removed the lint. Unlocked the door to the book room. Made a pot of coffee. Rolled up the metal shutter that covered the counter window where people paid for books. Then plopped down on the stool there and was ready to preside over the day.

The coffee wasn't even done brewing before this joker charged into the store. He looked like he'd escaped from a Nautica catalogue—all tanned up; salt-and-pepper hair flowing back like he'd been tacking against the wind; boat shoes, baggy white pants, red-striped seersucker button-down, sky-blue sweatshirt tied like a scarf around his neck. Even before he said a word, my alarm bells were going off. He was the sort of tourist every townie dreads; just off the boat, never been here before, sense of entitlement. American. Just being real. Look, I'm American too. Ten years ago, that wouldn't have been a big deal. But now, with all the crazy shit our president says about Canada, people in town are more guarded around their neighbors to the south.

Mr. Nautica stopped dead center in the laundry room, glanced around with a haughty sneer, took out his phone, and started jabbing it. Then he put the phone to his ear, marched up to me, and stared me down. My presence either disappointed him or barely registered; he craned his neck to look past me, back into my office.

"Got a phone in here?"

"No."

"Then how would somebody get a hold of you?"

"They would come in during business hours."

He glared at me. "Okay, but—but what if I had to get a hold of you during off hours. Say I wanted to order something."

I laughed. "Then you'd go to Amazon."

For a fleeting moment, I thought, *is this guy going to take a swing at me?* "Let's say I'm down at my cottage, and I've got a bunch of books I want to sell, but I don't want to lug them here. Wouldn't it be easier just to call and see if you had any interest?"

"I'd have to see the condition of the books."

The guy sputtered out a raspberry, like I was the one being difficult. "I just want to find out if you're interested in the titles."

I'd had it at this point. "You want my cell phone number? Would that make you happy?"

"Yes, it would." He acted like he had a God-given right to it. I wrote the number down on a scrap of paper and slid it across the counter. "Hmm," he chuffed, like he didn't believe me. "So, I could call this right now, and it would be ringing in your pocket."

"That's how it works."

"Okay." Then he tilted his head. "I would've thought your number was 519-396-9639."

"Nope," was all I said, but the look I gave him couldn't have communicated more clearly: *You, sir, are a whack job.*

With that, he stormed out of my store.

That's the sort of nonsense I have to put up with here. The drunk who passed out and knocked over an entire shelving unit of books. The woman who had a temper tantrum over losing a couple quarters and took a tire iron to my washer. The local guy who comes in, spouting conspiracy theories and complaining about the chip that the RCMP—think Dudley Do-Right—implanted in his head. All these eccentricities used to amuse me. Anymore? They're wearing down my faith in humanity.

One morning into the tourist season, and I couldn't wait for lunch. I never lock the place up, just the book side; I leave the laundry area open. There's a change machine on the wall, and if anything breaks while I'm gone, oh well. A man has to eat. And have a beer—or two. The problem is, there aren't many places close by where I can get a good meal and have a drink. Actually, there's just one: Wendy O'Shea's. That's the little gourmet hipster pub on the south end of town. Not that there aren't other restaurants around—the Tartan Tusk, the Aurora Quest, the Spider's Web, Hawg's Breath. It's just that Wendy's is the only place I haven't been kicked out of. I had a lot of anger issues after my divorce, and when I drank, I tended to have trouble keeping my mouth shut. I'll leave it at that.

The only reason I'm still allowed in Wendy's is Wendy. I've had one too many in her pub too, popped off, and found myself swinging fists. But even with that, she treats me decently, better than I deserve. I'm sure it has something to do with that first summer she opened, about eight years back, when one of the local drunks lunged over the bar, clamped her face like a vise, and tried to kiss her. His mouth was open, and his eyes were closed with this clumsy look of anticipatory bliss. This was maybe the third time I'd been in the pub, so it's not like Wendy and I knew each other. My protective instincts kicked in; I grabbed an empty bottle of wine and bonked the guy in the head. You know how in the movies the bottle always shatters when it meets the bad guy's skull? This one didn't; it just made a dull thud. The guy was out like a light. His whole body went limp, he let go of Wendy, and his chin hit the round edge of the bar. Then he keeled over backwards and thumped on the floor. Kincardine's finest came, and they were going to take me in—just another Saturday night for Terrible Tommy—but Wendy set them straight. I remember overhearing one of the cops, that Blair Henry hotshot, who's such a pain in my ass, tell Wendy, "This guy might've helped you out tonight, but sooner or later he's going to make trouble in here."

From then on, I made it my mission to be on my best behavior at O'Shea's. I wanted to prove Blair wrong—and I needed a watering hole. But that incident isn't the only reason Wendy cut me slack. It also had to do with her not knowing my history, then finding out from me, rather than going by rumors. She's one of the few people who I got to start with a blank slate. No reputation. No prejudices. Just the slightest chance to be thought of as good. That's at least how I look at it. I can't speak for Wendy. By now, she knows pretty much everything about me—current problems, past sins—and she still lets me come into her hipster hangout, take a seat at the bar, and order a beer and one of her gourmet sandwiches. She doesn't judge me. Of course, she doesn't ask anything of me either. I'm a faithful customer. That's about the best that could be said. As long as I behave myself, I'm welcome.

Every time I see Wendy, I'm struck by the capricious nature of time, how it can ravage one person and burnish the other. I'm 52, just 12 years Wendy's senior, but I may as well be 25 years older. Smooth tanned skin, almond-shaped brown eyes, buoyant smile, and lustrous cinnamon-colored hair, Wendy exuded so much youth I still thought of her more as a vulnerable girl than the fearless woman she was. She'd get after me for saying that, but it was true. Wendy has reminded me more than once how close in age we are. The last time she did, I said, "Then why do you look so young while time has taken sandpaper to my face?" I knew the answer: remorse, anger, despair, booze; some combination thereof.

But you know what Wendy said? "Lotion." That was her answer. She was just too polite, too professional, too…good, to blurt out the obvious. So, the next day, I went to Rexall and bought a tube of Neutrogena. It was too tempting a fantasy to think my problems could be smoothed away with a good skin care product and a little vigilance.

The great thing about O'Shea's is it's hardly ever busy around lunch time. I can get in, have a meal, and get back to work in 40 minutes. Great for me; not so great for Wendy. When she and her ex, Jay, first opened eight years back, you'd have to get here before 11:00 to beat the lunch rush, or else you'd be waiting in line outside. Wendy's soups and sandwiches weren't like anything else in town. It was like some chic New York foodie paradise had been air-dropped onto Queen Street. And the amazing thing was, the place didn't even have a full kitchen. Wendy prepped all the food at her little house 10 miles away in Point Clark, drove it in, then microwaved, toasted, or crock-potted the final touches on site.

Her biggest draw were the homemade butter tarts. You may think you've had a great pecan tart before, but you haven't lived until you've tried one of Wendy's. First of all, they're huge, hockey puck-sized, held together in this delicately balanced, flaky, buttery bowl of crust. Then there's the filling itself; soft, caramelized, sweet but not sugary, a perfect mash of chewy, melty crunchiness. When she first opened, Wendy would bring in a dozen a day. Then word got around. By the end of her first summer, people were begging to buy them dozens at a time. They were pulling their cars into the alleyway beside the pub and buying tarts out the side door like it was a drug deal. After O'Shea's third year, a TV station out of London did a story on Wendy and her wondrous tarts. After that, people were driving out of their way, and boaters were making the long hike up from the harbor to visit the pub. Then, reviews on Yelp and Tripadvisor took tartmania to a whole new level.

There was one problem with all that demand. Wendy couldn't keep up. Or, more to the point, her mother couldn't. It was her recipe in the first place. Baking a few dozen tarts now and then to help Wendy in her new business venture was one thing. Working 40-plus hour weeks, on her feet, over a hot oven, was something else altogether. Still, she didn't want to stop. It was Wendy who put her foot down. She decided they would make eight dozen a week during tourist season, and if they ran out, they ran out.

She had the right. Unfortunately, people also had the right to complain about it online. Before long, there were as many reviews extolling the delectability of Wendy's butter tarts as venting that she kept running out of them. Wendy took all of that in stride, until two summers back when her mom passed away. Then the whole subject of tarts became a sore point. She still baked a couple dozen on weekends—but if you happened to miss them, too bad. And if you were outspoken enough to press her on tart inventory, she'd walk away, leaving it to the waitstaff or some knowing regular to explain things.

The tart situation had an impact on Wendy's business, no question. But what really killed traffic was breaking up with Jay. It's not like he was essential to the operation. His only real value was freeing Wendy up to leave before the clientele switched from tourists looking to get fed to locals looking to get drunk. Wendy never liked that part of the business; she was too mannered, too subdued, to put up with the beer-swilling crowd. Jay, on the other hand, loved the late-night scene. To him, it was a big party, the only reason anyone would want to own a bar. They were a good complement to each other in running the pub. Unfortunately, they weren't so good at living together.

You wouldn't know it if you just saw them a handful of times. But if you were there as often as I was, you'd pick up on the tension—a head shake here, an eyeroll there, the clenched jaws, the gradual change from bantering to muttering to silence. I wasn't surprised when Wendy told me Jay was leaving, but it did knock me back to learn a week later that he was tending bar at the Aurora Quest, that tourist trap my gully neighbor Bogue owned, just up from the lighthouse on my walk into town. It stunned Wendy too, but not nearly as much as what happened soon after.

The Aurora started selling knockoffs of her best sandwiches— the crabmeat melt, the chicken parm, the brisket and mushrooms. The recipes weren't identical, and not nearly as tasty, but good enough. And since the Aurora was closer to the harbor and could serve burgers, fish, and fries along with the sandwiches, people found less reason to trek up to Wendy's. If it were me, I'd sue Jay, or give him a knuckle sandwich. But that wasn't Wendy. Besides, Jay wasn't the real culprit. It was Bogue. None of the other restauranteurs in town were cutthroat enough to do what he did. Then again, no one had been in business as long as he had either. With all the crap the Gartons were putting me through, you can imagine why I wasn't inclined to give Bogue the benefit of the doubt.

That's a long way around explaining why I expected O'Shea's to be dead when I pushed open the door on that first Saturday of the summer. Instead, I walked into a veritable town meeting. The two tables in back were crowded shoulder to shoulder, a good 15 people. It took a second for my eyes to adjust before I realized they were all farmers, faces I recognized. And the one staring straight at me was Newf, my old best friend. He didn't flinch right away; it was more of a delayed shudder. He knew I saw him, yet his eyes started flitting all over the place. Then his hands went into fidgety action, patting down his jacket, adjusting his collar, drumming on the table. It couldn't have been a worse performance than if some bad community actor pretended to pretend that he didn't see me standing in the doorway. And this from a guy who's usually as stone-faced as they come. I turned away, but I made sure to smirk first, so he knew I wasn't pretending not to see *him*.

"What's with the farmer's convention?" I said to Wendy after I sidled up to the bar. She was making a bunch of Bloody Caesars.

"Quiet, Tommy. I don't want you ruffling anyone's feathers."

I mouthed my next question: *who?*

"It's all the farmers with land from Amberly to the Tenth."

"Why?" I said, too loud for Wendy's liking.

"Later." She hustled off with the Caesars. When I turned to watch her, I caught Newf sneaking out.

"Newf!" I shouted, louder than I should've, loud enough that everyone in the pub heard me. Newf kept lumbering for the door. His hip had gotten worse since I last saw him in the fall. "Newf!" I shouted again, as the door closed behind him. What was his problem? By the time I got outside, he was well down the street, swinging that dead leg as fast as he could. As big and barrel-chested as he was, and as spindly as his legs were, even the strong one, I was worried he might crumple to the sidewalk.

He was in his truck and starting it up before I had another chance to shout him down. If he would've headed the normal way to Holyrood, I might've stepped in front of the truck and forced the issue, but he pulled a u-turn and headed north. I had no idea what his plans were for the day. Maybe he was headed to the Beer Store or had a hankering for Tim Horton's Timbits. Maybe there was some other way to Holyrood I didn't know about. Anyway, it sure seemed like he was trying to avoid me.

By the time I got back into O'Shea's, the farmers meeting was breaking up. Paul Ackert, the guy who owned the land from the Eighth, just south of Newf's property, past Concession 6, gave me this droopy frown of mock sympathy. "You doing okay?"

"Why wouldn't I be?"

He shrugged and filed out with the rest of the farmers. That left Wendy and me alone. "What the hell was *that* all about?"

Wendy ignored me. "How're you doing, Tommy?"

"Adequate."

She laughed. "I hear you." It was our routine. Wendy would ask how things were, and no matter what, I'd answer, "Adequate." I got that from my old man, and for some reason, Wendy got a kick out of it. I liked to watch her laugh. So I kept telling her I was adequate, even when I was decidedly less so.

Wendy started scanning the shelves of music CDs that climbed from the floor well over her head. There were easily 500, and yet I knew what she was going to play: The Tragically Hip. Whenever she was by herself, she played the Hip. In bigger crowds, she played summery music that went down more easily. Drums pulsing, guitars jangling, the voice of Gord Downie started right off with ominous intensity.

> *There's no simple explanation*
> *For anything important any of us do*
> *And yeah, the human tragedy*
> *Consists in the necessity*
> *Of living with the consequences*
> *Under pressure, under pressure*

Wendy told me once what the song was about, how it drew on some Canadian writer's book. But I'd forgotten her explanation. Now, it was just a worn groove we liked to retrace when we had a moment to ourselves.

"Not exactly a bustling lunch rush," I pointed out, scanning the now-empty tables. As if she wasn't already painfully aware.

"It's the first weekend of the summer."

"Yeah. It'll pick up." What I didn't tell Wendy was that when I passed the Aurora on my way here, the tables on their deck were full. "Hey—at least the farmers love you."

"Newf said they'd be in every Saturday all summer."

"Well, there you go. That's a nice little kickstart."

"It's not enough." There was something gloomier in her tone than the typical gallows humor she fell back on to brush aside her business woes.

I figured it was a good time to change subjects. "So did Newf just wake up this morning and decide it was time to drop any pretense of not hating my guts?"

"You got me." Wendy made herself busy wiping down the bar.

It wasn't a very convincing performance. "Come on, Wendy. What's going on?"

She stopped wiping. "I didn't hear everything."

"Okay…" Out with it already.

"Sounded like Newf sold all his land along the bluff."

That knocked me back. "*All* of it?" He owned the strip of land from Concession 8 to 10, a good half mile long and 100 yards wide. My cottage was directly below the south end of that swath.

"You can't let Newf know I told you. It's all very hush-hush."

"Who's he selling to? That's a shitload of money."

"That part I didn't hear."

"Come on."

"I said I didn't hear, alright? I've already told you more than I should've."

"Okay-okay." I ordered a Rueben and a Steam Whistle. But I couldn't resist circling back. "Ackert's the only one who'd have that kind of money," I mused when Wendy set my beer in front of me. "But he's got more land than he knows what do to with."

Wendy didn't bite.

"And why was Newf acting so weird about it? What do I care if he sells that land?" At that, she raised her eyebrows ever so slightly. "What?"

"Nothing."

"You can't do that to me."

She let out a groan. "He didn't just sell the land on the bluff."

"He sold the land on the other side of the Lake Range Road too?" That would be huge. Newf owned all the way out to Highway 21, a good six square miles. Four thousand acres.

"No…" Wendy let it hang.

It took me a few seconds to put it together. "Not the cottage?"

Wendy wobbled her head, then went off to finish my Reuben. By the time she came back with it, two couples had pressed up to the far end of the bar. The more I thought of it, Newf's sell-off made sense. He'd been pulling away from the beach for years, starting in the Nineties, but more permanently since he and I had our knockdown-dragout a few years back, when I caught my son and his daughter messing around. Why hang on to a cottage he hated coming to when he could unload it for a million dollars? But who would buy something that expensive?

Oh shit. As soon as Wendy returned, I put her on the spot. "It's Rob Garton, isn't it? It has to be."

"I told you, I don't know."

"What I don't get is the land. What's Rob want with all that?"

I didn't expect an answer, and I didn't get one. Wendy knew about my troubles with the Gartons; we had that problem in common. And she knew about my falling out with Newf. But she wasn't exactly steeped in Boiler Beach drama and had no desire to be. In her line of work, it wasn't advantageous to form opinions of people based on gossip.

A few more people came in, nowhere near a rush, but enough to keep Wendy occupied. I barely tasted my Reuben. The more I thought about Newf's sell-off, the angrier I got. It was one thing to cash in on his cottage; that was his right. It was another to run away from doing it. What was so shameful that he didn't have the guts to break the news to my face? And if it *was* Rob who bought everything, what did he want with all that land? The cottage made sense; Rob had coveted it for years. But 20 acres of farmland so far from shore, down a deep bluff, into sloping woods. Why?

By the time Wendy came back around, I'd worked myself up into a foul mood. "Stop stewing about it. You don't even know what's happened."

"Give me a shot of Skyy."

"Nope. You promised."

"One shot, Wendy."

"No liquor; that's our deal."

"One shot, and I'm out the door."

"Okay. I'll give you a shot. But you don't get the other thing I was going to give you."

"Fine," I agreed. Then I thought twice. "What other thing?"

Wendy held up a peace sign. "Two tarts. The farmers would've cleaned me out, but I held back two. For you…and Audie."

Great. Now she was bringing Audie into it. "Not fair."

Wendy cocked her head with a smug grin. She knew the power of her tarts—and the hold that Audie had on me.

"Awright. But nothing stops me from driving out to the LCBO and buying a whole bottle."

"Nothing other than sheer stupidity, no."

Wendy had me there. Getting back into hard liquor after six months off would've been a stupendously bad idea. I satisfied myself with the backwash at the bottom of the pilsner. Wendy went to box up the tarts. By the time she came back, I'd already put a 20 on the bar. "Keep the change."

"These are on me," she replied, patting the top of the box.

"Still."

"By the way," Wendy slid the tarts my way, "why do you need to warm them? They're just as good cold."

"I think they're better warm."

"Fair enough, but can you set aside some cold ones for me? I like mine freshly picked." I was at a complete loss. "The Tommy snots," she clarified. "I like them nose temperature."

"Very funny." Wendy loved to razz me about my sign.

"You have to admit, it's an upgrade from the Sodomy Mart."

"I'll give you that," I laughed. And for the briefest time, my mind skittered off my problems. Once I was out in the glare of the sun, though, with the long walk ahead, there was nothing to distract me. I got back to the Wondermat all out of sorts. Someone asked me about a Ludlum novel, and I gaped at them like they were speaking Swahili. I yelled at a girl who was shaking sand out of her towels. I had to get out of there, get my head clear. The only way that was going to happen was to have it out with Newf.

Half an hour after I'd gotten back from O'Shea's, I locked up the bookstore again and took off for Holyrood.

It's not my favorite place to go. You have to drive through Ripley to get there, and after all these years, I still try to avoid that little nothing town. You can hold your breath on one side of it and make it all the way to the other if you hit the four-way stop right. The two-laner out to there is called Boiler Beach Road because it's a straight shot from the public beach at Concession 8, up the steep hill, and all the way 13 miles to Holyrood. Of course, I was coming from Kincardine, so I had four miles on Highway 21 before I got to the road to Ripley.

I don't know why I was expecting anything different from the last time I'd driven that stretch, a few years back when I gave my son Cam a ride to see Newf's daughter Chloe. Hell, it really wasn't any different than it's been since I was a kid—same narrow lanes; same golden fields rolling to the horizons; same lonely farmhouses, deep creek beds, and meandering herds of cattle.

The only noticeable change over the last 15 years has been the outbreak of wind turbines. They're everywhere. Dozens surrounding Ripley, hundreds amassed along 21, a 90-mile phalanx from Grand Bend all the way to Southampton. Farmers get $8,000 a year to let a company put a turbine on their property. Some people have two dozen. Think about that. Nearly 200 grand a year, just to have a few giant pinwheels spinning around in their fields. Of course, not everyone is thrilled with the turbines. There have been thousands of complaints about the eerie, high-pitched waffling sound they make. Some can't sleep. Others claim the noise has caused everything from stress and nerve disorders to outright depression. Then there are those who object to turbines on environmental grounds. They do kill their share of birds.

For most, though, me included, the aversion to these whirring monstrosities is more visceral. I could say they ruin the view and leave it at that—but that doesn't begin to explain it. You have to know this place. You have to have in your mind what this place used to be. It's a feeling that goes far back. It isn't a memory. It's deeper than that. It's elemental. And when something as jarring as a wind turbine disturbs that feeling, it's like getting shaken awake from a beautiful dream.

So, I was driving to Ripley, and you could see forever. I was in my 1988 Lincoln Town Car, the grandpa-mobile, as Grant likes to call it. I don't deny it's a tad on the fusty side, but the vehicle has class. Black body and rooftop, black interior, blackened windows; it could pass for a limousine. The thing floats down the road like a hovercraft. It's also rock-solid; that's really why I bought it. I've had my fill of twitchy muscle cars. Today, though, I got a wild hair, pressed the gas, and watched the speedometer climb. Sixty. Seventy. Eighty. I was going to get to 100. See if it felt the same as it did 34 years ago. As the gauge passed 90, my heart tensed. Tighter...tighter...clenching. When I hit 100, I released everything—foot on the gas, my breath, that tension, the fear. I glided, letting myself slow down. And 70 felt so, so slow. By the time I hit the trees lining the outskirts of Ripley, I was already under 25.

I cruised past Ripley's only school, then between the smattering of ranch houses two blocks before the heart of town. I was still gathering my breath when I reached the MacKenzie & McCreath funeral home. Maybe it was because I was going so slow, but that was the first time I considered how strange it was for a funeral home to be mixed in so naturally with common dwellings. With its white siding, green-striped awnings, and that walk-out deck above the front door, it seemed like the most welcome place on the block. Then, on the other side of the street, came the old church—spare, narrow, windowless, sandstone brick. If you had to guess which practice the townspeople cherished more, the dull routines of faith or the festive occasion of death, you wouldn't pick living.

I was going too slow. For the first time since easing off 100, I sped up. Just a tap. But at that very moment, a tractor pulled out in front of me. Why? Nobody was behind me. I didn't want to risk passing so close to the four-way stop. So, I waited. The tightness came back. That knot in my chest. I took a deep breath to loosen it. I backed off the tractor, gave myself space, said out loud, *stay in the here and now.* We were stopped at the main intersection. There

were three cars ahead of the tractor and back-ups from every direction. You rarely saw traffic like this in Kincardine let alone Ripley,
and people weren't paying the best attention to when their turn
was. *Let it go, McTavish. Look around. Be present.*

At one time, someone had ambitions for a bigger downtown.
The building outside my passenger window was a stocky structure,
made from the same sandstone brick as the church, two stories
high, storefront on the bottom, windows on top, a modest attempt
at cornice work arcing below the flat-top roof. The building
reached around the corner, gathered in a few more stores, then
abruptly stopped. Same thing across the intersection; another L-
shaped building, except all but one of the storefronts were boarded
up. On the other side of the road, out my window, a warehouse,
an empty lot, a tiny park; nothing to match the early aspirations of
those facing structures.

My turn to go. Finally. As I crept through the intersection, out
of the corner of my eye, on the bricks beside a boarded-up door, I
caught the faded painting of a wreath, as big as the tractor's back
tire. Inside that circle, in ghostly calligraphy, the words were barely
visible: "Mary's Flowers. Est'd 1970." How had I never noticed
that before? The tractor grinded along in front of me. Forty-eight
years ago. Was Mary still alive? Did she ever drive past this shadow
of a sign, this pale emblem of her lost dream? Did she look away?

God, I hate Ripley. I checked oncoming traffic, hit the gas, and
pulled out from behind the tractor. A horn blared. The car that was
behind mine swerved onto the shoulder to my left. He'd been more
anxious to get out of town than me. I made eye contact with the
driver. He threw up an angry hand. I flipped him off. He roared
away, past the tractor, and out into the big emptiness before Holyrood. When I followed him, the old farmer atop the tractor looked
my way, not glaring, but disappointed. Like he knew who I was.
And what I'd done here.

Holyrood doesn't even deserve a name. It's a crossroads in the
middle of nowhere, with a collapsing barn on the near corner, a struggling abattoir across the road to Lucknow, a tacky

McMansion kitty corner from me, and a cluttered century-old general store. The one thing these four misfit places had in common was that Newf owned them. It would've been more fitting to call the corner Newfield's Hovel.

For some odd reason, though, Holyrood was crowded when I came to the crossroads. Cars were lined up on every shoulder. I had to park a good five cars before the stop sign. When I got out, there were two Mennonite women eyeing me from behind a roadside stand. I couldn't very well ignore them. We were practically facing each other. The older woman knew me, the one with the darker blue dress and the white bonnet. It had been a couple years since we'd seen each other, but she wasn't the kind you forgot, despite the self-effacing clothes. She was arrestingly pretty. And she had to be 40 by now. It was those piercing blue eyes, that snowy skin, her placid expression.

I'm sure I wasn't hard to recognize either—even with all the weight I'd lost and the buzz cut the barber in Kincardine talked me into after years of shoulder-length hair. The white patch of skin over my left eye was a dead giveaway. After the accident, they'd taken the skin from my thigh and tried to blend it with the color of my forehead, but it didn't heal exactly right. The pigments never matched, and I decided not to bother with it. Usually, I covered the scar with sunglasses, but I'd forgotten them at the Wondermat.

"How've you been, Beth?" I approached the stand like it was the reason I'd come to Holyrood.

"Fine," she said under her breath, eyes fluttering down to the merchandise crammed on two card tables.

"As soon as I heard you were selling your—your..." I scanned the tables: pickles, jams and other jars; wooden toys, wildflowers; asparagus, strawberries, eggs. "Your strawberries, well, I just had to drive out here and get some."

Beth was walking away before I looked back up. I gave the younger woman an awkward smile and grabbed a carton of strawberries. "How much for these?" She told me three dollars. I gave her a twenty. While she was making change, I took a closer look at the toys. There were three wooden arks the size of footballs, and several pairs of carved animals. They'd arranged them in a line, heading up a long ramp into the ark. "And what's this cost?"

Her cheeks flushed. She looked back for Beth, who was well down the dirt drive, on her way to the buggy beside the collapsed barn. "I'm sorry. I don't know. If you can wait, I'll go ask."

"Never mind." She seemed relieved. I was taking the change out of her hand when I had another thought. "How much for a bunch of wildflowers?"

She knew that; three bucks. While she was wrapping the flowers, I heard children laughing behind me. Across the road, a handful of little girls swarmed around a life-sized cartoon ice cream cone with googly eyes, a silly smile, and whipped cream-swooped hair. He was standing between two cupcakes with big, clown-like shoes, and there were holes in the billboard, right in the middle of the cupcake frosting. The girls were taking turns sticking their faces in the holes. One of the dads stood in the road, snapping pictures with his phone.

"What's that all about?" I asked the woman.

Her face lit up. "It's the Ice Cream Trail! We finally made the Huron-Kinloss Ice Cream Trail."

"We" who? Last I knew, Newf owned the Holyrood General Store. The Mennonites had nothing to do with it, other than being Newf's most reliable, year-round customers. I took another look at the billboard. Sure enough, there beside the smaller cupcake was a pink and chocolate-colored logo for the Ice Cream Trail. "Ah…" I nodded, like the gravity of being included on the Trail had dawned on me. "And what did you say your name was?"

She blushed. Of course, she hadn't. "Rachel," she murmured.

"Well, thank you, Rachel." I shook the flowers at her. Then I put them and the strawberries in my car and hurried to the store.

One look at the crowd inside, and you would've thought Justin Trudeau was making an appearance. That would've been about as plausible as if he showed up in my outhouse. The place wasn't so much a store as a hoarder's shack. Newf hadn't bothered knocking down the walls separating the chopped-up rooms. Some of the stuff had been there for decades: shovels and brooms and buckets;

mousetraps and fishing tackle; firewood and straw hats. You name it. There was a hallway devoted to spare parts for the Mennonites' buggies. And on the top shelves of the wooden racks behind the register, spanning the entire wall, a long line of rubber boots, at least 30 pairs, stood in formation, waiting apparently, for a rush of people panicked about the next epic flood.

I edged past the bottleneck of tourists waiting near the register. Newf was there, taking orders for ice cream. It looked like that was the only thing they were selling. Beside him, his daughter Chloe dug scoops out of tubs in three horizontal freezers. I managed to get past both her and Newf without them noticing me and got in line at the far end of the store. I was going to keep my face buried until I was right on top of them. I didn't want to give Newf time to figure out how to escape. And I just plain didn't want to deal with Chloe; I'm sure the feeling was mutual.

But after one glance her way, I couldn't take my eyes off her. She was as tall as I remember, and her blonde hair still had that childlike luster. But she wasn't skin and bones anymore. I was looking at a woman now. And her face had lost that guileless serenity. Maybe it was because she was working so hard, but Chloe hardly looked like the carefree girl from the cottage next door.

What really drew my attention, though, were her arms. Or I should say "arm," the one prying the ice cream out of those tubs. I didn't know many men with an arm as chiseled as Chloe's. Right on the spot, I thought of Popeye; that's how freakishly big it was, with that long cord of muscle from wrist to elbow and that bulging bicep. Her other arm, by comparison, looked deflated. How many hours of scooping would you have to put in to get such a gun?

"Mr. McTavish?"

I jolted as if I'd been caught staring down her shirt.

"Oh, for God's sake," Newf moaned. "What are you chasing me all the way out *here* for?"

"What are you running from?"

The people ahead of me looked alarmed. So I was louder than Newf, and my tone was a touch angrier. So what? Did they think I was going to jump over the counter and take a swing?

"You see I'm busy here, eh?"

I lowered my voice. "You sold all that land to Garton, you sold your *cottage*, and you didn't have the guts to tell me that to my face?"

"Chloe, get him an ice cream cone."

"I don't want an ice cream cone."

"Take the damn cone, go outside, and I'll be out in a minute."

"I can't eat ice cream," I muttered, embarrassed as I always am when I have to explain my dairy problem.

"Oh yeah. Chloe, give him some lactose-free butterscotch."

People were eyeing me now. The old guy beside me had the audacity to smirk. Fine, if Newf was going to put me on stage, I'd return the favor. "Why don't you give her a break and scoop the ice cream yourself. The poor girl's arm's going to explode."

A teenage boy laughed out loud. His mother gave me a smile of support. Newf just glared. "Mind your own business."

Chloe sculpted a hefty scoop and handed it to me. I took my wallet out. "No-no-no." Newf waved me off with an exaggerated sweep of his hand. "On the house."

I wasn't about to argue. As I took the cone, Chloe held out a little wafer of paper. "What's this?" I asked, reaching out for it.

"An Ice Cream Trail sticker. To prove you've been here."

Newf let out a booming guffaw. "He doesn't need that. He's not collecting the stickers, not with his tummy troubles."

Someone snickered behind me. I snatched the sticker from Chloe before she could take it back and stomped out of the store.

It was 10 minutes before Newf came outside. "You've got a lot of nerve, bringing Chloe into it."

"I wasn't kidding. Have you looked at her scooping arm lately? It's bigger than most men's."

"She's 18 now." Newf came down the steps. It took some doing, what with his bad leg. I had a fleeting notion to offer him a hand. But I knew he wouldn't take it. "She doesn't do anything she doesn't want to do. You of all people should know that."

Here he was, taking his digs at me, hinting at my son Cam's situation without coming right out and saying so. I let it go. We had more pressing issues. "I get why you want to change the subject. But I'm not leaving here until I find out why you sold out to Rob—and why you're so damned afraid to tell me about it."

A couple cyclists glided up to the store, stopped in front of us, and started chaining their bikes to the stair railing. Newf hobbled away, motioning me to follow, around the corner by the Ice Cream Trail billboard. "I don't know why you're shocked by this," he said. "I've been trying to sell that stretch of land for years. And you know I don't like going to the cottage anymore."

"So why run away from me? Honestly, Newf. I was worried you'd take a tumble and hit the pavement, you were going so fast."

"You making fun of *me* now?"

"No."

"Then don't give me that pity bullshit. I get around just fine."

This wasn't going the way I imagined. I was the one who was supposed to be mad. Newf was making it about ancient history. It didn't help to have that stupid, bug-eyed ice cream cone grinning over his shoulder. I stepped back so I wouldn't have to see him. Even still, I couldn't get my anger back. "Come on, Newf," I found myself begging. "I know we're not best buddies anymore, but I never thought we'd turn our backs on each other."

Newf wagged a finger, started to object, then quit with a growl. "I just need to be done with the beach," he finally spit out. "My life is here now. I know what you're thinking: *wasn't he always saying he wanted out of Holyrood?* That's what I used to think before Jill died, and Beth and I—" he glanced across the road. Beth had come out from hiding in the buggy and was straightening items on the card tables. "You know," Newf lowered his voice, "nothing says we have to do penance forever. Everyone deserves to be happy."

"I know."

"*You* deserve to be happy."

"Jesus, Newf. I didn't come all the way out here to get into *that*. Can we get back to the part about you slinking out of Wendy's?"

"I knew that's how you'd take this. I know I'm leaving you surrounded down there. Gartons on both sides now, Rob looming over you on the bluff. So, when I saw you in the bar, I just—I wasn't ready. I—"

"Looming over me on the bluff?" I interrupted.

"I—I don't know," he stammered. "He's got plans."

"What kind of plans?"

"I don't know, alright? Some venture. That's what he called it. And I didn't push him."

I didn't buy it. "Swear to God, you don't know?"

"Swear to God? What are we, Tommy? Ten years old? I don't believe in God, but I'm telling you, I don't know what he's up to, alright?"

"The guy who lives in the heart of Mennonite country doesn't believe in God…"

"And you do?"

He had me there. "I don't know. I just ran into Grant and got a big dose of the Lord. Guess it hasn't worn off yet."

"Next time you see him, tell him to stay away from Chloe. He managed to coax her down to that little revival of his and fill her full of nonsense."

I'd never heard Newf run down Grant like that before "I wouldn't worry." I stood up for him. "Grant's harmless."

"You honestly believe that—after all he did?"

"Whatever happened to the whole not-having-to-do-penance-forever thing?"

Newf scowled at me. We both went quiet. A car coming north from Lucknow turned and parked behind us. There seemed to be more I wanted to say, but I couldn't for the life of me think of what it was.

"I better get back inside." Newf broke the silence.

That unblocked things. "Sorry about Chloe. I shouldn't have brought her into it like that."

"You were mad. I get it."

I couldn't help myself. "I will say, though—just an observation—her right arm *is* noticeably bigger than her left."

Newf turned to face me full on. "And your point is?"

"Maybe a little time on the register wouldn't hurt."

"You done?"

"Or, I don't know, maybe developing the left hand."

I didn't mean it to be funny, but Newf lost the scowl and burst out laughing. "You are a piece of work, Tommy."

"Okay. Well, I'd say, *see you around*, but I guess I won't be any-more, will I?"

"Probably not." He looked hard into my eyes. "Go easy on yourself, eh Tommy?"

For some reason, that ticked me off. "Yeah. Sure," I said, making it drip with sarcasm. Then I turned my back on Newf before he could do the same to me.

As I hurried across the road, Beth was staring me down. I had my car door open and was getting in when I heard, "Fifty dollars."

I eyed her over the roof of my Lincoln. "Excuse me?"

"The ark. And the set of animals. Fifty dollars."

"Ah, yes. Good to know." I bent to get into the car.

"All handcrafted. Quite a bargain."

I straightened back up. She was holding the wooden ark in front of her now, displaying it expertly, like she was on some home shopping network.

"I don't have 50 dollars on me."

"We take checks."

Why is it so hard for me to tell white lies? All I had to do was say I didn't have my checkbook, get in the car, and drive off. But I *did* have my checkbook, and after all, I was the one who asked about the damn ark in the first place.

"Great," I said. After I wrote the check and exchanged it with her for the ark and a bag full of animals, there was a moment—I'd call it brief, except that so much seemed to be conveyed within it—where we looked flush at one and other. And for the first time.

"Your face doesn't look so bad," she whispered, squinting at my scar. I couldn't tell if that disappointed her or not.

On the way back to Kincardine, I got at least a dozen phone calls from Audie. I didn't hear the first couple because I'd left my phone in the car in Holyrood. I ignored the next few. Then the last ones, she hung up before I could answer. I pulled into Sobeys grocery store outside of town and checked my voicemail.

Audie always called me on the days I was coming over to ask if I'd pick up groceries. Her sister Allie from Owen Sound shopped for her once a week, but there were certain things—Pringles salt and vinegar chips, M&M Food Market brownies, Mackintosh Toffee, Player's cigarettes—that she refused to buy for Audie. That was my job, purveyor of vices.

Audie wasn't thinking about shopping. "I thought we agreed you were coming to lunch today," she said in her first message. (For the record, we didn't.) "Maybe you just forgot," was the sum total of the second. Message three: "I made soup, but I suppose I can refrigerate it." Number four: "I'm not mad. Just need to know what to expect." Five: "Are you alright? I don't see your car at the store." Then: "Tommy, if you're drinking, I promise I won't be mad. Just let me know you're okay." And finally: "Someone fiddled with your sign again."

It was true. When I pulled into the Wondermat, I was exhorted to TRY TOM'S DEMON MAW! Somebody had the temerity to deface my sign in broad daylight. This was a first. I stormed into my place, saw two teenage boys back by the washers, and marched over to them. "You know anything about my sign?" They gawked at me. Their heads swiveled in unison to share a look of confusion. "Don't play dumb with me," I told them—right before their dad came out of the washroom and asked what was going on. I played it off like I just wanted to know if they'd seen anything, and he seemed to buy it. But the entire episode left me edgy. I disappeared into my office without bothering to unlock the book room or slide open the metal shutter.

When I finally called Audie, she acted like I was phoning out of the blue. "Hey Tommy," she said indifferently. "How are you?"

"Oh, you know," I said, mimicking her fake apathy, "dead drunk, wandering the beach."

"That's not funny."

You can only joke so much with Audie. "I told you last week, you don't have to worry about me. I appreciate the concern. But if I don't answer after 10 calls, it's either because my phone's off, silenced, or lost."

"I didn't call 10 times." True. It was more like 15.

"Anyway, I never said I was coming over for lunch. I don't know where you got that. But if you want, I can come over now."

"Only if you want to."

I was hanging up when Audie asked, "What's a demon maw?"

"The jaws of the devil, I guess."

"Why would they put that up?"

"Audie, it's just some idiot jumbling letters."

"Still, you have to admit…" She hung up then, like she was afraid to finish the thought.

Audie's apartment building was right down from the lighthouse. Her living room window looked out over the harbor and south to the shore that bends for 10 miles to Point Clark. Somewhere in there is the run of 200 cottages that makes up Boiler Beach, where Audie and I met. Besides her sister, I'm the only person who regularly visits Audie. And if it weren't for Boiler Beach and what she went through there, I probably wouldn't bother. Visiting Audie isn't my idea of fun.

It took Audie a good two minutes to open her door, never mind that I'd just gotten through telling her I was coming. She didn't greet me when the door swung open. It was a game she liked to play, concealing herself behind the door as I took a few steps in and glanced around stupidly. Then, when I turned to her, I'd give a start, and she'd giggle. It was the same thing now as a hundred times before—hide-and-seek with a child who always picked the same easy hiding place.

"Woah!" I gasped in surprise.

She kept her head down, but I could see her smiling back, proud of how clever she'd been. When she looked up, the child in her was gone. It was those eyes, the tilt of them, like the outer edges had been weighed down by something hard and fixed, a force stronger than time. They were the only obvious sign on her face that anything, even time, was weighing on her. Whenever I see those eyes, it breaks my heart. That's why I try not to look at Audie too long—and why I keep coming to see her.

She moved out from behind the door and came right up to me, closer than anyone but lovers could endure. "What's in there?"

"These," I pulled out the wildflowers from Beth's stand.

"Oh Tommy." She cupped her hand over her mouth. "That's so…so kind. So—"

"They'll need water," I jumped in before she started crying.

Audie snapped out of it with an actual jolt. She went into a whirl of activity and flurry of apologies. "I'm so sorry. Where's my head? Let me find a vase." She flung open cabinet doors, crouched down to pull out drawers, rooted through her pantry.

"How about we just put them in that bucket for now?"

"Yes, yes! Of course, of course! I'll put them in the bucket," Audie repeated. "For now. Just for now." She pulled a red bucket out of the pantry, set it under the faucet, and started filling it. I handed her the bouquet and stepped away. Audie got nervous when I watched her. I walked out into her living room and, out of force of habit, glanced down the long wall plastered from floor to ceiling with Audie's old artwork. They were three high and eight across. If you weren't looking twice, you'd think they were a big quilt of pleasant local scenes. I'd seen them so often, they even washed over me. But now and then, one stopped me in my tracks. At the moment, I found myself lingering on an image of a little girl standing in the middle of the road that climbed the hill at the Eighth. A giant purple car was turning to bear down on her. I'd seen it hundreds of times. Still, my breath caught in my throat. I had to look away.

That was when I noticed the telescope. It was at the far side of the apartment, nearest to the lake, half hidden behind a drape and aimed over the harbor to the south. While Audie spluttered out bursts of commentary about her progress on the task, I sauntered over to the telescope. "I should probably get some scissors. Yes, I'll get the scissors," Audie absently announced. "And I'll cut the ends. At an angle, right Tommy? Yes, yes. At an angle. And—oh, oh, oh! N-n-n-no!"

I was leaning down to the telescope when her voice went frantic. "Don't! Please, no!" I gazed into the portal, through a break in the trees beside the gully, and right into the side window of my cottage. It was so close you could make out the stone chimney on the far side of my living room.

"I'm not spying on you!"

Clearly, she had been. And I wasn't pleased about it. Imagine some crazy woman watching you from three miles away, as close as if she were in the next room. "Crazy" is too strong. "Troubled" is more like it. What's the difference? It was creepy either way. And invasive. I should've told her that straight up. But I knew what any trace of anger might bring, how it would set her off. I took a deep breath and bit my tongue. So what if Audie was spying on me? I wasn't drinking. There was nothing to see. Still, I made a mental note: close the drapes on the bedroom window.

"Wow. That's got to be—what?—three miles away?" I made a show of my amazement to throw her off. "It's like you're right outside that window."

"Honestly, Tommy. I haven't been watching. It's just that— when you didn't answer the phone—"

"I already told you—"

"Allie gave it to me. Just this Monday. For my birthday."

Ouch. "I'm sorry, Audie. How did I forget that?"

"I'm glad you did." Typical Audie: *pretend I'm not here.* "These flowers are more than enough." She set the bucket in the middle of her dining room table. A child's red plastic bucket. She'd never get around to finding that vase. I just knew it.

"I do have another surprise. But didn't you say you had soup?"

"Ah! Yes, yes! Soup! Let me heat it up." She hurried away, retreating again into the kitchen.

I took the opportunity to have another look into the telescope. I tilted it to bring the mouth of the gully into focus. There were two young boys kneeling on the bank beside where the runoff pooled, dipping buckets into the water. So, the gully hadn't completely drained. No doubt, they were trawling for tadpoles, like Newf and I used to as kids.

The soup wasn't very good. Truth be told, nothing Audie made hit my taste buds right. She wasn't a bad cook. She just liked her vegetables overcooked without any added flavor. Even if she had put salt and pepper on the table, I wouldn't have reached for them, though. Her feelings were too easily bruised. Just that hint of dissatisfaction would've had her beating herself up, bustling around the kitchen in atonement.

"This is really good."

"It's not too salty? I did add some salt."

"No. No. It's…it's perfect." She watched me as I took my next spoonful. I closed my eyes, pretending to savor it, then nodded in approval. She nodded back, with a self-satisfied little grin.

"What's the other surprise?" Audie asked when we were done with the soup.

I went to the counter and pulled Wendy's box out of the bag. "Pecan butter tarts."

I may as well have presented a Christmas pony. "How did you get those?" she gawped.

"Wendy had a couple left over."

"You said she wasn't making any more." Audie picked up the tart by the fingertips and turned it around like some precious jewel.

"She still makes a couple dozen for the weekends."

Audie stopped spinning the tart. "And she saved two for you."

"We got lucky this time."

"So *that's* where you were when I called." She arched one eyebrow as she bit into the tart. Classic Audie glance. Her control of that eyebrow was uncanny.

"Audie. I was out running errands when you called." I wasn't about to tell her I went to see Newf in Holyrood.

"Oh," she uttered in a way that made it clear she didn't buy it.

Fine. Don't. Just let me enjoy my tart. Audie finished hers, then went through an overly elaborate show of brushing her hands and corralling all the crumbs into a tight pinch. She licked her index finger and pressed it onto the pile. Then she quickly snatched it away, leaving no trace, and nibbled the crumbs. I had this fleeting thought of a novice magician completing her first big trick.

"That was fast."

"Just as good as I remember," Audie replied.

I slapped my hands down on top of my thighs and pushed back the chair. "Well…"

She covered her open mouth and gasped like someone had died. "You just got here."

"I've got some work to do on a broken dryer."

Audie checked her watch. "Twenty to five. You're not going to the Beer Store, are you?"

"Good Lord, Audie. Seriously?"

"Well, you *have* done that before."

"Once. Two years ago," I found my voice raising. "And what did I tell you then?"

Audie crumpled like paper. "That you'd never do it again."

"And that I'd never lie to you about my drinking either. Right?"

"Go fix your dryer." She waved me away. That was enough to stop my rant. Because, of course, I *was* lying about that. And it was all because I wanted to get away.

"I don't have to rush off right now." I scooted back up to the table and gave her the best smile I could muster.

Audie inflated with one long, happy breath. It lifted her to her feet. "Good. Because I didn't get a chance to tell you *my* surprise."

I dug my nails into the underside of the chair. "Great." Usually, Audie's surprises involved bizarre pipe dreams that I was somehow roped into advancing.

"Are you ready?" she asked, throwing her hands out with an overly dramatic sweep.

"Lay it on me."

"Joan is up."

"No." We'd been down this road a dozen times over the years.

"I saw her."

"Where?"

She hemmed and hawed. "Through the telescope."

I glared over at that damned tube gazing dumbly out the window. No good was going to come of this. "So, you saw Joan from three miles away, across 34 years, through a little eyehole."

"I'd recognize that walk anywhere. And you know how she used to stand when she smoked, how she cocked her hip, with one arm folded and her hand raised? The woman I saw was standing by the water just like that."

"Like all the Duncan sisters."

"They were there too!" Audie fired back. "Karen and Sue and Nancy. I picked them out. Easy. And there must've been 20 people milling around. Men, women, kids."

Twenty people? At the Duncan cottage? It was too outlandish to believe. I'd never seen more than one family up at a time since Joan stopped coming. "Come on, Audie," I softened my voice. "You know what Joan said."

"Tommy, it was her. I know it."

I looked off, pretending to mull it over. Really, though, I was wondering how to change the subject. One thought was to toss the telescope into the harbor. She had to stop watching Boiler Beach. It was only going to torment her.

"You know what you could do?" she broke in. "You could walk down there, just pass by, and have a quick look for yourself."

There it was. That's what she was roping me into. Go visit the Duncans. I'd do practically anything for Audie, but I had no intention of doing that. "Speaking of the old gang, guess who I bumped into?" Audie gasped before I could even say. "Grant asked to see you. Just like last year. And the year before—"

"You know the answer. It's not going to change."

"Maybe it should."

Audie wilted. She crossed her arms, hands stretched out high on her shoulders, and started pacing in slow, tiny steps, feeling her way through whatever darkness it was that overcame her.

"It's been so long, Audie. Can't you just let go that much?"

She shook her head hard and fast, like a seizure. "You don't know," she said. "*You—don't—know.*"

"Grant isn't even the same person anymore." Where my impulse to defend him came from, I have no idea. "He's not that spacey burnout who got you in trouble."

" 'Got me in trouble,' " Audie echoed quietly, stepping in front of the harbor window.

"He's changed, Audie. Really."

She turned to me, a shadow framed in broken sunlight and rough water. "Everyone gets to be a different person. They wear themselves so loosely, they can just shed who they are, whenever they want."

She sounded envious. "I don't know about that. He is who he is now because of what happened with you. He knows he'll never be able to shed that. He just wants to say he's sorry."

Audie turned her back to me, grabbing her shoulders again. I thought of that trick we did as teens where you pretended by yourself to be making out with someone else. "So he can feel better."

"So he doesn't have to feel tortured all the time."

"Like me."

If Audie were anyone else, if she hadn't been through what she'd been through, I would've given her a good shake. I wasn't dealing with a normal person, I know, but she had it in her to be caring; she'd offered me sympathy countless times. Why couldn't she do it for Grant's sake?

"You know," I tried again, "not a day goes by that I don't wish I could beg forgiveness for what I did. I'll never get that chance."

It was small of me to go there, to play on her emotions like that. Audie went silent for a long time. Then she stopped clawing at her shoulders. "What about this: I'll meet Grant if you find out what's going on with Joan."

I had to smile. Who was playing whom? "Deal." I could sneak past Duncan's and check things out. No problem.

"But you have to be here when Grant comes."

"Fine."

"And if Joan really is up, you have to talk to her."

"Wait a minute."

Audie knew she'd pushed too far. "Alright, never mind. But how are you going to tell she's up without knocking on her door?"

Good question. I thought about that the entire walk back to the Wondermat. Then after I went inside and saw the place empty, I started thinking maybe one twelve-pack of Labatt Blue wouldn't be such a big deal over the weekend. Audie didn't have to know everything. As far as she was concerned, the Beer Store still closed at five; I didn't bother to tell her they'd changed their summer hours to six. Anyway, there was a big difference between having 12 harmless beers over the course of two days and getting my nose into a bottle of vodka.

I turned the lights out in the Wondermat and was on my way to the door when it dawned on me; I'd told Audie there was a dryer that needed fixing. For all I knew, she was watching my store from across the harbor with that infernal telescope. I checked my watch. I hadn't even been back 10 minutes. How believable was it that I could get the job done that quickly? And here it was now, a quarter to six. I turned around, flipped the lights back on, and retreated to my office. Forget the beer. Probably for the best.

Damned if the gully hadn't filled back up since I'd been gone. Not as bad as the morning, but too much for a day of low waves and no rain. I decided to get to the bottom of it. Maybe Bogue really *had* snuck a hose into the ravine and turned it on. I started walking along the bank on my side of the gully, from the front of my cottage facing the lake to the back, past the bridge, and into the trees toward the beach road. It was a good six-foot drop to the stream below. I would've climbed down there and tromped through the muck, but the side was steep, and I was afraid I'd fall.

I was all the way out to the road, and the stream was still strong. The banks flattened out there, so I could angle down into the water and get a closer look. Where the road crossed over the gully, there was an old, square cement culvert. The runoff from the bluff went through this tunnel before wending its way past my cottage. It had been there, pretty much in that same decrepit state, since I was a kid. Newf and I used to crawl into it and wait to feel the rumble when cars passed over. I couldn't get in there now. With my creaky back, I'd never get out. But what I did do every few weeks was clear the tangle of branches that collected at the culvert's mouth. One good rain, and it piles up so thick it blocks the opening.

I was clearing that debris when a car cruised up and stopped above me. Doors opened. I heard hushed voices. "How are we going to find this in the dark?" I could tell right away; teenage kids.

"Don't worry about that, Doug. Just watch the road," an older voice answered. They sounded so close, all it would take was a couple steps to the edge of the bridge and they'd see me. Quiet as I could, I pressed up against the slope beside the culvert. The car's trunk opened. I heard the clink of bottles. They were stashing beer.

The older kid said, "You got it, Brewski?"

"I'm good," came a third voice, younger than the other two. Brewski could've been 13.

"You can't take both cases at once."

"I got it."

"*And* the ice? No way. You're going to need two trips."

"What's taking so long?" Doug asked. He was right above me.

"Put one over there, behind that bush."

"I can handle it, Marcus," Brewski said. For such a young kid, he sounded like the least worried of the three. With a nickname like Brewski, it made sense. There was a clatter of clinking bottles, footsteps kicking stones, then rustling in the underbrush.

"Car!" Doug cried.

"Fuck," Marcus uttered. "Meet at the Eighth at nine. Alright?"

Brewski's muffled agreement came from the woods. The trunk slammed, doors closed, and the car raced off. Seconds later, a car cruised by, coming from the other way. I waited until Brewski's thrashing died away, then scrambled up onto the road. From there, I caught a glimpse of him waist deep in the brush. He hadn't listened to Marcus. Scrawny as he was, he should've. I marveled he could even lift that much weight, let alone stagger into the woods with it. It had to be 60, 70 pounds. Every few steps, he'd arch his back then move on. There was an old tottering outhouse way back where the hill made its steep climb. When he rounded that and veered left up the slope, I knew the path he was taking, and I had a pretty good idea where he was headed.

Fifty yards or so north, through a gauntlet of lodgepole pines, there was a fort dug into the hillside with a hinged top of two-by-fours, covered with twigs and pine needles. I know that because Newf and I built it when we were teenagers. Kids had stashed beer there ever since. I don't know if it was a secret handed down from generation to generation, or the inevitable consequence of kid's exploring the woods. A bit of both, I suspect.

When Brewski disappeared from view, I went after him. I wasn't going to confront the kid; I was just curious to see if they really were using the old fort. Not too far away from the outhouse, a case of Molson XXX was blocking the path. Molson XXX. Seven-point-three percent alcohol. Basically, a Blue and a half. These kids weren't messing around. Back in our day, Brador was the high-octane let's-get-stupid brew—and that was only 6.2%.

I stood over my discovery, pondering what to do. One idea: grab the case and go. That would solve my weekend problem, and a couple weekends more. Well, maybe not that long. *Take only what you need tonight.* That's what I decided. I was reaching to open the case when I noticed the kid, Brewski, a few steps away.

"Look what I found."

"What is it?" he asked, playing dumb.

"Your beer."

"Not *my* beer."

"Hmm…my mistake. I saw you lugging this through the woods and just naturally—"

"Are you going to take it?" He dropped the act.

"I probably should, as young as you and your buddies are."

The kid came at me—pretty bold, I'll say—and pointed at the case. "There's eight of us drinking that. Three beers is nothing."

"But six is something." I grabbed the case. Damned if Brewski didn't take another step toward me. You had to admire the balls.

"Six?"

"Come on, Brewski. Do the math. This case, plus the one I'll find when I get to the fort."

He stared me down, actually leveled me with a threatening glare. I couldn't help but smile. "How did you know?"

"I saw you walking up the hill with two cases."

"About my name. How did you know my name?"

"You and your pals aren't the quietest stashers on the beach."

As if to prove me wrong, he went mum. I shifted the beer case and waited him out. I was curious to see where this tough nut would go from here. "You're not going to take everything," he finally declared, like he could stop me. "You can't take it all."

"I'm not taking anything." I started down the path toward him. He didn't step aside until the last second. I refused to show him I was impressed. "Now, let's go see my fort."

"Your fort?"

"Yeah. *My* fort. I built it when I was younger than you." He cocked his head and stared at me again, only this time, it was a look of respect—as much as a kid his age could give. "I hope you haven't fucked it up," I said to him, straight-faced.

I was firing for effect, but as we headed to the fort, I felt like cursing a blue streak for real. What in the world were these kids thinking? Newf and I had made the fort hard to find. We went different ways to get to it, so we wouldn't wear a path. They had trampled down a thoroughfare. We thought of the fort as a hiding place, so we picked a spot with thick underbrush. They'd cleared everything to the pine needles. Not only that, but they'd chopped down a big circle of pines around the fort. Instead of being the most sheltered spot in the woods, this was now the most inviting. It was like one of those alien crop circles had magically whirled into the hill. That is, if aliens had a penchant for galactic littering. The place was overrun with candy wrappers, empty cigarette packs, pop and beer bottles, empty cases from past stashings. They'd even dug a firepit. Here, on a hill covered with brittle lodgepole pines.

"You guys need to make this easier to find."

Thank goodness Brewski had a sense of humor. "Yeah, who'd be dumb enough to hide their beer here," he joked back, as deadpan as I was. This kid was alright.

My mood didn't change until I saw the condition of the fort itself. Newf and I had spent a good two weeks building the thing when we were 13—digging a hole into the hill, carrying the deck boards his dad didn't need up there, nailing them together to make a cover. Then—our greatest innovation—hinging it to a railroad tie we took from the Gartons. It was a thing of beauty. You could close that cover like a trap door, spread branches over it, and no one would know the fort was there. Back then, young as we were, our idea was to make a place where we could hide out, close the lid, turn on flashlights, and spend the day reading comic books. By the time we were 17, the fort served a higher purpose: hiding beer cases. And no one, other than Newf, Rob, Grant, and I—not even the girls in our gang—had the slightest inkling it existed.

Fast forward to me standing beside Brewski, looking down on Newf's and my handiwork. Half the trap door boards were gone, the rest were rotted, and the whole thing had come unhinged from the railroad tie. Brewski had just leaned it over the top of the case, tilted tantalizingly for maximum curiosity. Hell, you could see one whole side of the Molson XXX box if you were wandering past.

"You guys sure are sneaky buggers."

Brewski jumped into the hole, pushed the ruined cover aside, and reached up for me to hand him the case. "Nobody's going to steal from Marcus."

It suddenly dawned on me who Marcus was. I knew I recognized that voice. Marc Garton, my neighbor Bogue's son, the punk who only ever gave me glancing scowls the rare times I saw him. But I heard his voice enough from across the gully, arguing with his parents. "Or they'll get roughed up, eh?"

"Marcus can get mad."

"Yes, *Marc* can." Marcus…where were we? Rome? "And this Brewski business. That can't be your real name."

"It's Bruce."

"Well, *Bruce*. How mad do you think Marc's going to get when you're short six beers?"

"What?"

"That's the rent for hiding beers in my fort. You're lucky I don't take both cases as payment for trashing it."

"I'd have to tell Marcus you forced me." He didn't mean it like a threat. He wasn't even saying it to me, really. More thinking out loud, looking ahead, dreading.

"Tell him his crazy neighbor across the gully took his beers. And if he'd like to discuss it with him, he's welcome to pop over." That made Bruce smile. "On second thought, it's eight beers for the rent. You and I are going to drink the extra two right now."

"I can't do that."

"Sure you can. Just tear open that case and start handing up beers. When you get to eight, stop, climb out, and I'll pop open two with this." I jingled the bottle opener attached to my car keys; my trusty church key.

Bruce did exactly as told. When I handed him his beer, he looked down the path. "If he saw me right now…"

"Yeah?"

He took a swig but didn't seem to enjoy it. "He wouldn't do anything with you here. But when you were gone…"

I took a seat on one of the logs they'd dragged over by the fire pit. "Tell you what," I said, after taking a nice, long draw off the XXX. "If we see him coming, I'll slap you around, so he knows I strong-armed you."

Bruce gave me a scoffing smirk as he joined me on the log. Either he didn't believe I'd do it, didn't think it would work, or couldn't see me overpowering him. I held out the neck of my beer. He just looked at it. "Cheers." He finally understood. We clanked our bottles together. "To friends who aren't assholes."

Bruce paused for a half-second before he drank to that. I was going to press the point, ask him why he even bothered with the jerk, but what was the use? Don't we all have a friend or two like Marc—or weren't we the Marc to some poor kid at one time or another? So, we sat there on that log in silence, sipping our beers and listening to the evening breeze shuddering high in those pines. All down the hill in front of us, orange shafts of sunlight pulsed, waved, and died. Now and then, through the mesh of trees, you could see a car fluttering past on the road below, like some old stuttering movie. I have to admit; it wasn't so bad sitting there. I could see why the kids took the chance of clearing out a campsite.

"So what cottage are you in, Bruce?"

"Eighty-one. Just on the other side of the Eighth."

I stopped my beer mid-hoist. "Eighty-one? The Duncans?"

"Something wrong with that?"

"No, it's just—" I stopped myself, trying to put the relation-ship together. "I know your Aunt Joan."

"That's my mom."

"Your *mom*? How old are you?"

"Fifteen."

That's about what I figured. That meant Joan was 36, 37 when she had him. Not ancient, but still. And she had a couple kids right after she got married. They had to be pushing 30 by now.

"How do you know my mom?"

I sucked in a deep breath and blew it out slowly. "We used to hang out together, like you probably do now with some of the beach girls, drinking at the gazebo, messing around."

"Nobody goes to the gazebo," Bruce said. I was glad he didn't ask what I meant by messing around. The gazebo was an old, unadorned lookout, perched on the bluff above my cottage, not that far from where Bruce and I were sitting at that moment. It wasn't much bigger around than a large hot tub, but you could fit 10 people on the benches, it was open on all sides to the elements, and it had a domed roof to keep out the rain. In recent years, some of the bottom logs had fallen off, and there was a hole in the roof now, but last I checked, it would still serve its purpose.

"What's wrong with the gazebo?"

"We just go to the clubhouse down at the golf course."

"You break into the clubhouse?"

"They leave it open. They figure if we're going to drink, better to know where we are."

"Do parents organize every aspect of kids' lives these days?"

"Not mine."

Back to Joan. "I didn't think your mom even came up to the beach anymore."

"She doesn't. I usually come with my aunt. But we have a big reunion this year, and Mom decided she'd put up with it."

" 'Put up with it.' " I had to laugh. "She sure didn't have that problem when we were kids."

"She says it's gotten too snobby."

"Can't argue with that." I finished my beer and thought of grabbing another, but I didn't want to cut into my six. "Well," I stood up. "Tell your mom Tommy said hi."

"Okay."

"Just don't tell her how we met," I added, stepping over to the edge of the ruined fort, where I'd left my stash of beers.

"I won't." Bruce eyed me jamming the bottles into my jacket.

I knew what he was thinking. "Don't worry about Marc. Just say I took them. That'll shut him up." He plastered on a thin smile. It reminded me of Audie trying to be brave. "If he gives you any shit, I'll buy you a six-pack, and you can say you stole them out of my shed."

"Thanks," he whispered, like there was a need to be quiet.

I left him sitting on that log, working on his beer. I was back in my cottage within minutes. I took the beers out of my jacket and put all but one in the fridge. Time for dinner. Nothing better than firing up the grill, cooking a burger, and downing a brew. When I was about to open that beer, though, I thought twice. I left it on the counter, went to my bay window, and gazed out at the lake. It was settling into rolling swells under a reddening sky. That's what I saw out the window, but what I saw in my head was Bruce, sitting in those shadowy woods by my old fort, alone and worrying.

The beach was suffused with that hazy golden sheen it gets when the sun's an hour away from a cloudless horizon, no longer so blinding we can't watch it shimmer and fizz like some giant pill dissolving as the blue giant below goes calm.

That first beer went down a lot easier than I would've thought. Part of it was telling myself that Bruce was scared of Marc for bigger reasons than the beers I took. The other part was clearing my head with a quick dip. At this time of night, especially so early in the season, hardly anyone ventured out on the beach. That was the way I liked it; no one to judge my 52-year-old wreck of a body. The water was cold; mid-June always is. When I finally got brave enough to dive in, that chill snatched the breath right out of me. I fought through it, though, gliding underwater as long as I could bear, reaching out into the dark murky currents.

There's always been an element of fear to swimming in these waters. The unfathomable expanse, the suffocating gloominess...

Lake Huron isn't the ocean; nothing will attack you—no sting rays or sharks. Its threats reveal themselves in more insidious ways: a looming shadow; a quick, shifting current; that cold muck your foot sinks into sometimes. Sure, these fears are more imagined than real. You could dismiss them as unfounded. But there were enough signs of things lurking under the dark heaving skin of the lake that you could never entirely free yourself from doubt.

About a quarter mile from shore, looming beneath the waves like some slumbering Moby Dick, is a gigantic white boulder. Everyone calls it Mammoth Rock, because as deep as it is that far out, to be able to see the top of the rock means it could be the height of a cottage. Once, Newf and I took a rowboat out there, dropped anchor on Mammoth Rock, and tried to walk along its top. It was deeper than it looked, well over our heads. We had to hop across it, plunging down for a couple steps, springing up for air, then plunging again. Newf went the whole way across; I set foot on it twice before getting back in the boat. After he was done, Newf dove down and followed the rock as far as he could to the bottom. It was a long time before he resurfaced, long enough to worry. When his head finally popped out beside the rowboat, he said, "I never got there." To this day, it still rattles me.

Every time I go in the water now, Mammoth Rock is in the back of my mind. How did it get so far offshore? Did it tumble from some antediluvian cliff that once towered above the beach? Or was it just one of a thousand similar rocks strewn across the bottom of Lake Huron, no more significant than the pebbles that washed ashore? If Lake Huron can hide something as huge as Mammoth Rock, what else is out there? Practically every day, I see dead fish washed ashore, most no bigger than my foot, but some as big as a child. If this is what the waves could muscle out of the lake, what's out there that can resist them? What unseen creatures share these same waters, swerving away from us when we dive in, retreating to unattainable depths, where things as big as Mammoth Rock go unnoticed? I know; it's just a big rock. It can't move. I'll never run into it. Still, it's out there. The fact of it. I don't know why, but that scares me, more now even than when I was a kid.

After that long glide, I scrambled out of the lake, wrapped myself in a towel, and ran for the cottage. It's the only time I run anymore. I got dressed, fired up my grill, molded a patty, then popped open beer number two. Standing there behind my cottage, with nothing to do but watch the burger cook and seagulls stream out from the eastern fields to where fish ran in the lake, I thought back to the morning. Ever have one of those days that never seems to end? Grant at the gully, Sharon with invites for everyone but me, Newf out in Holyrood, Audie and her telescope, and finally Bruce, Joan's son. All this on the first day of the season. Every one of the old gang, all the people who were there 34 years ago. Except Rob, who I was going to have to confront sooner or later. And Carrie…who I'd never get a chance to see again.

Ten seconds. That's all it had taken to go from 60 to 100 on the road to Ripley. I'd be paying my entire life for 10 seconds. Anyway. This wasn't the time to be thinking about that. There was a burger to eat, a sunset to see, and one more beer to drink. One. I ate my meal over the sink, per usual. Why dirty dishes if you don't need to? A paper towel on the counter was just fine for the burger, and as for the chips, what was the point of pouring them out of the bag? Just grab a handful and munch away.

By the time I was done, the sun was low enough to make a shimmering orange path across the settling swells. It was aimed straight at me, but that was an illusion anyone would see from any other cottage. It made me smile, though, to know that fewer people than usual were singled out this way. Most cottagers were in town to watch the season-opening parade of the Kincardine Scottish Pipe Band. Every Saturday evening throughout the summer, for as long as I can remember, a group of men and women, from children to old-timers, marched in formation with bagpipes and drums down the town's main drag, followed by hordes of adoring townies and tourists. They took the same route and played the same dozen songs they had since I was a child. And some of them, like the lumbering bear of a man who marched out front with his spear-like scepter and black feather bonnet, had been around that long, too. The novelty of the pipe band wore off for me about the time

Newf and I started stashing beers. And I haven't been back to see them in decades. Nothing against the band. It's just that there's this higher priority. Every Saturday, when everyone heads to town, I think, why waste this chance to see the sunset without kids screaming or couples walking across my view?

I rinsed out my sink and put away the chips. Clean-up complete. Now, that path had narrowed on the darkening waters to a rusty gauntlet. I went to the fridge and grabbed my last allotted XXX of the night. Then I got my old Phillips cassette boombox and took it out on the deck. I sat down on one of my two beach chairs, set the boombox by my side, and threw my feet up on the rail. I flipped over the tape—The Who's *Quadrophenia*, the same tape I'd been flipping over for weeks—and pressed "PLAY." The music came out tinnier, less potent than the last time I sat out there. I turned up the dial. Better, but The Who still had to fight over the breeze running through the brush around the gully. A bit louder:

> *Inside outside, leave me alone.*
> *Inside outside, nowhere is home.*
> *Inside outside, where have I been?*
> *Out of my brain on the five fifteen.*

I'd forgotten how hard the brass punched and the piano clanged, how furiously Keith Moon propelled the song. That was more like it. I shook my beer. Halfway gone? A dog bounded into view, chasing a ball in the surf. An old man followed behind him, carrying one of those plastic ball-launchers. He stopped smack dab in front of my sun and tried to scoop the ball out of the waves. His dog kept batting the ball back into the surf. How long was this going to go on? The sun was five minutes away from the water. I twisted the dial all the way up. The music wailed out of my ancient speakers, unhinged and distorted. The old man straightened and glared over his shoulder. I pointed at the sun. He got the hint and moved on. I toasted his retreat and tilted back my beer. Gone? And here the sun was still a sliver away from the horizon, flattening out into a deep red oval, like the lake was repelling it.

Executive decision: one more. You can't be empty-handed when the sun sets. I bolted inside, grabbed the cheat beer, and hustled back. The music was still on full, cacophonous blast. *Here by the sea and sand, nothing ever goes as planned.* No shit, Daltrey.

It didn't take long until Bogue's wife poked her head around the gully, making a show of her annoyance. I damn near kept the music blaring just to spite her, but it was starting to kill my buzz. Plus, I hadn't come to the right song yet. I hit "STOP" and fast-forwarded. The cartridge strained to advance the tape. No surprise there. This cassette was nearly 40 years old. And double albums like *Quadrophenia* had big spools. By the time it got to where I wanted, the sun had hit the horizon. Perfect.

Only love can bring the rain that makes you yearn to the sky. Nothing beat the hypnotic pulse of "Love, Reign O'er Me." The sun looked like it had been punctured by the sharp, dark edge of the lake. Red and purple spilled all over the water. *Only love can bring the rain that falls like tears from on high.* I took a long, glorious swig and stared down the bleeding sun. My head lurched to the song's great, heaving rhythm—one second hopeful, the next despairing. Why was this still so alluring? I knew the fiction of romance; I'd been paying for it for years. Yet somehow it still had the power to suck me in. *Love, reign o'er me, reign o'er me.* I guzzled the beer dry, already deciding I'd have all six tonight. Hell, who was I kidding? I knew I'd have all six the minute I took them. That's how easily I fool myself.

I leaned back in the beach chair, feet up on the railing, head arched back, closed my eyes against the vermillion sky, and let the music play out. The hushing of the waves, the narrow armrests, the demand to balance myself, I could've been gliding a canoe into that violet expanse. This wasn't the first time I'd imagined myself this way, bobbing in the water, elbows on the gunnels, drifting aimlessly into the dark. It was a little game I played: don't open your eyes until all the color drains from the sky. Just float.

Usually, I didn't fall asleep. But tonight, I must've. When I did finally open my eyes, I couldn't tell where water ended and sky began. The lake had gotten even quieter, from a hush to muffled breathing, like it was trying—preposterously—to hide. A few stars

stared down from the darker heights, and all along the beach, bonfires rimmed the lake. This was the time of night when I went walking. I could sneak down the shore under the protection of darkness
and the blinding glow of those bonfires and haunt my old stomping grounds. The ghost of Boiler Beach; that's me. I went inside,
grabbed the last two XXX's, and stuffed them in my jacket, then
headed down to the shoreline.

Once I was out from behind the brush that guards the gully, I
could see north, past the dwarfed lights of Kincardine, to where
the Bruce Nuclear Power Plant, the second largest nuclear facility
in the world, sizzled with its sickly fire. I'm told the plant is 20
miles away as the crow flies. At night, it seems much closer. Where
during the day, its steam towers rise off the shoreline like the last
few teeth of a broken comb, at night it burns out in the middle of
Lake Huron with an eerie greenish glow.

When I was a child, my dad nicknamed it the Emerald City,
after the Wizard of Oz's palace. I used to look out at those gleaming towers like they were the architecture of some wondrous, distant world. Then, one rainy day, my dad drove me out to Douglas
Point. We took a tour of the plant. It was a stark, lifeless place. The
workers were dead silent and grim. It reminded me of a prison.
Today, I know hundreds of those workers. They wash their clothes
and buy books at the Wondermat. I drink with them at O'Shea's.
The plant is the region's biggest employer. To get a job there is to
gain a lifetime of security. Now, when I look north at night, I don't
see an Emerald City or a prison. It's just part of the scenery, neither
magical nor menacing. Still, it *is* a nuclear power plant.

I headed south. Once I got past the Garton cottages, I popped
open my second-to-last beer. I had five minutes to down it before
the Duncans. No problem. It was nearly gone by the Eighth. As I
was passing there, I heard laughing up by the path that went from
the beach to the dead-end road at the bottom of the hill. Then I
heard a familiar voice—Marc, Bogue's kid—and I remembered:
they were meeting there before they went off to get their beer.

I snuck behind the bushes on the other side of the opening to
the road. Through the gap there, I saw dark figures milling around,

the back side of the diamond-shaped dead-end sign, and the road climbing straight up the hill. We used to meet in this exact place when I was a kid. With that road vaulting in front of us, it always felt like we were on stage. Now, so many years later, I was watching things play out from behind the scenes. One kid was hurling rocks at the dead-end sign. Another was rocking the porta-potty the Moores had installed to dissuade people from peeing on their dune. Someone inside begged for the kid to stop.

"We could push this right over!"

A shadow stumbled out of the porta-potty. "What the hell, Greg? I peed all over myself." It was Doug, the nervous beer-stashing lookout.

"Why would you even do that?" Bruce was getting after this Greg punk. "It's going to spill shit everywhere."

"Fuck you, Brewski," Marc chimed in. "That's the point."

"Yeah, well…" Bruce got quieter. "I'm three cottages away. I don't want to smell that."

"Listen to Brewski, growing a pair." Marc laughed. "Where were those balls when you handed over our beers?"

"I didn't hand them over." Bruce's voice fell to a mutter.

There was just a swallow left in my beer. I took a step back from the bushes to get the right loft and lobbed the bottle up into the opening to the dead end. It was a dumb thing to do; I could've hit somebody. The bottle crashed in the middle of the scene, just as I'd hoped. There were screams, then the kids scattered.

"Who did that?" Marc yelled. "Who the *fuck* did that?"

"Someone's here," Doug said.

"Shut up!" Marc hissed. "Colesy?" I stayed quiet.

"It's not Colesy," Bruce declared, with quiet certainty.

"Let's get out of here," Marc decided. With that, they piled into two cars, backed up the hill, and took off down the beach road to pick up their stash.

I walked out from behind the bushes, between the curtains of trees and around the guardrail which stopped cars that took the hill too fast. You could see enough under the stars to pick out glass shards glinting on the pavement. I couldn't help but snicker at the thought of that bottle exploding, Marc getting so rattled, and Bruce reacting with such cool. *It's not Colesy.* I bet he knew exactly who it was. Still, one beer grenade wasn't going to scare Marc straight. Once they were in the cars, he'd feel the need to bully someone. Probably Bruce. *Fuck me.* I was trying to help the kid out, but just making things worse.

As I passed the dead-end sign on my way back to the beach, I smacked it with the palm of my right hand. Bad idea. My wrist got wrenched in a funny way and needles shot up to my elbow. For the rest of the walk to cottage 81, I couldn't close my hand very well. The whole bottom part of my arm throbbed. I was sure I'd broken something. Served me right.

The Duncan cottage was set back further from the lake, hidden behind a dune. I could see lights through the beach grass, but I wouldn't be able to tell who was there unless I took the path over the rise. Then I'd be standing in front of the Duncan's picture window. Why go up there anyway? I already knew Joan was inside. Hell, I'd met her son. It's not like I was going to knock on the door and invite myself in. I turned to head home, then—I don't know why—I turned and hurried up that path, whispering all the way, *this is dumb, this is dumb, this is dumb.*

When I crested the dune, I could see the kitchen window lit up brightly at the far-right side of the cottage, a big circle of people sitting around the table, playing cards and drinking. There was Joan's brother and sister and her mom, too, so much older, but distinctively her. And there were a few younger people I didn't know as well, older than teenagers, but not by much. They were shouting and laughing. No one would've known I was watching them unless my face was pressed up against the glass.

In the living room, through that wide picture window, you could barely make out the silhouettes of the furniture against the meager light that leaked from the kitchen. And if you didn't know that room, you probably would've missed the figure crouching off to the side. Music started up. Buffalo Springfield. "Mr. Soul." That had to be Joan. She was the only one who ever bothered with the family's archaic record player. I waited for her to stand and join everyone else. She just kept crouching by the stereo.

Then my phone rang. Not loud. No one inside would've heard it. But in the moment, I panicked, grabbed for it, and forgot about my bad hand. It wouldn't close. The phone fell into the sand. I dropped to my knees and felt for it, but it wasn't at my feet. I started crawling down the sloping dune, brushing at the sand.

"Did I scare you?" I lurched back and keeled over on my side. The orange flare of a cigarette slashed across the dark screened-in porch where the path ended. It was as far away from the kitchen as you could get. "I just wanted to make sure that was you, Wonderman." The glow of a smartphone wobbled in the gloom. It threw a blue edge of light on one side of the man's face.

I'd heard that voice before but couldn't place it. I couldn't think of anyone who called me Wonderman, either. I was quick enough, though, to make an excuse. "Is this the Martyn's?"

The man let out a raspy laugh. "Nice try. Hey, while I have you here, I did find a book you might like. I just finished it. *The Scarlet Letter*. How's that grab you?"

That's when I figured out who it was—the guy from the bookstore, that jerk who wouldn't quit until he got my number. "Classics don't sell." I was tempted to go further, get after the guy, ask why he was such a prick. But arguing with a stranger in front of the Duncan's place, with Joan in the next room—Joan, who I hadn't seen in 34 years, and who'd abandoned the beach because of me—well, I wasn't so drunk I didn't realize that would be stupid. I picked myself up and made a quick scan of the dark sand. "If you find a phone, you know where I am."

I was walking away when he said, "I'll let her know you came calling." That's when it hit me: this guy was Joan's husband. Why had it taken so long to put that together?

I hurried away, over the dune and right down to the waterline. A wave hit my shoes. I didn't care. I stomped through the water all the way to the Eighth before I stopped. What was I running from? So I went to see Joan. So what? The way this guy was acting, it was like—what *was* it like?—like I was coming after his woman.

Where would he get that idea? Joan? No way. She might've told him a lot of things about me, but certainly nothing that would lead him to conclude I was a threat. Whatever. If he wanted me to steer clear of Joan, fine. There was just that one problem: my phone. No…I was going to have to see that prick at least once more.

How much further to my place? I looked up to the cottages tucked in the dark, unbroken stand of trees. They glimmered in a long succession, some glowing faintly, one soft light in a single room; others blazing brilliantly, sparked by the blue light of TVs. From there on the shore, all the way down the beach and around the bend to Kincardine, they looked so small, especially under the stars crowded in above me. Kindling for an endless bonfire. If you took the century of nights these cottages have stood beside Lake Huron and compressed them into an hour, this beach might look like a long branch in a crackling bonfire. Embers flaring up, dying out, flaring again. All our tiny lives flickering under those stars.

I would've passed the gully, still gazing into the sky, if it weren't for stumbling in the remnants of the trench I'd dug that morning. I sat down and took off my water-logged shoes. It wasn't that late, and I still had one beer left. I knew what I was going to do. Carrie's old cottage was 15 minutes away. *Go, sit on those steps, have the beer, beg forgiveness. Again.* There was no point trying to talk myself out of it, even though I knew what a dark place it would put me in. Every time I went to Carrie's, I fell into that same place. That Hell. Not Hell; the edge of Hell. Or Heaven maybe. But the edge, looking in. I knew I'd be broken and raw for days.

The heat was already rising in my chest. I walked around the gully and headed north. By the time I got to Carrie's, I was burning. I pushed through the high grass that had overtaken her old path and didn't break through it until I was an arm's length away from the cottage. Things had gotten so much wilder since March. The place was as dark as ever, all boarded up, no glass, no reflecting starlight. I followed along its side and found the steps that dropped from the front door. There were five of them, and they sagged and creaked so much when I stepped on them I was afraid they'd break. Still, I sat on the bottom step.

I opened the beer, still burning. I knew I'd have to start talking to her, I'd have to go back to that night. Again. At a certain point, shouldn't you get to stop apologizing? If Carrie were really listening, if this wasn't just me talking to myself, couldn't I take on faith that she'd heard and forgiven me? I raised my beer. A little wind rustled in the long grass around me. *Here's to love, Carrie.* I took a long swig. It wasn't cold anymore, but it calmed me. What to say now? Nothing came. I put myself back in that car beside Carrie. I tried to feel the same deceptively easy acceleration I felt today on the way to Ripley. I saw the pickup truck swerve. Our quick jerk to the right. The shadowy figures. The scream…

I downed the last of the beer in one gulp. Here I was again, on that edge. There was no answer coming to tell me how to live with this. Nothing in the stars or waves or wind. No. This was a decision I had to make alone. Could I forgive myself? Could I live with this? And if I couldn't? I tried to remember that last glance Carrie gave me. How did she say it? *What if I did love you—?* And I was going to say, *I'd give everything for you.* But I never got that chance—

Wait. Someone was coming down the shore. A dark, shambling figure, a stone's throw north of where I sat, walking across the shallow sandbar to the boiler.

Did I mention that Carrie's cottage was so close to the boiler? Have I even said there actually *is* a boiler on Boiler Beach? It's a big, rusted block of metal, half the size of a VW Beetle—all that's left of the Aurora Quest, a tugboat that sank a mile offshore in 1883, killing all six crewmen. Kincardine has made a cottage industry out of the disaster. From the back road, the same one that passes over that bridge behind my place, you can take a turn-off next to Carrie's cottage that goes to a three-car parking lot overlooking the boiler. In the Sixties, a few town merchants, including Mike Garton, pitched in for a stone cairn with a plaque that commemorates the shipwreck. It also shamelessly hawks the businesses that trafficked in the novelty of the disaster. After a confusing narrative of the tug's final hours, the plaque implores readers to go to Chapman's for "the town's biggest selection of Aurora Quest souvenirs." Chapman's closed 40 years ago. Then it ends by inviting people to the Aurora Quest restaurant. Mike Garton opened the restaurant in 1965. It's the same joint Bogue keeps pulling tourists into today—thanks, lately, to stealing Wendy's recipes.

When I was a kid, the myth of the Aurora Quest fascinated me. My dad couldn't drive by the boiler without me begging him to slow down so we could catch a glimpse of it through the broken line of poplars. I couldn't fathom how something so big and heavy could get pushed ashore from the distant depths of the wreck or how intense the explosion would have to be to throw it there. I marveled that it had withstood so many decades of bashing waves without getting pulverized into rusty splinters. As I grew older, I got jaded on the Aurora story. It didn't make sense. The cause of the wreck was listed as a boiler explosion. If the boiler had blown up, then what was that huge chunk of metal sitting just offshore? Wouldn't an explosion that could hurl a ton of metal a mile in the air blow it to smithereens? My dad thought the whole thing was a hoax. Of course, he also thought every pro sport was fixed. Except hockey. So, there's that.

Anyway. I didn't think much about the shadow circling the boiler. Kids were always goofing around there. When we were teenagers and it was 50 feet further into the lake, we used to try to smash our beer bottles on it. Of course, back then, only the very top of it stuck out. This summer, the boiler stood in ankle-deep water, and you could see practically the whole thing. In all my years, I'd never seen it so exposed.

What got my attention was when a rod of fire leaped out of the figure's hand. I heard a wheezy howl. Sparks flew everywhere. A blowtorch. The son of a bitch was taking a blowtorch to the boiler! Burning off a souvenir while the lake was low. I should've marched down there and given him the what-for, but I couldn't work up the gumption. What did I care if some guy cut a chunk off the boiler? If more people did it, the thing would be gone, and we wouldn't have to contend with sightseers cluttering the back road. Business at the Aurora might dry up. How was that a problem? Then again, there was still a part of me that wanted to spot the boiler between those poplars every time I drove by.

"Hey!" I barked. The blowtorch went dead. The figure turned his head, scanning the shoreline. No way he could see me. I was surrounded in black. He started the blowtorch again, kneeling behind the boiler on the lake side. Why there? There were easier places to cut. The boiler was nearly chest high; you didn't need to be kneeling in water. Now I *was* curious. I watched the guy work a few minutes more before the fire went dead. Then he rose and waded out of the water, blowtorch in one hand, slab of metal in the other. His souvenir. He walked a few cottages north, headed up for the road, and disappeared into the cover of the tree line.

I gave it a few minutes, then went down to the boiler. I rolled my pants up to my knees but didn't need to go that high. I still couldn't get over how much of the boiler was out of the water. In the Eighties, when the lake was so high it took out people's decks, the boiler poked out like a rusty iceberg, one jagged edge a foot in the air. But Lake Huron has been receding ever since. Old-timers talk about how the mailman used to drive down the beach. Today, you could drive three cars side by side along the shore. I sloshed across the sandbar until I was standing next to the boiler. There was no top to it; that had either collapsed, worn away, or never been there in the first place. I looked inside. A handful of thick metal rods were splayed out like gangly limbs.

I went around to where the guy had been working. There was a small puncture about two feet off the sandbar, the only sign of damage you'd expect from an explosion. If you didn't know better, you'd think the boiler washed ashore as compliantly as driftwood. The piece of metal the guy had burned out was right under that puncture, a hole inches from the waterline. I crouched down, traced my finger around the opening he'd cut, reached through, felt the other side. Why this piece? He could've made one cut across a flap of the puncture and made it much easier on himself.

I headed back to shore. The breeze was bending the beach grass toward Carrie's cottage. I should've gone back up there. I never got done saying my piece. No matter now. The burning wasn't in me anymore. And I was tired. Was it still Saturday?

I *wasn't going to go into the past. But you can't get away from it up here. I*
may as well start at the beginning: I met Newf before anyone else at Boiler
Beach, back in 1974, when I was eight years old and we were renting cottage
112. My mom was good friends with his mom; don't ask me how a Bloomfield
Hills socialite connected up with the wife of a cattle farmer. The two would lie
on the beach together, sunning and drinking Tom Collins for hours on end.
Newf and I had no choice but to become friends.

We made sprawling cities of sand and pushed our Tonka trucks around
them. We dug pits so deep we could barely get out of them. We braved the
biggest waves together. We got poison ivy at the same time. Newf threw an
errant rock that hit me in the head and caused seven stitches. I snagged him in
the ear with the hook of a bad fishing cast. We swatted flies against the back
of his cottage, snared them on fly paper, then learned to catch them in our
hands. We told each other ghost stories. We told each other dreams of who we
were going to be and lies of who we were away from the beach. And we knew
each other so well, that we could tell exactly when we were lying…but never
called each other on it. For six summers, until I was 14, my only friend at the
cottage was Newf. I've never had a closer friend.

Then Audie's family started renting the red cottage three places south of
Newf. The Bells from Darien, Connecticut. There were three children, includ-
ing Audie. Her brother Andy was two years older, and Allie was another year
older than him. That's right: Allie, Andy, and Audie. Who would name their
kids like that? Aaron and Ashley Bell would, that's who. They were the most
Bohemian couple I ever knew, on this beach or otherwise. He played trumpet
in the New York Philharmonic Orchestra; she was a painter and self-professed
psychic. They always wore black. Whenever he went outside, he'd wear a floppy
straw hat, coating his nose with white, old-school zinc oxide. She never strayed
further from her cottage than the sandbox-like perch that faced the lake off
their front porch. That's where she'd spend her time painting all manner of
waves—gliding, tumbling, crashing. When she wasn't painting, she was
hunching over a Ouija board. We learned not to ask what she was doing; her
answers invariably involved some wild premonition about our futures. She once
told me I'd end up doing what I was meant to do. When I asked what that
was, she just shrugged.

The Bell family's arrival changed my friendship with Newf, but not be-
cause of Audie, at least at first. It was Allie—and puberty—that turned us

from being content playing alone to chasing girls. It was inevitable. We were 14-year-old boys. She was 17, soon to be a woman. She wore an orangey-pink string bikini unabashedly and didn't pose or put on airs about it. There was a bit of tomboy in Allie, too.

The first day we met her, Newf and I were playing catch with the football in the empty field by their cottage. She came walking by, still wet from swimming. Newf threw one over my head. Allie raced over, scooped it up, and dared me: "If you want it, come get it." She was half a foot taller than I was, brown hair past her shoulders, a smirk on her face. That bikini. I froze. She shrugged. "Guess it's mine then." Newf charged right up to her and started swiping at the ball. When she held it over her head, he tackled her. The ball squirted loose. I came up with it, but Allie grabbed me by the waist and took me down. I managed to roll the ball to Newf, and he ran off before Allie could catch him. She laughed, brushed herself off, and sauntered away. We instantly regretted prevailing.

From that day on, any time we saw Allie on the beach, we started throwing that football around in front of her. Without fail, she'd get up and try to take the ball away. She'd tackle us. We'd tackle her. Sometimes she'd run into the water and we'd give chase. We'd splash and dunk her, and she'd do the same to us. Every day for the two weeks she was up, we'd play keep-away like that.

The next summer, we couldn't wait for the Bell's turn to take their two weeks in the red cottage. But in one short year, everything had changed. Allie didn't want to have anything to do with us. She'd found older boys south of the Eighth—or they'd found her. We still hung around their cottage and played catch on their stretch of the beach, hoping against hope, but we only saw her lying aloof in the sun, getting ready to go somewhere, or climbing into one of those older kid's cars.

That was the year we got to know Andy and his friend Casey, who he'd invited up to make his vacation more tolerable. They were two years older, bored, and looking for ways to kill time. We were convenient targets. Their favorite game was throwing rocks at us when we swam; small rocks, lofted high and piercing the water with ominous thunks. We'd dive underwater so they couldn't see us, come up somewhere else, wait until they wound up to throw, then dive under again. Neither of us ever got hit. It was only years later that I recognized how cruel Andy and Casey had been. The rock throwing wasn't the half of it. There was a trap door outside the red cottage that went down to a small, dank cellar riddled with toads. One time they tricked Newf into going down there and locked him in. I had to threaten to tell Andy's dad before they let him out. Another time, Casey chased me down, pinned me to the ground, and dangled a rope of spit as close as he could to my face before sucking it back up. He liked that trick so much, he repeated on Newf a handful of times. I wish I could say we did everything in our power to avoid him and Andy, but the truth is, we sought them out. We thought it was cool to be hanging out with older kids, never mind the abuse.

We didn't pay much attention to Audie those first couple summers. She was there, though, on the periphery, tagging along. She liked to gallop everywhere she went and would sometimes even whinny. Her sister would roll her eyes. That second year, Audie was taller and spindly, like she'd become the filly she wanted so badly to be. But by then, she was over horses. She spent most of her time with her mom, drawing or taking photos. Whenever we did see her, she had a camera aimed at us, that trusty Canon of hers. Every photo I have as a kid on the beach was taken by Audie and bestowed on me in the last couple years. She presents them like ancient artifacts, expecting me to receive them just as carefully. I oblige, lifting them from her palms by their edges. And I lean them against the mantel of my fireplace. They are exactly what Audie treats them like; relics from a lost world.

The only time Newf or I stood up to the bullying was when Casey teased Audie. They were teaching us to play poker one rainy day. Audie was taking too long to make decisions. Casey started razzing her. "Come on, Oddly." "Speed it up, Oddly." Andy let him get away with it, even laughing along. I felt bad for Audie, but I wasn't about to say anything. I assumed Newf felt the same way. When Audie bet all her chips and lost on a nothing hand, either trying to bluff or wanting to be done with the teasing, Casey declared her "Oddest of the Oddlies" and howled with laughter. Newf unleashed a roundhouse punch that knocked him off his chair and flat onto his back. He stood over Casey and growled "Don't call her that." Then he marched out of the cottage. I don't remember having any other problems with Casey and Andy, or ever hearing Audie called "Oddly" again.

The third summer the Bells came up, they took the red cottage for the whole month of August. That was 1982, when we were 16. It was also the year my parents sent me to Camp Chikopi in Algonquin Park for seven weeks. It was a swim camp. They said they wanted me to have a new experience. What they were really doing was working on their marriage. When I got back from camp, the Bells had already been up for two weeks. That's where I found Newf. He and Audie were at the kitchen table doing a puzzle. On a sunny day. When Audie looked up at me, I didn't know who she was. Then she smiled. That same timid smile she has today. It was Audie, and she was beautiful. Not like Allie. Not attractive in the way anyone could plainly see. Beautiful, like you were rewarded for noticing. Yes, she was more womanly. But it was the blush of her. And those eyes. There was a quickness to them, and a light, and so much feeling. She vaulted out of the chair. "Tommy!" she gushed. And she hugged me. Before that, I don't remember any other girl getting anywhere close to me. Besides Allie's tackles.

Newf had changed too. It wasn't as obvious, though; that is, if you hadn't been friends for so long. His smile was the same. And he belted out that gruff "Hey!" like he always did. But it was subdued. It wasn't like our friendship had cooled. He was just more serious. I sat, and we worked on that puzzle, and I told them about camp, and they laughed. And I don't remember ever playing again with Newf after that. Playing…like kids.

I learned soon enough one reason why Newf had become so solemn. My mother told me he had saved Audie from drowning one windy day. Audie had taken an air mattress out into the lake's morning calm and drifted off. Then the wind kicked up and swung to the east. An offshore breeze. Anybody with a boat on Boiler Beach knows you don't go in the water when an offshore breeze gets strong. Before anyone noticed, Audie was well past the second sandbar and a good 10 cottages north. People started shouting. Newf was close enough to hear them. My mom said he was pulling off his shirt as he came running down the dune. He stripped down to his underwear and dove right in. Newf wasn't the greatest swimmer. I was the one at swim camp, and it would've scared me to go that far to catch her. But Newf started flailing at the water and didn't let up until they saw him grab the air mattress.

By then, it had blown beyond the protection of the bluff, where the winds were even stronger, and the waves got choppier and white capped. Audie was hanging over the mattress crosswise, and all they could see from the shore were the two ends pointing up like crooked wings. Sometimes when the waves swelled, they couldn't see anything at all. Newf started pulling the mattress in. It was slow going because Audie couldn't help. Those with binoculars said she looked unconscious. At some point, 300 hundred yards out, the mattress shriveled out from under Audie, peeled off the water, and fluttered away. Newf got Audie on his back, clinging around his neck, and paddled her the rest of the way in. They laid her on the beach and gathered around while she recovered. Newf stumbled off to his cottage before anyone could thank him.

That explained Newf's doting on Audie, and their easy, unassuming intimacy. But I never understood why that meant they had to be together all the time. Whenever I went to find Newf, he was with Audie. If I had never come back from camp, they wouldn't have cared.

Those last few weeks of the summer might have been disappointing were it not for a chance encounter at the store on the top of the hill. That store had been around since the Forties. It was never much more than a roadside stockroom, catering to cottagers who were in too big a hurry to drive into Kincardine for conveniences. The store's biggest draw was penny candy, and its best customers were all the beach kids who couldn't think of anything better to do than jolt themselves with sugar. Sweet Tarts, Jujubes, and Chuckles, five cents apiece. Sugar Daddies, Smarties, and candy necklaces, three cents. Licorice and Pixie Stix, two. Tootsie Rolls, Bit o' Honeys, Bazooka Joe bubble gum, a penny apiece. Then there were the jawbreakers, multi-colored balls the size of marbles, three for a penny. You could stuff a bag with 75 of those for just a quarter. That's what I'd usually get, and they would be gone within a day. Old man Buehlow—Nelson, was his first name—would hover over that counter, reach under the glass, and count out your candy in that slow, deep voice of his. It had to be torture for him, waiting on little kids who made elaborate orders, only to change them again and again—all for a measly quarter.

The Buehlows sold the place to a young couple from Point Clark when I was 13. Jim and Sally Beam. That's right: Jim Beam. My dad got a big kick out of that. He was a laid-off handyman at the nuclear plant who'd come into some money when his father passed away and handed down a bunch of farmland outside Listowel. Mr. Beam never wanted to follow in his dad's farming footsteps. He sold the land and was sitting on a few hundred thousand dollars, wondering what to do with it.

As chance would have it, he'd run into Mike Garton, Rob's dad, at the Spider's Web bar a couple years before, and they got to talking softball, of all things. Beam mentioned he played on a team that faced the legendary Eddie Feigner, the so-called King, who barnstormed across the U.S. and Canada for decades, taking on all comers with a three-man squad; a catcher, shortstop, and first baseman. Feigner could underhand the ball 102 miles an hour. Legend has it, he threw 930 no-hitters and had an astounding 144,000 strikeouts over his 60-year career. In a 1967 charity game, he whiffed Willie Mays, Willie McCovey, Brooks Robinson, Maury Wills, Harmon Killebrew, and Roberto Clemente—all while Clint Eastwood stood in left field smoking a cigarette. Beam told Garton he hit a homer off Feigner in an exhibition outside of Waterloo that broke up a perfect game.

That was all Mad Mike needed to hear. That's what people called him behind his back; his friends called him Mighty Mike. Right on the spot, Mike invited Beam to play in the weekly Boiler Beach pickup game. Sunday softball had a long tradition at the beach. Cottagers were more devout about it than church. They'd show up at the ballfield behind cottage 50 early in the morning, form a line, then count off one-two, one-two to divide up teams. It was all in good fun—at least in the early years. A lot of men would come straight from the beach, in bathing suits and bare feet. One guy named Scorgie played third base without a glove. Then there was Louie Hornschmeyer, who'd stand in right field, smoking a cigarette with a beer at his feet, never moving a muscle unless a ball got hit right at him. That's because the right side of the field was tucked up against the bluff and so shallow, they made a rule that if a ball went into the woods there, it was just a single...provided you didn't touch it. If you did, the batter could take as many bases as he dared. Right field was the perfect place for Hornschmeyer; he could have a little hair of the dog and make a play or two if a lazy fly ball—what he called "a can of corn"—fell within reach. And the downside of his laziness was a lousy single.

Guys like Hornschmeyer and Scorgie don't play Sunday ball anymore. Around the time Garton met Beam at the Spider's Web, Boiler Beach softball got serious. Part of it was because in the Seventies they started a tradition of having a North-South rivalry game on the August civic holiday. Concession 8, that steep road where I lobbed my empty XXX, was the dividing line between North and South. By all rights, Garton should've been a Northerner. After all, he had eight cottages around the gully. But once Mike started renting out his cluster of properties, he decided it would be a good idea not to be so accessible to renters. He bought two cottages at the south end of Boiler Beach, knocked them down, and built himself a rustic mansion.

Once Garton became a Southerner, winning the annual game was an obsession. That might be because for the first six years, the North shellacked the

South. So Garton started bending the rules. If he heard of a good player any-
where south of the Eighth—on a nearby farm, along Lurgan Beach, or in
Point Clark—he'd get them to play for the South. Jim Beam was fair game
to Garton, and no one from the North complained about it—until he clubbed
four home runs his first year, and the South broke their losing streak. That's
when things got out of hand. The North started recruiting Kincardinites. The
South found a guy in Port Albert who'd played minor league ball for the
Detroit Tigers. That little Sunday pickup game was never the same again.
People started showing up with cleats. A crew of impartial umpires was hired
from Walkerton. There were practices scheduled practically every night. Louie
Hornschmeyer would've spewed his Molson all over his tiny spot in right field.

In spite of all the changes, one thing stayed constant after Garton recruited
Beam. He kept leading the South to victories in the annual game. Beam was
the Babe Ruth of Boiler Beach softball. Nobody could hit the ball within 50
feet of where Beam regularly sent it. Whenever he came to bat, people got quiet.
To watch him stride slowly to the plate, roll his head to loosen his neck muscles,
take a couple pitches like he wasn't even paying attention—then uncoil his
effortless swing and launch a moonshot higher than the bluff...well, that was
to witness greatness. Mad Mike owed a lot to Jim Beam; beach bragging rights,
money from bets he made on the game, his sense of superiority over other cottag-
ers. So, when Beam told him about his idea to buy the struggling beach store,
Garton was eager to help out. Some would say too eager. My dad thought
Garton took advantage of Beam. Whatever the truth, he endorsed the big idea
behind Beam's plan; to turn the store from a sleepy summer outpost into an
ambitious year-round collection of businesses.

The Buehlows wanted half a million for the store in 1979, an unheard-of
sum for those times. Beam offered $400,000 and got a loan from Garton for
half that. He could've put more of his own money into the store but held back
to fund his first wave of business ventures. He bought new shelving and a run
of refrigeration units, and turned the place into an upscale grocery store, the
kind that foodies would appreciate today. He hired a butcher from Amberly to
bring in meats; the hot dogs alone were a big draw. He even bought a delivery
truck and brought groceries door-to-door to cottagers—for a fee, of course. His
first driver was Grant. That's a story for later.

Beam had a lot of irons in the fire. But they weren't enough. Three great
months in the summer and a couple decent shoulder months couldn't compensate

for the dearth of business from October through April. It was Garton who finally came up with the brilliant idea that put Beam under. The only reason Mad Mike and his friends ever came up in the off-months was to snowmobile. When they did make the drive from the States, they parked in the dirt lot in front of the store. That's because the hill roads were often buried in snow. More than once, Garton had bemoaned that the store was closed.

What if, Garton suggested to Beam, he opened the store from December through February as a snowmobile haven? He could buy a couple used Ski-doos to rent, stock the place with the sort of stuff guys on long party weekends might want, make a trail map, and start promoting the place. Garton promised to be Beam's biggest customer; he'd organize a big retreat for his rich friends, fill up all the cottages he owned, and make sure Beam broke even the first year. And that's exactly what happened. Beam's first season running Sledheads— that's what he called the store in the winter—was so successful, he bought three more used Ski-doos. And he got a gas pump put in. And he built a big fireplace at one end of the store for snowmobilers to warm up and have a beer. And he hired a guy who knew how to groom trails and convinced farmers like Graham Newfield and Paul Ackert to let him cut routes through their fields. He even ran ads in the Detroit and Toronto newspapers. He went all in. And Garton helped out by booking long weekends for every cottage for 10 solid weeks.

After all that, it didn't snow until mid-January. And when it did, Highway 21 was so bad, no one could get up to take their weekends. Garton was there for his annual getaway when the blizzard hit. They were snowed in for five days. The drifts overwhelmed Garton's lodge; they had to dig tunnels to get out the back door. Beam took a bath that year. The next winter, less than half the snowmobilers returned. Garton even skipped out, electing to spend the winter in Arizona. To put it bluntly, Sledheads was dead, and the impact of that crippled Beam's summer business.

He didn't go down without a fight. With the last of his money, he started building a putt-putt course behind the store. It was a good idea—a play to win back the people who'd always been the store's best customers: all those bored beach kids. He'd alienated them by getting rid of the penny candy and replacing it with healthier options. Newf called the store the Funky Granola Hut, and that's pretty much how every kid viewed it. But a putt-putt course—now that was something the younger crowd could get behind. Unfortunately, Beam's timing was bad. He got six holes built, then the stretch of bluff where he'd put the course collapsed. It does that from time to time. Rains come, runoff gouges the soil, and a chunk of land slides into the woods. When those big, green-furred concrete tongues slid down the hill, it was the end of the Boiler Beach store. Beam couldn't pay back the loan he got from Garton, so he sold out to Mad Mike—for half of what he paid to buy it. Garton sold off the shelving, counters, and refrigerators, got rid of the gas pumps, tore down the fireplace, threw up some walls, did a little plumbing, and turned the store into a duplex, which he rented out for a pretty penny.

Whispers were that Garton had expected things to go badly from the minute he loaned Beam money; that it was all an elaborate plan to get that prime real estate on the cheap. I find that hard to believe. It doesn't make sense that Garton would play Beam, for reasons that are about to become clear. If that were the case, you'd expect there to be more bad blood between the two. But Beam never voiced any resentment toward Garton. He took his losses, licked his wounds, and went back to work at the plant. The only indication there might be any friction was that Beam stopped playing Sunday ball. And for 14 years, the South didn't beat the North in the annual game.

None of that had anything to do with the summer I was the third wheel to Newf and Audie, nor the evening I followed them into Mr. Beam's store. At that moment, all I knew about Jim Beam was that he could clout a softball farther than anyone I'd ever seen. I didn't know he had a family. I didn't know who the girl was working the register. None of that mattered. The only thing I cared about then, as it came my turn to pay, was that I was standing in front of the prettiest girl I'd ever seen. To say she was radiant doesn't do her justice. This girl shined in a way that was more incandescent than the light around her. It was after sunset. By all rights, her face should've succumbed somewhat to nightfall. But no. She had reddish cheeks and golden skin that had caught just the right amount of sun. And she had an easy smile, her mouth wide, teeth white, the tip of her tongue showing.

Those big, round eyes of hers fluttered up to mine and stuck. Audie gave me a nudge. "Tommy? Are you going to pay?" Apparently, the girl had told me twice what I owed. It was Sharon. Yes, that Sharon. Rob's Sharon. Whenever Audie recounts that story, she says I paid in "dumbstruck awe." Always those words. I don't know about that, but I do know I didn't speak, and I didn't hear anyone else until I was halfway down the hill. That's when Audie shoved my shoulder and said, "Someone's smitten."

Two days later, when Newf and I were lying on the beach, Audie appeared with Sharon beside her. I don't know what Audie had told Sharon. Maybe she said, "This guy's fallen for you." Whatever. We liked each other from the moment we met. Trouble was, there were just three days left that summer. On the last night, we had a bonfire, sat together, had marshmallows, and let the fire die. When it was time for Sharon to walk home, I went with her. We walked in easy friendship down to the Eighth, up the hill, and right to the front of the darkened store. Then we turned to face each other. She leaned in quick and kissed me. Then she kissed me again, longer, until we were both kissing. She stopped again, smiled, and hurried inside. I floated down the hill when I left her, then all the way back to Michigan, and all through tenth grade. I couldn't wait to get back up to the beach.

That next summer I got my first job: fee collector at the Boiler Beach Golf Course. I had to start the day after my last day of school, early in June. My parents didn't even come up with me the first two weeks. They drove me up, dropped me off, and left me alone at 112. Hardly any cottagers were there. But Sharon was waiting for me. Those two weeks in June when I was 17 were some of the best days of my life; free of cares, flush with innocence, full of possibilities. It was stormy the first week Sharon and I were together. The winds blew in hard from the north and the waves were huge, overtaking nearly all the sand so there was barely space to walk. Still, we went out every day, usually after I was done work and her dad let her leave the store.

We looked for beach glass. Before that summer, I barely noticed the little treasures. Sharon had been collecting with her mom for years. She was better at it than me. On a good walk, she might find 20; I'd get five. For whatever reason, I could only seem to spot the brown ones, the battered pieces of jettisoned beer bottles. Sharon was just as good with the browns but was uncanny with white beach glass. When the whites were wet, they were practically invisible to me. Sharon could catch their unusual glint yards away. And I've never found more than a handful of greens. They came easy to Sharon, too. She'd see the color out of the corner of her eye, bend at my feet, and pluck a mere sliver out of a bed of stones I'd been scanning.

It was competitive at first. Then, once I realized I had no hope of matching Sharon, it became a kind of idyllic diversion, something we could channel our feelings into without declaring them. We had our own language for seeking out glass. The thin, flat pieces were the most common, and we called them "wafers."

The thick pieces were "chunkies." And any piece that had lettering on it was a "clue." If the glass still had sharp edges, we'd say it was "raw" and throw it back in the lake. And we developed theories for how long it might take those raw pieces to "cook"—and where along the shore they might return.

Once every few days, we'd find a piece of blue beach glass, easily the rarest of all colors. We called them "sapphires," and they usually weren't much bigger than a shard. But the day before Audie and Newf were coming up, and our time alone would be over, Sharon found a chunky sapphire clue. It was the biggest piece of glass she found that week, never mind the color. Half the round opening of a bottle was there, with the thick lip and a hint of the screw threads. Then it tapered off the neck onto one shoulder where the word "MILK" was etched. It was from an ancient Milk of Magnesia bottle, but it may as well have been the Holy Grail for as thrilled as we were by it. Sharon wanted me to have it. There was no way I was going to deprive her of the find. She asked if I would at least hold it for her since she didn't have any pockets.

Later that evening, we sat in the dunes by 112. It was the only good sunset during those two weeks. The beach grass was so high, we couldn't lean back on our elbows or we'd lose sight of the sun. We watched it touch the horizon and go down, and we watched the sky go from orange to red to purple. And we watched each other, and we knew we were sharing a rare joy. And when we'd look away and then back to each other again, our hearts expanded with the changing sky. That night, when we laid down under the protection of the high grass and the boundless heights of that ripening night, our kisses were different, less anxious, more tender.

When I walked her home, Sharon asked for that magic piece of blue beach glass. I reached in my pocket. It wasn't there. We figured it had fallen out in the dune. I promised to find it in the morning. I knew exactly where we'd been. You could see where we'd flattened the beach grass with our bodies. But I couldn't find it. I ran my hand over the whole area, retraced our path through the grass, even got a rake and raked across the dune. I was heartbroken and dreaded telling Sharon. I went straight to the store anyway. As soon as I got up to where she was ringing in customers, I delivered the bad news. If it disappointed her, you couldn't tell by her reaction. "We'll find another," she said. We never did find anything like it that summer, or any other.

Once everyone came up, the summer changed. With Newf and Audie around, we looked for more things to do than walk the beach. When Sharon didn't have to be at the store, they'd all come down to the clubhouse and kill time until I was done working. We'd play Yahtzee or Euchre all afternoon. And I'd give them free grape sodas and Sweet Marie bars, paying for them with the meager money I made. A lot of kids from down that way came around too, and that's how our circle of friends widened. I felt more connected to the beach than I ever had; more, certainly, than I do today. I met more people, learned more stories, became more known myself. Boiler Beach was my world, I knew my place in it, and there was nowhere else I'd rather be.

At the time, I never stopped to think about what I lost with Sharon when those two weeks of togetherness were over. Today, it seems like a blissful dream. We didn't stop taking walks, but we rarely did them alone anymore. Newf and Audie usually came along, and Newf went so fast, we couldn't devote enough time to finding beach glass. As much as Newf had changed after he saved Audie from the offshore breeze, he was even less like the friend I'd grown up with that summer. For one thing, he'd gotten bigger, about as tall as he is today, a good six feet. And he'd lost that plump, childish face of his. He was more raw-boned, and sometimes he would grimace like his dad when I saw him working. He didn't laugh as much either. If he did, it came out in a coughing burst, more an affliction than a laugh. I'm sure I was changing too. But we never recognize it in ourselves as much as others, do we?

That was even more the case back then, when I was coming up to the cottage for such a long stretch of time. At home, I might see friends for a couple hours a day at school, maybe more on the weekend. And it would go on like that for 10 months. I'd rarely get enough time with any of them for an impression to form of who they really were, and there was never a long enough absence for change to make a difference. Here, where I was with my friends for hours on end, every day for 10 weeks, then apart for the rest of the year, I knew them better and their changes seemed more profound. Coming to Boiler Beach was like entering a time-lapse life, where everything around you went too fast, while your ability to take it in slowed to a crawl.

One day, we decided to walk to the Point Clark lighthouse, six miles south. It was Sharon's idea. Newf said he wasn't going to go, but once Audie asked if she could tag along, he marched off ahead of us. Two miles before the lighthouse, you have to cross the Pine River. This isn't some little creek like the one that flows through my gully. This is the confluence of hundreds of little creeks, a real river, 30 yards across, strong enough to form white caps of its own that clash with the lake's waves at the mouth with a deceptively volatile undertow. No matter where you started along the bank, if you didn't swim hard enough, the current would push you into that churn in a matter of seconds.

When he got to the river, Newf declared, "We can't go any further." Sharon and I looked at each other. We'd always known the river would be there, and we'd have to cross it. "The current's way too strong," Newf insisted. Then he started back north. "Come on, Audie."

Audie looked at us. "I've swam this lots of times," Sharon told her. "It's easy. Just swim upstream and don't stop. You'll end up right over there." She pointed across from where we were, well away from the roiling mouth.

"She can't go!" Newf suddenly boomed.

"I can do whatever I please," Audie said, and dove in. She started off toward where Sharon had pointed, flailing furiously, but the currents pushed her off course within seconds. Sharon was the first to dive in after her. I went next. The water was darker than the lake, and the current was much stronger than I expected. It tugged me as hard as any undertow I'd fought. Sharon swept against me. I looked up for Audie. She was well beyond where I thought I'd intercept her, head down, still flailing, still losing to the current. I told Sharon to get across, then set off downstream. Swimming with the river, I caught up to Audie just before the turbulence and guided her to the far bank. We climbed out of the water. Audie wasn't even breathing hard. "I didn't need your help." She loped off to meet up with Sharon. It was only then that I noticed Newf. He was down at the edge of the churn, where Audie might've wound up had I not caught her.

I don't remember reaching the lighthouse that day, or climbing up to the top of it, like we'd planned. Maybe it was closed when we got there. Maybe there was too long a line, and we decided not to wait. Maybe we went up and it was like any other time. My memory fails. All I recall of that walk was our struggle to cross the Pine River, how rattled Sharon and I were after it, how distant Newf was, and how giddy Audie seemed to be. When we came to the river on the way back, she wanted to swim it alone again. Sharon and I tried to talk her out of it. Newf never said a word, at least not until I told Audie I'd get in first, then she could float on my back. "She doesn't want any help!" he snapped. So, we let Audie swim the river again. But this time, Newf dove in right after she went and stayed close by, not so close that she knew he was there, but close enough to nudge her if she drifted.

We didn't see Newf for a few days after that. If Audie was bothered by his absence, she didn't let on. When he did finally show up, he was wading through the shallows, pushing a big raft our way. This wasn't the sort of raft we banged together as kids from lodgepoles. This was a well-crafted job, a square platform of perfectly laid two-by-sixes with a marine carpet covering it, big black floats so it stood out of the water, and even a metal ladder for climbing onto it. And to make sure that the wind and waves wouldn't move it, Newf had tied not one but two anchors to the raft.

We took that raft out nearly every day. We'd swim it out to the second sandbar, anchor there, and spend the whole afternoon lazing around, four bodies warming close together. When it got too hot, we'd dive in, splash around, and get back on the raft. When it got too cold, we'd huddle closer. We called the raft "The Island." Newf built a small bin in one corner where we put our towels and drinks and a radio dialed to CKLW out of Windsor. Then, to counterbalance things, in the opposite corner, Newf bolted on this short diving board he found at a garage sale. Finally, he added a couple small benches facing each other, so we could sit if we wanted.

If I close my eyes and think hard enough, I can still feel the sensation of lying on The Island, waves rolling under me, sunlight and clouds fluttering on my eyelids, Sharon warm beside me. Floating and floating. We were safe and secluded out there, together with nowhere to go. I could've gone on floating like that the rest of the summer.

Then one day, this awful whining roared up out of nowhere, and a wave crashed over us. We opened our eyes and sat up. There, sitting on a jet ski was Rob Garton, and behind him, arms tight around his chest, was Joan Duncan. And she was laughing at us.

I woke to thumping. It was so hard, the cottage shook. Or so I thought. I was hungover. I threw on my swimsuit and the first t-shirt I could grab and went to the back door. There he was, face up to the windowpane, peering through cupped hands. I came up from the side, opened the door fast, and startled him.

"Is this the new strategy, Rob? Just punch my cottage to the ground?" Rob didn't laugh. Rob never laughed. At least not around me. Rarely when we were kids, and certainly not now. That didn't stop me from trying to wind him up. He was as serious as a heart attack, standing there with that grim-lined mortician face of his, dressed like a lumberjack, despite the heat.

"You'll probably want to move your car," he said, looking off. The guy couldn't even make eye contact with me.

"What the hell time is it?"

"Nine," he stated bitterly, like sleeping so late was a crime.

"And I want to move my car why?"

"So you don't get blocked in." At that, he walked away.

I hurried after him. "Why am I getting blocked in?"

He pointed out to the road, where the entry to my driveway was. A mini bulldozer was parked between the two stone pillars. "Knocking those down."

The entry to my cottage wasn't on my property. My driveway fed into Newf's then met the road at a 45-degree angle in the far corner of his lot. Of course, the lot was Rob's now, but I wasn't supposed to know that. "So Newf's got you working for him?"

That got his goat. He wheeled to face me. "I bought his cottage. And all his land on the bluff." One side of his mouth twitched up in what qualified for Rob as a shit-eating grin.

He was waiting for me to be shocked. I wasn't about to give him the satisfaction. "Isn't that great."

His mouth unsmirked. "Don't say I didn't warn you."

Fine. I'd move the damn car. I went back to where I parked behind my outhouse and drove out to the entryway. Rob was coming toward me in the dozer. I had this fleeting notion he was going to ram me, but he turned at the last instant and brought it up next to my passenger side. I rolled down the window and shouted over the rumbling. "I'm going to pull into the field." He put his hand to his ear. I shouted it again. He turned the machine off.

"Okay if I pull into the field?" There was an empty lot behind cottage 94, the same one where we used to play keep-away with Audie's sister Allie. It was more of a meadow now.

Rob mulled it over, like it was a big pain in his ass for me to nose into the grass. "For today," he finally consented. "But you'll have to come up with a longer-term solution once I start building."

"Building?"

Rob worked his mouth like something was stuck on the tip of his tongue. Then he spat. "Knocking the cottage down and clearing that field, too," he said. "Need all this land for what I'm doing. Got to close you off all the way from the road to the beach." He swung his hand back and forth, tracing the property line, as if I didn't already get it.

"You building a wall, Rob? Want me to pay for it, too?"

"Well," he started, missing or ignoring the joke, "you *are* going to have to cut yourself a new driveway."

It wasn't until Rob said it that the full impact of his plans hit me. I looked out my driver's side window at the wedge of trees that blocked me off from the road. I got out of the car and walked the driveway to get a better idea of what I was up against. Rob came beside me. "Are you telling me if I want to park on my own property, I have to take down those trees?"

"I don't see any other way."

"And you think the township's going to let me put my entry next to that bridge?"

"Don't know."

"Well, that's great. Maybe the township will have something to say about you taking away the only means of access to my cottage."

"Already checked. I'm within my rights."

What a shock. The township greenlighted another Garton project. "How much did you slide under the table for that?"

"Watch yourself."

"Watch myself. You keep inventing new ways to push me out of my cottage—my home—and *I'm* supposed to watch myself."

"It's a driveway, Tommy."

"Then you pay for it,"

Rob rolled his eyes and snorted, as close to laughing as he ever got. "You can leave your car in the field for now. It'll be a few days before this gets closed for good."

With that, he headed back to the dozer. End of conversation. I got in my car, swung it around, and parked just off the road. Then I had a thought. He'd started up the dozer again, so I had to shout when I came up beside him. "By the way, thanks for the invite."

He turned off the dozer. "Invite?"

"To Carrie's dedication. Sharon stopped by and gave me one. It was nice of her, but I knew no way she'd do it unless you were good with it. So…thanks."

Rob squirmed in his seat. His jaw clenched. "Sharon would *never* give you an invite."

"Hmm." I rubbed my chin. "Maybe your wires got crossed."

I walked away. It was a while before the dozer started up again. I laughed to myself; I'd gotten to Rob. That had done it. Once back inside, though, I started replaying the exchange in my head. What kind of position had I put Sharon in? How would things go when Rob asked her about it? She'd tell him I was yanking his chain. He'd believe her. So, it's not like I was causing any real trouble. But it wouldn't make Sharon happy, and I still considered her a friend. Why piss her off? I needed all the friends I could get.

I was midway through my Cheerios when the phone rang. The cottage phone. I let the call go to voicemail. Then I heard my ex-wife's voice. I bounded across the cottage. "Kate?"

"There you are."

"There *I* am? I left *you* a message over a week ago."

"We just got back from Phoenix," she explained with that quiet remove she'd perfected since the divorce. "I got your message last night, and I called your cell first thing. I tried again this morning. Good thing I still had this number."

"I'm having trouble with my iPhone."

Kate got straight to the point. "So. You want something you know I can't give you."

"I'm fine. And how are you, Kate?" It was a smart-ass thing to say. And not at all calculated to get what I wanted. But I couldn't help trying to break down that officious shield of hers.

"Just fine, Tommy. And I'm not giving you Cam's number."

"How's Brad?" That's her new husband of…was it already a seven years? "And the kids. How are John and Cody?"

"Josh and Brodie."

"I always get that wrong."

"They're also fine. Are we done here?"

Any more of my crap and she would've hung up. So I started in on what I'd practiced saying over a week ago. "Kate, all I'm asking for is Cam's number. I'm not asking to know where he's living. I'm not putting the screws to him to meet me. I just think I should have his number, and he should have mine. Just in case. What if last week, while you were out of town—"

"It's not my call," she cut me off. "I've asked Cam if I can give you his number, and he doesn't want me to. Do you really think I should go against his wishes?"

"Wasn't that over a year ago?"

"Would you like me to ask again?"

"What I would like is for you to help me out. Plead my case. He listens to you."

Kate laughed. "I don't know what planet you're on. Cam hasn't listened to me for three years. I've seen him twice since his DUI."

That put a chill in the conversation. "How's *that* going?"

I could hear the shiver as Kate inhaled. "He got the tether off last week."

For a second there, it was like we were parents again. Together. "He never did cash the check I sent."

"He doesn't want your money."

"Last I heard, he didn't have any of his own."

"He's got a job now," Kate defended him. "It's just part time, but he's not paying any rent, so he's saving a little."

"How do you not pay rent in Ann Arbor?" I wondered.

She paused. "He's staying with friends in the student ghetto."

I groaned. "Don't tell me…the same numbskulls who've been getting him into trouble since high school."

Kate had had it. "I really don't want to waste my time listening to you gripe, Tommy."

"I'm sorry." I was out of arguments. All that was left was my flimsy hope. "I just—I just want to be a better parent."

Kate could've been mean. She had the right. "I'll tell him that," she said, with a tenderness I hadn't heard in years. "Just promise me, Tommy. Promise me you're not drinking."

"What? Why would you say that?"

"You know how you get. That self-improvement rage of yours. It comes after drinking."

"Well, I'm not, Kate. Do I sound like I've been drinking?"

She ignored the question. "I found some of your index cards the other day. You know those notes you wrote to yourself back when we were first going through this."

It took me a second to remember. "Ah yes. From Pastor Bob's sermons. During my brief time as a churchgoer."

"I could text you pictures of them, if you'd like."

"Just toss them."

"Maybe I'll send them to Cam. They might help."

"I don't think so."

"They helped *me*," she said. "I don't know what they mean, but you can tell you were wrestling with things."

"Yes, I was," I agreed, but only to move on. In truth, I couldn't remember what I'd written. It had been years since then.

Kate started reading the cards. "Number one: love God. With 'DO IT' circled beside that. And number six: let go—surrender. Number 10: love the other. And my personal favorite. Number 12: lust has no place in life. With 'lust' underlined. Twice."

I was getting mad. "And here I thought you were being kind."

"I was," Kate replied quietly, voice shaking.

"Well, there's nothing I can do about all that anymore."

"I wasn't asking you to."

"What I *can* do is be there for my son."

Kate stiffened again. "I said I'd talk to Cam."

There was a long silence. It felt like we were digging in for a standoff. "I have to go," I said finally and hung up fast.

I stood at the front window with the dead receiver in my hand, gazing at the lake. The waves were kicking up, coming from the north. A cold front was moving in.

What now? If I didn't get on top of the day, it would overtake me, pull me under. I was already thinking I could use a drink. Had they taken all the beers out of the fort? I was that close to heading up there. Then I remembered: I hadn't checked the gully since yesterday.

I hurried out to the outhouse, got my shovel, and went down to the shore. As strong as the tide was, it still came up short of the gully. I checked where the runoff pooled between the bushes. Sure enough, filled again. What the hell? It hadn't rained. I was grateful all the same. It was something to do, something to keep me from doing something I shouldn't. It wasn't a minute, though, before I heard throat-clearing. Out of the corner of my eye, on the opposite bank, I saw a pair of feet. I didn't look up. I knew who it was.

"Here we go again," Bogue said.

"Mmm-hmm."

"Nobody appreciates you junking up the water."

"Nobody has to worry about their cottage falling over," I said, head down, digging.

Bogue squatted so his face was level with mine. "What did I tell you? Dig the bank straight down, stack a bunch of railroad ties, then fill in the gaps with concrete. Done."

I finally looked at him. As close as he was, I could hardly avoid it. "And what did I tell you? That's why I'm having troubles. Your wall pushes the water over toward me."

He took a long, slurpy sip of coffee. "Some people solve their own problems."

"And some cause problems for others."

"So true," Bogue replied with a wicked little cackle. "So true."

I went on digging. A tongue of water slid into the trench. "As soon as you get that dug out, you know what I'm going to do?"

"No, Bogue. What are you going to do?"

"I'm going to fill it all back in. What do you think of that?"

"I think you've got to do what you've got to do."

"Damn right. It's just a shame to waste each other's time."

"I don't know about you, but I'm having fun." I tossed aside another shovelful, freeing the water that much further. In another five minutes, it would meet the shoreline.

"Suit yourself," he said, mouth tight and small. "I'm going to sit on my deck, enjoy this coffee, and wait until you're done."

"I'll give you a holler."

I dug like a demon after that. I wanted to free the dam as fast as possible, then make a show of working longer, so I could buy time for it to drain. I had the wind in my favor. With it blowing in from the north, the muddy plume would go south, out of Bogue's view, if he really was sitting on his deck.

After 10 minutes of watching the gully empty, I went to put the shovel away. I came around the back edge of my cottage. Bogue was across the bridge, practically mirroring me. I put the shovel in the outhouse as he took a shovel out of his carport. When I turned to face him, he turned to face me, framed in that open junkheap. I blew him a kiss. He gave me the finger. He turned for the beach. I turned to go inside.

I was halfway across the cottage, when I stopped cold. Was that a welding mask I saw on the ground, leaning up against the inside of the carport frame? I hurried back outside. I had to go to the edge of the bridge before I was sure. It *was*. And there was a blowtorch, with its neck pointing out.

Panic jolted me. I knew what I was going to do. I crept across the bridge, watching downstream for any sight of Bogue. Then I stopped on his side of the divide and listened for sounds in the cottage. Nothing. I bolted for the carport. There was the mask; there the blowtorch; and there, lying flat on the ground, was a placemat-sized oval of rusty metal. I snatched it up and took off running down Bogue's driveway for the back road.

My adrenaline didn't quit until I was crossing over the culvert where those kids stopped to stash their beer. Then a new jolt hit. There was Rob ploughing his dozer into a rubble of stones that was once the driveway pillars. I shoved the metal hunk down the front of my swimsuit and flipped my shirt over what stuck out. When Rob saw me, I gave him a casual wave, like there was nothing odd about showing up on the road an hour after he'd seen me walking to the cottage. If Rob was thrown by that, he didn't show it. He nodded, grim-faced, and went about his work.

As I approached my place, an instinct told me to leave. Get dressed, get to my car, and get out of there. I threw jeans on over my swimsuit and tucked the metal slab in them. They were so tight, my stomach kept pushing the metal out. I threw on a jacket, put my hands in the pockets, and hung onto the metal, so it wouldn't fall out. When I came up on Rob for the third time, I didn't even look at him. Who knows what he thought of seeing me again? I went straight to the Town Car and drove off for Concession 8.

When I got to where the back road met the hill, I stopped. I was out of adrenaline, out of impulse. I had to think this through. It was 10:30. I didn't open the Wondermat on Sundays until noon. Where to go? I looked down to where I grenade-tossed my empty. There was a private road that branched off south before the barrier. I could take that to the Duncans and get my phone. But then I'd have to face Joan and that oddball husband of hers, maybe even Bruce. I could drive to Grant's RV in the dunes near Concession 6. He'd want to hear the good news about Audie agreeing to meet. And I needed to tell him how angry Newf was over proselytizing his daughter. But no visit with Grant was quick. Best to save that get-together for the evening. So...

First things first: I took the metal slab out from under my jacket. One side was a smooth surface of rust. I flipped it over. The other side looked the same. Then I tilted the plate, and it caught the light. The slightest trace of three letters arced across the length of the oval like a faded scar: "SAW." This is what Bogue snuck out in the dead of the night to cut off the boiler?

There was a honk. I fumbled the plate. It fell down at my feet. In my rearview, a guy was glaring at me, hand upraised. I hit the gas and cranked the steering wheel. My tires spun on the gravel before catching and boosting me up the hill. I checked my mirror. The guy was still at the stop sign, no doubt deciding to keep his distance from the lunatic in the Lincoln.

So, it was on to Kincardine. Nothing said I couldn't open early, make up for all the times people bitched that I was late. I was going to go straight at the top of the hill and take 21 to town. But at the last second, I wheeled the car left onto Lake Range Road, past the rundown duplex on the corner that used to be Sharon's dad's store, and along the land extending to the edge of the bluff, the strip

Newf had sold to Rob. I looked for clues to what he planned to do. There was the old gazebo, still perched on the bluff, and there the creek bed that started in Newf's field to the east, snaked under the road, and crossed Rob's new property.

This was the source that fed into the gully beside my cottage. I eased the Lincoln onto the shoulder and got out. A strand of water snaked through the rocky bed and under the road. It was flowing, but not as strong as it was out of the culvert below. Somewhere between here, on the east side of Lake Range, and down beside my cottage, the current was getting stronger. Could that happen just by dropping down the hill? I looked west toward the gazebo. You could still make out the ruts we followed years ago to drive our cars out there. I thought of walking the creek bed to the bluff's edge. But what if Bogue came looking for me? What if I was out there when he came up on my car? I got back in the Lincoln and tucked the boiler slab under the floormat, then continued on. A couple hundred yards farther, a new entryway had been plowed into the field, and an excavator was parked, cramped in a small circle of flattened weeds.

On the outskirts of town, I ditched my plan to open early. I hadn't even had a cup of coffee yet. Bean's Bistro had the best coffee in town—and made a pretty mean bacon and egg muffin. But I decided to check out Wendy's first. If she was open this early, she'd have a pot going for sure, and I might be able to talk her into making me that crabmeat melt of hers. She needed the business more than Bean's.

I opened the door to an empty bar. The TVs were off, and no music was playing. Just as I turned to go, Wendy came bustling out from the back. She stopped, holding a jar of pickles, and gawped at me like I was a burglar. "Sorry. I didn't know you were closed."

"I'm not."

"Oh." I took a step toward the bar and stopped.

"You can sit. You just scared me. That's all."

"You sure? I can go to Bean's. I just need a cup of coffee."

"I've got a fresh pot." She set down the pickles and pulled out one of the glasses she used for Irish coffees. That wouldn't be such a bad idea; a little hair of the dog. No way I could ask her for a shot, though. She poured me the goblet of coffee and set it on the bar. I waited for her to ask how things were, like she always did, but she just silently went about the business of quartering pickles. When times were good, Wendy used to serve a whole pickle with every sandwich. Now, just a quarter wedge; one more sign of her struggles. She didn't ask, but I answered anyway: "Things are slightly less adequate today."

"Oh?"

"I lost my phone, caught a kid stashing beer in my old fort, got in a shovel duel with Bogue over the gully. And—oh—I learned that Rob *did* in fact buy Newf's property. And he's blocking off my driveway. So. Not quite an adequate day." That wasn't the half of it, but it was the most I could tell Wendy. Besides, I was trying to be funny.

Wendy didn't laugh. She did stop cutting the pickles, though. "Those Gartons," she muttered, shaking her head.

"Don't get me started." All it would've taken was her asking, and I would've told her about the metal under my floormat. "On the upside," I changed subjects, "Audie loved the butter tarts."

Wendy didn't exactly appreciate the compliment. "They're the last she'll ever get from here."

"Ever?" She chopped the pickles harder. "Sorry."

"I get enough crap without having to hear it from you."

"I know." She seemed out of sorts. "Everything alright?"

Wendy smacked the knife down on the bar, puffed a strand of her cinnamon-colored hair out of her face, and stared me down. "What? Now you want to talk about *my* problems?"

"I don't know. It's just—something is clearly upsetting you."

"Clearly? *Clearly?!* And you would know. Because we're friends, eh Tommy?"

"Wait a minute—"

"I've got news for you," she ranted on. "You're just a guy who comes in here and bores me with his problems. Like 50 other drunks in town. The only difference is, this is the only place you can go. So that makes you think I care; that I'm here at your disposal. You don't care about me, Tommy. Not really. You only care about how I make you feel about yourself."

I was floored. "Wendy…" I whispered. She swung her eyes to the ceiling. Then she started crying. Without a sound. Tears rolled down her cheeks. "If I've done something to hurt you," I tried. She kept staring away, face streaked with tears. I took out my wallet. All I had was a 10 and a 20. I set the 10 carefully on the bar. "I'm sorry." I couldn't for the life of me figure out what for.

"I don't want your money."

"You got me a cup of coffee."

"It's *coffee*," she snapped, like that ended the debate.

I picked up the 10. When I got to her front door, I looked back. She was still staring at the ceiling. "Just so you know," I called out, "I don't come in here for the drinks."

I was miserable all afternoon. I sat in my little closet of an office, gazing out at the store without really seeing anything. What had I done to set Wendy off? I should've never brought up the tarts. They were such a sore point with her. They'd made her famous, at least in this corner of Ontario. Then, in a few short years, they'd become a burden, chaining her to a routine she couldn't stop, a life she no longer wanted. And there I was, maybe not goading her like others, but definitely feeding her despair.

The tarts weren't the only problem, though. As I rewound our encounter, I kept coming back to how I started in with Wendy; by complaining—my lost phone, my gully problems, my boyhood fort, for God's sake. How did Wendy put it? I only cared how she made me feel about myself. Was that true? The only complaint of mine that seemed to get a rise out of her was when I railed against Bogue and Rob. *Those Gartons.* That's all she said. There was more of an edge to those words than all her other detached responses. Could you blame her, with the crap Bogue was pulling? Copying her best recipes, getting to her customers before they could even find O'Shea's?

All that took my mind off Wendy was wondering about the mystery metal under my car's floormat. *SAW.* Saw what? Why was it so important for Bogue to torch that off the boiler? There had to be someone who knew what those letters stood for. The lighthouse museum was a possibility. The last time I'd been there was with my son Cam, at least 10 years back. There was an old-timer named Myron selling tickets who'd been an actual keeper back in the Fifties. He knew a lot about the history of the harbor, and they had a little exhibit dedicated to the Aurora Quest. If he was still there, he might be able to shed some light on the boiler plate.

As soon as there was a lull in bookstore traffic, I locked the door, closed the booth shutter, and went to my car. I wrapped the metal slab in a towel I'd picked out of Lost and Found and headed for the lighthouse.

On the bridge across the harbor channel, I stopped to catch my breath, leaned over the railing, and looked down into the swirling waters. Once, during that last summer we were all together, Grant bet me 20 bucks I wouldn't jump off from here. I didn't hesitate, not because of the money, but because everyone thought I wouldn't do it. I kicked off my flip-flops, handed Sharon my wallet, climbed onto the top rail, and dove in headfirst. I'd never done anything so bold before, or so dumb. I had no idea how deep the water was beneath the bridge. After all, this was just the back channel where people docked their skiffs. I remember hitting the water, plunging under, and never touching bottom. Today, as low as the lake was, I wondered if I could reach it now. I looked to the bank, where the road past the harbormaster's hut dead-ended. It was just as murky there as the middle of the channel.

Would I survive that jump now? Why wonder such things? I backed away from the railing, suddenly dizzy. It took a couple deep breaths before I got my bearings and hurried on.

The old-timer was still selling tickets to the lighthouse museum. "You're Tommy from the Wondermat," Myron announced as I approached the counter.

"Yes I am." I set the bundled boiler piece on the counter.

"I think what they're doing with your sign, desecrating it with one vulgarity after another, it's criminal."

"That's what I keep telling Blair Henry."

"Beyond that, it's a blight on the town."

"You won't get an argument from me."

"It hurts all of us, it does." I nodded politely and unwrapped the towel. "You should do something about it. Get rid of that cheap road sign and paint something tasteful. This is, after all, the historic harbor district. That's my view, leastwise."

Ah yes…the historic Wondermat, Kincardine's first and only establishment proudly featuring musty paperbacks nobody wants and broken-down laundry machines people can't use. "You might have something there."

I pulled out the piece of metal and set it in front of him, with the *SAW* letters angled his way. "I was wondering if you had any idea what this might be." Then I added the story I'd made up on my way there. "I stubbed my toe on it in the lake this morning."

Myron's glasses dangled from a strap around his neck. He put them on, picked up the slab and tilted it. "Curious. Very curious. You say you found this in the lake?"

"Just this morning."

"It must've been thrown in there recently. These cut marks." He showed me the edge. "They haven't been worn down."

So much for my lie. But that wasn't what Myron said that got my attention. "How do you know it was thrown in the water?"

"I can't imagine any other reason a piece of a tractor should be in the lake, can you?" He peered at me over the rims of his glasses.

I felt suddenly on trial. "A tractor." I rubbed the back of my neck. "How do you know it's from a tractor?"

"See this lettering?" Myron traced over the three letters like I'd missed them. "It's part of a Sawyer-Massey emblem."

"Okay…"

"They made steam engines for tractors."

"Like a boiler."

Myron waggled his head. "Not quite. The boiler is just one part of a steam engine."

Alright. So people had ignored the distinction way back when and shorthanded the name. But why a tractor? "So, this Sawyer company, did they make boat engines, too?"

"They may have made them before merging with Massey. But after that, it was all tractors." He handed the hunk of metal back to me. "Paul Ackert would know. He collects Sawyer-Masseys. You know Paul?"

"I know Paul." It was just the day before when Paul gave me that pitying look as he left the meeting at O'Shea's.

"He'll have the answer," Myron slapped the counter.

A tractor. How could that be? I didn't remember my manners until I got to the door. "Thank you," I said, turning back to him.

"Fix that sign," he called out before I closed the door.

I debated heading straight over to Ackert's farm. But when I got back to the store, the front of Blair Henry's patrol car was poking out from where he'd backed into the space beside my Lincoln. Did he really need to back in? Was the action in Kincardine so intense Blair had to be ready to race off at a moment's notice? Before I went inside, I set the wrapped-up boiler piece on my front passenger seat. Blair was waiting at the counter of the shuttered bookstore booth.

"Looking for a romance, Blair?" He didn't laugh. "Don't tell me," I tried again. "You collared the sign bandit."

"I have your phone." Blair pulled it out of his pocket. This was a pleasant surprise, but as I took it from him, he gave a little tug before letting it go.

"You came all the way into town just to give me my phone. Isn't that nice?"

Blair ignored me. He was busy scanning the laundry room. A mom and her young daughter were back by the dryers. "Let's talk outside," he said. That was ominous. I was sure it had something to do with my sneaking around the Duncan cottage and Joan's crazy husband. We were filing along between our two cars when Blair wheeled around and hit me with this: "Are you missing a couple cases of beer?"

I nearly choked on my surprise. "Is this a trick question?"

Blair leaned back on his patrol car. "We found some kids drinking at the golf course last night, and the only one we caught said he stole the beer from your cottage."

I hadn't been drinking for a couple months now, at least not buying it, and I'd made that clear to Blair, who'd developed the impression that I was always one beer away from some drunk and disorderly episode. Who was this punk to lie about my drinking and drag me down? Then it hit me. Of course. Why else would Blair have my phone? "Don't tell me: Bruce Duncan."

"That's right."

"And you believe him."

"Well…you told me you weren't drinking."

"I'm not."

"So those cases weren't yours?"

"Nope."

Blair straightened up, pushed his OPP captain's cap off his forehead, and rubbed his chin. "But you *do* know the boy?"

"I know of him, sure. I've known his mother for years."

"So why would he make up a story like that?"

"How do I know? I can't fathom the mind of a teenage boy."

Blair scrunched his face. Then he started wagging his finger, not saying anything, just wagging, for dramatic effect. Who did he think he was? Columbo? "But why you specifically."

"Well, I do have a certain reputation."

"True. But he had to know that if you told me those cases weren't yours, I'd just come back and grill him more."

Then he lifted his chin slowly and stared at me. I stared wide-eyed right back at him. "What can I tell you? He's just a dumb kid, probably hasn't thought it through." Ah, but he wasn't dumb, was he? The little shit. He must've known I'd either have to cover for him or come clean about what really happened.

"Oh well." Blair said. "I guess it's back to the Duncans."

For cripe's sake. All this over a few kids drinking beer. Like that didn't happen every night on Boiler Beach. "Hang on," I called out as he was crouching to get into the car. He popped up as if he knew all along I'd give in. "You want to know truth? Fine. I saw Bruce carrying beer into the woods behind my house, followed the kid, and caught him stashing it in my old fort. So, I exacted a fee. For the use of my property."

"You exacted a fee…"

"I made him give me six beers."

Blair stepped away from the driver's side door, squared himself to face me across the hood of his car, jaw clenched, arms folded. Then he doubled over laughing. "And you can't fathom the mind of a teenager."

"I was making a point," I argued, not too convincingly, judging by the way his laughter rose to a howl. "Okay, so it wasn't my proudest moment."

"You stole beer from a 15-year-old. I guess it wasn't." He took a big, barrel-chested breath and deflated, lips flapping. "Now I've got to go back and get the real story."

Poor kid. He was a snake for putting me in this position, but he didn't do it to get me in trouble. He did it because he hoped I'd stand by him. "What if I say those cases *were* mine; that they got stolen just like the kid said. Is that going to hurt anybody?"

"But you said they weren't yours."

"What if I said they were."

"But they're not."

"Come on, Blair. I'm sure he's already catching hell for this. What's the difference if he gets in trouble or someone else does?"

"He didn't do it," Blair's voice got hard. "That's the difference. Now there's an underage kid out there still able to get beer."

"Like the hundreds of other underage kids."

Blair threw up his hands. "Alright. Forget it. The whole thing's a pain in my ass anyway."

"Think of it like this: you have more time to crack the case of the sign crook."

He didn't say a thing to that, just got in his car and revved it up. I stepped away. But before he could pull out, I had another thought. I banged on his window. He rolled it down. "What now?"

"Just wondering. That beer. Isn't it technically mine? I mean, if he stole my beer from me, shouldn't I get it back?" Blair leveled me with a scowl. "I'm just trying to stick to the story."

He rolled up the window and drove off.

I got out to the Ackert farm later than I would've wanted. Paul answered the door with a mouthful of dinner and a napkin tucked into the neck of his shirt. I apologized and told him I'd come back. He asked what he could do for me, and I said I found something Myron from the lighthouse thought he could identify.

"What is it?" Paul asked, looking at the bundle in my hand.

"It can wait." I started unwrapping the towel anyway. All it took was a glimpse of the lettering to get his attention. He pulled the napkin out of his shirt, set it on the stairs, and called out to his wife that he'd be a minute. Then he stepped out onto the porch with me. "That's a Sawyer-Massey," he said. "Where'd you get it?"

I told him the same lie, that I'd found it in the water. Paul noticed the same thing Myron did: "That cut's pretty new."

"Yeah, I didn't notice that. That's why my first thought was, it must've come from a ship."

Paul held his hand out for the piece. I gave it to him. He ran his finger over the *SAW* letters. "This is definitely their insignia."

"So, Sawyer-Massey never made any ship engines?"

"Nope. But judging from the arc of those letters, this comes from a bigger engine than I have. Let me show you." He handed the slab back and headed off down his driveway toward an arched hangar, shining silver and pristine, near the edge of the bluff.

"This is where I keep my toys." He grinned, punching in a code to open the big door. He switched on a row of high-intensity warehouse lights, but he didn't really need to. Even through the shadows, I could see six iron behemoths standing side by side, two rows deep, on skeletal wheels nearly as tall as me. Smokestacks sprouted from their fat round snouts. And there, repainted in white, arcing around the bulging end of those giant pipes, were the words "SAWYER" on the top and "MASSEY" on the bottom.

"These are my babies." Paul ran his hand along the side of a steam engine, like you might a prize horse. "This one took five years to restore." He pointed ahead, "But that's the one I wanted to show you." He stopped beside a hulking monster. It was thoroughly rusty, a rougher rust than the wave-worn plaque in my hand. With its wheels off, it looked like the exhausted elder of the pack, lagging behind his bright children. Still, even lying on its cylindrical stomach, the tractor was taller than most others.

"I pulled this beaut out of a field near Teeswater. Biggest Saw-yer-Massey I've ever seen. But that piece you're holding comes from something even bigger." I looked down at the metal like I had a prayer of figuring out why. "It's the size and arc of those letters." Paul motioned for me to give him the piece. "See this?" He held it up to the lettering on the front of his pet tractor. "Taller letters, wider arc, bigger smokebox. This thing was a beast."

"That's why I was thinking it had to be part of a ship. That, and the fact that it was in the lake. I imagine these tractors never got anywhere near the water."

"Well…" Paul cocked his head. "You'd be wrong about that. Back in the Sixties, I did a lot of work down on Boiler Beach, clear-ing boulders, tilling out stones, adding sand to make sandbars. Wasn't legal then. Isn't legal now. Difference was, if you got after it early enough in the spring, no one was around. Today, with all the retirees, you're right; you couldn't bring a tractor anywhere near the lake without someone griping."

Paul handed back the plate. So maybe the boiler *was* the steam engine of a tractor. What did Paul call it? The smokebox. "How old would the tractor be that this came from?"

"Somewhere between 1910 and 1915," Paul said. About when Bud Garton and Walt Newfield discovered the beach… Suddenly, I was anxious to leave. I asked Paul the time and said I had to go.

Up by his barn, we crossed over a drainpipe that took a stream from one side of the dirt drive to the other. I was a few steps be-yond it when the fact of that flowing ditch registered. "Where's all this water coming from?"

"Irrigating my soybeans."

Now it made sense why my gully kept filling up. Newf grew soybeans too, across Lake Range from the land he sold Rob. His runoff went through there down the bluff. But while my creek was a stream at the bottom and a trickle on top, this creek was the opposite; dry on the bottom, according to Newf, yet brimming here. "So, does this drain into the lake?"

"Lord no," Paul said with a quivering laugh. "*Oh-h-h-h-h no.* Used to. Not anymore. Not since the watershed initiative started up a couple years back."

"The what?"

"Oh…how would you put it?" He mulled over his answer. "They're a group of volunteers who started looking into why there was so much algae growing in the Pine River."

"And why was that?"

"It started with the corporate hog farm by Point Clark and all the manure they were generating. Then there was the increase in fertilizer everyone was using to boost crop yields. But the biggest culprit was the drainage systems we put in. They fed all that extra e-coli and fertilizer into the streams, down between the cottages, and into Lake Huron."

That explained why the water in my gully was so green and soupy. But if this group was doing something to stop that, why was the water there at all? "Where does all your runoff go?"

Paul pointed across the field to a thicket of bushes on the edge of the bluff. "See that circle of greenery? That's my retention pond. The runoff flows into there before it goes down the hill, then the water and all the nutrients seep slowly back into the ground."

"What happens to the old creek bed that goes down the hill?"

"Dries up, I suspect. Haven't really gone and checked."

"And every farmer along Lake Range has to do this?" I wanted to know about Newf, but the Ackerts and Newfields had always been close. I couldn't come right out and ask.

"Nobody *has* to do it. But the watershed people twist your arm pretty hard, and they get grants to make it worth your while."

So, there was my answer. If my gully was still filling up, then Newf's runoff was still coming down the hill, and he hadn't built a retention pond to catch it.

I left Ackert's farm with more questions than I had when I came. If the boiler wasn't a boiler, then how did the story of the Aurora Quest start? And why was Bogue trying to conceal the truth? More important, why did my gully keep gushing with water when everyone was working so hard to shut down the flow? Now that Rob owned the land, what hope did I have that the flooding would stop? It was in his interest to let it keep going until my cottage collapsed. And the most painful question of all: how much of this did Newf know? How could he stand by and let this happen to an old friend, no matter how far we'd grown apart?

I didn't remember I wanted to visit Grant until Concession 6 was right on top of me. I hit the brakes and yanked the steering wheel left. The back end of the Lincoln skidded onto the shoulder and threw a spray of gravel before I straightened it out and started down the hill. The Sixth is a longer incline than the Eighth, though not as steep. Unlike where my cottage is, there's a good 100 yards of flat, poplar-covered dune before you reach Gordon Street, the road that runs south behind the cottages. You can't turn north at the bottom of the Sixth; the county decided to keep the dunes as public land.

Actually, you *can* turn north—as long as you're willing to risk tearing up the underside of your vehicle. Grant has been steering the "Chief"—that's what he nicknamed his 1983 Winnebago Chieftain—through these dunes and setting up camp for the last several years. His campsite was hidden by a cluster of poplars and far enough back from the cottages that no one complained about him being there.

I parked my car in the dirt lot just off where the Sixth dead-ended and walked back to Grant's campsite. As I came up behind his RV, I heard voices. Kid's voices. They seemed to be arguing. I crept to the front of the Chief, crouched down, and peeked around the corner. Four teens, two girls and two boys, sat in a shallow arc on tree stumps, facing Grant. He had a Bible in one hand, and his other hand was held out, trying to tamp down flaring tempers. "Please! Be respectful. This is a gathering of friends."

"Friends," one of the girls scoffed. You could tell by the way she carried herself, sitting straight-backed on her stump, wearing a white tennis dress with her bright blonde hair pulled back into a ponytail, that she wasn't shy about her opinions, and was used to getting her way.

"Come on, Molly," Grant said. "We're not here to judge other people's beliefs."

"But God is."

"I didn't even want to come," one of the boys erupted. He was a wolfish looking kid, with a peach-fuzzy beard, jeans, work boots, and a Toronto Raptors cap. He looked like he belonged more in the fields than the cottages. "I'm only here because of her." He gestured to the girl beside him. She shifted on her stump and raised her head. It was Chloe. She didn't look like she wanted to be there either.

"That's fine, Derek. Really," Grant assured the wolfish kid. "Almost everyone who comes here struggles with their belief. *I* struggle with belief."

"Yeah, I don't struggle," Derek said.

The boy beside Molly groaned. He was pale and sweaty, and he kept gulping down burps. I knew a hangover when I saw one.

"You okay, Doug?" Grant asked.

"Do you have any water?" The name, that voice. This was the Doug on lookout duty when they stashed beer behind my place.

"I've got bottles in the fridge," Grant said. The kid pushed off the stump with another mournful groan, then started off on a shaky course to the Chief. I ducked back behind the RV.

"So why don't you believe in God?" Grant gently probed.

"Why should I?" Derek said. "Nobody's ever seen him. He's just inside people's heads."

"So, you won't believe in anything without direct evidence?"

"Pretty much. Like, I believe in Jupiter. Nobody's seen that directly either, but if you have a big enough telescope, it's there."

"Are we going to talk about anything on the program?" The sharp girl named Molly waved a sheet of yellow paper at him.

"There are just four of us here. Why don't we play it by ear?"

"No songs?!" Molly bellowed indignantly.

The door to the Chief slammed shut. I dared to crane my neck around the corner again. Doug was staggering back to join the group. "Anyone want to sing?" Grant asked the others. No one spoke up. "Let's wait until next week."

Molly made a big show of folding her arms, hunching down, frowning. Grant ignored her. "So those magic mushrooms you were joking about," he went back at Derek. "Do you believe in the things people see and feel when they get high on those?"

"You mean hallucinations?"

"Are we talking about *drugs*?" Molly protested. "Is this what youth ministry is going to be about now? I may as well go to Grove Chapel. You know who my grampa is? Larry Moore. He's president of the beach. He's not going to be—"

"Hang on a second," Grant cut her off. "Let me finish my point. So, Derek. If your buddy said he took mushrooms and started seeing serpents coming out of the floor or he floated over the lake, or he had some epiphany, would you believe him?"

"Epiphany?"

"A sudden understanding of the essence of things."

Derek cocked his head and looked sideways at Grant, like he was trying to figure out the trick to the question. "I guess so. But that's just what drugs do."

"So, you're willing to put your trust in that high because it's just chemicals. But you don't want to embrace God because you'd have to trust in him straight. Is that it?"

"Something like that."

"Dear Lord," Molly appealed to the sky.

Grant kept pressing. "What if I told you that having a spiritual encounter triggers the same part of your brain as drugs?"

"So?" was the sum total of Derek's comeback.

"It's the limbic system in your temporal lobes. Activate that and you get heightened spiritual sensitivity. That's all drugs do; they just spark the natural wiring inside us that connects to God."

"Drugs wear off," Chloe suddenly spoke up. "God has to be forever." She said it with a sort of distracted fatalism, like it was a truth she knew she had to accept but couldn't.

"Exactly!" Derek snapped his fingers and pointed at Chloe. "Once you believe in God, you never come back."

Molly stood up, walked to the edge of the poplars, and turned her back to the group.

"And you can with drugs?" Grant asked.

"Sure."

"So why do people get addicted?"

Derek didn't know how to answer that one. "All I know is getting high is fun. Believing in God is boring."

"Not if you're doing it right," Grant quietly proclaimed.

"Then no one I know is doing it right," Derek trumped Grant.

Molly didn't find it the least bit funny. She came stomping back into the circle. "Go ahead. Laugh. You know who's going to have the last laugh? God. He's listening to all this nonsense, and he's filing it away." She tapped her head. "Every word."

Grant blew out a long sigh. "Alright, Molly. Just amp down. We're here for fellowship, not punishment."

"God has a filing cabinet?" Derek joked.

"Shut up, Derek," Chloe snapped. Now it was her turn to get up and walk away. By the looks of it, she was leaving for good.

That's when I stepped out into the open. I had a reason for wanting Chloe to stay.

"Some fellowship," Molly sneered. "A druggie, a punk, and a heathen." With each slur, she gave the person a dismissive wave.

"I'm not a heathen!" Chloe screamed, wheeling around just as the rest of the group noticed me coming their way. They all froze, gaping at me as if Bigfoot just burst into the campsite. I was all ready to say something funny, like how Molly could add a drunkard to her roll call of nefarious worshippers, but the way they were looking at me, even Grant, so stunned and bewildered, I couldn't find the words.

"Sorry. I forgot it was youth night," I muttered. Then I joined them in their awkward silence.

"We were finishing up anyway," Grant said.

"It never got started," Molly swiped. With that, she strutted away and disappeared into the bushes.

I noticed Chloe eyeing me then, whether with bewilderment or disdain, I couldn't tell. All in all, the girl was a mystery. There she was in her sky-blue t-shirt with that googly-eyed cartoon ice cream cone, all timid and unsure of herself. And yet that ready-to-pounce stance, her flaring torso, the Popeye arm…it gave her an unsettling aura of menace.

"Hey Chloe. Glad I ran into you. Did you get Cam's new phone number?"

"Cam has a new number?" She bought it.

"When's the last time you talked to him?"

"A while ago. We didn't talk while he was…he was going through…" She didn't want to say it: rehab. "Through everything."

I took out my phone and swiped around on the screen for show. "What number do you have?"

She checked her phone. "734-642-0735." Easy as that.

I only had to remember the last four numbers; the others were the same as his mother's. "That's what I have. He obviously keeps you more up to speed than me."

Chloe shrugged and turned to go. Derek rose up to follow her. "I hope you'll come back next week," Grant called out before the two disappeared behind the trees. "I'll play some of those songs you like, Chloe."

There was no answer. For a moment, Grant and I stared at each other, him sheepish, me pitying. Then Doug wretched. "I'm going to go," he said, as if it needed to be announced.

"That's…fine," Grant responded.

As the kid shambled off, I called out, "Stop messing with the porta-potty at the Eighth."

It took him a second to make the connection. When he did, his whole body jerked. He gazed at me, eyes buggy and bloodshot, then hurried away.

Grant picked up the stump he'd been sitting on and lugged it over to a pile of logs beside the Chief. I grabbed the nearest stump and followed. There were about a dozen stumps there, apparently the limit of how many kids showed up for these gatherings.

"A visit from Tommy," Grant marveled after we'd retrieved the other two stumps. "To what do I owe the honor?" He had good reason to treat it like an occasion. I hadn't been down to Grant's campsite in a couple years.

"I bring tidings of great joy. Audie agreed to see you."

"You're shitting me."

"I shit you not. She made me promise to be there, too. But you'll finally get your chance."

"After 34 years. When?"

"Probably next Saturday, when I usually visit."

Grant's gaze fell, fixed, it seemed, on some blurry inner point. And his mouth twitched, as though secretly practicing his long-held plea. What if someone told me next week I'd be facing Carrie?

"I also talked to Newf." Grant was still stuck in his trance. "I said I talked to Newf. You need to be careful with Chloe. He's not happy that you're filling her head full of...your ideas."

That snapped him out of it. "You mean Jesus."

"You know what I mean."

"No, I don't."

Did I really have to explain it? "There's history, Grant. You can appreciate that, eh?"

"Chloe's a troubled girl," he faced me then. "You see the sort of kids she's hanging out with, this Derek punk. He's into any drug he can get his hands on. Around here, sooner or later, if not already, that means meth."

Grant had a way of exaggerating people's distress, particularly when it came to the sort of substance abuse he used to partake in. He relished his role as a cautionary tale. "So maybe you should go talk to Newf about that."

"I promised Chloe I wouldn't."

"Why the hell'd you do that?"

Grant hesitated. "She, Derek, and this other kid—Bogue's son—asked me to buy them beer at the Amberly Store."

I laughed. "Beer? Oh yeah, Grant. Real gateway drug there."

"They were already high on something. Chloe was so zonked she didn't even know me."

"When was the last time you'd seen her?"

"Three, four years ago."

"So, she didn't recognize some old hippie she'd seen five times in her life. I got news for you, Grant. To people our age, you're eccentric enough to be memorable. To a kid—"

"When I told them I wouldn't buy the beer, Derek said, 'She'll make it worth your while,' and they all laughed. Even Chloe."

That *was* a problem. "We need to tell Newf."

"I told her who I was then; that I was friends with her dad; that we'd actually met a few times. She begged me not to say anything. I said I wouldn't, but she had to come here, not just to youth night, but for one-on-one meetings too. She promised she would, and she's been true to her word. I can't go back on mine."

"*You* promised her. I didn't."

"Come on. We're making progress. Tonight went sideways. It's the first time she brought that Derek idiot. But I'm getting through to her. If she isn't better by July, I'll talk to Newf myself."

"Awright," I agreed, against my better judgment. "But that's your word to me."

Grant laughed. "Here we are, two old outcasts standing on our honor." He slapped me on the shoulder, and as we headed back to the front of his RV, he threw an arm around my neck and gave me a friendly squeeze.

"I hope you're not this touchy-feely with the kids."

"Aw, you're too uptight, Tommy," Grant pulled me into a quick headlock and planted a kiss on my cheek. I pushed him away. "A lot of these kids could use a hug."

"Or so you think."

"Or so I know."

I let it go. It was past dinner time and I hadn't even gotten to what I wanted most to talk about. For his part, Grant seemed eager to keep me there. He brought out a couple tattered folding chairs, set them beside a firepit he'd dug, offered me a seat, and asked what he could get me to drink. When I told him a vodka martini, he took me seriously. "That's not a good idea."

"I'll settle for a bottle of water."

When I leaned back in my chair, a strap ripped. I didn't want to bother Grant with it. He was so excited to have company—anyone, even me—that he was scurrying around like I was royalty. He got the drinks. He set a little table between us. He carried an armload of wood from around back. He arranged the logs in a tiny tepee, jammed some twigs and leaves inside, and got a fire started. I asked if I could help.

"Oh, no! Sit. Relax!"

He disappeared into the Chief. I heard cupboards banging, dishes clanking, Grant happily humming. Then he came bustling out with marshmallows, chocolate chips, and graham crackers. He set them on the table and settled into his beach chair with a big, satisfied grin. I must've been looking at him funny. "What?"

"Nothing."

"You don't like S'mores?"

"S'mores are fine." I reached over for the bag of marshmallows, punctured the plastic, extracted one, and popped it into my mouth. I may as well have bitten the head off a seagull.

"What are you doing?" Grant roared, aghast. "You can't just eat the marshmallows."

"I don't like it all together. I like marshmallows. I like graham crackers,"—I snatched the box of Honey Maids and started tearing into it—"and I like chocolate chips. Separately. They're ruined when they're all squished together."

"You really *are* nuts," Grant proclaimed. Then he pulled a Blue up from the other side of his chair and twisted off the top. "You don't mind, do you?"

"No," I dismissed him with a flick of my hand. I appreciate the thoughtfulness of people who ask for permission to drink around me. But I wonder why they think my seeing them drink should be such a problem. My triggers are a lot twitchier. I don't need the sight of a beer to set them off. Still, whenever Grant brought the bottle to his mouth, I couldn't help envying his cheap freedom.

"You sure?"

I realized then I'd been staring at the lip of his bottle. "Don't mind me. The only joy I get out of drinking anymore is watching other people."

"Okay," he said, but on his next pull he turned away from me.

"I figured out why my gully keeps filling up."

"I told you about my outhouse poster, didn't I?" Grant blithely ignored me.

"What?"

"Hang on." Grant sprung up and hurried into the Chief. He came out seconds later, holding a sheet of paper the size of a towel, pinching its top corners. He swung it slowly to his side, a bull-fighter with his cape. Sure enough, it was a poster of privies. "The Outhouses of Boiler Beach," it was titled, in an elegant font more appropriate for a wedding invitation. Below the title, in a grid of five rows and columns, were photos of all the outhouses on the beach, along with the number of the cottage they served. I picked out mine straight away. There was even a picture of the vine-covered outhouse in the woods on the way to my fort.

"How's this for a masterpiece?" Grant smiled proudly.

"I'm moved."

"You laugh, but this is going to get me through the winter."

"How's that?"

"It cost me a dollar apiece to print a thousand of these, and I'm selling them for 25 bucks."

"And people are buying them?"

"Heck yes! I've sold nearly a hundred in two weeks."

I get such a kick out of winding Grant up. "So, when do I get my cut?"

"What?"

"I don't recall giving permission to photograph my outhouses and use them for profit."

"Hold on—I don't—you can't—you're kidding, right?"

I held my hands out like it was out of my control. "I've got two of the 25 photos. That's eight percent. Let's say we split things fifty-fifty. So: four percent of 25 bucks is a dollar. What do you say we just square up every time you sell a hundred?"

Grant's mouth fell open. He started rolling up the poster, eyes working back and forth, like he was doing the grim math himself.

"I'm fucking with you, Grant." Poor guy; so gullible. My words didn't give him any comfort. "It's a great poster. Really."

"I guess I *should've* asked people to sign something."

"Don't worry about it. Nobody's going to come back at you."

"Geez, I hope not. I need the money for wherever I'm going to stay this winter."

That was a surprise. For the last several years, Grant had spent his winters in Rob's bunkhouse. That's what he called it, because that's what it used to be. But at the same time Rob built his glass palace, he renovated the bunkhouse, adding a kitchen, replacing the roof, insulating the walls. It wasn't big, but it could handle the winters—a lot better than my place. Letting Grant stay there was one of the few kindnesses I'd ever seen Rob bestow since everything went sideways with the gang. "Aren't you staying in the bunkhouse?"

"I haven't stayed there for a couple years." Grant fit a rubber band over the rolled-up poster and handed it to me.

"I'll pay you for it."

"No, you won't."

I took the poster. "So did Rob kick you out?"

"Sort of, I guess. He just told me he needed to use it for an office. He's been up here a lot the last few winters."

"I never see him."

"You don't get out much."

I grabbed the bag of marshmallows and shook out a couple more. "He was probably hiding away, working on his grand plan for whatever he's doing with Newf's land."

I was about to fill Grant in on what I learned about the sale. But then he said, "Oh, you heard about that."

"Wait. You knew about it?"

"Yeah," he said, like nothing was the matter.

"You saw me yesterday. I was wondering what was happening with my gully. And you didn't think it was important to mention that Rob now owned all that land above me?"

Grant looked at me like he genuinely couldn't fathom the issue. "I figured Newf would want to tell you that himself."

Fair point. In a different time, Newf would've told me as soon as he started thinking of selling. Hell, he might've even asked my opinion. But that time was long gone. "Nobody tells me anything anymore." I popped a marshmallow in my mouth and chewed it around. It was sickly sweet. I decided right then: I never really did like marshmallows.

"Well, I feel like a turd," Grant said, by way of apology.

"Don't worry. I'm not here to bust your balls about that."

"What *are* you here to bust my balls about?"

"Nothing." I got a little prickly. "I came here to tell you about Audie. I came here to warn you about Chloe. And I thought you might like to hear why my gully keeps flooding. Why do you assume I'm going to give you a hard time?"

Grant finished his beer. "I don't know. It just seems like every time we see each other, you're mean to me."

What were we, eighth-grade girls? "That's because you shove God down my throat."

"Shove? I *shove* God at you? I tell you about God, sure. That's my job. I can't help it if you feel threatened by it."

I had to laugh. "I'll try to be nicer."

"And I don't remember anything about the gully."

"That's because when I brought it up, you started going on about your crapper poster."

"Outhouse poster."

I didn't know whether to laugh or scream. "Honestly, Grant. For a guy who likes to get in touch with people's feelings, you don't listen very well."

"What did you say?"

"I haven't said anything yet."

"Okay…" He wobbled his head, like I'd just proven the crucial point he'd been trying to make.

I let it go. "What I was going to say about the gully is that I figured out why mine's filling up and others aren't. I was up at Paul Ackert's today, and his creek was filled to the brim. So, I asked him where all the water was coming from, and he said it was runoff from the fields he was irrigating. Turns out, a lot of farmers by the shore have figured out they can increase their crop yield by boosting irrigation. Then they divert the excess water into the creeks that drain into the lake. That includes all the corporate hog farms down by the Second."

Grant looked confused. "If Paul's creek is overflowing, why is the gully below him dry?"

"That's the big thing I found out. A group of environmentalists discovered that all this diverted water is pumping fertilizer and animal waste into Lake Huron. They're trying to convince farmers to build retention ponds that hold the runoff so it seeps naturally into the water table. I'm surprised you don't know about them."

You could tell the gears were turning in Grant's head. He reached for the Honey Maids, pulled out a cracker, and started chomping away. "Who's paying for these ponds?"

"The group gets grants, but the farmers have to kick in too."

"Tough sell," Grant said. "My guess is, Newf wasn't buying."

"Why would he? If he's selling the land next to the bluff, it's not his problem anymore."

"Exactly."

"What I can't figure out is why my gully only started overflowing this badly a few weeks ago, when the land was as good as sold."

"He probably wasn't diverting runoff to the creeks until then," he reasoned. "Maybe he didn't want these environmentalists in his face about it."

"But now that's Rob's problem," I followed along. Then the implication of what I'd just said hit me. "Wait. That would mean Newf is knowingly screwing Rob."

Grant cocked his head with his eyes wide. "It wouldn't be the first time a Newfield and a Garton have screwed each other."

I laughed. "Revenge. A century in the making." It was too preposterous. Then again, Newf and Rob never were that close after their falling out decades ago. And business *was* business.

"Or…or!…" Grant raised his voice like I'd been trying to talk over him. "Maybe your gully's been filling up for years, but you're only noticing it now because the lake's so low and the waves can't reach far enough to carve a channel for the runoff to escape."

That made more sense. But I couldn't help feeling vaguely disappointed by it. I was imagining more intrigue. "You may be right. Here's the funny thing, though. Just this morning, I checked the creek that cuts through the big stretch of land Newf owns between

21 and Lake Range. There's a trickle in it, but nothing like what's coming out of that old culvert at the bottom of the bluff."

Grant seemed as stumped as I was. Then he started snapping his fingers. "It's *Chinatown*!"

"*Chinatown?*"

"You know, the movie. They were dumping the water at night so no one would know." I was speechless. Then I started laughing. And I couldn't stop. Grant...what a character. "You laugh, but what else can it be? The creek's dry during the day. Then, in the morning, your gully's full."

"You should do a stakeout," I razzed him.

"Oh, I'm *definitely* doing that. I'll get to the bottom of this. If that means sneaking onto Rob's land, so be it."

"Just don't get your nose cut off, gumshoe."

"What?"

"Like in the movie."

"What movie?"

Was he kidding? "*Chinatown*! You know: 'you're a nosy fella; here's what we do to nosy fellas.' Then he cuts Nicholson's nose."

Grant was genuinely flummoxed. "We must be talking about different movies."

"How can you *not* remember that scene? It's the most memorable scene in the whole goddamn picture."

"Not it's not. 'She's my sister. She's my daughter.' " Grant stewed some more. "I honestly don't remember that. Maybe I picked that time to run to the washroom."

"For Christ's sake. Nicholson had a bandage on his nose the whole movie! Didn't you ever wonder why that was there?"

"For *whose* sake?" Grant was quick to pounce.

I pushed myself out of the beach chair and threw up my hands. "Awright. Time to go."

"Aw, come on, Tommy. I was just kidding. Stay! I've got hot dogs. It's a great night. We could watch the sunset. Probably the last we'll see for a while with the storm rolling in."

"I really have to go," I told him. "Just, whatever you do, be careful. If you check out that creek, you're technically trespassing."

"Like we were trespassing every time we went to the gazebo."

"It was different times. And it was Newf's land then."

"Different times," he repeated.

As I started off for my car, Grant's phone jangled. I had no reason to wait; his calls weren't my business. But then he announced, "Well lookie here. A text from Chloe."

That stopped me. "You're not going to answer it, are you?"

"What kind of a spiritual guide ignores texts?"

"The kind who doesn't get his head bashed in."

"Aw, don't worry about that. I've dealt with plenty of angry parents. No one's getting their head bashed in."

I would've pushed back on him, but he was already busy typing away. I left without another word.

I was going to make it quick. Zip down to Joan's, show her I wasn't a sad drunk, then warn her about Bruce hanging around with Marc—without contradicting the kid's beer stealing story. But what if Joan's husband was there? It was starting to sound a lot more involved than a quick drop-in. I was already debating pushing it off to another day. Then, as I reached the top of the Sixth and turned onto Lake Range, my phone rang.

"Hey Audie."

"Hey Tommy." She went silent. I thought we'd lost connection. Finally: "How are you?"

"Good. How are you?"

"Good…" Another long pause. "Is everything okay?"

"Yeah." Something clearly wasn't right. "What's going on?"

"Now, don't get mad. I was looking through the telescope, just drifting along the beach." The way she said it brought to mind some big ghostly bird. "And I saw all the commotion."

"Commotion?"

"Tommy, I see all the things you're throwing around."

"What are you talking about? I'm not even home."

Just as Audie said, "Oh no," I said those very words. Damn Bogue. Things were getting out of control. I hit the gas. "Shit. Can you see who's doing it?"

"I thought it was you."

"It's not!"

"I know! I know! Hang on…blue shirt. White shorts."

That didn't help. "What about the face? Or the color of his hair?" I swung onto the hill at the Eighth. "Could it be Bogue?"

"I guess so."

I fishtailed onto the back road. "I'm almost home."

"Oh God. No. You're not going *in*, are you?"

"Just don't—don't—don't worry. What do you see now?"

"They're still there."

"*They?*"

"I don't know. No. I don't think so."

"Then why—"

"I misspoke, alright?" Audie yelled. "This is too much. You're putting me under too much pressure!"

I parked in the field by my blocked-in driveway and started running for the cottage. "Is he still there?"

"I can't see him anymore. Maybe he's in another room."

My heart was thumping like a fist. I hadn't run that far in years. "Are you okay?" Audie called out. I told her I was, but the way I was huffing, you couldn't blame her for wondering.

The first thing I noticed was the pane on my back door. It was broken, and glass lay beneath it. Then I heard squeaking. The bridge was swaying, like it did after someone crossed it.

"I'm here," I told Audie. My outhouse door was open too. I saw the shovel at the last second, grabbed it, and crept up to my cottage. "They left."

"You sure?"

No. I wasn't. But I couldn't tell Audie that. "I'm going in to see how bad it is."

"Let me stay on the line and listen."

She had a point. If something happened inside, I'd want her to know immediately. "Awright." I was whispering now. "But I need both hands, so you're going into my pocket."

I put my phone in my pants, kicked aside the glass, and opened the door. The kitchen drawers were all pulled out, and one was on the floor, silverware spilled everywhere. All the cabinet doors were open, too, as were the microwave and oven. I held the shovel like a rifle and stepped through the kitchen. There was greater upheaval in the main room. My breakfast table was overturned, and the lazy Susan I kept in the center was broken beside it. Three rows of books had been swept from the shelves on the side wall and kicked across the floor. Every cushion on my two couches and three chairs had been yanked out and tossed aside. The toy ark and little animals I'd bought from Beth had been knocked off the fireplace mantel, along with the old photos Audie had given me. All my pictures had been yanked off the walls, two of which had been encased in glass. Not anymore.

The only sign this was anything more malicious than a hasty search was the picture outside my bedroom. It was a photo my dad had enlarged of he and Jerry Sharp playing Jarts behind 112. I don't know who took it, but it was stunningly crisp for a photo of that era, more alive in black and white than the faded color photos my dad had hung up. In the picture, he was in mid-swing with his Jart, beer in hand, an unfamiliar grin smeared across his face. Jerry stood beside him, head thrown back, beer sloshing out of his stubby Labatt 50, laughing with a gusto I'd never seen before. It was as if the camera had captured the one moment of joy that had eluded these sad men. And there, behind them, back by the cabin, fly swatter in hand, was me, maybe 10 years old, gaping at the men in wonder. This picture had been taken down and punched through. Its frame was broken in half, like Bogue had slammed it across his knee, and the whole twisted mess was flung across the room.

Could the message have been any clearer? Bogue was mad that I took his boiler souvenir, sure, but the real source of his rage was still the galling fact that I was even there, that the friendship of two pitiful men had taken something precious from him and his family.

"Hello?" I yelled out, stepping through the mess. I knew there wouldn't be an answer, but part of me hoped for one. As I pushed open the door to my bedroom, where the side windows perched over the gully, I was choking the top of the shovel. I wanted Bogue to be there. I wanted to be within my rights.

"Tommy!" I heard Audie's muffled cry. "Someone's there!"

I had a surge of panic. Then I realized: she was looking at me. I took my phone out of my pocket, held it up, moved to the window, and shook it. "It's me."

"How bad is it?"

My bedroom was like the rest of the cottage; mattress flipped up, drawers open, clothing scattered everywhere. "Just a big mess."

"Anything gone?"

I must've forgotten to answer, because Audie was pestering me now. "Tommy? Tommy?! Are you there? Tommy!"

I got angry. "Audie, I have to go now. I've got all this shit to clean up, and I don't have time to give you a running commentary."

"Okay," she replied quietly. "I just wanted to help."

"I know. It's nothing personal. I'm just upset right now. You can understand that, right?"

"I wasn't spying."

Bad timing. "What the hell else would you call it?" Silence. "I'm sorry. I don't mean what I'm saying." Still silence. "Come on, Audie. I didn't mean it. You were a big help." No answer.

"Awright. I'm going to hang up. I've got my own problems now." I stabbed the phone. Damn Audie, anyway. Was she so far gone she couldn't grasp basic human emotions? I was shaken up. I was scared. Who wouldn't be? So, I lashed out. It was understandable. Why couldn't she see that?

I went back into the main room and took in the wreckage. Then I found myself staring at the blade of the shovel. I was across the room, out the door, and careening over the shaky bridge before I took a second to reconsider. That didn't happen until I was pounding on Bogue's back door. It suddenly occurred to me his wife might answer. What would I say, standing there, armed with a shovel? Only she didn't come to the door. No one did. I peeked through one of the glass panes. Nobody was around.

It's amazing how easily glass breaks when you have the right tool. I barely tapped the pane with the butt end of the shovel. Once inside, the whole undertaking didn't take more than five minutes. I exacted an eye for an eye. I pulled out the kitchen drawers and made sure to empty one on the floor. I overturned the breakfast table, broke a plate, knocked a couple pictures off the wall. There weren't many books around, but I found a basket of magazines, upended it, and scattered the contents across the floor. I pulled out the cushions. I flipped the mattresses. I threw clothes around.

I thought I was going to have to leave without finding a suitable picture to destroy, but in a back bedroom, there was a photo of Les Garton, Mad Mike, and Bogue. He was holding a fish off the Kincardine pier. He was younger than I'd been in the Jarts photo, and he was the focus of the shot, standing proudly between the two kneeling men. I was all set to take my fist to it, then I held up. Bogue looked so meek in it, cringing at the wriggling blur he struggled to hold. The fact that he would frame this picture, this memento of weakness, and hang it above his computer, what did that say about Bogue? As big and blustering a jerk as he was, he seemed to know he needed this reminder of his vulnerability. I'd be fighting against self-interest to destroy it.

Still, I wanted Bogue to know I could've done the same thing with his picture that he did to mine. I wanted him to understand that I'd spared it. I took the framed photo off its hook, walked it to the front of the cottage, and set it carefully on the reclining chair next to the big bay window, so Grandpa Garton, Dad, and little Bo were staring at Bogue when he entered the room.

It was past 10:00 when I finished cleaning my cottage, plopped down in my recliner, and called it a night. All I had left to do was put the books on their shelves. But my back was aching already, so I left the paperbacks scattered on the floor. I'd opened all the bedroom windows that faced the gully to hear the reaction when they discovered the break-in. The longer it stayed silent, though, the more I dreaded what was coming. Bogue would know exactly who did it and why. He'd mutter a few curse words, but not much more. His wife, on the other hand, might very well scream. I decided I'd rather not hear that after all, but I was too tired to drag myself out of the chair and shut the windows.

Then my phone rang. Just the thing I wanted to do: deal with Audie. I was going to have to apologize to her soon enough, but not right then. I let the phone ring itself dead and checked if she left a message. The call didn't come from her. It was Cam. I called right back.

"Are you for real?" were the first words out of his mouth.

"What do you mean?"

"Tricking Chloe into giving you my number. You're pathetic."

"Hold on. Relax." I leaned up in the chair and planted my feet on the floor. "It's not like I killed someone. I wanted your number. Your mom wouldn't give it to me. So, I did what I had to do."

"And you thought I'd talk to you after that?"

"All I want to know is how you're doing," I lowered my voice to calm him. "Your mom said you were getting back on your feet."

"I got a job now, yeah."

"That's great. Where?"

"Comet Coffee in Nickels Arcade. It's the best coffee in town."

"Yeah?" I couldn't help myself. "Is it the best pay?"

"I'm just starting out," Cam bristled. "When I get full time, I'll get two dollars over minimum—"

"It's just part-time?"

I could hear Cam deflating. "You're incredible. I do something good, and you shit on it."

"I didn't mean it that way. Honestly. It's great. You're making some money. And I hear you found a place to stay. For free."

"Kemp and Riley are helping me out, yeah."

"Kemp and Riley..."

"I knew that's where you'd go with this," Cam seethed. "Look: they're trying to change themselves too. We're all trying to be better people, so just back off."

I'd heard it all before, but this wasn't the time to point that out. "I'm trying, too," I said. "You got my check, right?"

"I tore it up."

"Okay, fine. Do what you want. I'm just saying, if you need any help, I'm here."

"You're kidding, right? You haven't been here for nine years."

"There's nothing I can do about the past. But I'm still your father, and I'm here now."

He laughed again. It was farther away, like he was holding his phone at arm's length. "Come on. You're not going to pull that crap again? Look: you're not my dad anymore. Okay? You stopped being my dad when you started screwing your students—"

"And why was that?" I cut him off. "Why did I do all those terrible things?"

"I don't know. You tell me. On second thought, don't."

"Because I was drinking."

"That's not an excuse."

"No, but it's a fact." The phone was silent. "Cam?"

"I was just waiting for the part where you tell me you're not drinking anymore."

"I'm not."

"At all?"

I thought twice about it. "I had a couple beers yesterday."

"There's a shock. You know what? I don't even care. I just called to say I'm blocking your number. I don't want to hear from you. I don't need your help. You don't have to apologize. Let's just move on with our lives."

The words hit me hard. I felt like crying and screaming at the same time. "Come on, Cam. You don't mean that."

"That's exactly what I mean, D—" He caught himself. "I just think we're better off putting everything in the past."

"That's what I want to do. If we could just meet face to face. I'll come to Ann Arbor. We'll sit down, have a cup of that Comet coffee. We'll talk it out. Start over."

"It's too late," Cam's voice was hushed and hoarse. "I'll pray for you, though."

"You'll *pray* for me?" I was dumbstruck. "What about?"

"About finding a new way. You and me. All of us. We need forgiveness. And we're not going to get it by ourselves."

"What do *you* need forgiveness for? I'm the one to blame here."

"It might come as a shock to you," his anger flared, "but you're not the source of every problem. Think outside yourself for once."

"What's that supposed to mean?"

"Never mind."

"No. Say what you were going to say."

Cam was quiet, but I could hear his breath gathering. Finally: "Maybe you'd be better off if you didn't go around thinking your brokenness was worse than everyone else's."

"That's a low blow."

"Goodbye," I barely heard him say, like he'd gone even further away. "God bless you."

If I could've gotten my hands on some liquor then. Ah well, how many times had I thought that since I'd drunk the last of the Skyy bottles I'd hidden around the cottage back in October, when I vowed to stop drinking for good? Technically, one of those six bottles was still around; I just couldn't remember where. Served me right for hiding them when I was in the bag. Inside the cottage or out? My guess: out. Above ground or buried? I was good and drunk when I did it; digging seemed too ambitious. The outhouse was a likely hiding spot. None of the first five were there. But I must've checked it 10 times. I actually thought of heading out there with the flashlight and giving it one more once-over. I even started kicking a path through the books and back to the kitchen.

Then I heard Bogue shout, "We're not calling the damn cops!"

So they'd been home for a while. And his wife had taken the burglary quietly. Or, more likely, with muted shock. I stopped kicking the books to listen. There was a muffled squabble. Then Bogue roared again, "The hell we are! We're not telling Rob about this. He doesn't need to know everything."

I felt like laughing loud enough for Bogue to hear. He knew full well Rob would want to know something like this—and that he'd be the one to tell him. Keeping secrets from Rob wasn't a good idea. He was always two steps ahead of everyone and didn't appreciate disloyalty. Most importantly, he had the wherewithal to exact payment for it. Anyway, something told me Rob already knew Bogue had broken into my cottage and come up empty-handed. He wouldn't give a damn that I'd returned the favor; he'd probably laugh it off, because unlike him, I didn't have the power to punish. No, Rob wouldn't waste his time worrying about my antics. He'd be thinking about his next move.

*M*ost of us float through this world, never reckoning with the forces that push us along our lonely way. Some have enough of a grasp on how life works to steer themselves on a rough course. A few—the lucky or cursed, depending on your beliefs—see beyond the arbitrary currents of their lives to a power that operates on entirely different principles. Then there are those rare souls like Rob Garton, who are born with a burning compulsion to bend the tides their will. We all have a Rob Garton in our lives, well-meaning though they may be, who can't help but manipulate; who instinctively break things apart—nature, mechanics, commerce, people—to make a cold, calculating study of how they can be used to their advantage.

From the moment Rob roared up to our raft on that jet-ski, with Joan clinging to his waist, he was making plans. I don't mean that in a malevolent way. It was simply his nature to be thinking ahead, to factor the new variables before him into his ever-growing ambitions. "That's one bitching raft," he shouted, over the grumble of his jet-ski. "Where'd you get it?"

"I made it," Newf said with the slightest jut of his chin.

"You made this? How long did it take?" Newf tilted his head, trying to work out the time; too slow for Rob. "Couldn't have been more than six hours. Cutting boards, nailing them up, attaching floats. You don't need those seats."

"I could do it in less," Newf said, goaded into an uncharacteristic boast.

"We could use some of these down south." Rob cracked that near-grin he always had on the verge of a deal. "You could make some serious scratch."

"I've seen you before," Joan broke in. "You drive a tractor."

"So?" Newf snapped. She'd touched a nerve that's been raw as long as I've known him. Even though he lived nearby, Newf felt like an outsider around cottagers. Never mind that his great grandfather was one of the beach's pioneers.

"So, it's weird."

Rob twisted around and gawped at Joan. "What's so weird about it? His dad owns all the farmland from here to 21." Until Rob told Joan that, I hadn't grasped the expanse of the Newfield operations myself. Leave it to Rob to know who owned what, not just the cottages, but the surrounding land as well.

"It's weird that he's down on the beach," Joan said.

"He owns that cottage right there." Rob pointed to the place beside where I am now, which he'd buy 35 years in the future. "His dad could buy 10 of these measly cottages if he wanted to."

That was the other thing that impressed me about our first encounter with Rob. Given the history of the two families in founding the beach, you would've thought they already met each other. But they hadn't. Still, Rob knew who Newf was. Newf, on the other hand, had no idea about Rob, even though the Gartons were the social magnets of the beach. That goes to show how secluded Newf, Audie, Sharon, and I were up until that moment on the raft.

"I waved to you yesterday," Joan said to Newf. "You didn't wave back."

Knowing Newf, that sounded about right. He shrugged like I'd expect him to. But his cheeks flushed. Joan noticed. "Don't you like me?" she asked with big eyes and a small grin. Newf looked away. " Let's go, Rob" Joan decided. "I know when I'm not wanted."

"Think about the rafts." Rob revved up the jet-ski, and they swung away.

Ten minutes later, Newf swam The Island ashore and started walking it along the shallows to Rob's place. I was right beside him, and the girls followed along on the beach. Audie spent much of the walk teasing Newf. She had Joan's impression down from the get-go: the bat of her eyes, the purse of her lips, the way she flipped her golden hair, that husky voice of hers. "Newfie!" Audie lilted out. "Oh Newfie! Don't you like me?" Bat, purse, flip. If you didn't know their history, you'd think she was jealous.

I said none of us had met Rob before. That's not entirely true. Working at the store, Sharon had pretty much met everyone on the beach. And because of her dad's dealings with Mad Mike, she saw Rob more often than most, usually lurking in the background while his dad took care of business. The two had been introduced at least twice, reminded of that introduction more often than that, then left to make conversation. Neither felt compelled to do so.

"Are we really going to take this down to Rob Garton's cottage?" Sharon grumbled when Newf started guiding The Island away from our waters. No one responded. "As if the Gartons don't have enough toys." Then, moments later: "We'll never get it back, you know." As we steered the raft past the Eighth, Sharon stopped altogether. "What are we going to do there anyway? Just sit around with all the other wannabes?"

Newf reined in the raft, turned around, and glared at Sharon. But he didn't say anything. I didn't either. I was too surprised. Sharon never got this worked up. Audie fidgeted with her hands like she always did when she was anxious. "Honestly," Sharon said, "what's so special about the Gartons?"

"I want to go in a motorboat," Audie said. Newf laughed and went on. Audie gave Sharon an apologetic shrug and hurried to follow him.

"Come on, Sharon," I said. She was looking up the hill between the trees at that slot of blue sky; her way home. "If we don't like it, we'll just leave."

"You really want to go?"

I looked away. I didn't want to voice my reasons. They weren't good. I'd walked past the Garton cottage plenty of times, peered up at its imposing face, seen the long veranda and all the people spread across it, laughing and drinking. But I'd never climbed the wide staircase into that world. This was my chance. Never mind that I shared Sharon's disgust with all those upper-crusters who treated the beach like their extended country club.

Then there was the other reason I wanted to go: Joan. Seeing her straddling Rob on the back of that jet-ski, in her sky-blue string bikini, it was mesmerizing. Yes, there was the visual aspect of it; the way the side of her breast pushed outside her top, the long near-naked curve from there down around her haunch and along her shimmering legs. But more than Joan's physicality, there was the spirit that inhabited it. Sharon was developing into a woman too, but she didn't carry herself like Joan. Joan was more comfortable with her body, knew the effect it had, and relished using it. I'd made out with Sharon plenty of times. We were solemn and affectionate with each other; the way, I supposed, one should be. What Joan aroused in me was something else altogether. There was nothing sacred or loving about it. It was rebellious, willful. I wasn't about to tell Sharon all this. I barely understood the feelings myself.

"Let's just go for a little while."

Sharon shook her head at the sky. "If Rob starts showing off, I'm gone."

Even after agreeing to go, Sharon lagged behind. As we approached the groomed beach in front of the Gartons, I got out of the water to wait for her, and we crept up on the grounds together, as if we had to sneak onto them. It wasn't just the boats lining the shore that slowed us—canoes, kayaks, and jet-skis, the Sunfish and Laser, that sleek speedboat. It was the way the half-dozen yellow-and-white umbrellas and all the lounge chairs were so perfectly arranged in the raked sand. And, much as I hate to say it, it was the people too. Rob's older sister's friends, tanned and trim, lolling and laughing, posed like props in some California beach dream. And the adults, perched above on the long porch, slouched around tables drinking cocktails, all in bright regalia; an upper tier of angels. This was before Rob turned the place into a glass cube monstrosity. But it was still impressive back then, more a stately backwoods lodge than a cottage.

Standing on the fringe of that spectacle, it was as if we were taking in an illusion, a movie flickering on some sun-soaked screen. Even when Rob made an entrance, bustling out of the Garton's bunkhouse with an armful of paddles, it didn't seem real. He scurried down to the shore without noticing us, set the paddles in the kayaks, straightened a few boats so they were perpendicular to the water, then turned back to his cottage, hands on hips, surveying the setting as if he alone had placed everything and everyone where it was.

It wasn't until we heard a cry from up on the porch that the veil before us fell. "Sharon!" the call broke over the heaving of the waves. Leaning over the railing, a hippie in ultra-short cut-off jeans and a sweat-soaked tank top was waving both arms above his head. There in the midst of all those sporty adults, he looked like the hired help, just passing through on his way to dig up the next garden bed.

"What is he *doing here?" Sharon wondered.*

It was Grant. This was his third summer driving the delivery truck for Sharon's dad. Everyone on the beach knew Grant, but few had ever seen him doing anything other than standing in his old walk-in van, steering it along the beach road, and hustling back and forth to the cottages he served. What he was doing with all the beautiful people, flailing his arms around on the Garton's private deck, was an absolute mystery.

"It's Grant!" Audie marched ahead, through the raked sand, between the tanners, and right up to the base of those wide steps. I didn't realize until then that Audie even knew Grant.

"What is Audie's problem?" Sharon trudged after her. I helped Newf shove the raft ashore, and we followed the girls.

"Can you believe this place?" Grant raved to Audie and Sharon, as if none of the people around him could hear.

"Aren't you supposed to be doing deliveries?" Sharon said.

"That's the crazy thing—" Grant started.

"Well, look who's here. Little Sharon Beam," Rob's dad broke in, leaning back, elbow slung over the railing, cigar jutting out of his fingers. "You can blame your dad for bailing on softball. We needed another ringer."

A peal of laughter rose from the recesses of the porch. "What could I do?" he joked with his unseen audience. "You darn near dragged me off my truck."

"My dad's truck," Sharon muttered.

Just about then, the bunkhouse door swung open, and Rob came lurching out balancing a pair of water skis on each shoulder. There in the shadows behind him was Joan, with a kid's inflatable unicorn around her waist, a ship captain's hat cocked over her hair, and some sort of umbrella drink in her hand. "Hey!" she shouted with that brassy voice of hers. "It's our sheltered friends from the North!"

"Awright!" Rob proclaimed, not so much with enthusiasm as triumph, like he'd just clinched a deal. "Let's go for a ride. Grant, you wanted to ski, now's your chance. Newf, why don't we test out that raft of yours? Joan, get these four some life jackets."

"Aye, aye," Joan tipped her captain's hat and sauntered off, the unicorn tube rocking on her hips. Audie ran to catch up with her. Newf retreated to his raft. It was all happening so fast. Sharon turned to the shore too, and I thought we were going to follow everyone to the boat, but she just crossed her arms and froze, staring out over the lake.

"Dad," Rob called behind us. It didn't hush the chatter on the porch. "Dad?" he tried again. "Dad!" he shouted a third time. Finally, it got quiet.

"What is it, Robert?" Mad Mike threw his head back and stretched both arms across the railing.

"Look at that raft. I bet we could sell a hundred of those."

"Have at it, son," Mad Mike swirled his cigar to a smattering of laughs.

Rob's mouth fell open, hand still pointing at Newf's raft. Then he shook off whatever else he was going to say and tried again with Grant. "So, are you going to ski or not?"

Grant muttered something to his unseen admirers. Another swell of laughter spilled down. He pulled off his tank top to a chorus of ladies cooing and strode across the deck. "Alright, Big Rob. Let's see what your old man's new boat can do." As he passed Mr. Garton, Grant squeezed his outstretched shoulder. Rob was right there at the bottom of the wide steps when Grant came down, and though he led him to the shore, he kept turning back to check Grant's progress, like he might bolt away at any moment.

It's amazing to think there was a time when Rob looked up to Grant. Today, he treats him like a pathetic freeloader. If you would've told me when Rob was fluttering around Grant as he put on his lifejacket, picked up a ski, and waded into the water, that he would damn near denounce him one summer later, I would've laughed in your face. But no one could've expected the chain of events that would ensnare us all over the course of a year.

At that moment, though, following Sharon to the shore, I was excited. I'd never been in a motorboat before. And there was Joan, now wriggling out of her unicorn tube, now slapping her captain's hat on Rob, now falling back on the seat beside Audie, laughing and kicking up her legs. We were at the water's edge, the boat idling off the sandbar, and Rob was motioning us in. I turned to Sharon, but she wasn't there. She'd stopped beyond the reach of the waves and was sitting cross-legged in dry sand.

"What's wrong?"

"You go ahead."

This wasn't like Sharon. She always went along. "Come on. It'll be fun."

She dropped her head and shook it. "I'll just watch."

By now, the boat had puttered out toward Newf's raft. It was still close enough for us to wade out to if we hurried. I waved them off.

"You don't have to stay with me."

"I want to." That's what I said, as the speedboat thundered away, yanking Grant into his slashing run. But I found myself leaning from side to side with every cut he made.

"You should've gone." Sharon stood and started walking back north. I watched the boat pass one more time before running to catch up. She let us go a little way in silence, then turned abruptly in front of me. "We don't always have to do everything together."

"I know."

"I'm just going home."

"Me too."

So, we weren't really there for that first day with Rob, Joan, and Grant. And that was just the start of missing out. For Sharon, it was more about not wanting to be there. For me, it wasn't so much about feeling obligated to stick by her side as it was being tethered to my clubhouse job. Six days a week, from 10 to four, I had to sit in that stuffy, sunless shack and collect fees from the handful people who bothered to pay for the adventure of playing our quirky little course. Most didn't. Since there were only three holes below the bluff, five on top of it, and one, the infamous eighth, spanning across the wooded drop, you could sneak on up top, play as much as you wanted there, and no one would ever know.

That's one reason people didn't pay to play Boiler Beach Golf Course. Another was that the course was a joke. This wasn't golfing the way even a beginner would expect. The fairways were rougher than roughs, a mixture of spidering crab grass and rock-hard dirt, run over with a tractor once a week, if that. Poison ivy-infested woods strangled many of the holes. And the greens weren't greens at all. They were hard-packed sand, with cracks and bumps that would send a dead-on putt 90 degrees offline like that. Nearly all the holes were shorter than a typical par three, but the fourth was inexplicably longer than most par fives. Then there was the eighth, where you were expected to drive off the top of the bluff, between a wedge in the trees no wider than an alley, over the long incline of woods, and down onto a tiny green.

All this is why many beachers didn't bother paying the five bucks to torture themselves around the course. Heck, Newf and I never paid. We'd sneak on the top of the bluff barefooted, with one club and a pocketful of balls, and whack away until we lost them all. Technically, part of my job was to keep an eye out for such trespassers and roust them off the course, but I couldn't leave the clubhouse. So, for six hours a day, I sat at the window and earned 20 dollars for doing barely anything. I listened to cassette tapes, played solitaire, and read three books that summer: Catch-22, Slaughterhouse Five, *and Ken Kesey's* Sometimes a Great Notion. *It wasn't so bad; that is, until I started feeling like my friends were having summer without me. Even with Sharon visiting more often, playing gin rummy and sneaking kisses, I couldn't help but think we were getting left behind.*

I don't know why it bothered me. After all, I'd taken the job at the clubhouse and come up in early June specifically to spend time with Sharon. And there we were, with more time than we could've imagined. But something wasn't right. Little things: the way Sharon drummed her fingers on the table as I debated cards to play, how our talk would circle back into the same worn grooves, the wistfulness in her laugh. I told her more than once she didn't have to stay. She always said she'd rather be there with me. What sort of person would willingly confine themselves to long afternoons of boredom when they were free to do anything they wanted? Sharon's loyalty didn't endear me to her; it made me think less of her.

That's why, on the day everyone came to the clubhouse to see if we wanted to go to London to watch Return of the Jedi, *I all but shamed Sharon into agreeing. I couldn't go myself. But Sharon had no excuse—besides me. I argued with her that there was no point in staying. Audie begged her to go along. It was Rob who made the most forceful appeal. He sat down across from Sharon, looked her in the eye, and said, "We're beginning to think you don't like us."*

Sharon finally agreed to go. Now and then, I look back on that as the real moment Rob won Sharon over. It wasn't until the next summer that I recognized their attraction to each other. But I should've seen it then. If it hadn't been for something that clouded things minutes later, I might've. While Sharon followed Rob out the back door, Joan lingered behind. "You'd go if you really wanted to," she said.

"I'd get fired."

"So?"

"So, I need the money."

"Yeah," she nodded with a smirk. "But that's not what you want."

The road trip to London melted any resistance Sharon had to spending time with the gang. There was a stretch of bad weather when they piled into Rob's dad's Cadillac, the six of them, and went in search of fun. One day, they drove to Tobermory, on the northern tip of the Bruce Peninsula. The next day, it was Benmiller Inn near Goderich, a quaint old lodge Joan told everyone was where people went to have affairs. The next day, they drove to Collingwood, an artsy vacation spot on Georgian Bay, and didn't get back until after midnight. Listening to their stories, enduring their inside jokes, that was bad enough. But spending a whole night alone, with so few days left in the summer, was sheer misery. All that time they were together, all those hours driving lonely back roads, crowded in a car, three to a seat, what was really going on?

"Who sits where?" I asked Sharon.

"Different places," was all I got out of her.

With only the long Labor Day weekend left of the summer, the weather turned warm again, the lake calmed down, and there was no reason not to get back on the beach. I found everyone lying in front of Rob's place after work. As usual, he was bustling around, tinkering with boats, tilting beach umbrellas. What wasn't normal was the way Sharon was acting. Unlike that first time at the Gartons, when she kept away from everyone, now she was happy to be surrounded by people. And when Rob needed help, struggling once with an armful of paddles, getting too many drink requests another time, she came to his side, not Joan. When the two of them went off for drinks, Audie asked me, "What are you bringing tonight?"

I had no idea what she was talking about. "Didn't Sharon tell you?"
Joan broke in. "We're having dinner at my cottage. I'm making spaghetti, and
everyone's bringing a dish to pass."

"No, she didn't."

"Well…" Joan winked at me. "I'll give you a pass. This time."

When I asked Sharon why she hadn't told me about the party, she claimed
she had, and I mustn't have been listening. Maybe it was true. I'd never vouch
for my listening skills. At the time, though, I couldn't shake the thought that
she'd forgotten me intentionally. Was I losing her, after we'd meant so much to
each other earlier in the summer? I was determined not to let that happen.

I had no intention of showing up to the party empty-handed, not after being
on the outside looking in for so many days. When I went back to 112, my
parents weren't around. That was the year their marriage fell apart for good.
They were still cordial with each other, still playing bridge with friends, going
to cocktail parties, but the drinking had gotten worse for both of them. I'd been
taking advantage of that in small ways all summer long, getting home late,
drinking more myself, lying about where I'd been and what I'd done. The night
of Joan's party, though, I risked more flagrant transgressions.

Taking the M&M fudge brownies was one thing. They'd been in the
freezer all summer; my parents had likely forgotten about them. Stealing my
dad's last unopened bottle of Jack was downright dangerous. He didn't have a
history of violence, but his anger always contained that threat, never more so
than when alcohol was involved. For some crazy reason, that particular night,
I didn't care. I put the bottle in a brown bag, along with a stack of Dixie cups,
carried that in one hand and the box of brownies in the other, and hurried to
the back road. I hid the booze in the woods, then went on to Joan's.

Some places have an aura about them. They feel strange and familiar at
the same time, like some forgotten dream suddenly surfacing from an unfathom-
able depth. Joan's cottage seemed like a homecoming to a place I'd never been
and always wanted to be. The long welcoming dinner table. The bamboo door
beads between the kitchen and hallway. The French doors opening to the great
room that looked out on the lake. The huge vintage Motorola record player
with the beat-up album jackets forever scattered in front of it.

Many of my musical roots began at that Motorola. Neil Young, After
the Goldrush. *Janis Joplin,* Pearl. *Gram Parsons and the Flying Burrito
Brothers,* Gilded Palace of Sin. *Joni Mitchell,* Blue. Songs of Leonard

Cohen. *All these albums and more—the Byrds, Buffalo Springfield, Linda Ronstadt—I first heard in Joan's parlor. The whole collection came from the late Sixties, early Seventies. They belonged to Joan's older sister Nancy. She brought them up, lost interest in them, and left them in the console's cabinet.*

Given that there wasn't a single LP from our era—no punk or New Wave—you'd think Joan didn't have time for music. Not so. She actually wanted to be a musician. It's just that she had no interest in the rock trends of our teen years. Those 50 or so albums in the cabinet of that Motorola were the heart of her songbook. She was a throwback in that way, and many others, drawn to the free-spirited hippie ethos of her sister's generation, but embracing it more passionately than Nancy ever had. There was a wicker chair next to the Motorola, and leaning up against it was Joan's Gibson acoustic guitar. She would sit there, head bowed to the console's one big speaker, trying to mimic the riffs she heard spinning off the record.

The girls were cooking in the kitchen when I got there, and none of the other guys had arrived yet. Joan sat me down at the kitchen table, and Audie poured me a juice glass of red wine to the brim. I got the rare chance to watch the two of them and Sharon bustling around, laughing together, enjoying each other. They were wearing flowery sundresses, earthy yellows and oranges and limes, and they had all done up their hair and made up their faces.

When Rob and Newf and Grant showed up, they gave them red wine too, then showed us to the parlor. Joan came in, cozied up on the couch between me and Grant, and strummed a song on her guitar to entertain us. Joni Mitchell's "All I Want." I can't believe I remembered that. In the middle of the song, Sharon charged into the room with a look of anguish on her face. "Audie burned the bread."

Smoke hung across the kitchen. On the stove, a black loaf of French bread smoldered. Audie was standing with her back to us at the side door, mist swirling around her head. She wasn't making a noise, but her shoulders were shuddering.

Newf went to her. "We can get by without bread."

"But it's all I brought," she sobbed out.

"Let's not ruin the moment," Joan muttered. I don't think she meant for it to be heard, but Rob shushed her. Audie cried louder at that. Rob wheeled around and walked out of the kitchen. The back door clapped shut. We all went silent, stunned that the mood of the night had swung so suddenly.

Audie kept saying she'd get over it. Sharon asked Newf, shouldn't we go find Rob and tell him to come back. Joan said if he was going to be that pissy, why have him around? Grant figured it was a good time to break out a joint, the first I'd ever smoked, but clearly not the others. As it got passed around, everyone knew how to hold their fingers for the hand-off, pinch the joint, and draw a hit. When my turn came, Joan had to talk me through it. We quickly burned the joint down to a roach.

It was just as the weed was taking effect that the screen door clapped again. Rob came into the kitchen gasping for air. His face was beet red and he was sweating. He doubled over, catching his knee with one hand and holding out the other to Audie. There, poking out of a small brown bag, was a fresh roll of French bread.

Audie gaped, like it was a magician's trick. "How did you do that?"

"Ran," Rob gasped out. "Up to the store. One left."

Audie started crying again…good tears this time.

The dinner itself is the big moment we all remember from that night. Audie still brings it up. Grant gets to laughing about it now and then. And I can count on Sharon mentioning it once a summer, usually with this wistful sense of loss. In a way, it was the beginning of us—or I should say the myth of us, considering how short-lived that togetherness was.

I've never laughed as hard in my life as I did that night. It started with Rob regaling us about the details of his instantly legendary dash to the store. Apparently, when he got down by the dead end at the Eighth, he realized he had an urgent need to pee—and he wasn't going to be able to hold it through a run up and down the hill, with a store transaction thrown in.

He snuck into the bushes beside the Moore cottage and started relieving himself. What he didn't realize until he heard an angry shout, was that the Moores were entertaining guests on their porch, and he'd picked a spot perfectly framed for them to see through the pines. When Mr. Moore bound down the steps toward Rob, he took off running. But he wasn't done peeing yet, and the effort to avoid his own swaying stream slowed him down. Mr. Moore caught up to him and grabbed a fistful of Rob's shorts, tugging at him like he was on a short leash. He insisted that Rob stop doing his business immediately. But this was one of those long-held pees that just kept coming.

"Don't you dare urinate on my walkway!" Mr. Moore bawled. Rob wriggled free and broke out into the road. A Mennonite family was just coming

up from the beach; a father and mother, a boy and his younger sister. Rob nearly ran into them, shaking out the last drops. They stared solemnly, without a trace of surprise. Then the girl giggled and hid her face in her mother's dress.

"Sorry," was all Rob said. He zipped up, turned away, and started running up the hill. The family's buggy overtook him before the intersection. As they clopped past, father and mother sour-faced and staring straight ahead, the boy flashed Rob a smile, pointed at his crotch, and gave him a thumbs up.

"So, ladies," Rob ended his story, "I have the Amish seal of approval."

That got everyone roaring. Audie said Rob's run was the nicest thing anyone had ever done for her. Sharon told the rest of us we'd be hard-pressed to top Rob's chivalry. There was a long silence. "I pulled a calf out of a cow's vagina today," Newf reported, with a straight face

We all gaped to him. "I'll be sure to remember that," Joan said.

In the moment, it was the funniest thing I'd ever heard. I laughed until I started coughing, then I was crying, and I still couldn't stop. The whole thing—Rob's scurrying away from Mr. Moore (who, by the way, installed that porta-potty shortly thereafter), the Amish boy pointing at Rob's crotch, Newf elbow-deep in a cow, then Joan making note of that for the future. It was absurdly unreal, like some preposterous dream.

"Is this really happening?" I gasped. That was the sum total of my contribution to the conversation. But the question seemed so pressing and appropriate, I kept repeating it. After the fourth time, Grant clamped my shoulder and said, "Dude. This is happening. This is happening. This—is—happening!"

Everyone lost it. Yes, we were high, and the whole experience was joltingly new for me. But the feelings weren't any less authentic for the chemical inducement; it's just that we were all vulnerable enough to give ourselves over to them. (I sound like that Derek punk who was debating Grant.) Whenever anybody brings up the goings-on of that evening, they don't call it Rob's mad dash, or Newf's birthing adventure, or any of the other names that could've applied to what happened later. Everyone calls it, "Is-this-really-happening night." Like it's some sort of anniversary you shouldn't forget. September 3, 1983.

After we devoured my brownies, the guys left to get ready for the festivities at the gazebo. You had to be determined to go to the gazebo—and a little ballsy too. If anyone was there when you popped out of the woods beside the ravine it hung over, you were risking a confrontation. The first time Newf and I snuck up there, back when we were 15, we came face to face with three big kids passing around a bottle. "Get the fuck out of here," one of them said. We turned right around and trudged back down the hill. We didn't get very far before Newf stopped and looked up at the looming structure.

"That's my land," he fumed. "They can't kick me off my land."

"Maybe not," I told him. "But they can kick our asses."

That night, the gazebo was all ours—and, after all, we were the big kids now. We had time before the girls came to watch the sun go down, break out the Jack I brought, and have a toast. We stood in a tight circle in the middle of the gazebo, the sky burnishing the lake below us, faces radiant and close, holding our Dixie cups together. "To this moment," I said.

"To friendship," Rob added. After we downed the whiskey, he said, "I'm serious. I'll never have any better friends."

"Here, here," Newf agreed. "Friends forever."

Talk turned to next summer. Grant said it was a shame we couldn't spend the entire break together. Newf said that wouldn't be a problem for him. His dad had agreed to let him out of some chores, since there were already 20 orders for his rafts. I said my parents needed me to make money for college, but I could probably get my job back at the clubhouse.

"I'm not going to college," Rob declared. "There's so much money to be made on my own. Why waste all that time lining other people's pockets?" He swept his hand out across the Newfield land, the same stretch he would buy 35 years later. "Hell, even here, there are plenty of things I could do to make myself set for life. And as for that clubhouse job," he went on, "Screw that, McTavish. Cooped up in that dingy shack all summer. Making what? Twenty bucks a day? Come work with me. We'll be handymen. We'll set our own hours, and I'll cut you in on a percent of the profits."

So, it was settled. All of us would come up from the end of school to Labor Day and spend the entire summer of 1984 at Boiler Beach.

The girls didn't show up until dark. I poured shots. Newf opened a round of beers. Grant fired up another joint. Audie noticed the stars. We left the gazebo to find a place to lie down and look up at them. Newf knew just where to go. Most of the field bristled with cut cornstalks, but there was a spot across the ravine, a minute further along the bluff, that his dad had cleared to the soil. The spot was a wide circle, bigger than the footprint of a merry-go-round.

Joan was the one who suggested we place our heads together, fan out in a big blossom of bodies, and scour the sky for shooting stars. Laying there, heads touching, so close you could feel each other breathing, we were one sentient being, with the world stretched open further than any of us could see alone. There was a calmness to our purpose. Whenever anyone saw a shooting star, they didn't get overly excited. They couldn't without knocking into their neighbors' heads. There was this unspoken agreement that we'd wait to react safely past the time the last of us had a chance to see any slash of light. Even then, we reacted more in spirit than out of reflex.

I don't know how long the trance of that moment went on, but I had time to register the feeling, recognize its worth, and root it in my mind. I've had more intense, intentional, and transactional connections with people, but never so peaceful, never so deep, and never, ever with more than one person. There, with the cosmos spread out above us, sharing the secrets of eons, we were amazed... and elated...and together. Yes, we were high. And we were drunk too. But I know what I felt. And it was real. You can ascribe it to innocence, question its virtue, mistrust its promise. I would—if I didn't experience it myself.

At some point, Sharon and I went off by ourselves, further into the meadow. Wildflowers secluded us, and we laid together, bodies entangled. This wasn't the first time we'd dared such explorations, but there seemed to be more desperation in our embraces, a need to go further, to reach a conclusion. That's how it felt to me; maybe it was that need I'd felt for days to hold onto her. After a while, we fell out of rhythm. Our touching became fumbling. There was more effort, less floating.

Sharon sat up. "I can't. I tried. But I can't."

"It's okay," I said, dazed at my own relief. I put my arm around her. She shrugged it off—barely, but enough. I laid back down, flat on my back. The stars were spinning away from me. I blinked and they restuck, but only for an instant. Then they spun away again.

That night, after I collapsed into bed, moments came back to me—Audie crying over the bread...Dixie cups coming together in the dying sunlight...a shooting star gashing the night...Sharon's smooth warmth, thumping heart, shrugging shoulder. It was too much. The wonder. The wanting. There was something sweet about it, yet sad too.

I woke the next morning broken in half, throbbing from the center of my forehead to the back of my skull. Everything bright hurt, like those stars that prickled the night had ripped open at my waking. I went to work and slouched in the merciful shadows by the walk-up window. Then I began to feel the pangs of the night before and think again about Sharon, her body restless and electric, snaking away from me. I wondered where she was, what she was thinking.

And I felt lonely. Nobody had come to the clubhouse all morning. It was the Sunday before Labor Day. Most cottagers were packing for home. My dad had already made clear that we were leaving by seven the next day. (Thankfully, he never did find out about the Jack.) I was already missing the summer.

Just after lunch, Rob and Audie stopped by to talk me into biking to Point Clark. Grant and Sharon joined soon after, and they all put pressure on me to go. "It's your last time working here," Rob argued. "If they don't pay you, you're out 20 bucks. Here, I'll give it to you."

Lord knows, I wanted to go. It would be my last chance to be with Sharon beyond saying goodbye outside an idling car. But I couldn't do it. It didn't feel right. Part of it had to do with the hangover. Then I found out that Newf couldn't go because he had to mow the course. Finally, Joan showed up and said she wasn't up for going either. All that made saying no easier.

After the four of them left, Joan sat down across from me, propped her bare feet up on the card table, arched back, and let out a big sigh. "God, I'm glad you didn't want to go. It was boring enough biking here."

I laughed, and we fell into silence. After a while, Joan asked if I wanted to play double solitaire. She thrashed me the first game. I was better in the second, still losing, but more on the ball, getting my hand in under hers a few times. Before we dealt out again, she said she was hungry, and could she have a Freezie Pop? I was going to get one for her, but she said she knew where they were. A minute later, she was calling out, saying she couldn't find them. When I got to the doorway, she was standing in the middle of the narrow back room, more like a walk-in closet, just a step away from me. All she had on was her blue bikini bottom. The white sunless triangles of her breasts were heaving like she was out of breath. "Does it hurt to want so much?" she asked.

I didn't know what to say.

"I see you. Pining after Sharon, longing for something you'll never get. It must ache."

"I don't know…" I mumbled.

"If you want so much, why don't you come where you can get it?" She slid her thumbs under the strings of her bikini bottom.

Then the bell dinged. There was a call bell at the walk-up window that people could ring when I was away. I was going to let it go, but when I looked back, I could see the woman standing there, and I knew by how her head jerked away, she'd seen us. Joan stepped behind the door. I came hurrying out.

"Just one?" I asked.

"Yes," she said, looking down to get her money. As she handed me the five-dollar bill, we made eye contact. And I was looking at the most beautiful girl I had even seen—or ever would.

That's how I met Carrie Sinclair.

I woke to pounding—again. It seemed to come from all around the cottage. Bogue; it had to be. I threw on my swimsuit and the same shirt as the day before and stumbled out into the great room. I grabbed the fireplace poker on my way to the back door. Who knew how ugly it was going to get? On the way there, the pounding moved past me, along the side facing Newf's old place. I hurried to get ahead of it. Just before the sound got to the side door, I opened it quick, swung out the screen, and bounded onto the concrete walkway.

Joan let out a shriek. "My lord. Is this how you greet guests?"

"Sorry." I dropped the poker. "I'm on edge. I got broken into."

"About that." She stepped off the narrow path. Bruce was behind her, hands jammed in his pockets. "Bruce, what do you have to say to Mr. McTavish?"

"Sorry," he muttered.

"Young man, we address people when we talk to them."

Bruce raised his eyes. I couldn't tell whether they were pleading or challenging. "It's okay." I decided right then to keep our secret. "I've taken a few things that weren't mine in my day."

"It's very charitable to excuse the boy's behavior," Joan said. "But in our house, actions have consequences. Bruce needs to work off the cost of the beer he stole."

"It's fine. Really. I just hope he learns a lesson about who he chooses to hang out with. In my experience, kids don't go to these sorts of extremes unless they feel pushed." I left it at that. Bruce glared at me.

"In your experience." Joan laughed. That was the moment I appreciated that I was in the presence again of Joan Duncan. Her laugh was the same, a bit deeper, a bit rougher, but just as strong, just as unrestrained. And to look at her, you wouldn't think she was a mother there to teach her son a lesson. She had a floppy sunhat, rose-tinted aviator sunglasses, a see-through white wrap, and her blue bikini. And from what you could see of her face, time hadn't changed much. If anything, it was tighter, like the muscles had been working hard to hold that carefree veneer. But she was still magnetic, still attractive in that Joan way.

Bruce cleared his throat.

"S-s-so..." I stuttered out, shifting my eyes between them. "I don't really need the help."

Joan changed moods—bang—like that. "Bruce is *going* to work for you. I know how expensive two cases are. Ten hours at least. I don't care what it is. If you want him to sit in the corner, fine. Whatever. But he *will* do the time."

Bruce and I shared a hangdog glance. An awkward silence pressed in on me. "Now?"

"Now?!" Joan boomed. "Lord, no! You figure out what to do with him on your own time. Now, you and I are going to celebrate seeing each other again." She slapped a beach bag that swung on her hip. I heard the clink of glass, the tinkle of liquid shifting.

Uh oh.

"So, Bruce. You come back here tomorrow. Nine o'clock—"

"Ten," I jumped in.

"Ten o'clock. And you be ready to help Mr. McTavish with anything. Understood?"

"Understood," Bruce repeated, head still hanging.

"Okay. Now, get out of here." Joan waved him off. He glanced between me and his mom, then turned and walked away, in no special hurry. When he got to the back edge of my cottage, he looked over his shoulder. "Go on!" Joan flapped her shooing hand faster. Bruce jammed his hands into his pockets and sulked off.

"Teenagers." Joan eyed me with a confiding grin. Then she gave a wide-eyed gasp. "Look at you! You haven't changed. Still the hungry wolf. A little tired looking...but it's morning!"

"And you're still Joan."

"And I'm *glad* you're still drinking! Sharon told me you were being a good boy. Then I come to find out you're stocking up on beer! I can't tell you how happy I was to hear that. I make the best vodka mimosas."

"Look, Joan, about the beer—"

"I don't care that you're still drinking," she cut me off. "Come on. Let's greet the morning with big drinks and make fun of all the crazy runners punishing themselves up and down the beach." Joan pointed behind me, inviting me onto my own deck. I led the way out there like she had a gun on me.

"When did the beach get so boring?" Joan asked, after we were settled, and she'd topped off the vodka and orange juice in my flute with a dose of champagne.

I struggled for an answer. "It's never really been boring for me. Now, if you're asking, when did it stop being fun—"

"Oh, no. N-n-no!" she shut me down. "We're not talking about *that*. That's in the past. Like I told you then, what happened happened. You can't beat yourself up about it."

For the record, that wasn't what she told me back then. But I didn't have time to argue before she veered back to her point. "Like dinner with Rob and Sharon last night. We haven't seen each other in, well, ages. You'd think we'd have a little fun. But no. It was like being cornered at the worst high school reunion. Rob went on and on, bragging about this huge resort he's building. Mariner's Vista, or whatever. And Sharon just sat there, smiling stiffly. The good little wife. Then my killjoy of a husband got it into his head that we all wanted a lesson on the Mercantile Exchange—"

"Rob's building a resort up there?" I pointed over the low roof of my cottage.

"You didn't know? That's right. You and Rob don't talk. Nobody talks anymore. By the way, cheers!" She held out her flute. I clinked it. "Here's to us, damn few good people left on this beach." I took a sip, then thought, what the hell, and drained the glass. "There we go!" Joan cheered, reaching into her bag for the vodka.

As she mixed me a stiffer drink, I thought, well, as long as she broached the subject. "About that killjoy husband of yours…"

"Oh, God! I know. I am *so* sorry! I don't blame you for freaking out. Bryan spends every night out on that porch, hiding in the dark, spying on everyone. It's creepy."

"Yeah. But what got me was him coming into my store—"

"That's right! You own a store. A laundromat. *And* a bookstore. Two stores in one. How fun!"

"Well—"

"I have a whole big list of books I want to order."

"It's not that kind of bookstore."

"Oh." She got quiet, brooded.

"What I was saying was it was a bit unsettling for your husband to barge into my store and demand my phone number."

"What?"

"He stood in the middle of my place, poking at his phone. Then he wanted to know the store's number. When I told him there wasn't one, he insisted on getting my number."

Joan looked out over the swelling waves and sipped her mimosa, suddenly very still. I took the occasion to gulp down half my flute. "It never changes," she said, about as subdued as Joan gets. "The waves keep rolling in, like they always do. The sky keeps spinning over us. The sun, the sand, the sounds and smells. It's all the same. We could be babies. We could be dreamers. We could be dying—or dead. This beach doesn't care. *It* doesn't change. *We* do." She let out a big, sad sigh and went on staring.

I didn't want to contradict her, but the waves *weren't* rolling the way they always did. Something must've happened over night, because even though they looked bigger and were crashing hard and unraveling a long way, they didn't seem to be reaching very far up the shore. It looked like a new ankle-deep sandbar had mysteriously moved in overnight.

"Ready for another?" Joan rallied, taking off her sunhat and shaking out her hair. It was still flowing, still blonde, but not as long and not natural.

"Why not?" I downed the rest of my second.

"So, I've seen you now, Rob and Sharon last night, and Grant accosted me on the beach."

"Accosted you?"

"That's what it felt like." She handed me my new drink, then leaned back, opened her see-through wrap, and re-rubbed the sheen of suntan lotion into her stomach. "Honestly, when did he get so crazy?"

"When hasn't he been crazy?"

"I don't mean trippy like he used to be. I'm talking about all this God-forgiving, soul-saving, nature-reckoning nonsense. It wasn't a minute after seeing him that he launched into a sermon. I just sat there, twirling my cocktail, nodding my head, and wondering, when is he going to notice that he's boring me to death? Then, before I got a word in edgewise, he rambled off down the beach. The old Grant would've parked his ass in the sand, broken out a spliff, and sat through a good, long high."

"Oh, he's still got weed. You just have to get indoctrinated into the Religion of Grant before he fires one up."

"I'll be damned," Joan said. "That high and mighty fraud."

"He's no fraud. His problem is he believes every damn word he says. The guy has a heart of gold. Hell, he's helping me right now figure out why my gully keeps overflowing." Joan whipped her head around, like any second the water would come rushing over the deck. "Come to think of it, that's how Bruce can help me. If I can move enough sand up against the cottage, maybe the water won't take it away."

Joan was ready to move on. "Whatever you want him to do."

"Have him bring a shovel tomorrow."

"Yes, sir," she barked, saluting me. I laughed, and she laughed along. Then we couldn't think of anything else to do, but clink glasses again and work on our mimosas.

"Well," she finally said, looking over her shoulder at the waves, "I've done my duty. I've connected with everyone."

"You saw Audie?" I knew the answer.

"I didn't think Audie wanted to be seen."

Fair enough. "And Newf?"

Joan glared over the pink-tinted aviators. "You're encouraging *me* to go see Newf?"

"I was just asking."

"That's rich," she fumed, dousing her bile with a big gulp of liquor. And just like that, she was her cheerful self again. "I figured I'd be disappointed if I saw him. I heard he's Amish now, toiling away out there in the sticks."

"Who told you that?"

She ignored me. "Tell you the truth, you're the only person who *hasn't* disappointed me."

"The bar wasn't that high."

"You keep talking shit and you *will* disappoint me." Then she held her hand out for my flute. "Let's keep the good times rolling."

I was okay with that. I gave her my glass and eased back in my chair. That comforting current that always came when I drank liquor was flowing now, from between my eyes, down to the stalk of my neck, warm and thrumming. I rolled my head back and looked at the lake. "Damn," was the best way I could describe what I saw. The waves really were losing their grip on the shore. The sandbar that a minute ago was ankle deep was now a ledge of broken puddles.

Joan waggled the flute in front of my eyes. I straightened up and took it. When had the wind kicked up so hard? And it was blowing straight out from the shore. The trees between my cottage and Newf's were bending and losing leaves. I was about to take another stab at expressing my bewilderment when Joan said, "Did I mention that I'm finally getting somewhere with my music?"

I had to blink a few times to focus. The wind was blowing her hair everywhere. The rustling in the trees fought with her voice. Joan seemed oblivious. "No? Well, after 20 years of toiling away in little coffee houses around Chicago, I got off my ass and found an agent. Next thing you know, I'm booked at big venues, opening for big musicians. Regina Spektor. Lori McKenna. No? Anyway, just before we came here, I learned they want me to sing for six weeks on a cruise to Alaska and Japan. Isn't that fun?"

I pointed up at the thrashing trees. Joan didn't notice. "Bryan even agreed to stay up here and watch Bruce while I'm gone. And he absolutely detests the beach."

Just then a gust of wind came howling down the walkway, picked up Joan's sunhat and sent it tumbling like a wounded seagull over the beach. "Holy shit!" she shouted, turning to follow her hat's flight. It fluttered over the lake—at least where the lake used to be. It couldn't have been more than two minutes since I last noticed the waves coming up short on the shoreline. Now, they were a good 50 yards out. All up and down the beach, boulders were completely out of the water.

"I'll be damned. A seiche."

"A what?" Joan asked, standing to face the lake, hands on hips, like it had offended her.

"*Sesh. Sech. Seesh.* I'm not sure how you pronounce it, but it's when the lake sloshes away like a rocking bathtub."

"Well, screw that," Joan declared. She stomped across my deck, bounded down the steps, and staggered for the fleeing shore.

I chased after her. She hadn't deduced the other part of what a seiche did. By the time I came up beside her, we were at the edge of what had been the first sandbar, looking at an exposed vein of stones that meandered along the shore in each direction. It extended another 20 yards or so before angling into the thinning waters. Joan's hat was just beyond the exposed stones, but her attention was elsewhere. "Look at that!" she groaned out, pointing off to her left. There on the wrinkled sheet of sand, a chinook salmon, as big a fish as you'll find in this lake, flopped around, wrestling with what I thought at first was a bicycle tire tube. It was only when the fish stopped fighting and the tube went on wriggling that I realized what it was.

"Damn! A sea lamprey." The snake-like creature was nearly two feet long and had attached itself to the salmon with its fang-filled suction disc of a mouth. "They're like giant leeches."

"What the hell?" Joan gaped at me, as if we were witnessing the first grisly casualty of a horror movie. Then she scanned the whole strange panorama. Beached fish were flopping all around us. When our eyes finally met again, Joan bugged hers out and gave a theatrical shudder. Then she started giggling. "We've been bad." She beamed up at me with a bleary smile. "So, so bad."

I stepped across the slippery stones and snatched up Joan's hat. A strand of seaweed hung from the brim. As I picked it off, I noticed a big, white raft floating in the sunken waters a couple hundred yards out. It took a second to realize I was looking at the top of Mammoth Rock. That spooked me more than the sea lamprey. I hurried back to Joan and gave her the hat. After she took it, she looked south. At least 100 people stood on the naked slope of the lake. "The other part of a seiche, is when the tide comes back—"

"Do you think he can see us from here?"

"Who?"

"Bryan."

I don't know where my head was; floating away on the current of booze or stuck on the specter of Mammoth Rock. But I had no idea who she was talking about. "Bryan who?"

"My husband, silly!" Joan laughed and shoved my shoulder. I nearly slipped on the stones. "Oh, Tommy! You're exactly the same. *Is this really happening?*"

All the talk of me not changing was getting on my nerves. I pointed to the horizon. "When the water comes back, it's going to charge right up to the dunes like a tidal wave. We'll be on our asses and slammed against the shore." I brushed past her and headed back onto dry sand. She kept standing there, facing the lake.

"Come on, Joan." All at once, I was aware that there was no wind anymore. And the water had turned an unnatural green. The whole horizon seemed to lift and separate from the lake along a ragged white line. "Joan?"

Finally, she got the message. "I have to go." She stepped off the drained sandbar. "This was fun." She pulled me into a hug.

"Let me get your bag."

She looked up at my deck and back at the lake. White caps were tearing away from that ragged line. The wind had picked up, only now it had swung around and was blowing straight in. "Keep it," she said, starting down the beach.

"Oh, no. I don't want that here."

"Yes, you do." She kept walking.

"Damn it, Joan! I don't."

She wheeled around, turning into the wind. Her flimsy wrap flapped open. "Same old Tommy. You'd rather go on wanting than having what you want."

"I don't need to hear that shit anymore." Honestly, who did she take me for, some smitten teenager? She knew what I'd been through. What we'd all been through.

"It's a compliment, Tommy. No one wants for want's sake like you. You're the connoisseur—the wizard—of want."

I laughed in spite of myself, a gloomy snicker. "I'm just going to pour it out."

"What?" The wind was chuffing and wailing now.

"I'm going to pour it out!"

"Of course you are." She fluttered her fingers over her shoulder as she left.

The wind was blowing now just as hard into the beach as it had been blowing out minutes before. Beyond the second sandbar, the water had risen up like one giant wave. Gashes of whitecaps were seemingly vertical against that wall of water. A greenish-purple welt of clouds swelled over the horizon. I backed up toward the cottage. This was going to be bad. Joan was running along the shore now, maybe halfway to the Eighth. She wasn't going to make it home. *Stop at the Eighth, Joan. Get up to the road.*

Then the serious wind hit. It picked up my chairs by the scruff of their strapped backs and flung them against the cottage. It knocked me to my knees. I tried to get up once, then figured it was safer to crawl across the deck. When I went to open the screen door, the wind took it. It was all I could do to keep hold of that flimsy door and get the solid one open.

I got inside just in time to see that wall of water crash against the shore and charge up the beach. In seconds, it roared past the old high-water line and reached the bushes that bracketed the gully. And it kept coming, gobbling up sand, all the way to the bottom of my steps and under them. Then the rain came, a clattering sideways torrent that rattled my old windows. Everything was suddenly darker. Through the bleary haze, the waves seemed to be falling from the sky, thundering down right in front of me. My whole cottage shook and howled. This went on for a good five minutes. Then, quicker than it came, the storm abruptly died. No more wind. No more rain. No more gloom. The lake was still roiling, and the waves were big, but they'd retreated back within the confines of a usual day of high surf. The sun even peeked out, shimmering across my wet deck.

I figured it was safe to go outside. Joan's sun bag was blown over and open like the gasping mouth of a fat fish. The only container that survived inside was the orange juice jug. The champagne and vodka bottles had rolled against my cottage. So had the flutes, but they'd both shattered. The champagne was gone, but there were a solid five fingers left of vodka. I screwed open the cap and went to the deck's edge. I tilted the liquor up to the mouth, then held it there. *Wanting for want's sake.* What the hell. Why let it go to waste? I put the cap back on, set the bottle upright on the deck, then surveyed the damage along the beach. The sand had been swept smooth by the seiche, and the debris you'd typically see— driftwood and seaweed, raked piles and embers of old fires—was gone. Other than that, it was as if nothing had happened. I wondered: had Joan made it home?

I stopped scanning the shore at the gully. The waves were still big enough that they reached the bushes beside it. I took a deep breath and went to check things out, fearing the worst. To my surprise, the gush of water the seiche pushed into the gully had carved a wide channel on its way out, and everything was draining better than I ever could've done with a shovel. Maybe Grant was right. My gully wasn't filling up any more than usual; the drop in the lake level just wasn't draining it enough.

The day was getting away from me. The mess from the break-in. Joan and her mimosas. The battering of the seiche. Then, after all that, the vodka waiting there on my deck. After I brought it inside, I set it on the counter, and faced off with it. Damn booze. There was only one way to get rid of it: one jolt at a time. Take a swig, cap it, get out of here fast, and go about the day.

So that's what I did. One more swig—one and a sip—and I was out the door and heading across the backyard to my car. Even though the sun had been peeking in and out, everything was still wet from the sudden storm, and there were broken branches all across the yard, most small, but some big enough that I'd need help dragging them away. I hadn't run the mower across this field in weeks, so by the time I got out to the car, my shoes were soaked. I was brushing the wet grass off of them when I noticed a long strip of wildflowers that ran from the driveway down Newf's property line—now Rob's—all the way to the beach.

Of course, it had always been there, but it never stood out until then. The flowers were bent every which way, whipsawed by the shifting winds. Golds and oranges, purples, pinks and limes, jumbled, mangled, broken. A thought came to me. I ran back to my shed, found a yellow bucket Cam used to make sandcastles with, went inside, and filled it with water. I hadn't capped the vodka, so I took another swallow—one more for courage. Then I dug some scissors out of my knife drawer and hurried back to the car.

There were purple irises and daisies and some droopy star-shaped orange flower that had been crippled by the storm. I cut a mix of as many as I could fit in the bucket, carried it by the handle to my car, wedged it between my legs, and drove for the Eighth. The storm had done heavy damage there. Where the road dead-ended and the beach began, right in the spot I'd lobbed that XXX, big trees from either side had collapsed onto each other. This was where I wanted Joan to take refuge from the storm.

I roared up the hill and turned on Lake Range. I would've taken the flowers straight to Wendy, but I wasn't paying enough attention to the stop sign for Concession 10. I had to slam on the brakes to give way to a car rushing past from the highway. The bucket of flowers hit the bottom of the steering wheel and dumped nearly all the water into my lap. I needed more water and time to dry off. Plus, it was past 11:00. I should've had the bookstore open already.

TOMMY WAD MONSTER! Was there no end to this shit? How many embarrassing anagrams could one store name contain? Even as I was walking to the sign to rearrange the letters, a car drove by and someone shouted,

"Wad monster!" Myron was right; I needed a permanent sign. The whole thing put me in a foul mood. I stomped around the laundry area, getting what I had to get done, emptying the bill changer, filling the vending machine with soap and bleach, checking the washers and dryers. I caught an older woman giving me the eye.

"What?"

She looked away. Screw this town. What if I just closed for good? That's what I was thinking. Let the harbor crowd schlep their laundry up to that pricey, space-aged Sparkles rip-off of a laundromat. See if they thought this was funny then. Wad monsters. Wart demons. Randy moms. I didn't have to put up with this crap. The hell with opening the bookstore today.

I took the bucket of flowers to my sink and started filling it up. My phone rang. I didn't recognize the number, but it was an Ann Arbor area code. I answered it; probably Cam, in trouble again.

"Hi Tommy. It's Barb Bowen."

Even as lubricated as I was, the name, the voice, jolted me. It was my old doctoral advisor from the University of Michigan, the woman who guided me through my dissertation, advocated for my hiring, and ultimately counseled me to step aside and clean myself up. And here I was, drunker than I'd been in months.

"Barb Bowen. This is a surprise," I said. "How long's it been? Nine years?"

"I've tried to call a few times," she said.

"I try not to answer my phone."

"I have a longshot proposition." Barb got right to the point, like always. "There's a teaching position open, and I think you'd be the perfect fit for it."

I couldn't help but laugh. "I'm the perfect fit—the guy who drank and philandered his way out of the department. What's the class? Alcoholic authors of the twentieth century?"

There was a snag of silence. "Of course, this is predicated on the notion that's all behind you." Barb: still the dead-serious one.

"Of course. So…how are you going to convince the department head to give me another chance?"

"This isn't a Michigan job," Barb said. "I'm at Eastern now."

That was a stunner. EMU was a small college down the road in Ypsilanti, a solid school, but not nearly as prestigious as Michigan. "Weren't you up for tenure when I left?"

"They denied it," she replied, without a trace of disappointment. "You know that world; publish or perish."

"I *do* know that world. That's why I left it." Who was I kidding?

"It's different at Eastern," Barb ignored my revisionist history. "I'm running the department, and it's all about good teaching." She hesitated. "That's why I thought of you."

Something about that pause hit me wrong. I wasn't exactly known as a great teacher. "So, I'm the only one you called?"

"You're on the short list."

"Yeah? And how far down that list am I?"

"Do you want to hear about the job or not?" Barb pressed.

"Sure."

"It's Twentieth-century American Novels. Hemingway, Faulkner, O'Connor, Salinger, Nabokov, Morrison. Right up your alley."

"It's an intro course."

"It's a 100-level course, yes," she admitted.

"Do the kids know how to read?"

Barb went quiet. Finally, voice lowered, she said, "I thought you'd be ready to come back. I guess I was wrong."

"W-w-w-wait!" Damn Bowen, anyway; she always *could* shame me. "I was just joking around. What's the pay?"

"It's 32 thousand for the calendar year."

"What?!" That was half of what I'd been making when I left Michigan nine years back. "You must be moving down that list pretty quick."

Barb was undeterred. "Okay, so you're not interested. It was worth a shot. I'll let you go."

There was a finality to the way Barb dismissed me that stung. "Let me give it some thought," I found myself saying. "Can I get back to you in a couple days?"

"Of course," Barb said—and then she circled back to her first assumption. "I just want to make sure you understand; this all depends on you having your act together."

"I get it." I could feel my anger rising. Why did she have to go there? Could she tell I'd been drinking? "I'll call you back soon," I said and hung up before I added something I'd regret.

The faucet was still running. The bucket of flowers had long since been overflowing. I shut off the water, drained the bucket a little, and hurried to Wendy's.

When I walked into O'Shea's, the place was empty again. Wendy saw me coming. We made quick eye contact. But as I approached, she pretended to be preoccupied washing glasses. I took the seat right in front of her, set the bucket on the bar, and waited. She went on washing. This wasn't going to be as easy as I thought.

"Sorry," was all I finally said.

She dried her hands. "What are *you* sorry for?"

Damned if I really knew. "I'm sorry I upset you."

She stared me down for a good long second, then deflated with a sigh. "I'm the one who should be apologizing. The things I said. I was awful."

I thought she was going to cry. "You put up with a lot from me. You're entitled to put me in my place every once in a while."

"Those are lovely." She pointed to the flowers.

"I rescued after from the seiche."

"I heard about that. They say we had a tornado too."

"That explains things." I nudged the bucket toward her. "Anyway, these flowers got thrashed around in the storm. They looked so pretty. I never would've noticed them except for their damage. What does Leonard Cohen say? 'There's a crack in everything.' "

" 'That's how the light gets through,' " Wendy finished the line quietly. I thought she was going to choke up. I didn't expect it to get this emotional.

"All I had was that shitty bucket," I said to lighten the moment.

"It's perfect." She cupped her hands around the bucket and lifted it gently off the bar, like she was handling some porcelain heirloom. Then she set it high on the shelf behind her, visible from anywhere in the tiny pub, stepped back, and stared up at it. I wondered what was going through her mind. Was she waiting for me to say more, or hoping I'd get the clue and leave?

"I didn't know what the orange ones were."

"They're day lilies." She pulled a bottle of Whistle Pig Straight Rye off the shelf beside the flowers. "Have a drink with me."

"What?" This was in direct violation of Wendy's rule.

"This one time." She set the bottle on the bar, then crouched down and came up with two crystal tumblers I'd never seen before. "I have news." I didn't like the sound of that. As I watched her go to the mini fridge and get cocktail ice balls, I debated confessing that I'd already gotten my nose into it. But this seemed important to her. And it wasn't very often that my having a drink could be considered noble. Wendy placed the ice balls into the tumblers and gave us each a healthy pour. Then she slid my glass over and raised hers. "A toast. To what comes next."

I clinked her glass with a wince. She downed it in one go. I followed suit. For her sake. This wasn't the Wendy I knew. She poured us each another.

"I'm closing the bar after Canada Day," she said matter-of-factly. "Friday, July sixth is the last day for O'Shea's."

I was stunned. Wendy was eyeing me with her best attempt at a poker face. I put on one of my own. "I guess congratulations are in order."

"It's not what I wanted, but it's solving my money problem. This all came together yesterday. It was emotional. You caught me at a bad time, and I took it out on you."

"Forget about that." I took a long, slow sip, just barely breathing it in as I tried to make sense of what Wendy was telling me. "So, you're selling off, eh?"

"I'm getting the lease paid off. And in exchange for that…I'm doing a little consulting. And sharing a few recipes."

Wendy looked at me, eyebrows raised, mouth closed tight. She was waiting for me to get it. "The Gartons are helping you out."

"Bo is, yes."

I brought my glass to my lips but didn't drink. I needed to hide behind something. So, this was why Wendy got upset yesterday. In the heat of the deal, she didn't need me running down the Gartons. I wasn't about to make the same mistake. "As long as it's helping."

"I know you think he's a snake. So do I. But don't worry. I'm making out on this."

The front door creaked and clapped shut. A couple was standing in the entryway, looking around as if they expected a host. "Sit anywhere you'd like," Wendy called out. Once they picked a table, she came out from behind the bar to serve them.

That gave me time to think. Bogue was paying off the rest of Wendy's lease—a year at most—and hiring Wendy. Knowing Bogue, it couldn't amount to much. And for such a small investment, he eliminated his competitor, got her recipes, and prevented another restaurant from picking her up. How was this a good deal? *Give it up, McTavish. Give it up.*

"One more splash?" Wendy reappeared in front of me.

"I don't know—"

"How often do I relax my rule? And on the house, no less."

I tapped the rim of my glass. "After you close, there won't be a single place in town that'll pour me a drink."

"That's true." She gave me two fingers full then poured the couple their Sleemans.

"You could've worked that into the deal. No beer for Tommy, no tarts for Bogue."

I thought that was worth at least a chuckle. But Wendy took me seriously. "No way he's getting my tarts. That's my grandma's recipe. I'm giving him soup, salad, and sandwiches. The soups aren't easy to copy. But all you have to do is have a pair of eyes to figure out how to make the salads and sandwiches. I'm not giving up very much."

"The lease is probably enough of a bargain." I hid my eyes inside my drink, like I was just thinking out loud.

Wendy saw through me. "You want the particulars? Fine. He's paying off nine months of my lease. That's 45,000 right there. Then I get 4,000 a month over that time to whip his kitchen into shape. Eighty-one K altogether. Where else am I going to get that sort of money around here?"

She asked the question like she'd seriously consider an alternative. I shook my head. "Other than the power plant—"

"Right. And I'm not exactly a nuclear scientist."

Wendy scanned her collection of CDs. She put on Leonard Cohen, maybe because we'd just been talking about him. While she took the beers out to her customers, I took in Leonard's words: *Suzanne takes you down to her place near the river. You can hear the boats go by. You can spend the night forever. And you know that she's half-crazy but that's why you want to be there.*

"When I was a little girl," Wendy said out of the blue after she came back, "my dad was still manning the Point Clark lighthouse." She went to pour herself another snort.

"You sure you want another?"

"*You*, are asking *me* that?"

"What if it gets busy?"

"Just listen." She tipped more rye into her glass. "I used to sit there with him sometimes, at the top of the lighthouse, and look out over the lake. One day, as the motorboats puttered in and out of that little marina there, I asked why there even had to be a lighthouse. The shoreline was so sandy and the lake so deep. That's when he told me about the ridge."

"It's shallower off Point Clark than you think," I offered. "On a clear day, you can see the bottom a couple hundred yards out. My dad took me fishing—"

"Are you going to let me finish?"

"Sorry."

"You're always doing that, horning in on stories. You don't even realize it."

"Sorry. Please. I'll shut up."

She raised her drink for a toast. To what? To me shutting up? I clinked her glass.

"It's more than just a couple hundred yards of shallow," she went on. "It goes all the way across the lake. My dad told me that 9,000 years ago, the tide was 250 feet lower than it is today. And there was a hilly ridge that stuck out of the water as high as 100 feet and as wide as a few miles in places. It was a land bridge that went pretty much from our front yard all the way to Michigan, cutting the lake in half. Can you imagine?"

I didn't believe her. It sounded like a story a dad would tell.

"It was in the news two years ago. Researchers discovered an ancient hunting camp 100 feet underwater off the coast of Alpena, Michigan. Artifacts, hunting blinds, caribou bones, the works."

"No shit?"

"I was nine when he told me about that ridge. After that, I started having these crazy dreams. I still get them. I dream of islands, a whole fantastic archipelago trailing off to the horizon, some so close you could swim to them. Vaulting red-rock formations, waterfalls and streams, hidden coves, secluded beaches. And the funny thing is, in those dreams, I take the islands for granted. They're just part of the scenery."

Wendy stopped and looked past me. "Can I get you a menu?" she called out. The couple wasn't interested in food. The man came over, handed her a ten, and the two of them left.

"There goes the lunch rush," Wendy joked.

"It isn't even noon."

"Would you quit already? I don't care anymore."

"Fair enough." I stood. It took a little shuffle to steady myself.

"Where are you going? I haven't even finished the story."

"I thought you were done."

"What sort of story would that have been?" I started to answer, but nothing came out. The best I could do was sit back down. "I'm trying to tell you something."

Finally, I found words. "It was interesting. And descriptive."

Wendy laughed. "You are something else, Tommy."

"What?" I laughed along. It was good to see her smile.

"I'm trying to make a point. I'm telling you why I'm doing this thing you think is so shitty."

"I never said that."

"You didn't have to." She got quiet. Then she reached out, clawed the top of her glass, and swirled it on the counter. I had the good sense to shut my mouth and wait. "For years, I dreamed of those islands. So tantalizingly close, so beautiful, yet always just there, never acknowledged, never explored. One day, when I was in high school, my dad took me up in the lighthouse again, and he told me they didn't need a lightkeeper anymore. He said he didn't know what he was going to do, but he promised that, whatever it was, it would be sensible."

She let out a sigh and looked in my eyes. I gave a knowing grin. I had an idea where this was headed now. "I got so angry after he said that. He liked to do woodworking in his spare time, and he always talked about going back to his hometown way out east on Cape Breton. I told him, there was nothing stopping him now. He said he'd get there eventually, but he had to take things a step at a time." She shook her head and looked off.

Wendy's father had died five years back, in a tiny home under the shadow of the Point Clark lighthouse. If that's what caution got him, how did this explain Wendy's dealing with Bogue? "I can see why you'd be mad," I said to move things along.

She kept looking off, like she expected someone to come walking through the door. "So, we were sitting up there, and he was going on about what he *wasn't* going to do to make sure the family was taken care of, and I couldn't take it anymore. 'You don't have to worry about me,' I told him. 'I'm getting out of here as fast as I can.' He got quiet. Then, as calm as can be, he asked me, 'How?'

"That made me madder than anything. 'How?' I said. 'Easy. I pack up and go.' Then I pointed out the lighthouse window and told him, 'I think about that ridge out there all the time. I wish it was still there. I'd walk away from here and keep walking until I got to America, and I'd never look back.'"

She smiled and looked down into the glistening bronze of her whiskey, like she could see herself there, making that walk.

"*There's* a plan." I tipped my glass to her and finished it off.

Wendy's smile faded. "He leaned in close. His jaw was clenching like I'd never seen before. I thought he was going to hit me. Then he said, 'There's nothing wrong with wanting to get out of here. But don't dream big dreams you can't do anything about. Think about the little steps you *can* take, and then take them.'"

Wendy looked up finally and nodded, a grin bandaged on her face. I waited. There had to be more. Then I could tell she was waiting for me. "So..." I said, "that's what you're doing."

"It was good advice."

Maybe it was. But coming from Wendy, knowing where her father wound up, it felt like a surrender. "Well, the lake's definitely going down," I said, trying again to lighten the mood. "But I'm pretty sure that ridge isn't showing up in the next nine months."

"There you go," Wendy agreed.

"I better get back."

"One more."

"No." I was going to leave it at that. Then I thought, *Come on, McTavish. Out with it.* "Truth is, I had a rough morning. I was four or five drinks in before I even got here."

The look on Wendy's face said it all. She was decent enough, though, not to voice that disappointment. At least not directly. "Aw shit, Tommy. I'm sorry."

"I could've told you any time."

"And you finally did." She put a bright spin on things. "That counts for something, right?"

"Tiny steps. Like your dad said."

"Exactly." She came out from behind the bar. "Now, go take the next step. Get a cup of coffee at Bean's. Go back to the Wondermat. Finish the day. No more drinks."

Wendy gave my shoulder a pat. She held her hand there long enough for me to look over at it, then back up to her eyes. There was the slightest tug of a connection, then she was gently steering me toward the door. "When you put it like that..."

Wendy smiled and opened the door for me. "Thank you for the flowers. You couldn't have been drinking that hard if you remembered those."

"I guess not," I went along for her sake, stepping outside. The shock of the sunlight hurt my eyes. I must've blinked a dozen times to lock down the view of Queen Street. People were everywhere, mostly walking away from this remote end of the strip, up toward the heart of town. At the farthest point I could see, where the jagged façade of the buildings and the row of ornamental trees lining the sidewalks converged, the people seemed like one big, colorful mob, streaming into an impossibly narrow gauntlet.

I looked back at Wendy. "A thousand years from now, all this will be underwater. And someone else will be dreaming this."

"You might be right." Wendy mustered a smile and shut the door. I heard something like the click of a deadbolt. Had she locked it, this early in the afternoon? I was half-tempted to give the door a quiet try.

I didn't get coffee at Bean's. I passed the store and kept going, falling in with all the tourists shuffling up Queen Street. The more I thought of Wendy's story, the angrier I got. How was it that a woman bold enough to open her own restaurant could come to believe she was better off playing it safe? Damn the world anyway. Damn her father for encouraging her to think small. Damn Bogue for taking advantage of her troubles. And damn me for pretending she was right to be giving in.

I don't remember when the impulse struck me to barge into the Aurora, but I was up the steps and across their deck before I thought *this is a bad idea*. By then it was too late. I didn't think I'd get past the hostess stand. I'd tried the same thing last summer, and the woman who sat people for years stopped me before the door even shut. This time, no one was at the stand. I walked right past, ambled through the dining room, and came right up to the bar. I was sure I'd get caught then. Every bartender in town knew me. As luck would have it, I'd never met the guy who turned to serve me; must've been a summer hire. I had a vodka martini in hand and was swiveling around in my chair within minutes.

And there he was. Or rather, there *they* were. Bogue with Rob and Newf; the three-headed bane of my existence, huddled together in the far corner of the back room they kept closed off at lunch. Heads down, focused on a big sheet of paper spread across the table, they hadn't noticed me. I got right up and headed over. I had no idea what I was going to do, but I wanted to get to them before they had a chance to react. The element of surprise.

That got ruined when I stumbled on the step that separated the landing of that back room from the bar area. I spilled a bit of my drink but didn't fall. It was enough, though, to draw Bogue's eye.

"Look who's here. The wad monster!" Rob's and Newf's heads popped up.

"And it's the beach pirates," I fired back. "What's that, plans for your next raid?"

Bogue shoved back his chair and stood. Rob started rolling up the papers. They were blueprints, probably to his new resort. What did Joan call it? Mariner's Something.

"You know you're not allowed in here," Bogue said. "Do I need to throw you out again?"

I downed my martini and flung the glass at him. It shattered behind Rob and Newf. Now they were on their feet.

"You lousy piece of shit," I went after Bogue. "It wasn't enough to steal Wendy's recipes. You had to shut her down and humiliate her by forcing her to work in this dump."

"I'm helping her out. What have you done? Made trouble in her bar and cost her business. You're a real pal."

There were a couple chairs between us. I grabbed the back of one and threw it out of the way. Bogue stepped out from behind the table. Rob grabbed his arm. "Let it go, Bo. Tommy, do yourself a favor. Get out of here. You're drunk."

"That's right. I'm drunk. Isn't it terrible? Meanwhile, you're screwing over the beach with your bullshit resort."

"Alright," Rob cut me off. "That's enough. Let's just settle down and take this outside."

"Why? So you can explain how a tractor engine got where the boiler's supposed to be?"

Now Newf was coming out from around the table. "You need to shut the hell up." He put a hand on my shoulder. "Right now."

I slapped his arm away. "Or what? You'll flood me out?"

He put two hands on my chest and lowered his voice. "I don't know what you're talking about. But if you've got a problem, we can take it up some other time."

"You know exactly what I'm talking about. You know why my gully overflows. You're in it with him!" I pointed to Rob.

Newf's head snapped around. "What's he talking about?" he said to Rob.

Bogue charged at me. I tried to push away from Newf, but he had me by the shirt, fists boring into my chest. Bogue was going to take a free swing. I twisted to get out of Newf's grip and chopped down on his arms. It didn't work. I swung with my right. It grazed Newf's chin. I caught a blurry flash of his shocked face. Then my stomach shattered, and I doubled over. I barely felt the punch to the mouth, but that's what knocked me on my ass.

"Don't get up," I heard Newf say, and that's all I heard. No Bogue or Rob. No chatter in the restaurant. It was as if Newf and I were alone, like we'd been so many times as kids, settling once and for all our ancient grievance. I rolled over and started crawling. That's when I noticed the people watching by the bar. When I got far enough away from Newf, I got to my feet, but I didn't turn. Not yet. I wasn't ready. Instead, I faced the witnesses, hands on knees, catching my breath.

Finally, I straightened up, shook the ringing out of my head, and said quietly, "He's poisoning the lake." I don't think Newf could even hear me. But when I pointed at him, I shouted it. "He's poisoning the lake!"

Newf charged, bad leg and all. I got one swing in. It glanced off the top of his head. He barreled into me, shoulder to my chest, and drove me up against the bar counter. When I tried to push his head to the side, Newf rose up and smacked me a good one flush on the left cheek. I flailed at him with both fists, but he artfully ducked away. What was really happening is that I was falling, but I didn't realize it until I hit the floor, without even an instant to brace myself. The back of my head bounced on the wood. Blackness overtook me. I blinked it away, but it kept coming back.

Then I heard Newf. "Stay down, Tommy. Stay down."

The legs of a bar stool flickered into view. There was still a ringing in my head, and I could taste blood in my mouth. I'd be damned if I was going to give up. Slowly, like I was scrabbling up the ravine above my cottage, I pulled myself onto the stool, doubling over it on my stomach. Then I grabbed the bar rail. Then I planted one foot, then another. Then I stood and turned around. I wiped my mouth and looked at the blood in my hand. Newf was peering at me, assessing the damage. Rob and Bogue flanked him over each shoulder. The three swayed in front of me as if the Aurora was the mythical tugboat, ever so slightly rocking. I blew out a big sigh, shook my head, and managed a grin.

"All done," I said putting my hands up in surrender. Then I lunged forward and threw out a left-handed roundhouse. The last thought I had as my fist was about to connect with Newf's jaw was that I'd finally put one over on him.

I am rising. From the flat of my back, I am slowly tilting upwards. It's effortless, a kind of levitation. And now I am starting to slide. Something has been covering me. It's rolling away, peeling me naked. I open my eyes. I'm in bed, and the cottage is finally giving way to the gully. The bed glides across the floor. The footboard bangs against the wall. I am stood up straight now.

My bedroom window is at my feet. The side of the cottage hits the bank of the gully and keeps tumbling. The bed pushes against my back, forcing me face down. I edge out from under it just before the mattress slams over the window, then flips again onto the rafters that cross above the spine of the roof. I manage to hook my arms around two of the rafter boards. Then, as the cottage turns fully upside down, I swing my legs through the gap and throw them over the boards, like a gymnast on bars.

I brace for the jolt and crack that must surely come when the roof's spire wedges into the bottom of the gully. Instead, the whole structure quietly eases into floating, and I can see through the flipped window that the outside of the cottage is mere inches from the gully's side. Vessel and channel never touch. I realize with only mild surprise that my cottage has become a kind of ark, steering out into the lake.

I readjust myself on the rafters to face the bow of my ark. The window that used to look out over the lake is now half-submerged. I can see both above and below the waterline. Above, in the distance, there's a string of islands, stream-chiseled saw-tooths, the peaks of mountains. They are the islands of Wendy's dream, dappled with gardens, grooved with secluded bays. Below, the gloom of the lake slowly dissolves to pristine clarity, and I see its floor slope into the depths. Thousands of bright-colored fish—orange and yellow, purple and lime—crisscross the ark's portal.

My view brightens. The fish scatter. Icy whiteness is obliterating everything. It's Mammoth Rock, so close I'm sure I'll smash into it. In desperation, I climb across the rafters to the ceiling fan, sprouting like a giant spare-petaled flower. I grab two blades and find I can guide the vessel. I avoid Mammoth Rock. But within seconds, there's another white boulder in my way. I steer around that one, only to discover another. I'm slaloming between a succession of ghostly rocks. And now I find myself in a narrow gauntlet between two high-peaked islands. It ends at a rusty iron gate, bars draped with seaweed.

My ark clanks against the gate and stops. On the other side, seals and sea lions and walruses cover every ledge on the vaulting rocky shores, as high and far as I can see. Only they aren't exactly sea animals. Their faces are more elastic, more human. They're talking and laughing, yawning, scowling, pondering.

There's a knock at my side window. A giant sea lamprey, larger than a polar bear, is peering in at me. He has tiny fin-like arms, and he's rubbing them together in ravenous anticipation. Despite the gaping, fang-infested maw, he looks human, strangely familiar.

"Are you ready to forget?" he confronts me with a rasping roar.

"Forget what?"

"Everything," he says.

"Why?"

"To live."

I contemplate the transaction. A hollow thumping starts above me on what was the floor of my capsized cottage. It comes sporadically at first. Then I see white stones bouncing off the rocks in front of me, plunging into the water, pelting the serpent gatekeeper. Hail, I think. Giant hail. The wood all around me begins cracking and splintering. I realize it isn't hail pummeling me. It's golf balls. And now I know who that serpent is at my window.

"But I'm already alive," I argue. "What more is there?"

"Everything," he reassures me.

"So...give everything—to get everything?"

"If you'd like."

"What happens to me?" I demand to know. A plank above my head caves in. A cascade of golf balls pours onto the fan I'm still holding by the blades. The balls careen every which way, past the rafters and down into the steepled hull of my cottage.

"Who do you think you are?" the gatekeeper asks.

"Thomas Patrick McTavish." Another plank collapses. More balls pour in. The roof below me creaks and groans.

"Who?"

"Tommy!" My vessel is sinking under the rising trough of balls.

"Tommy?"

"Yes!" I scream. The golf balls are so deep they touch my feet. And now leaks are springing out between every board in the walls.

The serpent wedges his head through the window. "Tommy? Are you there?" he asks, so calmly I wonder if it's a test.

"Alright! You can have me!" The golf balls are up to the rafters, swallowing my legs. But the bigger problem is the water. It's rising, now to my chest, now gushing into the serpent's giant maw, now right under my neck.

"Tommy? Do you know where you are?"

The ship is sinking. The lake is lapping over my chin. I'm going to drown. "I don't want to be me anymore," I cry. "I don't want to be me!"

"Wake up!" the serpent roars, snaking toward me. He suctions my face with his sharp-toothed maw. I try to scream.

I gasped for air. I was looking straight at the rafters. Floating over them? Laying beneath them? Yes, laying, definitely laying, on my bed, flat on my back.

"There he is," a voice calmly reported. Grant's blurry face came into view, long hair dangling over me.

"There I am," I confirmed, blinking to focus.

"I was worried for a minute. You were thrashing around like you were having a seizure."

"I was drowning." My mouth didn't work right. My head hurt.

"A dream, eh? You're in luck." Grant wiped a washcloth across my forehead. He dabbed my nose. There was blood on the cloth. "My spiritual gift is interpreting dreams. Want to give it a shot?"

"Nope."

"Drowning isn't bad. It portends an emotional rebirth—that is, if you survive."

I felt my face. Everywhere felt tender. "What happened?"

"What happened? Newf laid you out in the Aurora."

"What I meant was, how did I get here?"

"Rob drove you home in your car. Then he called Sharon, who called me. Then—"

"Rob was in this cottage? By himself?"

"Taking care of you."

I tried to prop myself up. My head felt as heavy as a bowling ball. Where had I put the boiler piece again? Under the floormat or on the passenger seat? Either way, Rob could've easily found it.

"If it's any consolation," Grant said, "Newf's broken up about this. He wanted to take you home himself, but nobody thought that was a good idea. He even got into it with Rob, flipped over a table, spilled beer on a bunch of customers."

"And that's supposed to make me feel better how?"

Grant looked out my window, the same one through which I'd seen islands teeming with souls who'd surrendered themselves to forgetfulness. Now, it was just grey. "You're right. Newf's transgressions don't excuse yours."

"I was wondering when the scourging would begin."

Grant threw up his hands. "Honestly, Tommy. When's it going to stop? How much trouble do you have to put yourself in before you decide to change?"

"This isn't my fault. Those three are to blame. Trust me."

"So the vodka in the kitchen didn't have a thing to do with it?"

Shit. Joan's vodka. "Joan insisted we have mimosas."

Grant stared me down for a long, punishing silence. Then he burst out laughing. "Just like old times, eh? The whole gang's involved. Joan pulls the trigger. You, Newf, and Rob start fighting. And Sharon, me, and Audie are left to clean up."

Was he serious? I could feel the blood throb above my bad eye. "Since when did you ever clean things up? I seem to recall you throwing gas on every fire."

That wiped the grin off his face. "I wasn't talking about—"

"And what does Audie have to do with this?"

"She keeps calling. She wanted me to shake you, make sure you didn't lapse into a coma."

"How did she even know what happened?"

"The phone rang, and I answered it. She was calling for you."

"So, you told her. A woman consumed by worry. As if there wasn't enough to haunt her. I'm surprised she even talked to you."

"That first call was tough. But after a few times, she opened up. I got a chance to say some things I've been wanting to say for a long time. And I'm going to see her tomorrow. By myself. You don't have to come. So: there's some good that came from all this."

"I'm glad I could get knocked out for your benefit. What day is it, anyway?" The sky was so gloomy it could've been November.

"Same day," he said. "You've been out for five, six hours."

"Well, shit." I blinked my eyes wide. "I better get up."

"Just so you know, I poured out the vodka."

I swung my legs off the bed. "Aren't you a pal."

"And I'm headed to the gazebo right now, before it gets too dark. I'm going to find out what's really going on."

"I already know. Newf's diverting the irrigation runoff along the bluff into the ravine, there's no retention pond, and the low tide isn't helping. You were right about that."

"I'm just going to get some pictures. Before the rain comes in. They say we've got a lot of rain coming."

"Great. Maybe my cottage will float away after all."

Grant got very somber all of a sudden. He folded his arms across his chest, then started rubbing his chin. A doctor diagnosing a patient. As I rose to stand, he reached out, braced my shoulders, and peered hard into my eyes. "You going to be okay?"

"Yes, Grant. I'm going to be okay."

I walked him to the back door. When he opened it, there was a gasping sound. My bedroom door slammed behind us. A rising wind at night was never good. "You sure you shouldn't just go home tonight?"

"I'm going to get those photos." Grant waggled his blue paisley iPhone. "You'll know the story by tomorrow."

I barely got the door closed before my phone rang. The path across my living room was edged with books. Someone, more likely Grant than Rob, had lined them up cleanly on either side. Were they bored, or trying to send me a message?

"Hey Audie."

"Tommy! Thank God. I've been so worried."

"Your worries are over."

"What happened? I've heard two different stories."

I rubbed my temples with my free hand. "Can we talk about this later?"

"Oh. Right. Sorry. Now's not a good time. Maybe tomorrow, when you come over. With Grant."

"I thought that was just between you two."

"You said you'd come over."

"The way Grant told it, you and he had a breakthrough."

"I wouldn't go that far."

"Fine. Tomorrow." Audie's only response to that was fitful breathing. Huffs and gasps and sighs. "What else?"

"I don't like it here," she whispered like someone was listening.

"You've been there—what—eight, nine years? And now—"

"The new people next door, they don't like me."

"You don't know that."

"And when it's windy, like this morning, the windows rattle and leak at the top."

"Audie," I snapped with that hard edge reserved for times like this, when she was working herself up. "We nearly had a tornado this morning. My whole cottage shook."

She wouldn't quit. "Sometimes I feel dizzy up here. Like I'm out on a long, narrow ridge, exposed to the elements. Naked."

There was that word, the trigger that cast her back to that fateful morning. "Audie, I can't deal with this right now. We'll talk about it tomorrow. Okay?"

There was a pause. "I'm going to call you in two hours."

"No, you aren't."

"Tommy!" Now it was her turn to scold me. "Head injuries are nothing to take lightly. You could fall asleep and never wake up."

That sounded good to me. "Fine. Call me at midnight."

"Everyone just wants you to get better," she told me then.

"Who's everyone?"

"Everyone is us. Me and Grant and Sharon. And whether you believe it or not, Rob and Newf."

"All of you, except the one that matters."

"Well, we can't make you love yourself."

"Not me." Jesus, did I have to say Carrie's name?

"Oh," Audie got it.

"Midnight," I said and hung up.

I wasn't even sure what time it was. The light outside was no help. As grey and dull as it was over the lake, the sun could've already set. I went back to my bedroom to check: 8:45. I stood there, gazing out my front window. The sky was a ghostly pearl, all one color, hardly any distinction between clouds. It blended right into the water, erasing the horizon. And the lake was calm, its waves so rigidly consistent it looked like worn stone.

Then came the tapping. A finger. Another. Then another, gently tapping the glass. It wasn't until the pane in front of me started twitching and shifting that I noticed the raindrops. By then, there were dozens of fingers tapping. I could hear them on the big window in the other room. Then they were slithering down the glass, and finally, the sleek, grey heads of the drops seemed to slide onto the beach, halfway down the window. That's when I remembered the seals, crowded on the other side of the gate in my dream. No sooner had I thought of them than the rain came harder, and the whole window was smeared with silvery streaks.

It was a steady rain, the kind that goes all night, strong enough that I knew before long the roof leak beside my chimney would start dripping. I should've gone out and gotten a bucket to catch it. But I just stood there, listening to the clatter above me, watching the darkness close in, pile up. Even when I heard the drips start out in the living room, I didn't move a muscle. So what if a little water got on the floor? So what if the whole run-down shack collapsed? It might be a relief after all. No more worries. No more fighting. What was the bargain? *Give everything, get everything?*

The dripping came faster, from the pace of breathing to the ticking of a watch; now a rattle, now a draining. I jolted, blinked my eyes wide, and rushed to the outhouse. I was hurrying back inside with the bucket when a sound stopped me. Through all that rain, all the clatter in the trees, out to the road, and up the hill; a sound. Not a loud one either. Just a sort of lilting flutter. I waited. There it was again. I waited again. Then it wasn't there. I rushed the bucket to the leak and was on my way to get a towel to muffle the metal's ringing, when I wondered about that sound. Was that laughing? Was Grant still up there? Was someone with him?

*T*wo *things happened on that last day of the summer of '83, after Carrie Sinclair took her scorecard and left me. Like late-sprouting seeds, each held the kernel of the catastrophe that was to come a year later. The first thing happened when I went back to Joan. I opened the door to the storage room, and there she was, lying on her side across the long counter, naked, propped up on one elbow, eyeing me over her shoulder. "You didn't forgot about me, did you?"*

The second thing was that Carrie underestimated how long she could hit her drive on the par four. Normally, that wouldn't be a problem. But as fate would have it, Newf was mowing the last strip of that fairway. Later, Carrie would marvel that she never hooked a drive. An occasional slice, sure. But that day, right when she was about to strike the ball, she inexplicably tensed. The ball climbed higher than any drive she'd ever hit. Then it started drifting left, and as it fell against the backdrop of the curving peninsula, she saw the tractor. Inside the cabin, as Newf told it, the ball slanted into the side window, ricocheted off the windshield, and grazed his chin. He shut the engine off, glared back at Carrie coming toward him, and got out of the tractor. He was all set to let her have it. When she got close enough for him to take in the full impact of her presence, though, he bowed his head and found himself apologizing.

Carrie's appearance had that effect. The first thing anyone noticed when they met her was how tall she was. I'm six feet, and Carrie looked me in the eye. It wasn't her height alone, though, that was so remarkable. It was how she carried herself. I'd call it statuesque, but that suggests graceful majesty. Don't get me wrong; there was elegance in the way she moved, but she was lean and athletic, and she held her wide shoulders back and firm chest high, not because she was proud, but because that was her natural bearing.

After she said she was sorry, Newf muttered, "That's okay, ma'am." It was only when their eyes met that he realized Carrie was a girl, younger maybe than him. Carrie had the untroubled look of a child. You could've pointed out so many details to describe her beauty; those piercing blue eyes, the high flushed cheeks, that soft smile of hers, the luster of her tumbling caramel hair. But for me, it was the aura, the essential innocence that manifested everything else.

Newf finished mowing on the bluff before Carrie was done with the holes, but he circled around, cutting the same grass until she came looking for the eighth tee. He knew she wouldn't find it. You had to take a path into the woods. There was a platform hidden away no bigger than a toddler's sandbox, with such hard ground you could barely get your tee to stand. When Carrie started wandering across the bluff, Newf got off his tractor. As Carrie told it, he scared her to death when he came up behind her. "Looking for the eighth?"

She bolted upright. Her bag slid off her shoulder and clanked on the ground. The scorecard she'd been holding slipped from her grasp.

"Sorry to sneak up on you." Newf retrieved the scorecard and held it out to her. She had mostly twos and threes, with just a single four. Then there was the hole in one on the sixth. "You're having a good round."

"It's a short course." She gave a modest shrug. "The holes are buckets."

Newf laughed. "If they weren't, your score would be twice as bad."

Then she laughed. Newf said that was the moment he fell for Carrie. Her drive on the eighth may have also had something to do with it. When he showed her the sandbox of a tee and pointed out the green, barely visible through the pines and well below the bluff, Carrie dropped her ball and let it roll wherever—didn't even tee up. She pulled a seven iron out of her bag, took one quick glance between the trees, and hit her shot. No practice swing. No hesitation. And no pause to admire the drive sailing through the tight gap and drifting ever-so-slightly right to land on the green and roll within feet of the bucket.

Carrie offered a shy smile, thanked him for his help, and went on her way. The instant she disappeared down the path, Newf scurried up the hill, jumped on his tractor, and raced across the course. By the time Carrie got to the ninth green, Newf just so happened to be mowing the first fairway behind it. From the clubhouse, Joan and I watched him climb off the tractor and saunter over to her. The two talked for at least five minutes. I'd never seen Newf engage in that long a conversation with anyone, let alone a girl. We learned Carrie's story soon enough. Newf led her over, introduced us, then explained that she was new to the beach and working to become a golf pro. It would be alright, wouldn't it, if she practiced chipping up to the first green? I mulled it over to make sure Carrie knew who was in charge, then agreed.

She started lofting shots onto the ridge where the first green sat. The first few disappeared into the woods behind the green. But then she dialed in, and every shot thereafter was around the stick. We couldn't see where they landed, but some had to be close to the hole. We just watched, awestruck. Here was this girl calmly raining golf balls down on a target 150 yards away. It wasn't until the rest of our gang returned from Point Clark that anyone spoke up. "Holy shit!" Grant shouted after the first shot he saw clanked off the flag. "Did you see that?"

"She's been doing it for 10 minutes," Newf whispered.

Grant being Grant, he didn't get Newf's hint. When Carrie dropped the next shot beside the hole, he howled again. "Whoa! Who the heck is that?"

After the third dead-perfect chip, Rob wondered whether any had found the bottom of the bucket. Before long, Carrie was taking more time between shots, stealing glances our way, fidgeting in her stance. Finally, she hit a worm-burner, jammed the club into her bag, and marched off to retrieve her shots.

Grant was heading after her in a heartbeat. Newf chased after him. By the time the two caught up to Carrie, they were stride for stride, jockeying to get next to her. "They're going to tackle that poor girl," Audie said.

"You guys," Joan shook her head. "You're pathetic."

I looked at Rob. "I just want to see how close those shots came," he said, hurrying away. I shrugged at Sharon's glare and followed.

Of the forty-some shots Carrie had aimed at the flag, four were in the hole. Granted, it was a bucket, and that first green funneled into it from the back. But these were nine irons from 150 yards away. Carrie didn't seem particularly excited about her exploits. Grant whooped and danced when he saw the balls in the bucket. Rob peppered Carrie with questions, like he would on the verge of a deal. Newf just emulated Carrie, quietly picking up balls. He was using his baseball cap to hold them. I caught him a couple times, when Carrie wasn't looking, slicking his hair back and flattening it down.

We walked her to the parking lot. She didn't talk much. Grant and Rob hardly gave her a chance. Rob got out of her that her family had just bought cottage 142. Grant told her we were spending all of next summer together, and she should too. Carrie thanked us politely for helping her and drove off.

*I*f she'd done nothing else, Carrie would've been a beach legend for that day alone. As it turned out, by the next summer, she was a legend across Canada. The reason had a lot to do with her golf prowess. But it was more than that. It was Carrie's story—where she lived, how she grew up, who she was. She touched the soul of Canada in a way I'd only seen when the national hockey team beat the Russians in 1972 and Terry Fox ran halfway across the country in 1980 on one leg and a body riddled with cancer.

If you've driven Highway 21 south of Goderich in the last 50 years, you've seen where Carrie grew up. Most farmhouses there are set back from the road. But there's one that's so close to 21 you could mistake it for a boutique resort. What stands out is the gingerbread-like chalet on an island in the middle of a tiny lake. And the windmill at the apex of that chalet. And the rainbow-arced bridge that goes to the island. Even speeding past, it would be hard to miss all that. But you have to slow down to see the house itself. Tucked between two maples, it's more impressive than the chalet—a massive limestone farmhouse that had a fortune worth of renovations poured into it, from the steepled turret and slate roof to the huge wrap-around porch. The landscaping on the property is wondrously sculpted. Down the south side, a line of Dr. Seuss-like trees, with spindly trunks holding globes of greenery, extends as far back as you can see. Along the driveway, another line of gum-drop bushes leads to a white barn with a red roof. You don't have to be a farmer to know there isn't any farming getting done here. The barn looks more like a clubhouse—and for good reason.

Carrie's father, Carl Sinclair, is the most famous golf course designer in Ontario. As the story goes, he got involved in the sport in the mid-Fifties, when, at age 10, he started caddying at the Rockway Golf Course in Kitchener. Carl was the favorite caddy of the area's best golfers. The kid knew where to play the ball down every fairway, how to get out of trouble, how the greens would play from any location. More amazing than that, he could spot a flaw in even the best player's mechanics, and he wasn't afraid to speak up when he saw it.

There was just one thing Carl Sinclair didn't excel at in the game of golf— and that was playing it. In fact, he could barely hit the ball. It's a marvel he *even tried. You see, Carrie's dad was born with arms less than half the normal length, and hands that looked and worked more like flippers. He was the serpent gatekeeper in my dream. Knowing how much Carl loved the game, his dad made him a harness with a leather sheath into which the boy could jam the club handle and brace against his chest. Then he could squeeze his deformed hands against the shaft and rotate his torso to strike the ball. Carl tried it once and gave up. He told his disappointed dad he was never going to hit the ball with the majesty of a pro golfer, so he didn't see the point.*

When he was 15, Carl caught the eye of Moe Norman, the legendary Canadian golfer who Tiger Woods said was the most consistent ball striker in the history of the game. Norman was, to put it mildly, quirky. He was so obsessed with perfecting his swing he would hit a thousand balls a day until his hands often bled. From the time he bought a used five iron at age 11 until he died at age 68, Moe Norman kept at his quest. Plenty of people have witnessed him hit 250-yard drive after drive within feet of the hole. So why haven't you heard of him? Well, as perfect as Norman was on a golf course, he was a mess off of it. He lived out of his car. He only ate junk food. Today, you'd say he was on the spectrum. Still, his talents were undeniable. After winning two amateur titles in the Fifties, Norman joined the U.S. tour. For a time, he was a source of amusement for his fellow pros, a bumpkin Happy Gilmore. The clothes he wore were better suited for farming. He refused to use a caddy. He played so fast, never taking a practice swing or studying a putt—the only weakness in his game—that you'd think the point of golf was to finish fastest.

He was easy to laugh off—until he started climbing up leaderboards. At the Greater New Orleans Open in 1959, he was leading the tournament after the third round and wound up with a lucrative fourth-place finish. Legend has it that a group of threatened pros cornered him in the clubhouse, told him to change his clothes, fix his notoriously crooked teeth, and stop showing them up with his lightning style of play. He went home to Canada instead.

That's about the time he took notice of Carl Sinclair, though the boy was trying his best to escape detection. There just weren't many places to hide where Moe practiced. Who knows? Maybe that's what Carl wanted all along. One thing's for sure: from the moment Moe called him out from behind the bushes until Carl got married, the two were inseparable. Carl would walk alongside the eccentric legend, take in his stuttering sermons, and absorb them into his gestating ethos. As outspoken as Moe was about his "single-plane" swing, he also had a lot to say about the courses he played. He liked narrow fairways because they rewarded accuracy. And for the same reason, he relished the challenge of difficult holes, with doglegs and bunkers and water hazards.

At some point, Carl decided he could complement Moe's perfect swing by designing perfect holes. He got his dad to invest in converting a parcel of land near Bayfield into a par-three course. Within two years, it was making money. His dad bank-rolled another course near Southampton, then one south of Grand Bend. By the time he was 20, Carl had three courses turning a profit and was consulting on another handful of projects.

Then, to the shock of his parents, Carl got his high school sweetheart pregnant. No one even knew he had a high school sweetheart. Some, no doubt, were surprised anyone would have him, let alone a girl as popular as Kaitlyn Royce. A hasty wedding was arranged. Carl bought the land where he is today. And by the time Carrie was born, he had built his golfing Shangri-La. That's the part of the Sinclair property you can't see from 21. Behind the faux chalet and the lake and the limestone mansion, there's a wall of trees that hides a five-hole course Carl designed and often changed to experiment with ideas before he built them into his public courses. The only hint from the road that the owner had any interest in golf is a sign that spans the driveway, 20 feet high, from one pole to another. It's just sawed branches tied between two wires, arranged to spell "TROONORTH." You need to know something about golf to get the pun. Royal Troon is a course in Scotland known for tight fairways, deep bunkers, and punishing roughs—just the kind Carl would admire. On the other hand, every Canadian would get the allusion to the "True North." That's how Canada is described in its national anthem.

This was the household Carrie Sinclair was born into. It wasn't just about golf, at least not at first. She grew up doing all the things girls from that area did. She went to school, took horse riding lessons, got into curling, hung out with friends at the beach, loved to read, learned to cook. But everything was secondary to serving her father's vision to make her the perfect golfer—a Moe Norman, but with no quirks, more power, and a better putting touch.

I say it was Carl's vision, but Carrie's mom had a role in things too. Kaitlyn was a golfer herself, and a damn good one at that. She once had her own aspirations to make something of her talent, but a nagging hip problem limited her practice time. In fact, that was where Carl met her; on the practice tee at one of his courses. She was experimenting with swings that wouldn't strain her hip so badly. Carl watched from a distance, then moved closer, before he finally cleared his throat and gently suggested she might not want to torque her body so violently. He showed her Norman's single-plane swing, and while it didn't cure her injury woes, it did endear him to her.

It was only a year before Carrie showed up at Boiler Beach—after a full decade of her husband using their daughter to perfect what he called the "symmetrical-plane swing"—that Kaitlyn insisted they take a step back and put things in perspective. What finally tipped Kaitlyn over the edge was when Carl gave Carrie a daily quota of 200 swings and 200 putts.

"Moe Norman used to hit a thousand shots," he defended his directive.

"I don't want Carrie to be the Moe Norman of Canadian girls," Kaitlyn told him. "He might've been a perfect golfer, but he wasn't a perfect person."

Kaitlyn's worries for Carrie's well-being were the reason Carl bought 142. The idea was that she'd take a month every summer to get away from golfing and be a normal kid. But it wasn't a week into their first stay before Carl started getting antsy watching Carrie lounge around. He didn't come right out and insist she go golfing. Kaitlyn wouldn't have stood for it. What he did was wonder aloud why he spent so much money on a cottage if no one was enjoying the surroundings. He rattled off some things Carrie could do—have a swim, walk the beach, go down to the kids' softball game, maybe knock the ball around that crappy course they had. He knew his daughter well. She was too shy to show up for softball. Even walking the beach was putting herself out there. A swim? Sure, she'd do that, but how long would that take? He knew she'd gravitate to golf. Still, when she asked how to get to the course, Carl was smart enough to protest. Wasn't the point of the cottage to get away from the game? Anyway, if Carrie insisted on going, she should do it for fun. Not even keep score. The performance kept Kaitlyn's hackles from raising.

So that's how it came to be that we met Carrie on the last day of the summer of '83. I didn't learn all this until the following year. By then, everything had changed. A month before I saw her again, Carrie became a household name across Canada. Having won a couple amateur events in Ontario, she qualified for the Canadian Women's Open, which back then was a major on the LPGA tour. The timing couldn't have been better. Carrie was on top of her game. All the hard work she'd put in perfecting her symmetrical power stroke and tuning her putting touch paid off over four incredible days at the St. George Golf and Country Club in Etobicoke.

After the third round, Carrie was in second place, a shot behind renowned U.S. golfer Juli Inkster. If that were the end of the story, it would've been amazing enough: 17-year-old, self-taught amateur from Ontario's farm country challenges the LPGA's top pros. But what happened in the final round became the stuff of legend. Inkster got off to a hot start, while Carrie struggled. With six holes to play, she was in fifth place, seven strokes down. She picked up two when Inkster put her ball in the water on 14 and another two when she eagled the par-5 15. Then she stepped up to the tee at the par-3 sixteenth and lofted a five-iron toward the treacherous green. It hit behind the flag, took one bounce precariously close to the edge of a huge bunker, then reversed course and started rolling toward the hole, rolling, rolling, feet away, then inches, then hanging on the lip for one breathtaking instant before tilting ever so slowly into the cup.

If you had measured the decibels from the collective roar that rose across the country, it would've rivalled the cheer that erupted when Kincardinite Paul Henderson scored the goal to beat the Russians in '72. Suddenly, young Carrie Sinclair was a stroke off the lead, with two holes to play. After she and Inkster birdied 17, they hit their drives on the last hole right next to each other. It was such a long par four most players laid up. Carrie had other ideas. She took out her three wood and drilled a laser that rolled within three feet of the cup. Inkster decided to let it rip as well. When her shot found a bunker, it looked like the impossible might happen; a bogey for Inkster, a birdie for Sinclair, and a legendary victory for Canada. Then Inkster conjured up some magic of her own. With the gallery ready to roar at her misfortune, she nestled her feet in the sand, blasted out of the bunker, and holed out in two bounces.

Carrie made her birdie to lose the Canadian Open by a stroke, but she won the heart of Canada in the process. When the CBC tried to interview her walking to the scoring tent, she seemed as stunned by her feat as everyone else. She hung her head. She blushed. She fumbled her words. And then she started tearing up. Her father hustled her away. The gallery closed in. The cameras caught Carrie and Carl getting swallowed up by the crowd, but not before focusing on the father's fin-like arm fluttering on his daughter's shoulder.

Everyone descended on the Sinclairs for their story. Someone in Kitchener knew Carl from his caddying days and told the local station about his connection to Moe Norman. They ran the story that night. The next morning, television vans were parked outside Troonorth. Carrie came out with her parents, confessed she was overwhelmed, and begged everyone to give the family privacy.

Fat chance. Within days, the Toronto Globe and Mail *published a story on the unlikely rise of Carrie Sinclair, with details about Carl's golf course design genius, overhead pictures of the five holes hidden on his property, and quotes from locals about the demanding regimen he'd devised for Carrie.*

It was too much, too soon. Carrie couldn't go anywhere without people flocking to her. Most were polite; you'd expect nothing less of Canadians. But there were whisperings that, while Carrie's feat was incredible, her father was an odd duck, and was it really healthy to be pushing his daughter so hard? Carrie never heard such whispers. Neither did Carl. Mostly, it was Kaitlyn, the unrecognized member of the family, who overheard people when Carrie or Carl passed. She never mentioned these idle comments to Carrie. But she did tell Carl that Carrie needed a longer break than they'd slotted for that summer.

Carl grudgingly bowed to his wife's wishes. As for Carrie, she chopped off half her signature caramel hair, got it curled, and dyed it with sandy streaks. She changed her clothes too, abandoning her crisp golf wear for more of a grunge farmer look, with frayed jeans and tattered t-shirts. To complete her disappearing act, she hardly ever strayed from the confines of the beach, and on those rare occasions when she did, it was behind the mask of Ray-Bans and a beat-up Maple Leafs cap. For the first week Carrie was up, none of us knew she there.

Actually, one of us did; he just decided not to tell anyone. Living so close to her, Newf had been pursuing Carrie ever since she knocked her drive into his tractor. He killed time in Goderich, hung out on the practice tees at Carl's courses, showed up at Carrie's high school sporting events. It wasn't like Newf. He could barely get up enough gumption to make it his own classes; now he was running off to take in the extracurriculars of a rival school. Newf's mother was afraid he'd gotten into drugs. He had to come clean to get her off his back, and confessed it was about a girl.

When the two reconnected, it was purely by chance—at least as far as Newf knew. He was carrying a bushel of apples to the booth his mother had at Ripley's farmers market when he practically ran Carrie over. She was turning away from the booth with a jar of honey. Apples went everywhere. Stunned and tongue-tied, Newf scrambled to pick them up, hoping she'd walk away and spare him any further embarrassment. But she just stood there, waiting quietly for him to clean up his mess. What Newf didn't know then and found out only when they were recounting the story, is that while he'd been trying to run into her, she'd been doing the same with him.

*The two went out a handful of times from September to April. They saw
a couple movies together, walked the beach, snowmobiled around the gazebo.
Newf even had her out to Holyrood to see the rafts he was building. Carrie
invited Newf to Troonorth once, but it turned out to be a mistake. Carl knew
his daughter had been seeing a Holyrood boy, but when he saw them together
in his own home—how closely they sat on the couch, how Newf absently stroked
Carrie's hair, how she snuggled up against him—he got alarmed. After Newf
left, he laid down the law: she wouldn't have any free time with her first tournament a month away. Carrie knew better than to argue. Still, even after the
Canadian Open, Carrie would sneak phone calls to Newf. They never talked
about golf; they made plans for the summer.*

The rest of us finally found out Carrie was up when Rob and I got a job
insulating the cottage next to the Sinclairs. I'd been doing odd jobs with
Rob for a few weeks already, and things were turning out just as he'd promised.
We'd already cleared a patch of poison ivy behind 119, painted the boathouse
at 73, and mowed a couple dozen lawns. I made six hundred dollars in those
first two weeks alone. The job next to Carrie's was our first that went sideways.
The owner wanted us to put insulation under his cottage. Rob convinced the
guy we knew what we were doing. The lakeside of the crawl space wasn't a
problem, but as we slithered toward the bluff side, the joists angled into sand,
and we couldn't go any further. Rob went to get advice from his dad. I snuck
off to the beach to hide from the owner.

That's when I saw Carrie, tanning on the beach. I was going to call to her,
but I wasn't sure she'd remember me. Then there was the matter of her new-
found fame. Her beauty and reserve were intimidating enough; now she had the
aura of celebrity. Even Rob, when he came back with a new plan for getting
under the cottage (short answer: close-quarter digging), didn't feel worthy enough
to approach Carrie. When we shared the news with everyone else that she was
up, Newf came clean and told us he'd been seeing her. He wasn't sure how
comfortable she'd be mingling with a wider circle. "Aren't we good enough for
your famous girlfriend?" Grant needled Newf. "Afraid we'll corrupt her?"

Newf started bringing Carrie around. And we were all paired off—Newf
and Carrie, Rob and Audie, Grant and Joan, as much as either of them could
be tied down, and me with Sharon. Everyone was getting what they wanted out
of the summer, too. I was making more money than I ever could've imagined.

Sharon was learning about her dad's business so she could run it one day. Newf had more orders for rafts than time to build them. And Carrie was getting the downtime she so desperately needed while her father figured out her next move.

As for Rob, he had jobs planned through August and his cut in Newf's raft business. He and Audie seemed to complement each other perfectly. While he spent his days hustling for work and getting in good with local businessmen, Audie was off by herself, down by the shore, out in the countryside, sitting in front of an easel, painting landscapes. It sounds more liberating than it was. She'd been accepted into the Rhode Island School of Design and was worried that if she didn't get ahead with her portfolio, she'd fall behind come September. Her parents told her not to stress out so much. We managed to get her out most nights, but no one knew where she went during the day.

Joan was content hanging out with Grant, living for the moment. She didn't get good enough grades to get into UCLA and she didn't want to settle for community college. She was just going to get a job waitressing while she worked on her music. She was pretty sure she could get a gig playing at a coffee shop in Malibu, but they didn't pay anything. Anyway, she wasn't going to think about it until after the summer. Grant was even more militantly against planning a future. College was out of the question. His parents had died in a boat accident when he was 15, and his uncle, his only other relative, threw him out a year later. Even if he had money, school was the last thing he'd use it on. Grant thought college was a scam to extract money from well-heeled parents who still harbored illusions that a degree guaranteed a happier life. He'd bought an RV over the winter—the same Chieftain he was living in today—and he was just fine driving a delivery truck, being a beach bum, and going with the flow. It didn't hurt that he was making good money selling drugs around town for some guys in Grand Bend.

There are plenty of reasons why things spiraled out of control. God knows, I shouldn't be blaming anybody. But there's no denying Grant's part in it. He's the one who parked the Chief at Kozee Korners, the RV campsite on the shore road north of Boiler Beach, and encouraged us to hang out there. He's the one who made all the drugs available. Grant used to say drugs weren't a crutch for people who couldn't deal with reality; reality was a crutch for people who couldn't deal with drugs. He turned out to be wrong about that.

The first bad thing that happened was Newf's rafts started sinking. Two of the older ones went down in the space of a week. It had something to do with the connection between the platform and the flotation barrels. The barrels filled with water and took the rafts under. Word spread to those who'd got new rafts or made recent orders. Newf discovered there wasn't any easy fix. That meant returning money to buyers, money Rob and Newf had mostly spent. They had to go to their dads to make up the difference. No problem for Rob; Mad Mike considered it the price of a risk. Big problem for Newf. His dad paid up but put his foot down: no more ventures with Rob Garton. I got the impression that the history between the families had something to do with the edict. The end result of the raft fiasco was that Newf had more time to kill, less inclination to listen to Rob, and a greater desire to escape Holyrood. His immediate reaction was to hang out in the Chief, getting high and drinking beer.

That brought Carrie around Kozee Korners more often as well. Being with Newf wasn't the only reason she sought refuge there. She was having problems of her own with her dad. Despite assuring his wife he'd give Carrie a break, Carl couldn't help himself. It was one thing to suffer watching his daughter waste time with a boy from Holyrood; it was another to stop pushing her career forward. When Carl called Rob and me over after we finished the insulation project and asked if we'd ever built a garage, of course, Rob said we had (of course, we hadn't). That's how we started helping Mr. Sinclair make an indoor driving range. It wasn't much by today's high-tech standards; just a long, cavernous barn, with high rafters and a big net stretched across one end.

Carrie wouldn't set foot in the place. To her, it was a monument to a broken promise, her dad's craven way of punishing her for not practicing without confronting the issue. She was used to him playing mind games to get a golf club in her hands. What set her off was when he proclaimed one evening that he'd figured out her next career move. She'd be going to Miami in the fall. The coach of the Hurricanes was the best teacher of young women golfers in the world and had already helped seven girls go pro. That was the sum total of his justification for the decision. Carrie was stunned. But she didn't stand up to her dad. She knew there was no point. Instead, like Newf, she took refuge in the Chief.

Audie had the opposite problem of parental pressure. After she'd burned through her paint, her parents refused to buy more and told her to go have fun. Audie displayed her canvasses on their porch, leaning from the floor against the couches and chairs, lying flat on their cushions, propped on their backs. The early pieces were realistic landscapes. Then, Audie's work grew darker, more disconnected from reality. Her eye had turned away from the commonplace to the disturbing—a dead fish washed ashore, a toddler having a tantrum, a loopy looking old man buried to his neck in sand. The last time I visited, she'd started on a new phase. Using pencils, markers, and crayons, since she couldn't afford paint, Audie went back to landscapes, but in every piece, there was one element that was grossly oversized. The boiler as wide as a building, blocking dwarfed beachers from the water. A child poking a stick at a dead fish as big as a house. When Audie asked me if I liked that one, I just smiled. I didn't know what to say. It was brilliant, but scary. What was going on in the mind of someone who could produce such a thing?

When she did finally start coming around the Chief, it wasn't so much to take refuge as to establish a base of operations. Audie brought with her a backpack crammed with art supplies. She didn't mind getting high, but refused to vegetate after the weed kicked in. Drugs gave Audie a kind of manic energy. If she didn't get up and do something to work it off, that energy started gnawing away at her hold on reality. Rob witnessed Audie's mania firsthand when we stopped by once on a break. I wasn't that alarmed; I'd seen it before. But Rob was so unnerved he chewed out Grant. He promised he'd go easy on the weed when Audie was around. Then, unbeknownst to me, Rob asked Sharon to keep an eye on Audie when the partying started. Sharon wasn't big on hanging out in the Chief. She was still working for her dad, learning bookkeeping at the store. Her way of helping out Rob was to bring a stack of board games to the Chief. Monopoly and Life. Stratego and Sorry. Even Candyland.

Everyone got absorbed in those games—except Audie. The result couldn't have turned out any better, though. Grant stopped stoking up Audie's eccentricities, and she found a new compulsion to preoccupy her. It wasn't with the games themselves; she steadfastly refused to play them. No. Her obsession was with game pieces. That was the one part of playing, the picking of the pieces before the first move, that Audie was psyched to get in on. She always had to be first to choose, and when she got her piece, she'd go off in the corner, bring it close to her face, and squint over every detail.

We didn't discover until later what she was using the pieces for. Rob and I were painting a cottage near Kozee Korners when I spotted Audie, standing on the shore's edge, peering through pinched fingers, like she was measuring the length of a distant boat. Then she got on hands and knees, flattened out on her stomach, and took another pinching measure of the lake. I had to see what she was up to. I snuck up behind her. She was drawing what looked like a huge metal high-top sneaker rising as high as a house from the lake. Kids were swarming all over it, crawling up on the humped toe, sunbathing on the upper ramp of the shoe, diving off the loop jutting from the heel. I cleared my throat. Audie jolted as violently as if I'd screamed in her ear.

"How'd you come up with such a weird shoe?"

She plucked something out of her lap and held it up the same way she'd pinched the horizon. It was the metal sneaker from Monopoly. Audie proceeded to tell me, in her breathless, frenetic way, how she was turning game pieces loose on our vacation paradise. She flipped back in her sketchbook and showed me a drawing of the Kincardine Harbor with a green Candyland piece—you remember the flat gingerbread-like kid with the hollow eyes and creepy smile—straddling the pier like the Colossus of Rhodes. He was twice as tall as the lighthouse, outstretched arms wider than the harbor channel. Boats passed under the steepled space between his stubby legs. The vision was unnerving enough, but what made it truly disturbing was the understated execution. This could've been a pleasant rendering of a sleepy harbor town. People were walking across the bridge, milling around the docked boats, fishing off the pier, and no one was paying attention to the giant Candyland boy. It was genius. And I told her so. She gave me a faint smile, sunk her gaze, and turned the page.

There, a red Stratego piece, with its gap-toothed battlements and a shining gold bomb, tilted forward from the Boiler Beach pitcher's mound. The monolith loomed over the trees that surrounded the field. As with the Candyland scene, the drawing's attitude is what gave it such eerie mischief. You were looking out at the massive slab from the batter's box; the bomb seemed like the ball that would somehow get hurled your way. But the fielders behind the piece behaved like this was any other Sunday game. The third baseman was sharing a laugh with the shortstop. The rightfielder had a beer in hand. Only the centerfielder seemed bothered by the giant wall of a pitcher. He craned his neck to see around the oversized piece, with a vaguely detectable scowl.

Like I said: genius. But there was a strain of madness there as well. Audie was showing me the next sketch when Rob called out from the boathouse. I told her I had to go. She kept on talking even after I'd backed away. Rob and I got back to painting. But I'd catch him now and then, glancing down at Audie, hunched over her sketchbook. "She really is amazing," I felt compelled to offer.

Rob stopped painting. "She has to quit. That's what her parents say."

"She won't know what to do with herself."

Rob heaved a heavy sigh. "I've got to figure something out."

"What's to figure out? Let her do what she wants. Be a good boyfriend."

"I'm not her boyfriend."

He'd sure been acting like one. "Then why are you always going off alone?"

"I don't want to let her down," Rob said. "Everyone has someone—Newf and Carrie, Grant and Joan. And you and Sharon, right?" He looked at me, a miserable hope in his eyes. If I hadn't mistook that look for a moment of weakness, we might have spared ourselves a lot of animosity. "So, I figured, it's just summer. Why not play along, let her be happy?"

You can say a lot of bad things about Rob. He's cocky, standoffish, conniving. But one thing you can't say is that he's heartless. Rob takes care of his own. These days, it's family and business partners. Back then, it was friends. "I just wish I understood her better," he added. "Like you." He went back to painting, so I did too. But there was something about the way Rob let those last words hang. When I glanced over, he jerked his head away.

*A*fter the sinking rafts, the next bad thing that happened was the closing of the beach store. Mr. Beam was behind on his loan payments, and when the putt-putt course collapsed, Mad Mike ran out of patience. He bought out Sharon's dad, converted the store to a duplex, and rented both sides for a pretty penny. As I've said, there are those who think Mad Mike had been scheming from the start to get his hands on that property. I don't know. After all Jim Beam did to help Garton win softball bragging rights, it's hard to believe he would treat him that coldly. Then again, the counterpoint went, "It's the Gartons. They've been scheming since they put Boiler Beach on the map."

After the store closed for good, we got together at the gazebo to reminisce about that all-important trek we took as kids to the top of the hill. Audie recalled how scared she was of Nelson Buehlow's gravelly voice. I remembered searching for empties at the roadside for two extra cents. Newf's favorite thing was feeding the rabbits they kept caged outside the store. "I'm glad you find this fun," Sharon suddenly erupted. "One day, when your dad gets cheated out of his land and they bulldoze the gazebo to the ground, we can all tell stories about how we used to be friends." Then she stomped off into the night.

That shook Rob up. He started after Sharon. I held him back. "Let me." When I found Sharon crying at the edge of the bluff, I told her my best memory of the store would always be the day I met her. She smiled. Seconds later, *though, she was despairing again. "That was so mean of me. Should I tell Rob I'm sorry?" That was the first inkling I got that there might be stronger feelings between the two than friendship.*

I did have one chance to talk to Rob about it, the day after Sharon's outburst. We were finishing up framing Mr. Sinclair's golf shelter when Rob brought it up. I was holding a board, and he was about to nail it down. He lined up the hammer, lifted it, then froze. "About Sharon," he started. I took a deep breath. "I feel terrible. I have to do something."

"She'll be alright. She just got upset."

"You can't blame her." Rob hammered down the nail. "I have to make this right. I need to get her a job."

What could I say? He was trying to help. And he did finally get her a job waitressing. We'd done work for a guy who was friends with the owner of Pelican Pete's, a restaurant that came and went within five years. But it was the hot place to eat at the time. Sharon said she never left there without at least a hundred bucks. So, it all worked out—at least for the time being.

That wasn't the only fallout from the store's closing. Grant lost his job doing deliveries. That gave him more time to cause trouble at Kozee Korners. People in the RV park were already irritated with how loud we were and how much we partied. Once Grant had nowhere else to be, his neighbors got openly hostile. The guy parked beside him, a sour-faced cuss named Dean, got so tired of our infringing on his space, he staked an ankle-high fence of string around it. Grant being Grant, he didn't see the string, rambled through it, and got the whole mess tangled in his feet. Dean charged out of his RV and gave Grant an earful. He listened intently, nodding and furling his brow, and when Dean was done ranting, Grant blew him a kiss and sauntered away, trailing the stakes behind him. We had to hold Dean back from tearing into Grant.

Not long after that, Grant started talking about going on the road, exploring Canada. "Why should I stay here, crammed into this tiny lot, taking all this shit?" he complained, after the owner of Kozee Korners came down to warn him to shape up or leave. "I've got no job holding me here, no one breathing down my neck, and nothing to look forward to. Why not see something new?"

"You better take me with you," Joan piped up. We thought she was joking. But Joan had her own reasons for discontent. The store's closing intensified them, too. She'd been floating all summer, lounging back in the corner of Grant's RV, playing her guitar, working on songs she never finished. Carrie

asked her once if she'd play one. Joan started strumming, stopped, tried again, stumbled on her words, and went quiet. "I can't play for you guys. I need an audience, people I don't care about."

Rob snickered. "You can't play here, but you can play up on a stage?"

"Don't believe me. I don't care. I know myself. I need that pressure."

After Rob got Sharon the job at Pelican Pete's, Joan lit into him. "You put in all this time to help Sharon, but you won't use any of your connections to get me a gig."

"When did you ever ask me?"

"You knew what I wanted. You just don't believe in me."

It took a couple weeks, but Rob managed to convince someone to give an unproven singer a shot. The owner of the Windsor Hotel was struggling to stay afloat and had started opening his bar early to grab a piece of the town's lunch business. It wasn't working out. The Windsor was way down Queen Street. There was no reason to walk that far, past so many better restaurants. The owner needed a draw. He met with Joan and decided to give her a shot. It didn't hurt that she auditioned in her bikini. And when Rob took him aside and said he'd pay the 20 bucks she wanted per show, the deal was clinched.

That's how the closing of the beach store came all the way around to bite me in the ass. With Rob so preoccupied helping Sharon and Joan, he had less time to help with the jobs on our plate. I found myself alone for the better part of a month. But when we got paid for our work, Rob took his usual 60 percent. I called him out once. He argued that if he hadn't stoked up the business, neither of us would have anything. I fired back that if I didn't do the work, we wouldn't get paid. "A deal's a deal," Rob countered.

The project that ultimately did me in was Carrie's golf shelter. Rob and I worked together on the framing, but after that, I had to do all the shingling. And, as luck would have it, those days were the hottest of the summer. If you've ever worked on a black roof in 90-degree heat, you know how miserable it is. The longer the heat wave wore on, the angrier I got. I cursed Rob for using me like that. I beat myself up for letting it happen. Then I started thinking I should up and quit. If it were any other job, I would've straight away, but I had over a thousand dollars coming to me.

Besides, I had another reason for sticking with the Sinclair job: the morning breaks. After Rob started ditching me, Carrie began showing up to offer me a glass of lemonade. The first time she asked if I needed a break, I told her

I liked to work through lunch to beat the afternoon heat. From my perch on the roof, I could see her shoulders slump. "What the hell," I decided as she was walking away. "I'm at a good stopping point."

From that day on, for two solid weeks, she brought me a drink. At first, it was no more than a couple-minute break, a little small talk while I downed the glass. Then she started asking questions that took longer to answer. One morning, I noticed a wood stump set up between two chairs. She came to that break with a pitcher of lemonade and a plate of watermelon slices. "It occurred to me," she said, sitting down, "you're building my prison. Once you're done, my dad will have me in there forever."

"So, all these breaks are just an elaborate plot to slow me down."

Carrie grinned and patted the empty chair. "Have you ever been to Miami?" she asked after I sat.

"No, I've been to Disney World, though. All I remember is that it was really hot and everyone's skin was so leathery, they looked like lizards."

"I don't want to go." Carrie's breath caught, as if she was trying to suck the words back in. She stared at the ground, those piercing eyes suddenly lost.

"What else would you do?"

She had a ready answer. "Newf says we could find work anywhere— Toronto, Calgary, Vancouver."

I was stunned. "Newf lives in Holyrood. He slings shovels full of shit. You swing a golf club and can make tons of money doing it."

"That's the men. The average woman makes less than 15,000 dollars."

"You're not average."

Carrie put her hand on my knee and graced me with her tender smile. "That's nice of you to say," she whispered, like it was a secret only we knew.

Another time, after we were done with our break, and I was climbing back up the ladder, she called out, "You think you and Sharon will get married?"

I nearly choked at the idea. "No."

"You've never thought about it?"

I was 18. Why on earth would I think of getting married? "Not once."

Carried looked troubled by that. "Newf and I talked about it." I must have looked at her funny, because then she said, "What's wrong with that?"

"Nothing. Not if you think you're ready."

She let me get on the roof, then shouted, not loud, but loud for Carrie, "You don't have to be mad about it."

I finished the project the next day. Then, after Mr. Sinclair paid us, I quit. We were about to get into Rob's pickup when I did it. Rob stared at me across the front of the truck. "You're putting me in a bit of a bind."

I knew what I was going to tell him. I'd played out the moment for days. I'd say I was quitting because he'd abandoned me, taken me for granted, used me. And when he pleaded with me to stay, I'd insist my mind was made up, and he had no one to blame but himself. But now that the moment was here, I didn't say any of that. "I just need a break, Rob. I'm headed off to college in a month, and I need some time to kick back."

Rob didn't plead like I expected. "It's alright. I'll figure something out." Damned if the son of a bitch hadn't made me feel sorry for him. After he dropped me off at 112, the complaints I was going to voice came back to me. Muttering them aloud as I retreated to the cottage, they sounded petty. The fact was, I'd broken my word with Rob, and there wasn't any justification that was going to make me feel better about that.

*T*hat was the day the summer turned for me. Back then, I would've said *infinitely for the better. I had money, time, and freedom. And I was convinced I'd earned the right to kick back. That's what I told Sharon I was doing whenever she'd ask what was wrong. Nothing was wrong. Everything was absolutely right. I was done denying myself, always wanting, like Joan said. I see now that quitting on Rob was more of a surrender than a liberation. Yes, I had money, but none of the foresight to use it for what I needed. And I had time, but I wasted it all. And there was no one around, really, to point me in the right direction. My parents had finally split. My mom stayed home in Michigan, and my dad holed up in the cottage and drank.*

The one thing he did for me actually fed my rebellious streak. One day, I heard the rumble of a hot rod roaring up on our cottage. I went outside to find two cars idling in the driveway. One was a K-car. The other was a 1973 Charger, snarling away with a 440 Big Block V8 engine. This was 1984, but the car looked brand new, its classic "plum crazy purple" paint job shimmering, the iconic black bumble bee stripe wrapping the trunk. A rail thin, old man got out of the Charger and asked if this was Frank McTavish's place. I said it was, but he was asleep. By this time, the guy's friend in the K-car had come up beside him. They looked like friends of my dad's, which is to say fellow alcoholics. "Well, get his ass up," the first guy said. "We got a car for him."

As it turned out, the guy driving the Charger borrowed money from my dad, lost it gambling, and offered his prized car as repayment. My dad had no interest in a muscle car. But being such a soft touch with friends, he agreed to take it and erase the debt. After the men left, my dad walked around the Charger once then came back my way. As he passed, he tossed the car's keys at me. "Don't say I never gave you anything," he muttered.

I didn't feel like I had the power to let go until I got that Charger. As fast as I drove that car up and down the beach road, I'm amazed I never crashed it. Once, Grant got talking about how all the hypercompetitive weekend warriors had ruined Sunday softball, so I veered into the infield and did three donuts. The damage was so bad, they cancelled the next game. Rob suspected I did it and accused me to my face. I denied it, and everyone backed me up. When we were alone, Newf said, "Rob thinks he's entitled to everything. He's not even Canadian. And this is Canada. Fuck him." Fuck Rob. Damn straight. Fuck everyone. That became our motto late that summer, at least some of us. Definitely Newf and I. Definitely Grant and Joan. Even Audie and Carrie, in their own ways. But not Rob. And not Sharon. They were together in that…and more.

I stopped into Pelican Pete's once after getting overserved at the Spider's Web to surprise Sharon at work. She was in a corner booth with Rob. Once she saw me, she popped up and hurried over. "This is a nice surprise."

"This is a surprise," I snapped. I looked past Sharon to Rob. "But I don't know how nice it is."

"Rob knows the owner. He's in here all the time."

Rob stood up then. I took it as a provocation. "All the time, Rob?" I was pointing at him now, pressing against Sharon. "Is this where you were when I was busting my ass on Sinclair's roof?"

He started coming toward me. Sharon wouldn't let go. I nearly tripped. A table toppled over. Then the cook was in my face. Then Pete.

"Come on, Tommy," Sharon begged. "Please stop. Please?"

I let them back me up to the door, most of the fight gone out of me.

"You were hiding this," I said to Sharon in a hushed voice. Rob came up beside her. "Both of you."

"Can you blame her, Tommy? Look at you."

"Look at me?" Pete started pushing me out the door. "You're stealing my girl, and look at me?" Rob didn't hear that last part. I was already outside.

Then Rob threw his hands at me. I don't know why, but that set me off. I put my fist right through the glass. Everyone froze. Sharon dropped her gaze. I looked at my hand. There was a chunk of glass wedged into the meat of my palm. I pulled it out, tossed it away, and left.

It was a couple days before Sharon and I talked about what happened. One evening, she came to 112 and asked if we could walk. We went well down the shore before she told me she thought we should stop seeing each other. I didn't argue. I apologized for Pelican Pete's, and she forgave me. Then I asked if she and Rob were together. She said he'd been helping her through a hard time. I could've pressed it, but I didn't. When we turned to walk back, Sharon gave me a quick, tight hug and said, "Please take care of yourself, will you, Tommy? You're not the same person when you drink so much." I told her I knew. When she left, I watched her go all the way to the Eighth. And what I felt wasn't sorrow or remorse, or any of the proper feelings you'd expect after losing someone you cared for. I felt relieved, elated even. Why couldn't I have seen then what was wrong with that?

When I told everyone Sharon and I were on the outs, no one seemed surprised. I viewed that as support. Grant told me he thought the whole business of pairing up was a problem, not just Sharon and I, but Carrie and Newf, or anyone else. Why should we make claims on each other when we were all just beginning to explore our freedom? Going steady, getting married, falling "in love"—they were all obligations society promoted so you'd do your part to advance the species. It made sense at the time.

*G*rant's idea of taking a road trip started becoming more than talk. He bought a map of Canada and took a red marker to it, tracing a crooked line from Kincardine through Parry Sound, Sudbury, Sault St. Marie and Thunder Bay, to Winnipeg, Regina, Medicine Hat then Calgary, and finally on to Vancouver. He concluded we could do the drive non-stop in 48 hours. "But we have all the time in the world," he stressed. "We owe it to ourselves to savor the soul of Canada." Half of us were American—Joan, Audie, and me. I had the temerity to second-guess Grant. If we took a U.S. route across Michigan, into the plain states, out near Yellowstone and through Seattle, we could cut 10 hours off the drive. "This isn't about time," Grant thundered. "It's about expanding our consciousness, getting closer to what's real."

"And you can't do that in the U.S.?"

Grant didn't take the bait. That's one thing you'll find with Canadians: They're careful about telling Americans what they really think of us. For the longest time, I didn't see much difference between an American and a Canadian, so I hardly ever checked myself in expressing opinions. Now, I'm as cautious as Grant. Having lived in Canada for nine years, I can tell you, as much as I've tried to blend in, my Americanism remains an undisguisable piece of my identity. Of course, given what happened that summer, I can understand why some hold my nationality against me. But even those who don't know what I did still think of me as an American first—and a beacher, a drunk, or that Wondermat guy second.

In the end, Grant had us vote on the route to take. Canada won, five to one. We picked a date two weeks out—the morning after the barbecue, when parents would either be at the North-South softball game or sleeping off the party. Then we figured out who'd drive; Grant in the Chief, Newf with his pickup, and me in my Charger. We all could've gone in the RV, but Grant was worried it might break down. I volunteered because my dad wouldn't care if I left—and I wasn't sold on going all the way to Vancouver, though I kept that to myself. Finally, everyone thought through their escape. For me, it was easy: grab what I needed the night we were going and leave. Others, like Carrie, had to concoct more elaborate plans. As attentive as her father was, packing and lugging a suitcase out of the cottage would be impossible. Newf came up with the idea of smuggling out Carrie's belongings piece by piece. He got a spare suitcase from his house, threw it in the back of his pickup, and every time he went to visit Carrie, they snuck out with something for the trip.

That included 300 dollars. Grant decided we'd all need to pony up that much to make sure money wasn't an issue. The only person who had a problem with that was Joan. Her gig at the Windsor had done wonders for her confidence and showmanship, but it hadn't put much money in her pocket. When Grant set the price of the trip, Joan realized things had to change. She went to the Windsor owner and asked if she could go from three to six days a week. No problem. Then she told him she thought her pay should be doubled to 40 dollars a set; lunches had definitely picked up since she started. The owner laughed. "If you want a raise, go ask Rob. That's who's paying your way now. As for the lunch rush, don't flatter yourself. You've seen the act that comes after you, eh?"

The real secret to the Windsor's turnaround had nothing to do with Joan. It was the stripper who took the stage at 12:30, just in time to give plant workers an eyeful before they drove back to Douglas Point; fifteen minutes of tits and ass in a town that had never allowed such a thing. You'd think the actress who took off her bikini in Fast Times at Ridgemont High *was putting on a show. Phoebe Whatever. This stripper was hardly her. Grant and I had hung around after one of Joan's sets to see her. She was an older woman, in her thirties, with a pleasant world-weary face, a scrawny body that made her boobs look deflated, and a Caesarian scar. Joan said she was some struggling farmer's wife out of Kintail. It was sad, really. But you wouldn't know it by the reaction she got. And I have to admit, the fact of her nudity was thrilling. I say nudity; she still wore pasties and a G-string—tame by today's standards.*

Joan thought it was tame even at the time. She complained that the woman was the least sexy stripper she'd ever seen, and she was embarrassed to be her warm-up act. So, I wasn't surprised when after the Windsor owner insinuated that sex was what filled up the restaurant, Joan asked how much he'd pay for her to play nude. As she told it, the guy practically fell off his chair. Joan was offended he hadn't raised the possibility first. All he wanted to know before offering her an extra 30 bucks, was whether she was 18.

"What if I didn't wear the pasties and G-string?" She had to wear the G-string; that was the law. Pasties were optional. The stripper had insisted on wearing them, her little nod to modesty. If Joan didn't want to wear them, she didn't have to. "What I'm asking is, how much more is that worth?" The owner couldn't see how that would attract more business. "Well," Joan said, pulling up her bikini top. "I think this is how." They agreed on six shows a week, 75 dollars a show, and an extra 25 whenever the bar take got over 1,000 bucks—which it always did. Then tips on top of that.

Rob was furious out about the deal. I was there when he barged into the Chief and got after Joan. Why would she make a joke of her music like that? Nobody would listen to what she sang if she did it nude. Was it about the money? If she needed more, he could help her out. Joan went right back at Rob. She told him she was insulted that he'd foot the bill for her to play.

So: there was my altercation at Pelican Pete's, and Joan's dispute over singing nude. But those were just two of the run-ins we had with Rob in the days leading up to our escape. Funny thing is, we were trying hard to watch ourselves around him and Sharon. We didn't want them to know about our road trip. I don't know why. We just thought the trip would go better if they were as surprised by our leaving as everyone else.

If we were trying not to draw attention to ourselves, though, we did a piss-poor job. Grant and Newf got banned from the go-karts for playing chicken. Joan got mad playing putt-putt, swung her club at the windmill guarding the last hole, and knocked off a blade. I got the bright idea to yank the papier-mâché head off Blinky, the town's cartoon lighthouse mascot, at the pipers' parade. I thought it would be funny. The grizzled guy who lugged the band's bass drum around on his big belly didn't. After the tween-age girl under Blinky's head started bawling, the drummer, who Rob told me later was her grandfather, charged me, wielding his mallets. Depending on your point of view, the sight of a portly man in a kilt chasing around a gangly punk he had no hope of catching made for a comic or pathetic scene.

Rob landed on the not-amused side. "Damn it, McTavish," he roared, "I work with people who witnessed your antics. They know I'm friends with you guys. When you pull crap like that, it comes back on me."

"Sorry, Rob," Joan sniped. "We forgot this was all about you."

That's when Sharon spoke up. "It's so rude!" She pierced us all with a withering glare. "You're all just so rude."

It wasn't like Sharon to snap. Maybe if we'd taken her words to heart, we might've avoided more trouble. Instead, things got worse. We were in town one day, when Grant spotted a rack of coveralls in an alley beside the cleaners. On impulse, he snatched them and took off running for Newf's pickup. In broad daylight. The rest of us—Carrie and Joan were there too—had no choice but to run after him. It was insanity. Anyone could've seen us. At the time, though, we didn't think about that. We just went running hellbent for the pickup, laughing and screaming in our own private madcap movie.

The coveralls were dark blue with red letters on the back. BNDRT. Newf knew enough to identify what the BND stood for: Blue Nuclear Development. But no one could figure out what RT meant. Grant proclaimed that it stood for "Road Trip," then proceeded to throw out new ideas for BND. He landed on "Brand-New Day Road Trip," and we decided the coveralls, which hung on us like scarecrow suits, were the official uniform of our adventure.

Later that night, at a bonfire in front of Newf's cottage, where we all showed up in our new outfits, we learned what RT stood for—and got our worst tongue-lashing from Rob. "For God's sake, you know where those are from? That's the Radiation Testing group. You can't wear those around. You're messing with the Canadian government."

"You won't have to worry about us in a few days," Audie let slip.

Everyone went silent.

"What's that supposed to mean?" Sharon asked.

Newf leaped up and started unbuttoning his coveralls. "It means we're opening our own nudist colony." He let the coveralls drop and stood before the bonfire in all his glory. Everyone howled in surprise. Newf raced down to the lake, galloped into the water, and dove in. Joan was stripping off her coveralls in seconds. Grant was right behind her. Then Audie went shrieking away.

Carrie and I walked together to the water's edge. I stripped down and quickly went in over my waist. "Come on, Carrie! Don't be a downer!" Newf yelled out. She unbuttoned her suit slowly. I dove in and swam underwater as far as I could. I never did go for the rowdiness of skinny dipping. To me, it was a solitary act, floating in the liquid dark, naked under that vast infinity of stars. When I came up, I was past everyone, beyond the sandbar. Audie was already back on shore, Grant was getting out, and Joan and Newf were still thrashing nearby. I couldn't find Carrie anywhere. Finally, I saw a dark head gliding out by the second sandbar like some stealthy seal. Then Carrie's shoulders broke out of the inky gloom. She shook her head, hair gleaming, and offered a tentative wave. I thought it was for Newf. But when I saw how dark his silhouette was, I knew it was meant for me. I waved back, thought about it, then swam out to her. I stopped a safe distance away, far enough that she wouldn't feel threatened, but close enough to see her face.

"Just because I don't want to splash around, doesn't mean I'm a downer."

"If you're a downer, I guess I am too."

She drifted my way. If we had both reached out, we could've touched hands. Still, we were blanketed to our shoulders in a glimmering plain of darkness. "I just like to be alone sometimes," Carrie said.

"Nothing wrong with that."

"It's going to be different on the road..."

I thought she was fretting about being crowded in the Chief. Then I remembered: Newf would be driving too. Wouldn't she be in his pickup? "If you ever need to be alone, you can take my car and drive it yourself."

"I can't drive your car. It's too fast."

"You don't have to race it around like I do."

Carrie looked in toward the beach. "Newf wants to stay out there, get jobs in Banff, and learn to ski."

She didn't seem excited. "I'm driving back early," I said. "If you decide you don't want to stay out there, you can always come back with me."

Carrie sunk slowly under water, was gone for a heartbeat, then breached right in front of me, her face pointing up to the star-packed sky. As it tilted back upright, I saw those stars glittering in her eyes, like she'd caught them falling. She came close, gave me a hug, and gently broke away before swimming hard to the shore. To this day, I can still feel her body's imprint. It wasn't a tight embrace, but it was full. She had taken care to stamp herself against me, from her arms and breasts down to her stomach and the tops of her thighs. It was warm and smooth, like the softest branding. I shuddered in the water.

Later, when we were around the fire again, back in our Brand-New Day coveralls, Carrie leaning against Newf, Joan cuddling up with Grant, and Audie bracing against me as I lay on my side, the talk swirled around Rob, who had left with Sharon.

"You think he'll tell someone about the suits?" Newf wondered.

"I wouldn't put it past him," Joan said.

"You want to know what's really eating at Rob?" Audie spoke up then. "He can't control us. That's why he's being the way he is."

"Yeah, but he can still cause problems," Grant said. "Sharon too. You can't be talking about the trip, hinting that we're going somewhere."

I could feel Audie tense up against me. "Sorry. It just slipped out."

"What's sorry," Carrie added, "is that we have to keep it from them."

"Sorry! Sorry! Sorry!" Audie burst out angrily. Then she started giggling. It was the sort of laughing you were worried might turn to crying.

"You have nothing to be sorry for," I tried to comfort her.

"Yes, I do." She seemed excited. "We're all sorry. That's the game."

She was quivering like a live wire in the crook of my body. I put my hand on her shoulder to calm her. "Audie," I whispered. "Audie…"

Shit. It was 12:14. I'd forgotten to call Audie. She answered before the first ring ended. "Thank God."

"I set the alarm for noon by mistake," I lied.

"You can't do that to me, Tommy. I get bad thoughts."

"Anybody would, Audie."

"Did you sleep? The concern was whether you could wake up."

"I dozed off." Another lie.

"And the cottage is okay?"

I didn't get what she meant at first. The rain had been so hard and steady that its drone had lulled me into my reverie. "I think so. I should go check the gully."

"Oh, no, Tommy. Don't." I may as well have been contemplating jumping off the harbor bridge for as alarmed as Audie got. "You can't go out in this. Not in your condition."

"Okay."

"I'm going to call you in the morning," she told me. "Nine o'clock on the dot. If you don't answer, I'm calling 9-1-1."

There wasn't much choice but to agree. I got off the phone and went into the living room. The bucket I'd set by the chimney was overflowing. A stream of water ran across the room to where it pooled by my side door. I emptied the bucket, got a push broom, and shoved as much water as I could to the door. When I opened it to push the puddle out, the full roar of the rain shocked me.

I ventured out onto my deck. I was drenched within seconds. Even out in the open, exposed to the expanse of the sky, I could barely see. What little light came through my windows was no more than a melting swell, worn dim behind a sheet of water cascading off my roof. I didn't know I'd made it to the deck's edge until I banged my knee on the railing. I could barely make out the ground below. The humped outline of the bushes by the gully was barely visible. I listened for a rush of water beneath the roaring rain. Everything sounded the same.

I hurried back inside. I couldn't have been more wet than if I'd jumped in the lake. The bucket was half full again. I emptied it and put it back under the leak. Then I took a shower. Drying off, I caught myself in the mirror. My jaw was misshapen and purple, nose red and swollen, eye black and partway shut. Jesus. Why *hadn't* they taken me to the hospital? I leaned in for a closer look. It wasn't the injuries so much that caught my eye. It was my skin, how papery it looked. The wrinkles around my eyes. The spidery veins on my cheeks. Was I that old already? I backed away and turned off the light. Then I turned off the living room lights, went into my bedroom, and turned off those lights. There was only the faint

numbers on my clock. I watched their slow, methodical progress—
1:03 to 1:04, 1:04 to 1:05. The rain kept drumming on.

I burrowed under my blankets. My mind was swirling. How
bad would it get by morning? Would the bank beside my cottage
hold? It was already eroding without rain. And why was that? I'd
find out in the morning. Grant would have seen the gully before
the rain and after water flowed into it. He probably already knew
the answer. I could've called him and avoided lying there wondering. But he would've called himself if there was something to worry
about. No, I'd wait. Get my rest. Take stock of the cottage when I
woke up. Then call Grant. And Audie. *Can't forget Audie.*

*The last I'd seen of Audie's artwork, she'd been placing pieces from the
Game of Life in perilous locations. Remember the tiny convertibles you
filled with blue and pink pegs, one for you, then your spouse, and the children
you collected? There were six holes you could use; perfect for our gang. The
picture I remember most vividly had the car at the top of our hill. The peg
people were as tall as water towers, round heads looming over trees. The view
was from a little girl's perspective, as though we were walking behind her up
the Eighth to the store. The car was swerving onto the hill, straight for the girl.
It was unclear who she was, but her shoulders were thrown back like Carrie.
A pop bottle had slipped from her hand but had yet to crash on the pavement.*

*Not exactly uplifting material. Grant said, "I like your funny ones
better." Audie argued that this was funny; a little unsettling, sure, but funny
still. Who could be scared by a flimsy plastic car?*

*The criticism had been enough to paralyze Audie. She moped in the Chief,
smoking more weed than usual, gazing out at the lake. Carrie asked why she'd
stopped doing drawings. "Because they're demonic," Audie said. I defended
them. Even Grant acknowledged they were brilliant, just too disturbing for
him. "They're supposed to be disturbing," Audie muttered.*

"Why are you even listening to us?" Joan weighed in. "You're the artist."

*The one game piece Audie had yet to use was the pawn from Sorry. But
after her "sorry" rant, she couldn't render her visions of the game piece fast
enough. You know the piece I'm talking about. It looks like a droplet frozen
in the act of bouncing off a still pond. Audie drew them like faceless aliens,
with flattened oval heads, long elegant necks, and sloping shoulders. She did a*

family portrait with her mom and dad smiling on either side of the yellow pawn. In another piece, you were looking around the slender neck of the white pawn, into the shallows, where five pawns were stationed in an arc, around the back of the boiler. Their egg-shaped heads were tilted ever so slightly toward the relic, whose gutted metal innards were ablaze. Floating above the boiler, shreds of burning paper rose into the evening sky. Most were small ashes, but on one smoldering piece, Archie was sharing a milkshake between Veronica and Betty. Veronica's eyes were closed, enjoying the shake. Archie was glancing her way. Betty was mooning over Archie. Naturally.

Audie wasn't crazy about that one, and she was even less pleased with her next attempt, a shot of the Point Clark lighthouse between two pawns twice its size. The three monoliths stared out from the drawing's left edge. In the lake, a line of pawns waded ashore, extending to the horizon, like they were walking along that ancient land bridge. Of all the Sorry drawings Audie did, that was my favorite. It was just after sunset, and the lighthouse beacon was barely visible against the vermillion sky. The wake swelling around the pawns gave you this tangible sense of these creatures powerfully striding ashore.

As soon as Audie finished that drawing, she let loose a wounded howl. I thought she stepped on glass. When she had all our attention, she threw her hands at the sketchbook. "Why do I keep getting shittier?" I told her it was good, and she knew it. If she'd really thought it was that bad, she would've come to that conclusion a lot earlier and spared herself the pain of finishing it.

Audie's face got red. "If I stopped drawing the instant I thought something sucked, that whole book would be filled with one-line scribbles. Art is an act of faith. You'd know that if you did it."

I don't know why, but Audie's words cut me. So I slashed back. "What kind of faith makes you so unhappy all the time?"

To this day, Audie finds snide ways to throw those words back in my face. If I visit when she's doodling, I can't compliment her without her muttering, "I didn't feel too unhappy with this one," or "I suspended my disgust," or some such dig. I've come to realize that Audie's art is more an act of hope than faith. She gets a burst of creativity and runs with it, always optimistic she'll reach some rare, enduring freedom. But, inevitably, her mind gets chased down by the hounds of self-hatred, and she winds up feeling more demoralized than if she hadn't attempted her escape. Then the next chance comes again, and she breaks away. Only to get overtaken. Again. And again.

*A*udie still blames herself for everything that happened after we argued about her sketches. It was just a few days before we planned to slip away. Joan had been working for two weeks at the Windsor and bragged that she'd pulled in over a grand. "I get more in tips than the hundred I get paid," she told us. "I just hike that garter way up on my thigh, and all those men line up to paw my skin and jam their dollars in there. You should come watch."

"I'm in," Grant said.

"If you insist," Newf chimed in.

"I'll go," Audie added.

Newf tried to dissuade her. "You don't want to be in a strip bar with a bunch of grubby pigs shorting and hollering."

"Do they really cheer?" Audie wanted to know.

"They howl," Joan grinned. "Like wounded cats. It's a rush. To have that power, to know when you take a deep breath, a roomful of men gets weak."

"I'd like to see that," Audie said quietly.

The whole thing annoyed me. Maybe it was because she'd had me under that spell the summer before, and I knew now it was just a game to her. Maybe it was because she hadn't tried to seduce me like that since. I walked out of the Chief. "You're coming, eh Tommy?" Joan called out. "I know you want to."

We went to the Windsor the next day. I drove. Grant, Newf, and Audie came along. She brought her sketchpad. It wasn't until we were in line to get in, and you could see the shabby bar through the open door, with its tiny stage and the yellowed spotlight on the empty stool, that Audie had second thoughts. She froze at the threshold. It was so sudden, the guy behind us bumped me. "I'm going to the harbor," Audie said.

"What's the hold-up?" the guy chirped.

"Here," I gave her my keys. "Take the car. That's a long walk."

"Can we get moving?" the guy griped again.

"Just fucking relax," Newf broke in.

"What the hell did you say?" one of the guy's friends leaned in. They were plant workers, four of them, not much older than us, but big guys, not the sorts we needed to be messing with.

Fortunately, Audie backed away. "I'll be back at one," she said.

"You going in or not?" the guy behind me pressed again.

"What's your problem?" Grant shot back.

"You're my problem."

Newf was glaring at the four guys now. I shoved Grant through the door. Then I turned to the workers. "We're good."

But we weren't good. Not even close. The place was packed by the time we got in, and we had to sit off to one side of the stage. The plant crew that had been behind us joined another group right at the front and center table. There was a huge scrum around the bar to get drinks. All they served at lunch was beer in plastic cups. Newf came back with six, as many as he could hold.

When Joan came out from behind a black sheet at the back of the stage, a howl rose from the smoky crowd. They weren't just plant workers. There were middle-aged men too, farmers and townies, even beachers. Joan didn't play to her audience the way a common stripper might. But she knew exactly what she was doing. Every move was innocent, but there was something enticing about the way she made them—the barefooted tiptoe across the stage, as though she were sneaking out, the turning of her bare backside to take her guitar off the stand, the rocking of her hips as she sat on the stool—then the heave and hold of her breasts as she waited for the din of yearning to settle. Like parishioners, the men reciprocated with a reverential hush.

Then Joan started playing. The song was Joni Mitchell's "All I Want," which she played for us the night of the dinner party. When she sang, "I wanna be strong, I wanna laugh along, I wanna belong to the living," the room was dead quiet. Her singing was pure and impassioned, urgent in a way I'd never heard. After she sang, "I wanna wreck my stockings in some jukebox dive," Joan kicked her foot ever so slightly and wriggled on the stool. The huddled men erupted with a lusty roar, and you could barely hear her asking, "Do you wanna take a chance on maybe finding some sweet romance with me baby?" When she ended the song, the crowd's applause was—how else to put it?— genteel, like it was coming from discerning theatre goers.

She thanked them with a whisper, then went about fiddling with her guitar pegs. As her arm stretched to twist the tuners, her right breast danced above the guitar's waist. After she finished one string, she arched her back and shook her hair out of her face. It was all calculated; most importantly, the way she straightened her leg, so her heel rested on the edge of the stage. After a respectful pause, a grey-haired man came up, reached out with a five-dollar bill, and gently tucked it under the white garter Joan had pulled up high on her thigh. Joan gave a startled shiver, like she never saw him coming, then put her hand on her breastplate. "Isn't that nice?" she said with a breathless air of surprise.

Another man came. Then another. Soon there was a line. And all that while, Joan tuned her instrument, or at least pretended to, stopping periodically to thank her admirers. This went on for a few minutes before the line dwindled. Joan tucked her leg under the stool and gave her guitar a punctuating strum. A couple men heading up to the stage dutifully returned to their seats.

She started playing the chords to "Love Hurts," a Gram Parsons tune we'd heard her spin over and over to get the finger play right. For once, it seemed that she was going to nail it, but then she lapsed into a gentle strum. "It's a special day," she said. "My friends came to see me." Joan turned to us and held out her hand. All the faces in the crowd swung our way. The plant guy who bumped into me made a point of craning his neck and fixing on us a sneering squint. A stare-down formed and hardened. Then Joan started singing "Love hurts, love scars, love wounds and marks." She hadn't gotten through the first verse before that guy rose up from his circle of workmates, held up five twenties for all to see, then shook them at Joan like he was trying to befriend some frightened animal.

When he put a foot up on the stage, Newf's chair scraped back. I grabbed his arm. He yanked it away. The plant worker slipped the twenties under Joan's garter. She kept singing, but there was a quiver in her voice. When he was done, the guy leaned into Joan and whispered something. She forced a brittle smile. Then he straightened, swung his hand back like he was appealing to the crowd for quiet, and gave Joan a hard slap on the side of her ass.

Grant and I were up in a heartbeat. The guy's buddies blocked us. He returned to his seat under a muddled outcry of protests and catcalls. Just before he sat down, he jutted his chin out at us. Not two seconds later, Newf swung a pool stick into the worker's face. How he got the stick, I don't know. The guy never saw it coming. He lurched sideways, hit the ground, and didn't move.

Then all hell broke loose. The last clear image I had was Newf swinging that stick and Joan, arms crossed over her breasts, looking on in horror. After that, it was a blur of arms and fists, chairs flying, tables overturning. There were people for and against us. I was swinging wildly at anyone who swung at me. But punches came from everywhere. I took one from the side, spun, and got one flush on the nose. My eyes watered up. I covered my head and dropped to my knees. Suddenly, my jaw clamped shut, my teeth crushed together, and my head burst with light. Next thing I knew, I was getting dragged across the floor. There was still yelling, still fighting, still a riotous dance of flailing bodies, raining beer, and flying furniture. When I was shaken to my senses, the face looking down on me was Jim Beam, Sharon's father.

"Where am I?"

"You're in the Windsor. God knows why."

"But where?"

"Behind the bar." He shook his head. "What are you kids doing here?"

I could've asked the same to him. To this day, I've never told Sharon her dad was in the middle of the Windsor brawl. I don't even know if he threw a punch. All I know is he pulled me to safety, then went back out into the melee. A couple minutes later, he pulled Grant behind the bar, too. We were both in bad shape. I had a bloody nose and the beginnings of two black eyes. Grant got it worse; a nasty gash across the bridge of his nose, a split lower lip, and a broken pinky finger he made me pull out to set straight.

The fighting stopped soon after Mr. Beam saved us. One moment, there was chaos, then silence. Then the Windsor's owner was swearing. The bar looked like a tornado had swept through. Not a single chair or table was upright. Cups were everywhere, and the old floor was sopped with beer. Pictures had been taken off the walls and wielded as weapons, their mangled remains strewn everywhere. Even the front window had been broken.

"He slapped her ass," Grant said, by way of excuse.

"He slaps her ass all the time," the owner said. "Not that hard, though."

"Where is she?" I wondered.

"In back. I got her off stage as soon as I could."

"I'll check on her," I volunteered. "I can't get this bleeding to stop."

I went down the corridor behind the stage to the men's room. I didn't think to knock. There was Newf with Joan. He had his back to me; she was bent over, bracing herself on the sink. They both gaped in the mirror. "Shit." I rushed away. Newf called out behind me. I can still see him there, as clear as yesterday, face contorted with desperation, fumbling at his pants, the washroom light spilling out behind him. "Sorry, man," I said and hurried away.

In the first few minutes after I left him, a fever of shame flashed through me. I felt as if I were to blame for something. I helped clean up as far away from the stage as I could, dreading the moment I'd face Newf and Joan again. But as time wore on, I started thinking more about what I'd seen, what it meant, what I'd do about it. I started thinking about Carrie, how much it would hurt her if she knew what I saw. Then I was mad.

Joan finally made an appearance. Just Joan. She was dressed for the beach, in her cover-up, bikini, and flip-flops—and she had her sunglasses on too, even though the bar was dark. Her face was smeared with tears.

"You okay?" *the Windsor owner asked.*

"I just want my money."

"No chance. Look around. There's a thousand dollars of damage here."

"That's not my fault."

Was she for real? "Gimme a break," *I grumbled.*

Grant looked at me like I was a traitor. I stared right back at him. "Is Newf okay?" *he asked Joan.*

"He has an ugly welt on his head. I'm going to take him to the hospital." *Joan glared my way.* "You okay with that, Tommy?"

"Why wouldn't I be?"

"You seem upset."

"We're all upset, Joan." *With that, I went outside to wait for Audie.*

Grant came out later and sat beside me on the curb in front of the Windsor. We eyed each other. "Do I look as bad as you?"

"Worse," *I joked. Nothing was said for a while after that. Grant flicked pebbles into the road. I peered down Queen Street. Audie was late.*

"Joan told me," *Grant finally broke the silence.* "What you saw."

"Is Newf going to tell Carrie?"

Grant stood and looked down on me. "You really think that would help?"

"She has a right to know," *I argued.* "They're running away together. She told me. They don't plan on coming back."

" 'She has a right.' " *He flung the rest of his pebbles into Queen Street.* "Why? So she can be unhappy? She doesn't need to know about this. He's not hers. She's not his. And who are we?"

"Friends."

"That's right. We're all friends. That means we look out for everyone." *It was the usual free-love, happy-family Grant crap.* "It's not right."

Grant sat back down. "So, what are you going to do? Tell Carrie?"

"I'm not telling her. Newf should."

Grant went silent, like he was giving it some thought. Then, looking away, he said, "Did you ever tell Sharon you screwed Joan?"

I didn't see that coming. "How'd you know about that?"

"Joan and I don't keep secrets."

There wasn't anything more to say. I wasn't going to tell. Newf wasn't going to confess. Carrie wasn't going to know. We were all going to drive west like nothing happened. It nagged at me, though, not just what I saw, but how Grant and Joan were conspiring. "Maybe I should've *told Sharon.*"

I started walking. I was done waiting for Audie. Grant followed. When we got to the bridge, we looked across the harbor for my Charger. You couldn't miss that plum purple paint job. But it wasn't there. I leaned over the rail and peered down at the road that ran past the harbormaster's hut and ended at the channel. Audie always liked hidden places. She wasn't there, either.

Grant leaned over the railing next to me. When he caught my eye, he said, "I stood in this very place the first day I came to town."

He went on looking at me, waiting. "Oh yeah?"

"After my uncle kicked me out, I stayed with a friend in Parry Sound. He told me they were hiring at the nuclear plant in Kincardine, and if I got a job there, all my worries would be over. So I packed up that shitty Pinto I traded in for the Chief, drove down, and went out to the plant. Of course, there weren't any jobs for a 16-year-old."

I remember wondering at the time, why is he telling me this? *I wasn't in the mood for a long Grant story. But he kept going.* "I kicked around for a couple days, slept in my car, tried to find a job. I was ready to give up when I stopped here on this bridge, leaned over like we are now, and looked down into the channel. I thought to myself, I don't have anyone. I could disappear and no one would care. I could leap off this bridge, like you did when I bet you wouldn't do it, dive into those waters, and will myself never to come up.

"And that's exactly what I resolved to do. But it was broad daylight, and I couldn't risk some good Samaritan saving me. So I decided I'd head down to the beach, kill time until after sunset, and make the jump when it got dark.

"When I walked down to the harbor, I passed that French fry truck there in the parking lot." Grant pointed out the truck between the thicket of boat masts. It's still there to this day. "I was halfway to the beach when I thought fries sounded like a pretty good last meal. So I went back and got in line."

Grant seemed to be getting off the point. "We should get going," *I told him. I was starting to worry about Audie.*

He ignored me. "I'm standing in line for fries, and this guy files in behind me. It's a long wait, so we get to talking. I happen to mention I just got into *town and I'd given up trying to find a job. And he says, that's funny, because he just bought a store and can't find anyone to drive his delivery truck.*

"It was Sharon's dad, the same guy who just saved us in the Windsor." Grant laughed, surprised by the connection. "Needless to say, I didn't jump that night. I took the job. Then I met all of you."

I thought he was done. I stepped back from the bridge railing. Grant grabbed my arm. "I don't have any blood relations anymore," he said. "I just have you guys. You're my family. I have to keep us together."

Those were the last words said before we got to Kozee Korners and saw the police car in front of the Chief with my car parked beside it. Audie was leaning against the hood, arms folded, head turned away from the officer talking to her. His partner was listening to Grant's disgruntled neighbor Dean. He saw us coming and pointed at Grant. Audie shouted, "I'm sorry! I'm really sorry!"

What had happened was this: Audie went to the harbor like she said she would. But once there, she decided she'd done too many harbor drawings already. She wanted to find a setting she hadn't done before, so she drove out to the highway. That's when she saw the radio tower. It was on Concession 8— still is—a half mile from the old store. It wasn't a tower so much as a triangle of three rickety ladders vanishing at a dizzying height over two hundred feet in the air. Newf tried to climb it once, but he didn't get halfway up in the tight, three-sided cage before the wind forced him down.

When Audie saw the tower looming over the lake, she had what she called "an epiphany." That was the perspective she needed for her Sorry masterpiece. She drove down the gravel lane, grabbed her sketchbook, then started climbing. Audie said she went all the way to the top, and her drawing confirms that. She's captured the coastline with a level of reality that could only come from lofty observation. It extends all the way north, past Kincardine, to the power plant. Later, Audie would bury six monstrous Sorry pieces half as tall as the tower, up to their sloped shoulders along the bluff, tilting back, like they were gazing out into Lake Huron. They looked like relics from Easter Island.

When the OPP pulled up behind my Charger and ordered Audie down, they took her sketchbook. She explained that she was an artist; she was seized by an inspiration and compelled to climb the tower. She urged them to look through her book. They wouldn't do it. She was more offended by their disinterest than worried about the consequences of her climb. It was only when they started peppering her with questions that she realized she was in trouble. They asked where she lived. Audie told us she imagined how her parents would react if she showed up at her cottage between two OPP officers. She made a snap decision. "I'm staying with friends at Kozee Korners."

That's how a policeman came to be standing in front of the Chief, getting an earful from Dean, the neighbor we'd had such trouble with. In the end, nobody suffered any punishment for Audie's trespassing. The police handed her sketchbook back and told us we needed to be better neighbors. They didn't even ask about the bruises and cuts on our faces. But right before they left, one officer said to Grant, "Don't make us to come back here. Next time, we'll look through your RV, and I don't think you want that."

That alone was sufficient to worry Grant. But later, when Rob said Pelican Pete told him his friends had gotten in a fight and put someone in the hospital, Grant freaked out. That "someone" could've very well been the guy Newf smacked with a pool stick. If he decided to press charges, the police would be back in a heartbeat. They'd tear the Chief apart, find evidence of drugs, no matter how hard we cleaned, charge him and Newf, maybe even me, and we could forget about Vancouver. We were three days from leaving. We couldn't afford to hang around Kozee Korners, waiting to be caught.

So, we made a new plan. As soon as he could pack up, Grant would pull his RV out of Kozee Korners. And he'd tell everyone there, especially Dean, that he was headed east to Montreal. Then he'd drive the Chief to Holyrood and park it behind Newf's father's barn. Newf would tell his dad Grant needed a place to keep the vehicle for a few days because he was short on money. That was step one. Step two was to move up the time we left by a day. That meant we had just two days to lay low. And he wanted to be on the road, pulling out of Holyrood, the evening of the barbecue.

As Carrie listened to Grant sweat over the possibility that the police might come back, she wondered about those coveralls we'd stolen. Shouldn't we get rid of them? Joan and Newf didn't want to. Those were our Brand-New Day Road Trip uniforms. We couldn't go cross-country without them. Grant was too paranoid to take a chance. We had to make them disappear. Question was, how? It didn't seem that difficult; ditch them in a field. Grant argued they could check for hair fibers to find out who wore them. That was the first time I wondered whether the drugs were getting to him.

In the end, Audie came up with the solution: a ceremony. On Saturday night, we were all going to catch one last sunset, then drive off to Newf's and start our caravan west. Why not stop at the gazebo and build a little bonfire of the coveralls? Make a party of it. One last blowout at the old stomping grounds. A kind of Viking funeral, burning our Brand-New Day husks before we headed off naked into the great unknown. Everyone loved the idea. There was just one question: should we invite Rob and Sharon? We'd kept the trip a secret from them for weeks. If we had a bonfire at the gazebo, burned the uniforms, then piled into two cars and took off, they'd wonder what was up.

"Let's just tell them," Audie said. "What can they do to us now?"

"Plenty," Grant complained. "Rob'll try to talk us out of it. Then the whole party will turn into an argument."

"It won't matter by then," Newf said. "They can say whatever they want. We're going. What are they going to do? Call the cops?"

Joan was with Grant. I was too. Carrie didn't care. In the end, we decided to keep it from Rob and Sharon. I wonder sometimes how different things might've been had they been there that night.

M aybe if our escape wasn't days after what I saw at the Windsor, I would've come to terms with it. But the shock of Newf's betrayal still jolted me. To see him there on the couch in Grant's RV on the last day at Kozee Korners, arm slung around Carrie's neck, I couldn't help but fume. How had Grant put it? She wasn't his? Well, the way he had her neck in the crook of his arm, it sure seemed like a show of entitlement. I got up and left.

Later that day, I came back to the Chief to pick up a map of Canada Grant bought me for the road. I walked in on Joan and Grant lying on the couch, with Carrie between them. It reeked of weed, and there was a near-empty bottle of vodka on the low table where their legs were tangled together. They were all wasted. Carrie was in the worst shape. Head rolled back on the pillows, eyes fluttering to stay open, she was in nothing but her bikini, and the top had been pushed up, so a white lobe of her left breast was exposed. Joan was beside her on that side and she had a hand on Carrie's stomach. Grant's fingers were snagged in her hair.

"Tommy!" he roared. "Let's get cozy one last time at the Korners!"

"Tommy?" Carrie slurred out in wonder. Her head wobbled up and she gave a bleary smile. "Hey! We're playin' a game You'sh'd play. You'd win."

Joan laughed, traced her finger along the top of Carrie's bikini bottom, then leveled me with a smoldering stare. "Wanna play, Tommy?"

I went over to the couch and swung Grant's legs off the table. I got a hold of Carrie's arm and pulled her off the cushion.

"You wanna dance?" She popped up faster than I expected and fell into me, arms flailing around my neck. I had to squeeze tight to keep our balance.

"Dance with her, Tommy!" Joan implored me.

"It's a slow...such a slow, slow dance," Carrie murmured dreamily. I struggled to hold her up. She had her head on my shoulder and was swaying recklessly. "I like you, Tommy. I like you so much," she whispered.

I got us out of the Chief as fast as I could. The whole way across the Kozee Korners lot, Carrie thought we were dancing. We stumbled through our graceless waltz out to the road. It wasn't until she saw the lake that Carrie tried to break free. "Let's go swimmin'!" She slipped out of my grasp and staggered into the shore road. I intercepted her before she toppled to the pavement. "Jus' run into the water," Carrie kept mumbling, as I propped her against the car to get the door open. Her bikini was still riding high, exposing the bottom white curve of her breast. I pulled the top down. She lunged to embrace me. "Let's float away, Tommy. You n' me." Then she kissed me, a hard, sloppy kiss.

I pushed her back by the shoulders and maneuvered her into the car. "Let's take a ride." She didn't fight me. I reclined her in the bucket seat, then hurried around to my side. Carrie was passed out before I even started up the Charger. Or so I thought. As I rumbled up the hill at Concession 10, she latched onto my arm and yanked it off the wheel. The car lurched right, but I managed to correct it with my free hand.

"Why didn't I hit you with that ball?" Carrie muttered. "Why didn't I get to love you?"

I shook out of her grasp. "Lie back. Get some rest."

"Aw Tommy, you're no fun. Jus' like Joan said. Jus' like she said."

I wondered then—what had Joan been saying? And what had I walked in on? Grant and Joan loosening Carrie up, wearing down her resistance, corrupting her. This wasn't some spontaneous dalliance. This was an initiation. Did Newf know? I didn't doubt it.

I couldn't take Carrie home in her condition or go to my cottage either, not with my dad bingeing. So I drove into the countryside, through Teeswater and Formosa, out to Walkerton and Hanover, then back west to Tiverton, and finally down to Kincardine. All that while, Carrie slept by my side, peaceful, guileless. I stopped at the Hi-Way Variety south of town to get her a Coke and some mints before I took her home. When I turned off the Charger, she reached for me. Her hand fell inside my thigh. I moved it away.

"What happened?"

"Do you remember being in the Chief with Joan and Grant?"

"Sort of."

"Remember me taking you out of there?"

"Did we go swimming again?"

"No." I opened the car door. "Just wait here."

I was up at the register, in line to pay, when Carrie came ambling in, barefooted, just in that bikini. She looked drowsy and tranquil, like she'd woken from a good dream. As she came to me, someone said, "You're that golfer. Carrie Sinclair." There was a hush in the store. Everyone stopped what they were doing and gaped at her. "No, I'm not," she said. "Not anymore."

I edged to the front of the line, threw a five-dollar bill on the counter, and hustled Carrie out of the store. She didn't say a word the whole ride home, just drank her Coke and gazed out the window. When I pulled into her driveaway and stopped beside the golf shelter, she said, "I wish it all never happened."

"No, you don't."

Carrie gave me a brittle smile and opened the door. Before she closed it, she leaned down and said, "You're a good friend, Tommy." Then she walked away and disappeared into her cottage.

The evening before we were set to go, when the sun was still too far off the horizon for people to watch it set, I hurried down the shore, past the 30 cottages between mine and Carrie's. I couldn't keep quiet any longer. I had to say something, take some kind of stand to change Carrie's mind. Her mother called her to the door. When she saw me, Carrie hung her head. Was she ashamed? Had she pieced together what had happened in the Chief? Even as she led me down the steps in front of her cottage, she seemed agitated. "What are you doing here?" she asked when we were out of her parent's view.

"I wanted to talk—"

"If it's about the other day…at the Chief, I don't—"

"It's not about that." Carrie let out a sigh and sat down on the bottom step of the stairs. I sat beside her. "I need to tell you something."

"You're not going, are you?"

"Maybe just to Thunder Bay."

"I didn't think you'd go all the way."

"*Why?*"

"*Everyone else is excited. They talk about it nonstop. You get quiet now. Even Newf noticed.*"

"*Newf?*"

"*No one's forcing you to go.*" Carrie put her hand on my knee. "*I just wish—*" She pulled it back.

"*What do you wish?*"

"*That night in the lake. Tommy, if I led you on...*"

Was I hearing this right? "*What? No. This isn't about you and me.*"

"*Newf sees how you look at me. After I told him, he said I needed to be more careful. With you.*"

"*You told him? About what?*"

"*The lake,*" her voice lowered.

"*You told him you* hugged *me?*" I understood now. She'd confessed to a second of contact not knowing Newf was hiding the ultimate betrayal.

"*I shouldn't have done it.*" Her voice shook. "*I was confused. I'm still... I don't know—sometimes I don't know what I feel.*"

"*Carrie. I don't think you should go.*" It came out just like that, in the heat of the moment. "*That's why I came. It has nothing to do with me.*"

"*I have to go now. We promised each other.*"

"*You can still change your mind. You're not like the rest of them. Joan and Grant, they don't have anything else but this trip. Audie's scared. And Newf...he just wants out of Holyrood—*"

"*With me,*" Carrie interrupted.

"*He'd go even if you didn't.*"

"*No he wouldn't.*"

In her narcotic haze, she'd reckoned love as capricious as an errant golf shot. "*You say you love him. Okay, but does he love you? Are you sure about that?*"

"*Yes...*"

"*Has he told you that?*" She didn't answer. "*Carrie...*" She wouldn't look at me. "*Carrie...*" I touched her shoulder. She flinched. Then she faced me. She was crying.

"*Maybe he loves you. Maybe he doesn't. I don't know. But what I do know is that you have a gift. And a chance to do something great. If you go on this trip, and it doesn't work out, how will you feel?*" She shrugged and sniffled.

"You have this moment. And it may never come again. Do you want to let it go—for a guy who can't even say he loves you?"

"Why shouldn't I give him a chance?"

This was the time to tell her about Newf and Joan. And...I couldn't do it. I couldn't break her heart. "If you're having doubts before Thunder Bay," I told her instead, "you can come back with me."

"I won't have any doubts." Carrie trembled with defiance.

I stood up and tried to think of more to say. Nothing came. She'd made up her mind. I went slowly down the dune. When I got to the shore, something struck me. I turned before I'd even formed the thought.

"What if—" I stopped. Carrie was staring at me like she'd been waiting for this moment. Maybe that's what distracted me. Maybe I had a fleeting notion to tell her about the Windsor. Maybe I simply forgot what I was going to say. Whatever the reason, what had struck me was gone.

"What?" she called out.

"Never mind." I was halfway home before I admitted to myself what I'd wanted to say: "What if I said I loved you?"

*E*very night around dinner time, instead of worrying about what to eat, my dad would pour himself a rocks glass full of Jack and ask if I wanted a drink. I always said no. When he asked me that night, I told him I'd have a little one with him. He was surprised. He'd already settled into his chair, drink in hand. He made a half-hearted gesture to pry himself out of the cushions then gave up. "Hell, can you make it?"

I went out to the kitchen and poured myself more Jack than I would've accepted from him, then snuck a big swallow before I went back out.

"I said a drink," he mocked, "not a splash." Then, realizing he'd ticked me off, he held out his glass as a peace offering. "I'm just busting your balls."

I clinked it. "Maybe I don't like my balls busted."

"Fair enough." He brought his drink to his lips and waited. Then he dropped it back down. "You're supposed to drink after you toast."

"I didn't know we toasted."

"That's what the glass touching was."

"I thought you had to say something."

"Nope." I drank. It's not like I never had Jack before, but I did give a shiver. My dad let loose a wheezy cackle. "A little too strong, eh son?"

"Sorry I don't like liquor." I held my glass out to him. *"Here. It's your thing anyway."*

"Aw shit. I'm sorry." He swung his legs off the ottoman and leaned up to pat it. *"Sit. Sit! Finish the drink. Sip it if you want."* I sat down in front of him. *"I should be happy you don't have a taste for it."*

"You should." I took a sip. We sat in silence, long enough to hear everything else around us—the squawking of distant gulls, the rhythms of the waves, the clinking of ice cubes.

"This is it?" my dad said finally. *"Your one drink with me all summer and you've got nothing to say?"*

"What do you want me to say, Dad?" These days, he interpreted everything as an indictment of him. I figured he'd welcome easy silence.

"I didn't think you'd drink with me unless something was on your mind."

"Alright. Here's something. What would you do if a friend of yours was cheating on another?"

"Another friend?"

"Yeah."

"I don't have that many friends." He laughed wistfully.

"Seriously."

He threw back a hefty swallow. *"I'd mind my own business."*

"What if you couldn't?"

"Then I'd get after the creep who was doing the cheating. Tell him to stop."

"And if he wouldn't?"

"Jesus!" My dad blew up. *"What are you asking me for? I'm not the one to be giving advice on anything."*

"I'm just wondering. What if he wouldn't stop?"

"Hell, I don't know." He deflated with a rumbling sigh. *"What do you want me to say?"*

"Would you ever tell the friend who's being cheated on?"

"That depends"

"On?"

"On whether you're ready to lose two friends." He didn't wait to explain himself. *"The cheater won't forgive you. And the cheated-on either won't believe you or will resent you for telling."*

I gazed down into my drink. Then I downed what was left and got up.

"Where are you going?"

"You haven't cared about that all summer."
"You're the one who asked me to give a shit tonight."
"Well, you can stop giving a shit now."

I woke in ghostly grey. The clock showed 5:26. I buried my head under the pillow. I needed more sleep. My jaw hurt. My ears clicked. I heard water, not rain, not a leak. Water flowing. I thought of my dream, the cottage capsized, floating out of the gully. I lurched up, planted my feet on the floor, listened. Definitely water, fast and close, lapping at the walls. I went to the front window. I couldn't see down to the deck, but when I looked beyond it, I knew something bad had happened. Something catastrophic. A channel of muddy water, a good 10 feet wide, was gushing out from under the deck, cutting deep through the sand as it flowed into the lake.

I dressed and hurried outside. I was going to go down to the beach to assess the damage, but the steps from my deck had been torn away by the force of the rogue river. I crossed the deck to the edge that ran along the gully. What I saw there devastated me. The runoff was so high it had washed away the whole bank, back to the bridge that crossed over to Bogue's. The water was running up against my foundation. Who knew if my basement was holding up? Why hadn't the downpour run out of the opening? I leaned over the rail and looked down that way. All the flotsam coming off the hill had piled up at the end of the gully. I'd need a chainsaw to clear it out. Or we would, Bogue and I. Then again, probably not. I scanned his bank. It was intact. The wall of railroad ties he built there had held. Figured. Without it, the flooding probably would've spread out more and not hit my cottage so hard.

It was too early to call and find out what Grant knew, but I wanted to see for myself what the storm had done from the top of the bluff. I put on some boots and left out the back door. On my patio, gully debris lay strewn about, and the stone slabs that marked the walkway had been pried up and pushed against the cottage. Thankfully, the water had receded, but when I walked over to the bridge, I saw that the gully was still filled to the brim, so high the bridge's middle boards sagged into the murky discharge.

I followed the creek back toward the hill, along the edge of my property. The floor of the woods was a quagmire that sucked at my boots. Before I even got to where the runoff squeezed though that old culvert, I knew something very bad was awaiting me. Water was pouring over the sloped edge of the road, carving furrows into the muddy shoulder and cascading in front of the tunnel opening. It was hard to see behind the splashing chutes that spilled off the road, but the culvert looked plugged with branches and whatever else the rain had pulled off the hill.

I had to go back toward my blocked driveway for flat footing to cross the road. I was met there by a disaster; standing water all the way down to cottage 92, and on the other side of the creek, around the bend past Bogue's driveway. I'd never seen anything like it before. The whole road, for at least two hundred yards, was underwater, not just an inch or two, I realized as I sloshed over to my Town Car, but nearly over the top of my boots. First things first: I checked for the boiler piece. It wasn't on the passenger seat. I actually said a prayer as I reached under the floormat... Thank God, it was there. Amazingly, Rob had missed it.

I locked my car and sloshed across the road. Then I plunged into the woods and forced my way through the brush to a spot on the edge of the ravine that overlooked the culvert. You couldn't see the tunnel's opening. The runoff was slamming into a huge tangle of branches and spouting into the air. Had it really rained that much overnight? I took out my phone and checked the time: 6:17. Late enough. I called Grant. It rang and rang.

I climbed the rest of the way up the bluff. The path zig-zagged away from the ravine then back to its bank. Every time I came close, I looked down over the edge. The water was just as strong the higher I got, flowing like rapids in the rockier stretches. Where was all this water coming from? The rain had stopped long ago.

When I got to the top, I was south of the ravine, beside the gazebo. Good thing. Across the gorge, a swath of water, nearly half the grassy field, was sliding toward me, converging with the swollen creek that came from Newf's land across Lake Range and tumbling over a newly collapsed stretch of the steep bank. Where I

was, at the gazebo's opening, the ground was just soggy. But after
I leaped across the creek, a safe distance from where it fell into the
ravine, the field was underwater, not deep, up to my ankles. At a
distance, you might not even know water was running through the
wild grass. Standing in the middle of it, it felt like the earth was
sliding away.

I looked north along the bluff. A hundred yards or so further,
where we laid down and watched the stars, a green wave rose out
of the field. The closer I got, the better view I had. It was the berm
of a retention pond, like Paul Ackert's. So Newf *did* have one after
all. I walked out far enough to see the breach where water spilled
over. On one side of that gap stood a pile of earth, higher than the
berm. And a backhoe was beside it. Newf's backhoe. The son of a
bitch. He'd dug a trench to drain his pond, no doubt weeks ago,
when I first noticed my gully filling up. Now, with the heavy rain,
he'd caused a disaster, jamming up the culvert, washing out the
road, possibly destroying my cottage.

I wish I'd connected on that roundhouse in the Aurora.

I went back to the ravine, sloshing through the field, following
the current. As I came close to where the spillway tumbled over
the edge, I veered toward the gazebo. Who knew how long that
ground would hold? That's when I saw the broken railing. On the
side overlooking the rubble of boulders that tumbled into the
creek, a guardrail that served as back support for one of the
benches had broken off from a post and was dangling over the
incline. Its spindly grey tines hung like fingers over the chasm.

There was a thud in my chest. The storm couldn't have done
this. I backed away from the bluff, hurried into the gazebo, and
stood in front of the bench with the broken guardrail. All I could
see beyond it was open air, then the far side of the ravine. I leaned
over. Just a couple feet from the side of the gazebo, the ground fell
away into a rocky precipice.

I tried Grant again. No answer. It was still early. No need to
worry. Not yet. This damage could've been done any time over the
last few weeks. I was standing there, pondering, when something
under the bench caught my eye. A scrap of paper. I crouched down

and picked it up. It was a round sticker, the size of a half dollar. I turned it over. On the front was a smiling cartoon ice cream cone with the words "Huron-Kinloss Ice Cream Trail" above it, and "Holyrood" below. Newf gave out these stickers at his store.

Now I *was* worried. I put the sticker in my pocket and tried to call again. Same story. Ring and ring, then nothing. Crazy notions ran through my head. Newf surprising Grant. An argument. A push. The railing giving way. The fall. Were there footprints, too? I looked around. I could see where I'd walked up to the bench and now where I was leaving, but no other prints. Should I wipe mine away? I decided against it.

I went down the hill on the opposite side of the ravine from where I came up. The path hugged the edge all the way down. It was so close to the pond's runoff, the path had a rivulet of its own snaking beside me, making the whole descent a slippery, treacherous mess. When I broke out into the open, I got my best view of how the runoff was slamming into the clogged culvert, spouting up onto the road, and flooding it out. I hadn't noticed before that the earth above the culvert had collapsed, making a giant trench across the road. You could see the ghostly top of the cement tunnel submerged under murky water that swirled around a knot of branches then dropped into the gully.

I was on the wrong side of the flood when I came out of the woods. If I kept going, I'd wind up at Bogue's cottage. I looked for a place to cross. The washed-out shoulder where I'd first seen water cascading over the culvert's opening seemed passable. I could hop over the two-foot gap between the edge where the road fell away and the top of the tunnel, slosh across the cement, then hop back onto the other bank of the caved-in road. One thing I didn't anticipate was how slick the cement would be. When I was about to take my leap onto the other side, my foot went out from under me. I fell to my knees and had to brace my hands on a nest of branches wedged beside the culvert.

It was a close one. I could've gone headfirst into that deep slot. As it turned out, I was just kneeling in a foot of water atop the culvert. I sat back on my haunches, let the water flow around me, and allowed myself a long leaking sigh. It was only after I scanned the magnitude of the flood, from where it spread, now well past Rob's run of cottages, to where it gurgled in front of me, that I saw the white limb sticking out of the nest of branches.

A crooked elbow. A twisted arm. I tugged away a branch. There, his hand. And there, his head. His face bone white, under a slithering glaze of water, even with all the cuts. Eyes closed, mouth open, hair flowing; my friend, my fearless friend, Grant.

I wasn't there when they pulled Grant out of the crevice between the culvert and the collapsed road. I was in my cottage talking to my old buddy Blair Henry and some other officer. I walked them through everything that happened from the moment I took a swing at Newf to when I saw Grant's crooked elbow in the branches. I admitted I was drunk when I entered the Aurora and angry with Bogue for his treatment of Wendy; admitted I got after Rob and Newf about their land deal on the bluff; admitted I got what I deserved.

Then I told them how I woke up later in bed with Grant looking after me; how he planned to get to the bottom of why my gully kept filling up; how I woke to the flood and decided to see for myself what was wrong. Climbing the hill. Seeing the gazebo's broken railing, swung open to the ravine. Then going down, crossing the culvert, and seeing Grant stuck in the nest of branches. I told them everything. Except two details: accusing Rob of hiding the truth about the boiler and finding that Ice Cream Trail sticker. I even volunteered to retrace my path up and down the hill with them. They declined the offer.

As they left, Blair let his partner go ahead. "You always seem to be around trouble, eh Tommy?"

"I don't need that shit today, Blair," I snapped at him. "I just lost one of my best friends."

Blair hung his head, chastened. "Sorry. You're right. My bad."

After the police left, and it was coming up on nine o'clock, when Audie said she'd call, I debated letting my phone go to voicemail. *Go ahead. Call 9-1-1.* I'd rather give the paramedics a false alarm than tell Audie what happened. I even left my phone behind in the kitchen when I opened the trap door there and ventured down into my basement to see what damage the flood had done. As if hiding away in a bunker would avoid the inevitable.

I only went down in the basement when there was a problem—the furnace went out, the water wasn't working, strange noises were coming from below. It had been a couple months. I should've gone down there when the gully started rising, but I was afraid of what I'd find. Now, I had to see. With the runoff right up against my foundation, the threat of disaster was too real. The only lighting in the basement were two bare bulbs with chains. When I pulled the first one beside the top of the steps, I was happy to discover that the concrete floor below was dry. If the worst had happened, I'd be looking down at a muddy pool.

The second bulb was in the middle of the dank space. When I pulled its chain, the news wasn't as good. All along the floor on the gully side of the cottage, big tongues of water lapped out, converging into a stream that snaked into the drain near where I stood. The wall there was cracked in more places than I remembered, and a handful of leaks were seeping out and trickling to the floor. This was the moment I'd been dreading. The crisis was here.

My phone rang above me. I was going to let it go, then changed my mind and bounded up the stairs. The phone stopped ringing before I could get to it. I called right back.

"I was just dialing 9-1-1."

"Audie—"

"I told you. Nine o'clock, and I was going to call."

"Audie."

"Did you just wake up?"

"Audie, there's been an accident."

Finally, she let me talk. And I told her. I was going to ease into it, start with why Grant went to the gazebo in the first place, explain how I came to find him. I took a deep breath—then blurted it all out. Grant was up at the gazebo, a railing broke, he fell into the ravine, and died in the flood. I was ready for the gasp. I was ready for the scream. I was ready for wailing and weeping. What I wasn't ready for was silence. I had to ask Audie if she was there. She said she was. Calmly. Then…more silence. You know how it gets with silence between two people. You start to feel like you're being waited out.

"I don't know what to do now," I found myself confessing. Then it was me weeping.

"Call Sharon. She'll know."

Sharon would know? *Sharon?* She'd know how to stop my cottage from collapsing? She'd know how to plug up a retention pond; stop her husband from building his resort? She'd know what to do with the ticket in my pocket and the metal in my Lincoln?

"Did he ever say if he wanted to be buried or cremated?" Audie went on in that calm manner. "Do you know if he had a will?"

A laugh spouted up out of me. "A will? Grant—with a will."

"If it were me. I'd get cremated. Turned right to dust. Remember that, if anyone asks."

"I'll do that."

"I'm not joking."

"I didn't think you were."

"I mean it about Sharon. Call her. She'll take care of the funeral if you ask."

Okay. Sharon *would* know that. "She'll take care of it even if I don't ask her."

Audie laughed. And just when I started to get my composure back, she burst into tears. "Oh Tommy. I'll never get to forgive him to his face. He died, and I'll always be unmerciful."

It was hard to argue with that. "Well, he *did* find a higher grace. Remember that. Maybe without you, he wouldn't have."

Audie tried a few times to gather her rattling breath. "Aren't we a pair? You, with no one to beg forgiveness. Me, with no one to forgive."

That hit me like a gut punch. "When you put it that way…"

"We could make this a lot easier. I could just forgive you. And we could be at peace."

"Just like that?"

"Just like that."

W e were right about Sharon. I didn't have to ask her to take on Grant's funeral. She came down a day after the flood and said she was already making arrangements. Grant didn't have any next of kin. He always told us that with his parents dead, the beach was his family. There didn't seem to be a will either. Sharon had checked and hadn't found a thing.

So, we made decisions over a cup of coffee—or I should say Sharon proposed decisions that had already been made, and I didn't object. He would be cremated. We would have a service in the church grove four days from then. The pastor who'd hired Grant as a youth minister would preside. After the service, we'd scatter his ashes in the lake. There would be an obituary in the *Kincardine Record*. Sharon would write it, and I'd look it over. Someone would go through Grant's belongings and decide what to do with them.

"We were thinking maybe Newf," Sharon said.

That was the only suggestion I pushed back on. "I can do it."

She took a long sip of her coffee. My cottage was still a mess from the flooding, and there were still books lined up across the floor. "You sure you're up for that?"

Of course, this had all gone through Rob. "I'm sure."

The last thing Sharon said before she walked back out to the road was, "Someone will have to talk at the funeral." Then she looked at me with raised eyebrows.

"Someone will," was as much as I committed.

I didn't bother to ask Audie if she wanted to come to the funeral. It was hard enough to get her down to my cottage, and she only ever did that in the off-season. Showing up for a big, public beach ceremony was Audie's idea of Hell—everyone surrounding her, the glances, the whispering. Never mind that it was 34 years ago. Never mind that few cottagers who saw her that fateful morning would be at the funeral, and that fewer would recognize her. There was no arguing with Audie over her fear of being a spectacle.

So, it was a surprise when, just two hours before the ceremony, Audie called and asked what time I was picking her up. Like it was a foregone conclusion that she'd go. Like we'd already talked about it. I didn't want to make a big deal out of things and scare her off. I told her I'd pick her up in an hour.

We were a half hour early to the ceremony, but Tout's Grove was already packed with cars. Rob was directing traffic, and when we came up alongside him, he told me I'd have better luck parking down by the clubhouse. He didn't notice Audie until she leaned over and said hi. I had no idea when the last time was that the two had seen each other. Judging from the stunned look on Rob's face, it must've been a while.

After we pulled away, Audie said, "That's what I'm afraid of."

By the time we parked at the clubhouse and walked back to the church grove, the service was almost ready to start. We came into the grove through a break in the hedges and found ourselves at the left side of the rows of green benches. The little outdoor church was packed. People were standing in the back and all along the opposite side of the benches where the cars were parked. I even saw two buggies out by the woods, their horses grazing. Joan waved at us from the front row on the far side. She was sitting next to Newf and Sharon. Audie was already walking toward the back of the congregation, so I followed her. We managed to wedge into the corner of the last row, back where the kids were sitting. I recognized the girl beside Audie from Grant's youth gathering. The puritanical tennis player. What was her name?

I looked for Chloe. She wasn't in our row. I scanned the heads in front of us. There she was, within arm's reach of Audie. Even in profile, I could tell she was shattered, face flushed of color, the one eye I could see red and blotchy. Chloe hung her head over clasped hands, as if in desperate prayer.

"Molly?!"

Joan's son Bruce stood beside me. He had his hands out toward Audie, presenting her as some sort of evidence.

"Hey Bruce," I greeted him.

He shuddered. "Sorry, Mr. McTavish. I didn't see you. It's just, *someone* was supposed to save my seat."

I traced the direction of his glare past Audie to the blonde-haired girl I'd met at Grant's campsite. Molly. That was her name.

"I'll stand," Audie offered.

"No. You sit. My back's bothering me anyway." I let Bruce file in beside Molly, and Audie slid down to the end of the bench. I stepped away, across the aisle, and up against the pine hedges.

"We've been friends with Grant since the age of 15," I heard Audie tell Molly. Then a moment later, loud enough for all the kids around her to hear, she said, "Imagine if one of you died in a horrible accident, and the rest of you had to live with it. It would be like that."

Whether out of politeness or genuine empathy, the kids around her—Molly, Bruce, Chloe, and others—contemplated Audie's words with far-off gazes. I was going to let it go, then she added, "Actually, two. Imagine if two of you died."

I reached over and nudged Audie's shoulder. "Enough."

She gave me this uncomprehending look. I stared her down. She dropped her head. "No, just imagine one," Audie felt compelled to amend the slip. "One of you dying is enough."

I backed up about as far away as I could get without leaving the grove altogether. That's when I saw Joan's husband Bryan edging past people standing along the far side of the benches. He was poking at his phone. Then he stopped, brought it to his ear, pulled it away, and scanned the gathering. Frowning at the outcome, he went another few rows, stopped, made a new call, and watched the crowd again. Just like in the Wondermat, he was looking for a person to match that number. He kept going. Another few rows. Another call. More watching. All the way to the back, opposite from where I was standing. He looked my way, but it wasn't me he noticed. It was his son. For some reason, that angered him. He started striding up behind Bruce. Then he finally did see me and stopped short. His face contorted. He wheeled around, marched up the middle aisle, and plopped down next to Joan.

The service began minutes later. The pastor spoke about how he came to know Grant, how skeptical he was about his idea for a youth group, how Grant's enthusiasm won him over, and how he came to appreciate his "unorthodox" methods. I was one of only a handful who laughed at that. A kid in front of Audie got up next and talked about how Grant had helped him through difficult times. Sharon's mother, of all people, spoke too. She was at least 80. I hadn't seen her in years. It was painful to watch her hobble with her walker. But she had come. She'd made the effort, and she reminded everyone what a fixture Grant had been as the delivery man for the beach. She said he was the son her deceased husband Jim never had. Then she started weeping. After trying a couple times to go on, Sharon helped her back to her seat.

The last speaker was a gaunt man from the Stony Point First Nation. That was the band of indigenous Canadians who lived on the land the government took over for an army camp from World War II until a decade or so ago. He spoke softly, almost muttering into the microphone on the stone lectern. As I strained to hear, I realized I'd met him before. Grant introduced him once when I helped drop off supplies at the camp. Cecil; that was his name. That day, he walked alongside the Chief as we puttered through camp, pointing out where we could and couldn't go on the rutted roads. He claimed there were bombs left behind by the army and buried all over the property. I didn't believe him until I read a story about it in the *Globe and Mail* a few years back. The man had aged alarmingly. His long ponytail that was once jet black, was now bone white, as was the scraggly goatee he'd grown since then.

He didn't speak for long, and I don't know how many people heard what he was saying. I had to walk up five rows to catch his words. He was talking about the Ipperwash protest in 1995, when a small band of Stony Point members occupied the army camp. The Ontario government sent in an OPP riot squad as a show of force, and when things spiraled out of control, one protester got beaten up and another was shot to death.

"Grant was there," Cecil said. "He was the only non-indigenous protester in the crowd. And I thank the Great Spirit that he came to be with us. If it weren't for Grant, I might've been beaten to death. But because he cared about his fellow man, because he hated injustice, because he was brave—and, yes, because he was white—he was able to step into that huddle of policemen, with all those clubs flying, and make them stop."

That's when I made the connection. This was the man who'd been beaten at Ipperwash, whose treatment had sparked a riot among the Stony Point protesters. And that riot had prompted the OPP to start firing, and that's why Dudley George had died. It was a stunning revelation. I never knew Grant had been with the protesters. None of the reports mentioned a white man on the scene. And to think he'd stepped into that flurry of clubs, risked his life, and ultimately saved Cecil's. Could I see Grant doing it? Yes. Could I imagine him keeping it secret? Honestly, no. Yet here stood the proof. How much did I know my friend after all?

After Cecil was done, Sharon told the congregation that if anyone wanted to say something, they'd be walking microphones down the aisles. A kid took the mic and said a lot of people his age didn't understand Grant, that he was so passionate, he weirded them out. That all his bear hugs and back slapping had become a joke to the hard cases. If they only gave him a chance, he said, they would've discovered how genuine Grant was. No one wanted to follow that. Sharon and the pastor paced the center aisle, shaking the mics as if hawking spurious elixir. I waited until Sharon's head was turned, then snuck over to get Audie and leave. Not fast enough. Sharon spotted me and glowered. Why wouldn't *she* talk? Or Rob? Or Newf? Why me? "Here's one more," she said, striding my way. There was no escape. I stepped forward and took the mic. One of us, the people who knew him best before he became who everyone thought he was, had to speak.

"Grant Rose was a pain in the ass," was the first thing out of my mouth. I didn't mean it to be funny. Anyone who really knew him knew that was true. There was a smattering of laughter, though I heard gasps too. I hung my head and pushed on. I didn't want to know how people were reacting. "I don't mean to be disrespectful. But let's call a spade a spade. That's how Grant would want it. He was highly principled, highly opinionated, and highly full of you-know-what. As caring as he was, he could drive you crazy. You wouldn't know that, though, unless he happened to catch you pulling out beach grass or drinking in the morning, or you disagreed with his views on the fallacies of love, or the spiritual value of hallucinogens, or the difference between Canadians and Americans." My mouth was suddenly dry. "That didn't come out right," I said, louder than I wanted. My voice coughed out of the speakers. "I should've thought more about what to say." I looked out at the crowd and tried to smile.

There, all the way on the other side of the benches was Wendy. Of all people. She barely knew Grant. "The truth is," I struggled on, "Grant always had my back, no matter what kind of trouble I was in—and I've been in some serious trouble. He was a good friend to me. I just wish—" I stopped. My breathing lurched. "I just wish I was a better friend to him."

I gave the mic back to Sharon. She took it with a tight-lipped frown. She was disappointed. Fair enough. Then don't force me to talk. Audie's head was bowed low, shoulders quaking. Tears. Of shame or grief, I didn't know. At least not anger. Heads turned away from me in unison, following the pastor up the aisle as he announced that the ceremony would be moving to the lake, where they'd scatter Grant's ashes. Wendy caught my eye again. She was looking straight at me. She hadn't turned away.

"Funerals aren't for the dead," Wendy told me when I said I didn't think she knew Grant that well. We were by ourselves, sitting in the grass on a dune overlooking the ash scattering. A couple hundred people had been at the grove ceremony. Only 30 or so had come to spread Grant's remains. Many were people he knew from his church work, some of the kids he taught were there, then there was Sharon and Rob, Joan, Newf, and even Audie, who had fallen in with her old friends, unassuming as ever.

"Not into the whole ash spreading thing, eh?"

"No…" Truth was, I didn't feel much like standing beside a guy who knocked me out and another who was trying to force me off my land. "If Grant knew we were using his very being to pollute the lake, he'd die all over again."

It was an excuse, but it was probably true. I turned to Wendy, expecting a laugh. Instead, she squinted into my face, then reached out and ran her fingers across my jaw. "That doesn't look good."

"It's okay. I can move it now." I waggled my jaw.

"I appreciate the chivalry, but you shouldn't have done that."

"Is Bogue going any easier on you?"

Wendy thought about it a second, gathered her breath, and said, "He keeps pushing on the tarts. Every time I see him. 'I want those tarts. We could make a mint on those tarts.' It's tiresome."

"They're your fucking tarts!"

"And it's my fucking problem. That's why I don't like to tell you things. You get…angry. And then you get hurt."

"You meant to say 'drunk,' right? I get drunk. Then I get hurt." She shrugged her admission. "I just hate feeling responsible."

"It's my fucking problem." I nudged her with my elbow. There was that laugh of hers.

The pastor called for everyone's attention. He held up Grant's urn, an old glass milk bottle, the kind Grant used to deliver, with the boxy body and the indentations for holding. He said something we couldn't hear and handed the bottle to Rob. He poured some ashes into the waves, then gave the vessel to Sharon. She followed suit, then passed it to Newf, who took his turn and gave it to Joan, before it was finally in Audie's hands. She held the bottle over her head and waded into the water, her long dress floating around her like some ghostly jellyfish. She froze for a moment, gazing into the mouth of the bottle, then sunk over her head with Grant's last ashes. She didn't just duck under either. She stayed there, long enough that Newf started in. But before he reached her, Audie broke out of the water, face aimed skyward. As she waded back to shore, she had this beautiful, beaming smile, a smile so uncharacteristic she looked like a completely different person.

Later, when we were walking up from the beach, Audie and Wendy on either side of me, I said to Audie, "*You* looked happy."

"I just let go of everything. I told myself—I told Grant—as you dissolve in the water, I'm dissolving. All my anger, all my shame, all my fear; it's floating away. And when I came out of the water, I promised him it was done. I was better."

"Well, you could definitely tell something profound had happened," Wendy jumped in.

Audie gazed down at the road and smiled, her old smile, shy and secret. Then she stopped suddenly and faced us. "Do you tell Wendy I thank her every time you bring me something she made?"

"I think so."

"Did he tell you how much I love your butter tarts?"

Wendy's smile froze, open-mouthed. "Yes. Yes, he did."

"I could eat them every day. They're just perfect. Chewy, crunchy, soft, not too sweet. Food for the soul."

Everyone's soul, apparently, but Wendy's. You could practically see hers shriveling as Audie fawned. "I wish I could make more," she said, and left it at that.

When we got back to the church grove, Wendy said she had to leave for work, and quickly departed.

"Audie, I told you about the tarts. It's a sore point for Wendy."

"I couldn't remember what you said. I just thought it would help her spirits to know how much people loved them."

"Yeah, well, that kind of love came with a lot of pressure."

She kicked at the stones as we walked along in uneasy silence. "No one else is mad at me anymore. I don't know why you are."

"I'm not mad at you."

"Maybe no one ever really *was* mad at me. Maybe I just need to get out more."

"I won't argue with that." I laughed. Audie didn't. She wasn't joking. When we got in sight of the clubhouse, she hurried ahead, before I had the chance to tell her we weren't staying long.

Twice as many people were in the clubhouse as at the ash scattering. That's what a table of food and a tub of beer will do. I was ready to grab a quick bite, find Audie, and get out of there. Grant would've despised making such a spectacle of his death.

That didn't stop Joan, though, from taking the occasion to sing a song. Before they uncovered the food, she called for everyone's attention. Seeing Joan standing there beside the closed door to the storage room where I lost my virginity to her, I didn't know how to feel. I should've felt wistful, nostalgic. There was *some* of that. But as I watched Joan try to get the mingling crowd to listen, what struck me more than anything was sadness. Regret. Loss in the truest sense, not just of my innocence, but of something more valuable. My basic goodness.

Joan told the crowd she was going to sing Grant's favorite song, and she wanted everyone to sing along. She took out her phone, put it up to the mic, and played the karaoke version of "Get Together" by the Youngbloods. He really did love that tune. Unfortunately, the internet signal was spotty. The song stuttered in and out, and Joan didn't know the words very well. She got through the first verse before the signal cut out, and she knew the chorus by heart, but she mumbled through the second verse—something about how we were a moment of sunlight in the grass. Then the chorus came again, and she implored everyone to sing along—to smile on your brother, get together, try to love one another.

It was the essence of Grant's free-love ethic. But Joan wasn't delivering it with any conviction. The instrumental clicked in and out, the crowd's uncertainty came across as muttering, and she was distracted, waving her phone to catch a signal. Sharon rushed up, took it, and carried it to the veranda where the signal was stronger. It was a good thought, but Sharon didn't realize Joan didn't know the words. She struggled through the first line—"If you hear the song I sing"—then extemporized. "I don't have the words," she joked in song, "Sharon took them all from me. Now I'm lost for sure." Everyone laughed. She tried to rally the crowd for one last crack at the chorus. But they were already flocking to the food.

I felt bad for her. Not bad enough to sing along or offer a word of encouragement. It was more empathetic than that. I felt her need to escape. Why stick around and risk getting asked about Grant? The way rumors spread, most probably knew I was the one who found the body. Some, I'm sure, knew my cottage bore the brunt of the flood. I suppose a few were even aware of the gazebo's broken railing and my ongoing feud over the gully. I could only imagine how people were connecting those dots.

When I went to get Audie, I found her talking to Rob and Sharon. Rob saw me coming. He rocked back on his heels like he was expecting me to take a swing.

I tapped Audie's shoulder. "Ready to go?"

Audie screwed up her face. "Now?"

"Yeah."

"Sorry I put you on the spot," Sharon broke in. "With the speaking. I thought you agreed to do it."

"I said *one* of us ought to. I didn't say me."

"It was fine." Rob surprised me by weighing in. "Hell, it was honest. Grant *was* a pain in the ass."

"That's not all I said."

"It was perfect," Sharon said, giving Rob a quick scowl.

"I said it was fine. What do you want?" Rob stalked off.

"I want to stay longer," Audie declared, ignoring the squabble.

"Well, I want to go." I was done arguing. Audie, of all people, should've understood how uncomfortable being there was for me.

"I can take her home," Sharon suggested.

Audie was as stunned as I was. "You don't have to do that."

Yes. She *did.* I had no intention of sticking around and left right away. The front of the clubhouse was jammed with people. I didn't want to wade through that. I slipped around back, into the thicket of poplars that offered cover to the road. I had just stepped under the trees, when I heard arguing deeper within.

"What does it matter anymore?" Joan's voice was a whispering snarl. "It's over."

"Not for me."

"I can't deal with it anymore. I can't. You, waving your phone around, making your show of tormenting me. Just stop it. Stop!"

"So, you're the victim now."

There was rustling behind me. I turned. It was Bruce.

"Hey, Mr. McTavish. Have you seen my parents?"

His voice was louder than what I'd overheard in the thicket. I shook my head, hurried out to the road, and headed for my car.

"What time should I come over tomorrow?" He followed me out to the road.

I waved him off. "There's nothing to do." Behind Bruce, within earshot, Bryan stepped out of the poplars. "There's your dad." I pointed, then rushed to my car.

I backed out the Lincoln and swung it around to escape up McCosh Hill. Newf stepped in my way. I didn't want to have it out with him there, a stone's throw from a crowd. As he came around to the driver's side, I had a fleeting urge to race off and leave him in a cloud of dirt. I rolled my window down instead.

"We never got a chance to talk." Newf bent down to eye level.

"No."

He pointed at my face. "It doesn't look too bad."

"It doesn't feel too good."

"Well, sorry for that."

"That's it?"

Newf was confused. "That's all I wanted to say, yeah."

"No apology for flooding out my cottage?"

"Look. I didn't have anything to do with that."

"Newf, I saw the retention pond. I saw the trench and your digger. I saw the water flowing out."

Newf straightened up, looked over his shoulder, then leaned back in, closer to my face this time. "Let's not talk about that here."

"You know who else saw it? Grant. The night he died."

Newf's eyes narrowed. I could hear him breathing. "I don't know what you're trying to suggest. The police ruled what happened to Grant an accident."

"I know," I said, digging for my wallet. I pulled out the Ice Cream Trail sticker. "But I wonder what they'd think of this."

Newf glanced at the sticker, then glared back at me. "So?"

"So, on the morning they pulled Grant's body out of the culvert, I found this under the broken railing in the gazebo."

"So?" he challenged me again.

"So, I guess I'll give it to Blair Henry if it's no big deal to you."

"Why didn't you?"

"Maybe I'm trying to help you out."

"Maybe you want something."

"Okay. Maybe I want something."

"Like?"

"Maybe I want to know what the hell's going on."

Newf rubbed his neck. "I have no idea how that sticker got where it was. It could've been there for months. Grant could've come out for ice cream. Lots of things could've happened."

"I'm not talking about the sticker."

"I didn't kill Grant," Newf blurted out.

"That's not what I mean. Will you listen for a second?" Newf's eyes darted around. His breathing was ragged. "I want to know why you're trying to flood me out. Is Rob putting you up to this?"

Newf glanced behind him again. "I *can't* talk about that here."

"Don't make me threaten, Newf."

He pointed at my hand. "So, that's what the sticker's for, eh?" I waited him out. "How do I know you even found it at the gazebo? Didn't Chloe hand you one that day you came in?"

"I wouldn't do that to you."

"You already are." He had a point, but I wasn't about to give in. Not now. I stared him down. He stared back. "Come out to Holyrood," he finally said, looking away, like he was talking to someone else. "Wednesday afternoon."

"Holyrood," I agreed. Then I sped off, up McCosh Hill and away from everyone clustered behind my veil of dust.

I tried every contractor in town. The only one willing to come assess my cottage's damage was Paul Magnuson. He didn't have the best reputation on the beach. Word was, he did an okay job, but was always late. Beggars can't be choosers.

Magnuson put the cost for fixing the foundation at 10 to 20 thousand dollars but couldn't guarantee repairs would last. Worst case: I'd have to pour a new foundation—for 75 grand. The prognosis on the gully wasn't much better. Magnuson estimated I'd need 70 cubic tons of rip rap, basically a 150-foot wall of wire-wrapped, football-sized stones, to shore up my bank. The cost: 40 to 50 thousand. All told, I was looking at 50 to 125 grand to solve my problems. Where was I going to get that kind of money?

I was taking in all this bad news as we came back up from my basement and out behind my cottage. I didn't see Rob and Bogue, but Paul did. He called over to them. They were on the other side of the gully, standing in the water, inspecting the bridge abutment. Paul asked what they were doing. Bogue said what did it look like? Then Rob asked Magnuson what he was doing. I said none of your business. After that, I hustled Magnuson out to his truck.

When I got back to my cottage, Rob was on my side of the gully, looking over the end of the girder that rested on the abutment. "We're going to have to fix the footings for this," he said, without looking up. "Looks like that flood did a number here."

"You mean the flood that came from your new land?"

"Fuck right off, eh?" Bogue barked from his side of the bridge.

"Shut up, Bo." Rob stood from his crouch and took a few ambling steps toward me. "You're not seriously thinking about having Paul Magnuson fix your cottage, are you?"

"I am."

"I like Paul," Rob said, stopping in front of me, "but I wouldn't trust him with anything more enterprising than a deck."

"I was going to do that myself."

Rob kicked at the dirt. He had a lump of chew under his lower lip, like he used to when we worked together in '84. Damned if it didn't feel like then too, standing there, thinking through a project. "Well…Paul doesn't know the first thing about foundations."

"I don't have a lot of choice."

Rob put up his hands like a crossing guard; here it came. "If you ask me—and I'm being completely straight here—you got two choices." I knew what one of them was going to be. "Pay a hundred grand to pour a new foundation. Or—and I know how you feel about this—sell the place for upwards of a million dollars." There it was. I didn't even bother to voice an answer. "You're going to go bankrupt fixing this place, you'll still have a broken-down cottage, and you'll be surrounded by a resort, having to put up with the sort of high-brow people you detest. Why punish yourself like that?"

"It's *my* cottage." I sounded like a pouting toddler.

"Okay. But I'm doing what I have to do. Nothing personal."

I just pointed to the ruined bank of the gully. "This might not be personal for you, Rob, but it's very personal to me."

He didn't have a reply, just a tight mouth and empty upraised hands. "The least you could've done was warn me Newf was draining his pond."

Rob gave that some thought. "What would you have done?"

"About that, I don't know. But I could do other things."

"Like?"

"Like maybe people should know their cherished boiler didn't come from a shipwreck."

Rob gave me a sideways squint. "Go ahead. Tell them. It's not going to change what I do. You'll just have a lot of people pissed off to learn that they live on Tractor Beach."

Was he bluffing? "I'm sure there's a story there."

"I'm sure there is," he agreed, poker-faced.

I laughed. "So…we both do what we have to do, eh?"

"Guess so. I just hope you don't wait too long. There'll come a point where you can't give this place away." It sounded like a threat, but you wouldn't know it by Rob's defeated look.

Right then, Bruce came around the corner of my cottage, a shovel slung on his shoulder. He didn't even wait for me to object. "My mom said I *had* to come."

"You're making a kid dig in the gully?" Rob grumbled.

"I'm not making him do anything. Joan is. It's a long story. This is her son, Bruce."

"I know who he is."

"Hi, Mr. Garton," Bruce muttered, head down.

"You shouldn't be going down in that gully," Rob browbeat the poor kid.

"I'm not sending him into the gully."

Rob folded his arms and spit. Then he walked away. But as I mulled over what to do with Bruce, I caught him glancing back from the bridge. Did he think I was lying to him?

"I've got an idea what you can do." I motioned Bruce into the cottage. He followed with the shovel. "You can leave that."

I got a push broom, mop, and bucket, and took him down into my basement. I hadn't done a thing about the leaks since I discovered them. The puddles hadn't gotten worse, but all along the gully side, the water went over the sole of my boot. I offered Bruce two ways to handle the problem: shove the water halfway across the room to the drain or sop it up with a mop and squeeze it out in the bucket. He gazed at the floor like it was a life-or-death choice.

"Am I just doing this today?"

I could understand where he was coming from. It was sunny finally, and here I'd confined the poor kid to the dungeon of my basement. "I can find something outside."

"Can't I just stay inside?"

That was a surprise. "Look, you don't have to be here at all."

"I *have* to be here," he stressed again. "It's just, I'd rather not go outside. Mr. Garton's always yelling at me."

"Rob?" I could understand Bogue. But Rob?

"He doesn't like me."

Rob could be a jerk, no doubt. But I'd never known him to yell at kids. "Just steer clear of him. He's got a burr up his ass about something. I'm sure it doesn't have anything to do with you."

Bruce snickered but quickly lapsed into brooding. Poor kid. Every time I saw him, he seemed more unhappy. I was going to talk to him about it, but the phone started ringing upstairs. I hurried away. And all the while up the stairs and over to my landline, I kicked myself for leaving. So, maybe it was fate, karma, or some such cosmic comeuppance that the person on the other end of the line was Cam, the kid whose problems I'd also never had time for.

"Cam!" I sounded like I'd been waiting by the phone all day.

"You busy?"

"No. Well...there's a lot going on."

"I heard about Mr. Rose."

"That. And the flood. If you wait too long, you may not have a cottage to come to anymore."

Cam took it the wrong way. "You know I can't get across the border right now."

"I know." The DUI situation again. The restrictions. The endless legal loops.

"But I've been thinking about what you said. About getting together. Maybe we *should* do that. Talk things through."

"Yeah. Absolutely." Where was this coming from? What had changed since we last spoke, when he was going to block my number, never mind getting together? "Changed your mind, eh?"

"The Bible tells us to forgive men their trespasses."

I couldn't help myself. "Did you just get to that chapter?" Nothing on the other end. "I'm kidding, Cam. I don't care why you changed your mind. I'm just happy you did."

"Actually, it was Chloe. She told me about you and her dad."

"Oh?" That could've meant so many things.

"Chloe said you weren't looking so hot at Mr. Rose's funeral."

Ah. The punch. That made sense. Chloe wouldn't know any of the other problems between Newf and me. "I'm better. To tell the truth, I wasn't entirely the victim there. I had a little relapse and went looking for trouble."

"Well," Cam let it hang. "Chloe was worried you didn't have anyone looking out for you."

"That's nice of her."

"She's coming down for a concert this Friday. I was going to have a friend pick her up and bring her across the border, but she said, 'Why not ask your dad? Have lunch. Give him a chance.' "

He rushed the words out like they were rehearsed. Maybe they were. Maybe he was worried I'd say no. I could've given him a harder time, but why risk putting him off? "Well, I'm glad she did."

"Great. I'll figure out a nice place to meet in Port Huron and get back to you. Friday noon sound good?"

"Sure. I can come all the way to Ann Arbor if you want."

"No!" he cried out. "The concert's...um...it's up closer to Port Huron."

Something wasn't right. Cam probably didn't want to risk my seeing the dump he was living in with Kemp and Riley, his slacker buddies from high school. "Whatever you want, Cam. Who are you seeing?"

"What?"

"The concert. Who's playing?"

"Oh," Cam took a long pause. "You wouldn't know them."

"Probably not. Is Chloe going to need a ride home, too?"

"No. My friend can take her back."

"Alright. Well...thanks for doing this."

"Alice Cooper," Cam blurted. "We're seeing Alice Cooper at Pine Knob."

I laughed. "You thought I wouldn't know who Alice Cooper was? That's my generation."

"How would I know that? I didn't even know it was a guy."

"Why did you decide to go then?"

Cam jumped down my throat. "What does it matter? I'm trying to do a good thing here, and you're busting my balls. We're going because Chloe wants to go, okay?"

"Sorry. It's just—Alice Cooper? 'School's Out.' 'I'm Eighteen.' You really don't know who he is?"

"No, I really don't."

"Take earplugs."

TRY TOM'S MADWOMEN! Hell, why not? You want them crazy? Angry? Fanatical, wild, impassioned? I can scare them up. After being gone so long, you'd think I'd be anxious to fix my sign. Who knows how long I'd been hawking crazy women? But I got out of my car, looked at the sign, and thought, *screw it*. I change it back and it's just going to be something else. Mad women didn't seem so bad.

The place was a mess. Trash cans were overflowing. Someone had sprinkled detergent on the floor and torn up lint sheets. A piece of paper was taped on a dryer with the message, "Fix this!!!" scrawled on it. And the washer that was running when I came in thumped like it was full of shoes. "You got shoes in there?" I asked the guy sitting beside the rattling machine. He shook his head., didn't even bother to pull his nose out of his newspaper.

"Something's not right." I rocked the washer to test its wobble and got down on my knees. One of the back legs had broken off. It had happened before, but not this badly. Usually, wedging a paperback there would do the trick for an hour or so. But the book would inevitably slide out of place. What could I jam in there that was more permanent?

When the idea came to me, I laughed and went straight out to my car. I made no effort to conceal the boiler plate on the way inside. There was just that one guy in the Wondermat. For all he knew, I had a pile of scrap metal for just such occasions. I couldn't reach back to the broken leg. The wedge between washers was too narrow. I'd have to wait for the guy's load to finish. Would I have to move the one beside it too? Lying there on the floor, eyeballing the dark gap between the two machines, it was hard to tell.

"Mad woman reporting for duty." Wendy stood over me.

"That sign might be a keeper."

She helped pull me to my feet. "You *do* seem to attract women on the madder side."

"That's me, Tommy McTavish, dealer of deranged dames."

"It has a ring." She laughed, then pointed to the metal hunk. "Remind me not to ask you to fix anything."

"You'd be surprised what sort of problems this solves."

"Well, I'm not here to question your choice of tools. I just want to give you this." Wendy thrust a green piece of paper at me.

I took it. *Wendy O'Shea's says goodbye.* It was an invitation to a farewell party. On Friday, July 6. Just over a week away. I tried to show Wendy a smile.

"It's a celebration." She was trying to be happy too.

"Damn straight it is."

"Just for regulars. And it's all free. I've already closed, so technically I can't reopen the business. But I have all that spare booze."

"Free alcohol for a bunch of people who don't particularly like each other. What could go wrong?" I was joking. Wendy, more than anyone, knew her regulars and how they could get on each other's nerves. Still, she seemed bothered that I pointed it out. "Don't worry. We'll be on our best behavior."

Wendy let out a wistful sigh. She said she had a few more invites to hand out before her shift. But she didn't make a move for the door. "I could use a walk." I took the hint.

"I'm going down to the harbor."

I suggested again that I'd join her, to make sure I wasn't misreading signs. This time, she agreed, and we started for the door.

But the washer stopped right then, and I still had that metal plate in my hand. "I should fix this before I go."

After the guy fished his clothes out of the washer, I got him and Wendy to pull out the machine and tilt it while I placed the slab so it was out of sight and the washer was stable.

"I didn't know you were going to put me to work," Wendy said as we walked across my lot toward the harbor.

I pointed to the sign. "My madwomen have to earn their keep."

We crossed Huron Terrace and walked along the dirt road on the edge of the marina toward the harbormaster's hut below the bridge. "I'm at the point where I'd take a job as a madwoman," Wendy said. "I'm getting great experience."

"I take it things aren't going well."

She stopped in the middle of that dirt road that dead-ended at the channel. "I don't know if I can handle this for nine months. Whenever I do something Bo doesn't like, he reminds me how much I owe him. Guess who has me reporting to? Jay. My dirtbag ex. Like he didn't know what torture that would be."

All of it was so predictable, except how much it hurt Wendy. "Like you said, you didn't have much choice. Just remember: your money problems are going away. By next spring, you'll be free. How did your dad put it? Small steps."

Wendy threw her head back and gazed at the masts rocking over the harbor. Then she slumped down on a nearby bench. "Wanna know the latest crap Bo's pulling? He's buying these shitty factory-made tarts and telling customers I made them."

"No…"

"Hoping I'll be humiliated enough to give him the real thing."

I sat down beside Wendy. "Want me to go get my ass kicked again? I'll put my jaw in the way of his fist for you any time."

Wendy leaned her head onto my shoulder and laughed. At some point, though, it turned into crying. "Oh Tommy. Why did we waste all these years?"

What did she mean? Sure, I wasted the last decade, more than that. But her? Chasing her dream, making it real, becoming some-one. "You didn't waste any years. You had a great run. You'll be back. You'll leave Point Clark, like you've always wanted to, and do something great somewhere else."

I could feel the tension draining out of Wendy. She lifted her head and stared at me with bewilderment. What did I say? She blinked, looked away for a moment, then gave me a soft, resigned smile. "You're a good friend, Tommy," she said quietly. With that, she got up and went into the harbormaster's hut. I didn't know whether she wanted me to wait for her or leave. Even after she came back out, I couldn't tell.

"I'm out of time," Wendy said. She headed toward the harbor's channel, striding like there was no other recourse but to dive off the ledge there into those murky waters. I hurried after her. I'd forgotten there was a staircase under the bridge that went up to the high road. She took it two steps at a time. They were steep and metal grated. I got winded trying to keep up. I had to stop. My heart was pounding. Was I this out of shape? I didn't bother to call for Wendy to wait up. She was anxious to get where she was going—or leave where she'd been.

"You okay?" I was surprised to hear her ask above me. She had come back down and was standing one flight away.

"I'm fine. Just got a little dizzy. Go on. I know you're late."

"I'm not late. I'm just worn down. You know how it is when nothing's right, and you don't how it's going to get better."

She wasn't asking if I knew. She assumed I did. She wasn't wrong. I'd known that feeling for 34 years. I climbed the flight and leaned beside her. The whole harbor was below us, the lighthouse loomed to our side, and the channel to Lake Huron was calm and wide. If only I owned a boat. If only we didn't have these worries. Funny how long a minute is when you're so close to someone and neither of you talk. We were just looking over the swaying masts to the vast shimmering emptiness of Lake Huron. If only…

"What should I do?" The words came out of me like they were someone else's. "Should I sell my cottage? If I walk away with a million dollars, I'll never have to worry about money. And all this conflict goes away. But I'll never have a piece of Boiler Beach again." Wendy went on looking at the lake like she didn't hear me.

"I always thought I'd give the cottage to Cam, like my dad did to me. Where else will I find a place like this?"

"Well, you know what I'd do." Wendy waited for me to look at her. "Give yourself a chance to be free. A chance to hope."

"What if you don't know how anymore?" I asked, looking away. I didn't want to see how she'd react. It was wrong of me to inflict my despair on her like that.

"It doesn't take anything to hope, Tommy."

"You're right," I said to be done talking.

After Wendy walked up Harbour Street and disappeared into the Aurora, I looked back to where the road ended beside Audie's apartment complex. Should I go see her? Usually I had a reason—groceries to bring, something to fix. There was nothing at the moment. Worse, I had this unsettling sense that I'd disappointed Audie at the funeral, or, more to the point, that she'd figured out how little she really *did* need me. I should've been happy about that, her out among people, unashamed, unafraid. So why wasn't I? I didn't deserve Audie's company, not in this frame of mind. Yet I headed down for her place anyway. Maybe for once, instead of acting like I was comforting her, I should admit I was going so she could help me. Another madwoman to try.

I knocked on the door three times, and Audie still didn't come. I knew she was inside. I could hear her banging things around. When it got quiet, I thumped again. Finally she opened the door—threw it open, really—and stood before me, wild-eyed, panting.

"What are *you* doing here? I didn't ask for anything."

"I was just—I was walking into town, and I thought of you."

"I'm fine." Audie was never anything but desperately welcoming. Now, here she was, arm stretched across the doorway, barring my way. Behind her, there was upheaval, cardboard boxes on counters, rearranged furniture, stripped walls. "I can't invite you in right now." Audie closed the door to squeeze my view. "I'm busy. With something important. Very, very important."

"It looks like you could use a hand."

Audie looked back, assessing the disorder. Then she scowled at me, like I was to blame for it. "I don't want any judgment.

You've been very judgmental lately." With that, she lowered her arm and swung open the door.

I didn't know if I wanted to go in now. "I've been judgmental?"

"It's the way you look at me. I can tell."

I took a second to mull that one over, putting on as stony a poker face as I could. *Don't look at Audie. Don't look at Audie.*

"Do you want to help me or not?"

I hung my head and walked inside. The place was in even worse disarray than my glimpse from the door suggested. All the drawers and cabinets in the kitchen were open, and stacks of dishes, glasses, bowls, and pans cluttered the counters. The books had been pulled off their shelves and dumped into one big pile in the middle of the living room. And there wasn't a single picture still hanging. Every piece of Audie's artwork had been shunted to the corner, the framed pictures leaning against each other in a long row, the others rolled up, rubber-banded, and standing in a big huddle of tubes.

"Wow."

"See? There!" Audie jumped at my reaction. "That's what I mean. Judgment."

"I'm not judging you, Audie. It's just—" *Careful, McTavish...* "There's a lot of work going on around here."

She grinned and fixed her fists to her hips: "Yes, there is. Yes—there—is."

"What's it all for?"

"For my move."

"You're moving? When?"

"I don't know. Some time. Any time, really. I have to be ready."

Audie: thinking about moving, leaving this self-imposed prison of—how long had it been?—nine years. I never thought I'd see the day. "That makes sense," I replied matter-of-factly. I didn't want to spook her with my amazement.

"But there's just so much junk!" she marveled.

"What can I do?"

Audie pointed to the pile of books. "You can help with those. And those pictures." She waved a dismissive hand at her artwork. "Take them to the dumpster."

"The dumpster?"

"I don't need them anymore. They're just ghosts."

"You can't throw them out," I argued—gently. "They could be worth something."

"I have nowhere to show them. Take them if you want."

We agreed that I'd swing by after work, load the books and pictures into my car, and she'd never have to see them again. Then I spent the next hour helping Audie. The way she went about things, it's a wonder she'd made any progress. While I filled boxes with books, she fluttered around the apartment, picking up random items—a vase here, a basket there, a bagpiper figurine—putting them in boxes with no rhyme or reason, moving them to new locations, setting them right back down where they'd been.

"What got you started on this?"

"Wondering how Grant would want me to live," she answered without hesitation.

"You don't think he'd want you living here?"

"I think if I forgave him, he'd expect me to change."

Grant always *had* wanted Audie to break out of her shell. "You're probably right."

"That's how I'm going to live now. I'm going to act like we had our meeting, he apologized, and I forgave him."

"Good for you," I said, but I didn't mean it. Pretending. If it was that easy, why not pretend none of it ever happened? As long as we were engaging in fantasy, why bother going through the motions of apology and forgiveness?

"You should try it," Audie suggested.

I retreated to the corner, where the artwork was, at the far end of the window overlooking the harbor. "You think Grant would want you to give up on your art?"

"I'm not giving up on my art," Audie said, coming my way. "I'm just getting rid of the old art, so I can start over. That's what Grant would've wanted. It's time to get back out there." She was standing beside me, pointing down the coast, where the telescope beside her was aimed. "Out in nature, in the sand, with the wind and waves, the clouds and birds. It's time...for reverence."

"Sounds like you want to get back on the beach."

"I'd love that."

"Got a million dollars?"

Audie took me seriously. "It wouldn't cost that much."

"That's what I'd get if I sold out to Rob."

"You're not thinking of doing that, are you?"

I let out a long sigh. "I guess I am."

Audie grabbed my arm. "You can't."

"Why not?" I pulled my arm away. "What's wrong with taking Rob's money and being done with all these headaches? You said so yourself: it's time to let old things go."

"But that's not moving forward. That's surrendering."

"Who's being judgmental now?" The nerve. She was allowed to change, but I wasn't?

"You're right. Forget what I said." Audie thrust a rubber-banded packet of photographs at me. "Here. I divided up all the old photos I have of everyone. These are yours." On top of the inch-high stack was one of me sitting beside Carrie at the gazebo. I'd never seen it before, couldn't even remember the moment it was taken. She was laughing, and I was smiling at her. We could've been a couple. "Whenever I have to decide something now, I just ask myself, what would *Grant* want?" Audie retreated to the kitchen. She left it at that. But I knew what she was leaving unsaid.

"So you don't think Carrie would want me to sell. Is that it?"

"I never said that."

"You didn't have to." I stomped off for the door. Screw this.

Audie stepped in my way, hands up in surrender. "Wait, Tommy. Stop! I'm sorry. I just hate the thought of you letting your cottage go. And I hate that Rob's doing it to you."

Sure. But that didn't stop Audie from clinging to Rob and Sharon at Grant's memorial. Old habits die hard. He was always more a guardian than a boyfriend to her back then. Why wouldn't they fall back into familiar roles? Never mind that I'd been looking after her for years. And what did I get for all that caregiving? The first chance Audie got, she scurried under Rob's wing.

I edged past Audie. "I'll come in an hour and get the pictures."

"Don't leave mad," she begged me.

"I'm not mad."

"If you have to sell the cottage, you have to sell the cottage," she kept trying. "I shouldn't have said anything."

"Okay," I replied. Then I left. Mad.

On the drive back to the cottage, I got a phone call. The instant I saw the number, I knew who it was.

"Barb! I've been meaning to get back to you." It was Barb Bowen. I hadn't given a second's thought to her teaching offer.

"I don't mean to press," she said, "but if you're not interested, I have to move on."

It had been—what?—maybe a week since Barb floated the teaching opportunity. I found it hard to believe a go-getter like her was waiting for an answer from a disgraced pseudo-academic like me. "Nobody else raised their hand?"

"I wouldn't put it that way."

How would she put it? Any self-respecting professor would turn down a 32-thousand-dollar job at a second-tier college on the spot. "I think I'll have to have to pass. I've got a lot going on here."

"I get it," she said. "Sometimes, I wish I could go on permanent vacation."

I don't know if she meant it as a dig, or I was still seething from my encounter with Audie, but the comment rubbed me the wrong way. "You think that's what this is?" I snapped. "You have no idea what's happening here; no idea what I've had to deal with."

"I'm sorry," Barb backed down. "I remember you saying—"

"I've got to go," I cut her off, stabbing the phone dead.

"A man needs a maid." That's what jolted me as I was bringing the first armload of artwork into the cottage.

"Jesus!" the rubber-banded scrolls spilled out of my hands. Joan was lounging back in my favorite chair up by the picture window, obscured in early-evening shadows. "Please, Joan. Make yourself at home."

"I figured since Bruce was working here."

"He's been gone for hours." I crouched to gather the artwork.

"How am I supposed to know that?" As if being his mother conferred no advantage. She leaned forward in my chair, straddling the footstool. She was dressed like always, in a bright see-through cover-up and a bikini that any other woman her age wouldn't have dared attempt. But this was Joan, and she could still pull it off. I didn't realize she'd been working on a joint until she took a quick hit and held it out to me.

"No, thanks."

"It's shitty weed, Tommy. Come on. Take the edge off."

"Look where that got me last time." I stood up with the armload of Audie's scrolls and hurried to the back bedroom. I didn't want her seeing what I had. I dumped them on the bed, turned, and there she was, blocking the doorway, back arching against one side, bare legs angled out, feet propped on the other side.

"Nobody told me you weren't drinking."

"*I* told you."

"I didn't think you were serious." Joan held the joint out to me again. "One lousy hit."

I took it—the price for getting freed from my own bedroom. Joan straightened and let me pass. I sat in the small chair that bookended my front window and left the lounger for Joan.

"Why don't you want Bruce working here?"

"There's nothing to do. I've got big issues, not little chores."

"I told you he could sit and do nothing if you wanted."

Joan was right. The weed was shitty. I reached out for the joint. "The whole thing's B.S. anyway. Bruce didn't steal anything. He's just protecting his friends."

Joan wasn't surprised. "He lied," she said without hesitation.

"So, he lied. It's not like he was trying to get out of trouble. Hell, he put himself in deeper shit. Knowingly."

Joan sucked the joint down and squashed it on the table between us. As she exhaled, her head dropped back on the cushion, and her eyes fixed on the ceiling. "I don't really care what he did or why. Truth is, I need a reason to get him away from Bryan."

"So, you need a favor. You could've just asked me."

"It's not the sort of thing you come right out and say. 'Hey Tommy. My marriage is in shambles. My husband's dangerous. I'm scared. Can you take my kid?' "

"That bad, eh?"

"He thinks I've been fucking around up here."

I laughed. Then I made myself stop. Then I laughed harder. "How far back's he going?"

Joan didn't see the humor. "I'm talking about recently. He got a hold of my phone and found a few 519 numbers. Then he started combing through our records. One number kept coming up over the years, so he's convinced something's going on."

Now it all made sense—Bryan grilling me at the bookstore, walking the aisles at Grant's funeral, hoping to get someone to answer his call. "Whose number was it?"

"I don't know. I've called Sharon over the years, Grant, Newf, Rob. Lots of people. He's just a jealous sort."

"He sure didn't pick the right gal to marry, did he?"

I thought Joan would think that was funny. I don't know why. "He knew exactly who he was marrying," she snapped. "He knows I messed around before we met. Back home, up here."

"Up here? You told him about up here?"

"I told him we had our fun." She started picking at her pink toenail polish. "Then he wanted names...so I told him about you."

"Me?!"

"I had to give him someone."

"Not Newf? Not Grant? None of the other handful of strangers up and down the beach you must've—"

"Watch it."

"Only me," I fumed. "For that one time."

She patted my knee. "I knew he wouldn't see you as a threat."

"So. Coming to my store, grilling me—that was just amiable fraternizing, eh? What a relief. I'd hate to be threatened."

"Trust me. You would."

I looked out to the lake. A young couple was walking the shoreline, each holding the hand of a child between them. They'd swing him up in the air, settle him safely to his feet, then do it again. "So, your bright idea was to hide your son away with the guy his father thinks might be having an affair with you. Good plan."

"He doesn't think we're having an affair. Not anymore. Not after he met you."

I laughed in spite of myself—actually, *at* myself. It was just dawning on me. "So, in addition to being harmless, another big point in favor of naming me was my unattractiveness."

"Come on, Tommy."

"I get it. Why not tell your husband you messed around with the one guy you'd never dream of having an affair with now?"

"Want to have an affair, Tommy?" Joan bristled. "Shall we just fuck right now so you can feel more dangerous and desirable?"

"Sure, Joan. Let's do it."

Joan glared at me like she was trying to decide if I was serious. Then, apparently having made up her mind, she dismissed me with a bitter laugh. "You *are* a piece of work."

"*I'm* a piece work?" The way she said it…I couldn't let it go. "So…who *are* you having the affair with?"

Joan's eyes burned into me. "You know I haven't been up here for a summer in ages. But try explaining that to Bryan. He doesn't deal in the realm of logic."

Joan had a point. She really *hadn't* been up for the last 30 summers or so. I knew that. I was just giving her a hard time, like she'd given me. Now, we were both silent, licking our wounds.

"Where's more weed when you need it?" Joan finally said. "We could deal with a little mellow right about now."

"That we could." I looked at Joan squarely then. "I'm sorry you're going through all this. If you need somewhere for Bruce to be, he can hang out here."

Joan pulled herself up from the lounger and came toward me. "If you can't figure out things for him to do," she said, motioning toward the mess at our feet, "I'll write you a list."

After she left, I brought in the rest of Audie's artwork. I put it all in the back bedroom, leaning the framed pieces against the wall and setting the rolled-up drawings on the bed. A rubber band on one scroll snapped, and it uncurled enough for me to see what it was—the Sorry pieces congregating around the boiler. Veronica, Archie, and Betty. I rolled it out and took in the full picture. Why would Audie get rid of these? With the right exposure, in some big gallery, they could've made her famous. When I let go of the edges, the paper sprung back into a wide circle. Was it really a good idea to store these rolled up? I started freeing them from their rubber-banded shackles, flattening them on the bed with the help of two pillows. There was the Candyland gingerbread boy straddling the harbor channel; there, the Stratego bomb on the pitching mound; and now the one where the Sorry pieces waded toward the Point Clark lighthouse. I had almost all of them flattened when I unrolled the drawing of the gigantic purple Life car with its six treetop-dwarfing pegs about to roar down the hill into the path of that frozen girl, standing with her shoulders thrown back. Like Carrie…

I rushed to the fireplace with the drawing half-curled in my hand. The wooden matches were by the log bin. Audie said she didn't care what I did with these. I lit the lower right corner of the canvas, where the road dropped below the girl's feet. It took a while for the fire to spread. Eventually, though, the flame grew. It started licking at the feet of the girl. So close…

I slapped the fire dead. Then I scraped the black off the burnt corner, carried the picture back into the bedroom, and buried it on the bottom of Audie's stack of art. I left the room and closed the door. It was dinner time, but I'd lost my appetite. Thank God, I thought, that there's nothing here to drink. Then I wondered: *was there?* And I went looking for that missing blue Skyy bottle. Again.

By the time I packed what I was going to take for our road trip, drove up the hill, and followed the ruts through Newf's family cornfield to the gazebo, it was nearly dark. I was late. We were supposed to be there for the sunset. Still, there was a faint glow over the trees and, oddly, in the low branches too. When I came to the end of the gauntlet of cornstalks, I saw what had made that eerie glow. They had started the fire without me. It was flickering just outside the entry to the gazebo. We'd never had a bonfire so close. I wondered how wise it was. The structure's domed innards were pulsing with a dim orange light that carved at the shadows of my friends' faces.

As I walked toward them, Newf's face fell and went dark. Carrie was beside him. She looked away too, but kept glancing up, her face flashing in and out of shadow. Joan glared at me through the glow, eyes burning hard. I didn't see Grant until he leaped off one of the benches and blocked the opening, arms upraised. It was obvious: I'd caught them talking about me.

"There he is!" Grant bellowed. "We were starting to worry. Did you bring your uniform?" He pointed to a pile of coveralls by the fire.

"Shit. I forgot."

"Then go get it," Newf said behind Grant.

"Nobody's going to find it," I said. "It's hidden away."

Joan huffed. "The whole point of this is to burn the suits."

"Hey-hey-hey! Come on," Grant tried to calm everyone. "We're all cool."

Screw it, I thought. Why even go now? No one wanted me along. I should just go home. Put everything behind me. Clean myself up. I was that close to leaving. Then Audie burst from the shadows and danced up to me. "You're here!" she gushed with spacey wonder. She ran her fingers down my face, eyes wild and jittery. "You're really here."

"Audie got an early start," Grant said, as if that explained everything.

She didn't seem to hear him. She just kept gazing at me with that open-mouthed awe, raking her fingers over my face. "You know me, right?"

"Yes, I know you," I answered, laughing.

"I'm the yellow piece," she said. "And you're the black one."

I should've known by the way Audie was dancing around and rambling out nonsense that something more than beer was fueling the celebration. Grant had broken out mushrooms for the occasion. They were crushed into a powder and put in gel caps. He took me aside and tapped a pill out of his vial. "Since you're driving, one is enough. And go easy on the alcohol."

"How many has she had?" I pointed to Audie, who was skipping around the fire now, hands clawing up at the emerging stars.

"Audie got ambitious and went with three."

"Three?!"

"Three isn't bad. Trust me. Four beers would mess her up worse."

I don't know if it was the drugs or what, but there seemed to be a malignant energy to the proceedings. Grant leaped up and straddled the benches across the gazebo's opening. He was spread-eagled above the fire, with his back to it, blocking our exit. He got us all to quiet down, then told us, in a kind of

shamanic intonation, how this might be our last night on these hallowed shores;
how our Eden had been corrupted—by the plundering of corporate farmers, the
greed of spoiled retirees, and the toxic seduction of nuclear conglomerates.

"And we've succumbed to the wickedness," he proclaimed with a gravity
so heartfelt Joan's laughter trailed off. Newf plunked down next to Carrie and
went silent. I stopped smirking. Our faces gleamed with the flickering sheen of
the fire's glow. "We stole without conscience. Our spoils are the trappings of
evil." Grant shook the suit he was wearing by the collar. Then he started
unbuttoning it. "Now, we must strip away these costumes before we head off
on the journey to purify our souls."

Grant pulled his arms out of the suit and let it drop to his feet. All he
had on was his underwear. He stepped out of the legs, picked up the coveralls
by the neck, leaned out, and dangled the empty suit over the fire. The flames
took a minute to catch, then leaped up the legs. Smoke escaped out of the neck;
a fleeing ghost. Just before the blaze reached his arm, he let go of the suit. It
snuffed the fire dark. Then the flames fought free and overwhelmed the fallen
heap. With that, he grabbed the rafter beam above him, swung back, and
launched himself over the fire.

Everyone else did their own version of the ritual. Joan went first, shaking
the folds out of her coveralls, dropping them in the fire, then screaming as she
flung herself over the pit. Audie wanted to try swinging as well, but Grant
convinced her to stand beside the pit and broad jump across. Even at that,
spaced as she was, she nearly tumbled back into the embers. Carrie got up on
the bench, stepped over to the edge, and tossed her jumpsuit in the fire.

"Come on, Carrie. Get down." Newf said. "You don't want to get hurt."

I was the only one in the gazebo besides the two of them. "Let her do what
she wants," I muttered. "You always do."

I couldn't see Newf's face very well; Carrie's coveralls had smothered the
glow. But I could tell by the cock of his head and its dead still aim, he was
staring at me. "Why don't you fuck right off, eh Tommy?"

Maybe it was the mushrooms kicking in or too much alcohol to go with
them. Who knows? But I didn't consider how Newf would take my words
until he got so angry over them. Then, instead of telling him I didn't mean
anything by what I said, I decided I must've meant it. And I got angry myself.

Carrie stepped back, charged to the end of the bench, and vaulted well
beyond the bonfire. Newf brushed past me, hopped up on the bench, tossed his

suit in the fire, then, without any further ceremony, made his leap. His foot hit a log at the pit's edge, slid out, and sent him airborne. He landed on his back, head by the fire, wind knocked out of him. If Carrie hadn't acted so quickly to pull him away, we could've had a serious problem.

The fall rattled Newf. He angrily waved off Carrie when she came to see if he was okay. I felt bad for him, but given the clash we'd just had, I didn't want to go anywhere near him. When he came back into the gazebo to grab another beer, I snuck out to join the others.

"Why aren't you making the jump?" Newf grumbled behind me.

"I don't have a suit."

"So?"

"So, the whole point was to burn our suits."

"N-n-no. The point was to get pure. You've got to jump."

"Fine." I walked to the edge of the fire and hopped across it.

"That's not enough!" Newf screamed.

Until that moment, I don't think anyone else realized Newf was mad at me, never mind the force of that anger. I wish I'd kept my cool. "It's not enough?" I pushed back.

"No. It's not."

That's when I snapped. "You're right, Newf. Jumping over a fire isn't enough. Let's do something real. Let's all give confession. Let's name what makes us so impure." I waited. Newf seemed to be waiting, too. The next thing that was said would decide how explosive things got.

"That's cool," Audie broke in behind me. "Liking confessing our sins."

Grant finally grasped where things were going. "We're not doing that. Nobody has to do that."

I ignored Grant. "You go first, Newf. Tell us what makes you so impure."

"You're an asshole, Tommy," Joan snapped, coming up beside Grant.

"What's going on?" Audie wondered.

"Just tell her," I challenged Newf. "Somebody needs to tell her."

Newf shoved me. I stumbled back, got my feet tangled, and hit the ground. Before I could get up, he was looming over me. "Shut up! Shut the hell up!"

Carrie was suddenly between us. "Stop it!" she pleaded, hands on Newf's chest, pushing him away. "What is happening?"

Newf put his hands up in surrender and let her back him into the gazebo. "If you don't tell her, I will."

"Go on, Newf," Joan said. *"You're going to have to now."*

Everyone turned to Newf. There was a heavy silence. His hands were still in the air. He kept looking past Carrie as she tried to make eye contact.

"Just tell me everything's okay," she begged, tugging at his raised arms. *"That's all I want to hear."*

He pushed her away, stomped past us, and fled into the darkness. Carrie chased after him.

"Something's wrong," it finally dawned on Audie.

"I can't believe you," Joan hissed at me. *"You're ruining everything."*

Newf's pickup rumbled to life. Its taillights lit the cornstalks red. Carrie screamed. I started running. Before I could get there, the truck was hurtling away in a careening tunnel of light. Carrie was trying to keep up, pleading at the driver's window, then banging on the pickup's side, then chasing after it until it broke out of the field, fishtailed on Lake Range, and headed for the Eighth. And all that while, she kept yelling, *"WHY?!"*

When she came staggering back to us, no one knew what to say. I'd never seen her so distraught. I wanted to tell her it was just as well that Newf left, that it was better for her to know the truth now than learn it hundreds of miles away. But it wasn't the time for talk, and it wasn't clear whether Carrie knew anything at all—except that something was so wrong Newf had to escape. We were all out by my car, watching her pace, uncertain how to console her.

"What's going on?" Audie was first to speak. *"Why is this happening?"*

"It's alright," Grant said. *"He's coming back. We'll talk it out."*

"The hell we will." Joan stomped off toward the gazebo.

"Give me your keys." Carrie held her hand out, eyes avoiding mine.

"Why? You're not going to chase him?"

"Tommy." She looked at me, eyes pleading now. *"Give me the keys."*

"They're in the car."

Carrie broke away and went straight for the Charger.

"You can't drive," Grant said, following her. She closed the driver's door on him. *"She can't drive,"* he appealed to me. *"She took two pills."*

I hurried to the passenger's side and got in as the Charger lurched forward. *"Wait!"* I yelled. *"Why are you doing this?"*

"He has my stuff. Everything we snuck out of 142. Including my money."

She slowly steered the Charger onto the road. We cruised to the stop sign at the Eighth. The effort of driving appeared to calm her. She leaned forward, *squinting through the windshield. And she flipped down the blinker to signal our turn toward Holyrood, even though no one was around. She seemed okay to drive, much more so than me. My head was swimming—with drugs and alcohol; with the shock of the moment; with warring voices—should I be letting her do this or not?*

"What did he tell you?" I asked Carrie.

"That I shouldn't go."

"Did he say why?"

"He told me I wouldn't want to know."

We eased away from the intersection. Carrie flicked the brights on. The road instantly leaped into the distance. The fields crowded in on either side.

"Do you?"

I waited for an answer. It didn't come. Carrie stared straight ahead, mouth pressed shut. Then I felt us accelerating.

That little girl in the picture Audie drew. I was past the place on the hill where she had stood. I looked over the wall of trees at the intersection. Of course, the giant car wasn't there. No towering peg people, no threat of a collision. Still, as I neared the hill's crest, I slowed down more than I needed to. Mine was the only way without a stop sign. But there was good reason to be careful; two summers ago, someone got t-boned cruising blindly into the intersection. In truth, though, I never hesitated before.

There was brilliance to the day's colors, a deep, unreal saturation—in the greens of the pastures and distant trees, in the gold of the big rolled bales of hay, even in the stark black and white of the roaming cattle. It wasn't because of the sun so much as the low, tattered blanket of dark blue clouds the sun shone through. You know the skies I mean. You've seen this as a storm began to gather or break apart. Everything seemed charged with urgency.

As I gathered speed past the radio tower Audie climbed, I checked my breath in the cup of my hand. The night before, I finally found that hidden bottle of Skyy. It was behind a bunch of tiki torches I'd stored in the basement. It hadn't been full, thank God, but it was more than enough. I could still smell the tinge of sour liquor in my hand. I'd have to stop in Ripley and take care of that. No way I could stand in front of Newf, reeking of booze, and talk through what had to be said.

I took my foot off the gas well before Highway 21 and let myself drift up to the lonesome intersection someone had decided to name Pine River. The place made Ripley look like a thriving metropolis. There was a single clapboard house on three of the four corners, and on the last one, an abandoned gas station. Twenty years ago, I could've stopped there and bought some mints. Now, the windows were boarded up, and the lone island where the gas pumps used to be was infested with weeds.

It was a busy time on the highway. I had to wait for a caravan of cars coming north, stuck behind a cattle trailer. Cows to slaughter. Tourists to the shores. When I did finally cross the intersection, with nothing but open road and Ripley five miles ahead, I set the cruise at 50. There was no hurry, no need to test the deception of speed like before. A car roared by. Then another. I saw a third, still a way off, gaining in my rearview. I was tempted to step on the gas. But I didn't. The car kept coming.

"*Slow down,*" *I told Carrie as we roared up to the highway at Pine River. The store there was still open. "I should drive. Pull over here."*

She didn't listen. We cruised through the stop sign and started gathering speed again. "Why doesn't he want me to go?"

The question didn't surprise me. I'd been the one pressing for everything to come out. I just never thought I'd be the one to tell Carrie the truth.

"Did he ever tell you he loved you?"

"Why shouldn't I go?"

"What if I said I loved you?" As soon as the words came out, those words I couldn't say before, I wondered at their audacity. "What if I said that?"

Carrie didn't answer. She was thinking about it, though. I could tell, watching her eyes blink and shoulders heave, hearing the shiver in her breath.

"I do. I can't help it."

She glanced at me then, the slick sheen of sudden tears reflected in the dashboard lights. "I don't know what to feel anymore."

I didn't realize how fast we were going until the red taillights of Newf's pickup started rushing up on us.

"Whoa!" The speedometer was past 80. I put my hand on Carrie's arm. We roared up so close to Newf's truck we could hear the engine rev and clatter as he tried to pull away. Before long, we were both hurtling down the narrow road at 90 miles an hour. No more than two car lengths away from each other. Then 95. Then 100. "Carrie! Slow down! What are you doing?"

"I have to end this," she sobbed out. She flicked her brights on and off. Newf's silhouette leaped to life before us, vivid then shadowy, over and over.

When we hit the outskirts of Ripley, Newf's brake lights flared up. Carrie was forced to slow down. It was either that or ram him. As slow as it felt, we were still going 80 through town, between that gauntlet of sleepy houses. It didn't seem real. The way our brights flung an eerie glow against the buildings as they streamed past, we could've been racing through a ghost town. As we came to the four-way stop in Ripley, Newf barely tapped the brakes. Carrie started accelerating, too.

"Let him go."

She dared a glance my way. "If I did love you..."

"Then I'd give—"

Newf's truck lurched left, swerved back hard, and started flipping.

"Oh no," was the last thing Carrie said. Then the rearing horse's frantic eyes were beaming at us. The Charger jolted to the right. I saw the black outline of the buggy, just before we barreled through it. There was an awful cracking, a hail of splinters, a shriek. Then the tree trunk was there through the windshield, right in front of me. Carrie's hand stamped my chest. She wrenched the wheel. The tree swung across the windshield, away from me, over to her. My head hit the glass. And I was flying.

I came to the four-way stop in Ripley and turned off the main road. I needed to get something—a mint for my breath, a minute to think, a drink to calm my nerves. I pulled into a spot in front of the Mini-Mart. A tiny LCBO was attached to the store. I'd never stepped foot in there, but I was sure they'd have a pint of something that worked. As I stood on the sidewalk, wrestling over whether to go in, it started raining, not a downpour, but not just drops either.

A collective groan rose up behind me. A group of bicyclists, festooned with colorful jerseys, spandex shorts, and sleek helmets, came pouring out of the storefront a couple doors away. I saw Wendy seconds before she saw me. Had she not caught me staring, I might've ducked into the LCBO. Now, there was nothing to do but go to her. She seemed anxious as I approached. The last time we'd seen each other, down by the harbor, neither of us had been at our best. "Your timing isn't great." I pointed to the sky, trying to put her at ease.

Wendy glanced back at the store. It was a restaurant. Fig. I'd never seen it before. "I forgot something,' she said, retreating back to the door. Just then, it flung open. Bogue came striding out.

"McTavish!" he bellowed. Wendy cringed; she hadn't wanted me to see him. He came up beside her, threw an arm across her shoulders, and squeezed. "Trying to sweet talk my manager into drinking at the new place?" Bogue grinned, watching me squirm. "Tell you what, I'll give you a chance here. But one strike and you're out. Right, Wendy?" He shook her and walked away.

Wendy pushed her wet hair out of her eyes. "Tommy—"

The other cyclists were on their bikes now. "You've got to go."

Wendy stepped forward and gave me a quick hug. "I can explain," she whispered.

"No need."

She broke away. "You should try the coffee." She pointed into Fig. "It's strong."

So you *could* still smell liquor. "It was last night."

"Is it ever going to stop?"

I looked into the window of the restaurant. "I don't know," I admitted to our reflections. Then I hurried inside.

It was an impressive place—new wood floors, black fleur-de-lis patterned ceiling, white granite-stacked walls. It put every other store in Ripley to shame. There wasn't anywhere in Kincardine that was this stylish; of course, with the exception of O'Shea's. I sidled up to the long, blond-oak bar and waited for the woman down the way to pour a trayful of mimosas. Wherever that tray was going, that was where I wanted to be. Then again, there was an entire wall of booze in front of me, gleaming in a glassy spectrum from vodkas through gins, to rums and scotches and whiskeys. I'd nearly talked myself into having a shot when I noticed the glass-domed cake stand in the middle of the shining run of bottles. It was filled with a pyramid of puck-sized butter tarts. When the bartender came my way, I ordered a coffee to go.

"Those tarts," I said, as she sealed a top on the paper cup. "Are they homemade?"

"No. They're from Wendy O'Shea's in Kincardine. You know about her, eh?"

"Yeah, I know about her."

I left without another word. It was raining harder. I hurried to my car, got it running, then took a sip of the coffee. Damned if it wasn't good. Five minutes earlier, that would've been a welcome surprise. Now, it made me mad. When did Wendy become manager of this new restaurant? I'd just seen her the day before, and she was still holding out against giving Bogue her tarts. What the hell happened? Why did it bother me so much, anyway? Her life was her life. It had nothing to do with me, with the showdown I was about to have with Newf. *Let it go, McTavish. Let it all go.*

I headed back to the road for Holyrood. I had to put the wipers on high. Even at that, I could barely see the road, and everything outside the sweep of my wipers was a blur of smearing streaks. Just as well. I didn't want to see that lane the buggy was turning out of when Carrie hit it. Seconds later, I was out of Ripley altogether. I couldn't go any faster, though. The rain washed up the windshield in waves. My wipers couldn't clear them fast enough. And it beat the road to a quaking froth.

Suddenly, there was a shadowy stain on my windshield. And now it was a phantom floating in the downpour. Someone was on the side of the road; a Mennonite woman, getting buffeted along in sheets of rain. Her long black dress was drenched and flapping, enveloping her in a skin-tight husk. I pulled up beside her and rolled down the window. "Can I give you a ride?" She staggered on, like she hadn't heard me. She may not have even seen me. The rim of her bonnet was sopped and drooping below her eyes.

"You need a ride?" I shouted louder.

She finally turned to me. "No, thank you."

I recognized her. She was the young woman who didn't know the price of the carved ark. "Are you going all the way to Holyrood?" She nodded. "That's six miles. You can't walk there in this rain. Come on. Get in."

"I cannot."

So that was it. She couldn't get in the car. A Mennonite principle. Poor girl. She was shivering. This wasn't a warm summer rain. With the wind, it felt like 60. No way she'd make it to Holyrood.

"Nobody's going to know you got in."

"*I* will."

"I'm not going to leave you here and find out later somebody ran off the road and hit you." She stopped walking and peered at me. I could barely see her eyes under the fallen bonnet. "Please."

She got in the car. "I can't go all the way to Holyrood."

"I'll drop you off before we get there."

I eased back up to speed and into the torrent. We drove for at least a mile without a word, just the chattering of the rain and the shrill squeak of the wipers.

"I'm Tommy. Sorry, I forgot your name."

"Rachel," she answered with that meek voice of hers.

She was sopping wet and shivering. I turned on the heat, felt behind my seat for the towel I used to wrap the boiler plate, and gave it to her. She dabbed her face and wiped her dripping bonnet.

"Your friend at the vegetable stand, does she own that?"

"She's not my friend. She's my mother."

I didn't say anything at first. I was too busy disguising my shock. I don't know why it surprised me; maybe because I only ever thought of Beth in one way—young, orphaned by our fateful accident, helpless. "I've known your mother for a very long time."

"She told me."

A splattering of color blossomed through the rain on my windshield. We were passing the cyclists. Rachel slunk down in her seat. When Wendy streamed by, I saw her gazing into the car.

"We didn't meet under the best circumstances." I watched the pack recede in my rearview.

"I know."

*W*hen I woke up in the Goderich Hospital after the accident, the only person in the room was my dad. His eyes were bloodshot and squinting through red swollen circles. He'd either been crying or drinking. I learned from him what had happened—that we'd hit a buggy, killed a horse, and a man and woman; that the collision hadn't slowed us enough to prevent my Charger from skidding across a yard and slamming head-on into a tree; that the force of that impact propelled me through the windshield, and they found my body 50 feet away from the car; that I'd broken my arm, three ribs, my collarbone, and an ankle, suffered several cuts on my head and face, the worst of which was above my eye and would need a skin graft; that the policemen on the scene said it was a miracle I'd survived.

"What about Carrie?" He sucked in his breath, let it out, gathered it again. "She's dead, isn't she?"

"She hit the tree." I remembered then how the tree had swung from me toward her in the windshield. Had she steered me away from death? My dad scooted up his chair. "Son, why'd you let her drive the car?"

"I was in no shape to drive."

"Neither was she. She was a point-oh-five, under the limit. But did you know she was 17? She can't be drinking anything."

"Why are you whispering?"

"The police are going to ask these questions." His voice was still low, like they were just outside the room. "They're wondering if she had anything else, something more than alcohol."

I didn't say anything to that. Wouldn't they already know that from a blood test? And if the test didn't detect mushrooms, I wasn't going to be the one to tell them that. "So, we killed all those people in the buggy…"

"No. There was a girl in the back. She got thrown clear. Barely a scratch."

"What about Newf?"

"He's okay. His left leg is pretty badly broken, and he broke his collarbone, too. Cuts and bruises on his face as well, but not as bad as you."

I don't know why, but learning that Newf hadn't suffered more severe consequences made me angry. It was a terrible, shameful way to feel. I turned away from my dad and closed my eyes, hoping for sleep.

"He's right next door. When you feel up to it, we can get you together."

I've been waiting for that moment for 34 years.

Rachel had me pull up short of Holyrood. It was a good quarter mile away from Newf's store, but the rain had let up enough that she wouldn't get drenched. I couldn't very well disrespect her wishes. She thanked me abruptly, got out, and was on her way before I had a chance to say anything.

By the time I parked across from the Ice Cream Trail sign, the cyclists were coming down the rise. I got out of the Lincoln. Within seconds, they were streaming by, wheeling around the corner south to Lucknow. Bogue passed me with a sneer. A few riders back, there was Wendy, head up, not leaning over her handlebars like the others, watching me. When she came close, she cocked her head and offered an enigmatic frown.

There wasn't a soul in the store, not even Newf or Chloe. I called out, but no one came. I was ready to head across the street to the house where Newf lived. But as I got to the door, Chloe came bursting in. As soon as she saw me, she turned around and left. I didn't know what to do. Thankfully, Newf came through the front door himself. He didn't say anything either, but at least he didn't run from me. Before I could break the silence, Chloe followed behind him, eyeing me with a hangdog look.

"Lock the door and change the sign," Newf said. She turned the deadbolt and flipped the sign so CLOSED faced out.

Was this where Newf wanted to talk—in front of his daughter? "Chloe has something to tell you." He turned to her. "Just tell him what you told me." His voice was uncharacteristically gentle.

She hung her head. "The sticker you found at the gazebo. It came from me." Chloe looked up and waited. She was expecting me to say something. I was too stunned. "I was up there that night, meeting friends. Then it started raining and they decided not to come. Before I could leave, Pastor Rose showed up. We sat and talked. It was fine at first. Then he started talking about God."

Suddenly, she was fighting back tears. "I got uncomfortable." Her voice was smaller. "He was pressuring me so much. And touching me. He moved closer, put his hand on my shoulder, touched my face. Then—I—just—reacted..."

"You reacted..." Newf prompted her.

Chloe shuddered and came back to us. "I swung my arm out," she made the motion with her right forearm. "I didn't think it was that hard." The arm she scooped ice cream with all day long; she pushed him with that. "He fell back and lost his balance. But he was sitting. It didn't seem that bad. Then the rail behind him cracked, and he kept going over backwards, his arms swinging, his feet in the air. And then…gone."

"Did you say it was dark?" Newf prompted again.

"It *was*," she insisted, like I wouldn't believe her. "With the rain, there were no stars, so I heard him hit the ground, but I couldn't see it. Then he groaned and tumbled back. I tried to find him—I did—but the ravine was pure black, and the banks were so muddy, I was afraid I'd slip down there too. I called and called his name. I listened for any noise. But the rain was loud, and the water was flowing against my feet. I didn't know what else to do."

Chloe started crying then. Newf stepped forward and folded her into his arms. He motioned with a cock of his head for me to leave. I unlocked the door and went back outside. Should I go home? Suddenly, the flooding of my gully didn't seem so important. Why would he have Chloe confess to me anyway? There were any number of reasons the sticker could've wound up under that bench. It would've been a hell of a lot easier just to say he didn't know anything about it, call my bluff, and see if I'd really go to the police. I doubt I would've.

I was out around the corner of the store waiting beside that Ice Cream Trail cartoon cone. He stared at me with that big, dumb grin and those glazed eyes. I reared back and punched him in the nose. I knew the wood was too thick to give. I knew I couldn't wipe that stupid grin off his face. As I shook my aching hand, the cartoon kept on smiling. I drove the heel of my other hand back into his face for good measure.

"Kicking the shit out of my sign now?" Newf said behind me.

"Why would you have her tell me that?"

"Because we're friends. And I trust you."

"Bullshit."

"We're not friends?"

"I don't know. But you don't trust me. That's for sure."

Newf pressed his lips into a tight grimace. "I wanted you to know that you wouldn't just be hurting me with that sticker."

"So, you're using your daughter to play on my sympathies."

If looks could burn, Newf's glare would've bored to the back of my skull. "The situation's a bit more serious than that. What if the cops start wondering if Grant didn't fall by himself?"

I pulled out my wallet, found the sticker, and gave it to him. "Now they don't have any reason to."

When he took it, the tension flushed from his face. "I appreciate this. But all it would take is one of the friends Chloe was supposed to meet saying the wrong thing to the wrong person, and we'd be in serious trouble. I need to get her out of here. If she's just sitting around here waiting for something bad to happen, she'll go crazy."

"Where would she go?" I asked—and right when I said it, I thought of Cam and the ride he wanted me to give Chloe. "Wait. You know anything about Chloe going to a concert in Michigan?"

"No."

"I think she's decided she needs to get out of here, too." I told him about Cam's call, how he wanted me to drive Chloe to Port Huron and said a friend would drive her back.

"I was happy to be asked," I told Newf. "Cam said he thought I might want to drive her because he'd changed his mind about meeting with me. I haven't seen him in nearly two years."

"So, what do you think?"

"I don't think anyone was going to bring her back to Canada."

Newf mulled it over. "Who were they going to see?"

"What?"

"The concert. Who did he say was playing?"

"That's what got me wondering. When I asked Cam the same question, he said I wouldn't know the band. Then, a minute later, he told me it was Alice Cooper."

"*The* Alice Cooper?"

"Like I wouldn't know an old rock-and-roller from my era."

"Like they'd want to see him."

Ever since I'd left the store, the sun had been struggling to break through the clouds. Now, it was shining in the open, and everything was glistening—the leaves in the trees, the grass, the rusty sheet-metal on the collapsed barn across the road, the buggy parked beside it. "Maybe it's not such a bad idea—" Newf started to say. Then he turned abruptly and retreated into the overgrown lawn behind his store, hobbling off with that lurching gait of his.

I didn't know what he was doing until I saw Beth across the road, carrying a card table stocked with boxes of her wares. It was quite a balancing act. She'd obviously done it before, but probably not while getting surprised by someone. When she saw me, the table wobbled, a box of vegetables slid off, she overcompensated, then the maple syrup bottles went, and finally everything hit the ground—flowers, jars, bread, ark carvings.

I went to help her. Beth stood there, holding the table by one leg, staring me down. "I don't need your help," she snapped sternly. I froze in the middle of the road, put up my hands, and backed away. "And we don't accept rides in automobiles."

"That wasn't her fault. I made her get in the car. She could've gotten hurt in that rain."

"It's not your place. You, of all people."

"Beth…" Newf was there behind me. He said her name gently. She bowed and went about picking up her goods. Newf motioned for me to follow him. We went across his backyard and behind a shed. There were two folding chairs there, hidden in a cluster of bushes and looking out on the fields that rolled up to the distant stand of woods along the eastern horizon. Everything from here to those woods and well beyond was Newf's. He sat in the chair with a pile of cigarette butts beneath it. Judging by the worn grooves of dirt at his feet and the grass around my chair, I gathered Newf came here often and mostly sat alone.

"See all this land?" He swept his hand toward the rising fields. "I gave it all away. To the Mennonites. It was too much work for me. They needed it, and I felt like I should help them out. Because, you know…" He didn't need to say more. The papers said at least 500 people came to the funeral of the couple killed in our accident.

The Mennonite community was devastated. I've been afraid to come to Holyrood ever since. But Newf had to keep living here.

"After my wife died, I thought about moving." Newf took a pack of cigarettes out of his coat pocket, tapped one out, and lit up. He blew out a big gust of smoke and continued. "Then Beth's husband died, and it seemed like we were bumping into each other more often. Or maybe I just noticed her more.

"I'd always kept my distance. Everyone out here knows I was in the accident. Some blame me for it." He took another draw off his cigarette. "If I wasn't speeding away from Carrie, she wouldn't have been speeding after me. You think you're the only one who carries that guilt; I've got a lot of it weighing on me, too."

I suspected Newf felt a measure of remorse over what happened, but until that moment, he'd never come right out and said it to me. "You carry it better," I told him.

He offered a sheepish smile. Newf's smile, a smile I wasn't sure I'd seen since we were 15 years old and the whole world of Boiler Beach was just him, me, and our dreams. "We don't see each other all that much these days, do we?" he stated the obvious.

"Something tells me we won't see each other *that* much ever."

Newf wobbled his head like he wasn't so sure and took another puff. "I'm never going to leave here. I've been in love with Beth for 15 years now. Maybe longer. Maybe from the moment she got thrown out of that buggy."

"Are you allowed to love her?" It didn't come out right, but Newf got my meaning.

"There seems to be some question about that. I'd have to convert to their religion, for sure. Then I'd have to go before the elders and get permission."

"You'd do all that?"

A couple fields over, on the rise to the eastern ridge, a group of Mennonite men, with grey work clothes, straw hats, and pitch forks, were getting back to collecting hay after the rain.

"That's why I'm selling the cottage and getting rid of that land by the beach."

"You make it sound like a sacrifice. You're making millions."

"True. I don't have to worry about money. Never did. The only worry I have"—he threw his thumb over his shoulder—"is that girl in there."

"Nothing's going to happen," I tried to reassure him. "They called it an accident, and there's no proof Chloe was there."

"Even if that's true, I still have to do something about her." Newf dropped the cigarette butt and stomped it out. "If she's still here next summer, scooping ice cream and sneaking off with druggies from Owen Sound, she might never leave this place. I owe her the chance to dream of something bigger."

"Maybe I *should* drive her to see Alice Cooper," I half-joked.

"Welcome to my nightmare." Newf laughed, but he quickly lapsed into thought. "My sister Bryne *is* still in Florida."

"You're not saying you want me to drive Chloe down on Friday, are you?" Newf shook his head. "Good. I was worried you were making a drastic decision."

"I've been making a lot of those lately."

Now seemed as good a time as any to change the subject. "Like emptying out your retention pond?"

Newf's eyes slowly shifted toward mine. His face got red. "I sold that land three weeks ago."

"And my gully's been flooding since the spring. When did you put that pond in, anyway?"

Newf got quiet. "Two years ago. Before I knew I was going to sell. The watershed people got to me."

"So, when did you dig the trench to drain it?"

"Hang on—"

"Come on, Newf. I was up there. I saw your backhoe. I saw the trench, and the water rushing down into the ravine." I softened my tone. "So, you didn't expect we'd have such a heavy rain. You didn't consider that the culvert might fail. It's either that, or you did it on purpose. Maybe Rob put you up to it. Part of the deal. Help flood out McTavish and you'll get—"

"Enough!" Newf cut me off with a hard jab. His open palm stopped inches from my face. "I lent Rob my backhoe, okay? He said he had a problem he needed to fix. When it came to the pond,

I told him I'd plug the pipes beneath Lake Range and build a new pond across from the resort. The old pond would seep away by the fall. He obviously didn't want to wait that long."

Either Newf was a better liar than I suspected, or he was telling the truth. He seemed angrier about the whole thing than I did. "He drained that pond because he was impatient?"

Newf pinched his nose. "He wants your land—badly. I told him just to wait you out, that you'd come around. I said forcing the issue, turning it into a feud, was the worst thing he could do. I warned him: don't fuck with Tommy's Irish temper. He's got nothing to lose." He gave me a crooked grin.

"I wish that were true."

"Well…" Newf slapped my knee. "You might've saved yourself a punch in the nose."

I laughed. "You're probably right about that."

"I said I was sorry."

"It wasn't the most sincere apology."

"Well, I'm not going to say it again," Newf insisted. "Sorry isn't a word I use too often."

"Sorry's my entire goddamned life." I meant it as a joke.

Newf didn't get it. "You can't be so hard on yourself."

"Yes, I can. That's the one thing I've learned. I can never be too hard on myself."

"You should do something about that."

"I've got enough on my hands trying to keep my cottage."

"You might find self-improvement easier."

"I hope that's not some sort of warning."

"Just friendly advice," Newf said. "Rob's not giving up on this. He's got a huge model of the resort in his bunkhouse. There's a big blank where your cottage used to be. And the gully's a river. He's got something planned. You'll see at the party."

"The party?"

"Carrie's dedication. They're installing new greens at the Boiler Beach course. Real greens, no more rock-hard dirt. And they're renaming it: Sinclair Golf Club. Then on Sunday, they've got some big fundraiser tournament called the Carrie Open."

"Oh yeah." The party at Rob's place. I'd forgotten all about it. "Sharon was handing out invites. Shockingly, I didn't get one."

"Shit. I'm sorry."

"It's not her fault."

"Anyway, point is, Rob's got big plans. Hell, he's got all the movers and shakers in town behind this. He can't afford to let you stand in his way."

"I wonder how they'd feel about the chunk of metal Bogue burned off the boiler." I'd been waiting to bring that up.

"They're worried about it," Newf admitted. "No doubt about that. The day you came into the Aurora, Bogue was freaking out. He had all sorts of crazy ideas to strong-arm that thing away from you. Rob had to talk him down."

"I could give the plate over to the police any time I wanted. You tell him that."

"I'd be careful making threats. You don't know what you're dealing with."

"Why do the Gartons care if it's a tractor boiler, anyway?"

Newf lifted his eyebrows and shook his finger. "That's a good question. There's a simple reason, then there's the real reason."

"I already know the simple reason—same reason Rob does anything: money. He's going to have a hell of a lot easier time selling a resort named Mariner's Whatever if he has the mystique of a shipwreck to market than an antique farm implement."

Newf screwed up his face. "I give him a little more credit than that. Rob cares about the beach. If it came out that the sinking of the Aurora Quest wasn't real, part of what makes the place special would be lost. A legend would be tarnished."

"A legend…"

"Crazy as it is, that boiler is the emblem of the beach."

"The relic of a shipwreck that never was," I corrected him. "Rob's not that sentimental."

"Don't get me wrong. Rob's concerned about his business, too. Losing the folklore of the Aurora Quest would put a crimp in his plans. And think about what it would do to the family restaurant. But never underestimate how much Rob loves Boiler Beach."

"Right," I scoffed. "Buying it up, building a monstrosity, bringing in tourists, capitalizing on our sanctuary. If he loves the beach, he's got a funny way of showing it."

Newf laughed. "Just remember, to the people who live here, you're all tourists along the shore. And to the Ojibwe, we're all centuries-old interlopers."

"Still."

"But that's the only way Rob knows how to love," Newf argued. "Possess it. Make your mark on it. Use it up."

For a guy who kept his emotions bottled up, this was a pretty deep insight. I saw his point about the beach, but Rob knew no other way to love? "Sharon may have something to say about that."

"I didn't mean it that way," Newf backed down. "Anyway, that's not the biggest reason Rob cares about people finding out the boiler's a fake. Fact is, your question wasn't even the right one."

"No?"

"What did you say—*why* do the Gartons care if the boiler came from a tractor? The *how* is a lot more telling than the why." Newf raised his eyebrows again. Was I supposed to figure out what he meant from that? "How did that tractor engine get in the water? And how did they know it was there in the first place?"

I hadn't pondered things quite that way. The hoax would've had to pre-date Rob and his dad. When I looked at Newf, he was giving me the eye. "You know, don't you?"

"I do," he said.

"So?"

"So, I'm going to tell you," Newf decided. "You need to understand why the Garton's are so desperate to get that piece from you. Sure, it's about business, and preserving the mythology of the beach, But, more than anything, it's about covering their asses, protecting the family legacy."

He let that sink in for a while. It seemed like he wanted me to draw some conclusion that should've been obvious. I was anxious for him to keep going. "Am I missing something?"

"You might ask how *I* know all this."

I waited. Apparently, he wanted me to voice it. "How *do* you?"

"I know because my family's involved, too," Newf leaned forward in his chair, elbows on knees, head down, inches away from me. And he started talking, like he might in a confession booth.

"This goes back to the summer the beach was founded, when my great grandfather and Rob's were clearing away brush on their original lots. Nobody else knows this, but old Bud and my Great Grampa Walt picked a spot well north of where they ultimately built their first cottages. That spot happened to be right in front of where the boiler is today, next to Carrie's old place.

"The way it was told to me," Newf went on, "they liked it there because Concession 10 was open, the Eighth wasn't there yet, and the beach was bigger. But there was one problem: no sandbar. Just like today, that north shore was all rocks. They decided to clear the rocks away with a fancy new steam tractor Bud had sold Walt."

"A Sawyer-Massey," I spoke up.

"That's right," Newf said. "Rob was afraid you'd figure that out. Anyway, this was no ordinary steam tractor, even for its day. It was a beast, the biggest the company ever made. They chained a plow onto the back of it, drove it into the shallow water, and started dragging it across the bed of rocks.

"By all accounts, it was going well. They'd cleared the whole width of the lot, well into the lake. Then Garton got greedy—at least that's what Walt related to my dad. There seems to be some dispute, though, about who was driving the tractor. Rob says his dad told him it was Walt. Whatever, they were both to blame."

Newf shook out another cigarette. If unburdening himself of the truth was causing him angst, he wasn't showing it. On the contrary, he seemed relieved to be telling someone the long-held secret. "So?" I prompted him.

"So, they went too far. There was a steep drop-off from that first ridge of stones. The wheels on one side slid into the dip, the tractor started tilting, and with the top-heavy weight of that huge smokebox, it went over. The boiler made an awful thumping sound when it hit the water. Walt and Bud thought it hit a boulder. They were worried enough to swim away from the tractor. Good thing, too, because seconds later, the thing exploded."

Newf took a draw off his cigarette and let the smoke seep out. "Pieces of the tractor went everywhere, splashing all around them, flying up on the beach. Luckily, neither man got hit. They were in water up to their chest, so the wreckage was submerged. Still, steam was billowing everywhere. They were afraid the boiler might blow again, so they hurried ashore and waited up on the dune for the wreckage to simmer down.

"It kept pumping out so much smoke, they worried someone might see it in town and come check it out." Newf scratched the back of his neck at that. "I never did get a good answer why that should bother them so much. Maybe clearing the woods by the shore wasn't strictly legal in those days. It sure as hell isn't today, not without a mountain of paperwork.

"They abandoned that spot half cleared. Then they tried to cover their tracks. They spent a few days pulling everything they could off the tractor. With the explosion, it was pretty well unrecognizable. They did find a couple of the back wheels intact and a few scraps of metal that might identify the remains as a tractor, but the smokebox—what we call the boiler today—was just a big, gnarled hunk of metal. Plus, it was completely submerged under water. They knew someday someone would find it, but they figured by then, they'd be long gone.

"What they didn't count on was the lake level dropping. Two summers later, well after they'd built their original cottages where you and I are now, the top of the smokebox started poking out of the water. Nobody but the Garton and Newfield families were around to see it, so it wasn't that big a deal. But it did get the two men talking again about how to explain its presence on the beach."

Newf finished his cigarette, tamped it out on the edge of the chair, and started laughing, a long rumbling laugh, the kind you kept to yourself. "It started as a joke. Both men's versions of the story agree on that. They got to drinking around a bonfire and decided it would be a lot safer if they claimed discovery of the wreckage rather than have someone else do it and set the narrative.

"It was Bud who came up with the idea to pass it off as a shipwreck. The Newfield contribution to the hoax was giving the ship its name. Credit for that, all agree, goes to my Great Grammie Norma. While the families were sitting around that bonfire, right out in front of our cottages, the Northern Lights started pulsing above the curve of the peninsula. That's when Norma suggested the Aurora Quest as the name for the mythical ship, after the Aurora Borealis—and, I suppose, the two men's quest to hide the embarrassing and likely criminal truth of its origins."

Right then, the screen door to the house creaked open behind us. "Dad?" It was Chloe. She looked flustered.

"What's wrong?"

"We just got a big rush."

"Alright," Newf replied, standing up. "Be there in a minute."

She went back into the store. I stood up to go. I'd heard all I needed. But Newf had more to say. "They started telling people they found a ship's boiler in the water. All very casual. Then they kept adding to the story, talking about the explosion of the Aurora Quest like it was fact, making up details—the sailors who died, the storm that grounded the ship. A few years after their fiasco, the water had receded so far that the smokebox was 20 feet offshore. By then, everyone knew about the wreck of the Aurora Quest. Fiction had become fact simply in the frequency of retelling."

Newf started walking out toward the Ice Cream Trail sign. A good dozen cars were parked now on either side of road. "It was just a few years after that," Newf went on, "the early Twenties, that Bud named these shores Boiler Beach and started capitalizing on the mythical shipwreck. He had commemorative coins pressed, postcards made, toy ships. Then Mad Mike opened the restaurant in '65. As my dad told it, Walt was not happy with those developments. It was one thing to concoct a story about a shipwreck to cover up your own bone-headed mistake. It was something else to profit from it. People think the reason Rob's and my family fell out was because of cottage squabbles. Truth is, it was all because of that mangled smokebox and the Garton's greediness."

When we came around to the front of the store, a line was out the door. "I better get in there," Newf said, holding his hand out. I shook it. An hour before, I wouldn't have.

After Newf left, I headed for my car. Everything felt so different from when I arrived in Holyrood. Instead of ominous skies and rain, it was sunny, and the clouds were thinning. Instead of lonely crossroads, the four corners were clogged with cars. Across the street, Beth stood behind her card table, straight-backed and still, expressionless, eyes locked, it seemed, in a stare-down with that googly-eyed ice cream cone. I could've stayed on the cone side of the road, bypassed Beth, then crossed at a safe distance to get to the Lincoln. I was on my way to do just that.

Then I was making a beeline to Beth. Her eyes shifted ever so slightly to me. I didn't look away, even when I was in front of her. I didn't attempt my usual small talk either. I just said what I should've years ago. "I never told you I was sorry. I never just came out and said it. Truth is, I couldn't be sorrier for what happened. I try. To be…more than sorry. I punish myself, too much, too hard. It doesn't help anything. It doesn't help you. I wish I could help you. I wish I could undo it all. But I can't. Just know… I *am* sorry. You don't have to forgive me or stop hating me. Just know."

I said that all in one hurried outburst, then I walked away.

"I do not *hate* you, Tommy McTavish," Beth called out behind me. I stopped, but I didn't turn around. "Forgiveness isn't easy, either. I pray for you, though. I do. Every day."

I closed my eyes. The tears came, and they stung, and I shut my eyes harder. Then they burned. I hurried to the Lincoln, started it up, wheeled around, and headed back for the beach.

When I came to the stop sign by the old store, I saw trucks and workers in bright orange vests and white hardhats lining the road beside the land Rob bought from Newf. I should've coasted down the hill, minded my own business. But last time I passed that way, there was police tape across the ruts to the gazebo. I turned to check it out. They were putting up temporary chain-link fencing, eight men, working in teams of two, fitting the long panels into bright yellow feet that marched away along the strip of field as far as I could see. The panels were tall, eight feet at least, and they had a green mesh privacy screen on them. Most did, anyway.

As I drove along the barrier, every 10 panels there was a big vinyl banner tied to the top and bottom bars. I pulled over on the wrong side of the road to take one in.

COMING SOON! MARINER'S VISTA. RESORT LIVING.

In the lower left corner, there was a gold double-G logo with "Garton Group" below it. All that information was overlaid on a lush, colorful drawing showing a high-angle shot of the resort, the bluff, and the lake. The view reminded me of the picture Audie drew after climbing the tower. Instead of gigantic Sorry pieces in the fields, there were clusters of bungalows, with decks jutting out toward Lake Huron, and perfectly slim, faceless architectural people lounging on them. Overlaid on the unnaturally cerulean waters were three circular inset images, highlights of Mariner's Vista living—a sprawling tentacled pool, a line of sailboats waiting on the shore, a group of people solemnly surrounding the boiler.

I eased back onto the road. At the entry to the field, where just a week before an excavator could barely fit between the cornstalks, a dirt road wider than Lake Range had been cleared, and a fleet of construction vehicles was lined up midway to the bluff. This entry was protected by swinging chain-link security panels. As if they weren't enough, there was a heavy-duty iron gate in front of them. Across the top of the fencing, razor wire coiled around the bars. Perched on the posts that held the swinging panels were two security cameras, one pointing down on the field's entry, the other pointing over to the construction equipment. Rob must've expected serious opposition from locals and cottagers. Whether it was wind turbines, hog farms, or nuclear waste dumps, there was always a faction who vehemently resisted any undertaking that disrupted the region's pastoral serenity. Some of the more militant ones took to vandalism to make their points. A resort as expansive as Rob's billboard promised was sure to draw fire, and not just from a disgruntled old beacher like me.

I heard beeping. Rob was in my rearview, face close to the windshield. I put my car in gear, but before I could drive off, two workers blocked the way. Then another came striding toward me from the gate. I debated not rolling down my window, but he looked like the sort you didn't want to upset. "Something I can do for you?" he barked. His vest had the Garton Group logo on it. With that hard squint and the jut of his jaw, I pegged him for the project's superintendent.

"Just curious. Is that a problem?"

"What's the trouble?" Rob came up beside the guy.

"Am I not allowed to take a look?"

"I got this," Rob told his men. They all went back to work.

"What's with all the henchmen?" I needled Rob. "Plotting to overthrow the world?"

"You know how people are around here. Some aren't that fond of change. If you don't keep an eye out, they'll try to hurt you."

"I hear you. I've got a failed cottage to show for it."

"You can always solve that problem," Rob reminded me.

"Why would I sell when I can live in the bosom of such an idyllic resort community?" I cocked my head at the sign with its happy architecture people, just slightly more evolved than the Life pegs Audie used to draw.

"Suit yourself." Rob backed away.

"I'm especially excited to take a pilgrimage to the hallowed boiler." I pointed at the inset picture with the circle of worshippers.

"Yes." He acted oblivious to the sarcasm. "It's quite the historic attraction."

"I don't know about that…"

"Oh, I know," he said. "You have a good day, Tommy." He tapped the top of my Lincoln and strutted away.

I drove off, heading north. All along Rob's half-mile stretch, workers were putting up fencing. Every few seconds, I'd pass the Mariner's Vista sign—the radio tower view of the bungalows, the peg people, the sailboats, the boiler shrine. Did he really need so many signs? And that smirk he gave me when I brought up the boiler. Newf said Rob was worried about that. He didn't act like it.

I cruised down the hill at the Tenth and turned left at the bottom, taking the back road opposite the way I usually did. Before long, I was passing the lot where tourists parked to visit the boiler. I saw a young couple going hand in hand to the beach. Then I was in front of Carrie's old cottage. The property was staked off with surveyor's flags, the cottage waiting to be leveled. The golf shelter Rob and I had built still stood, but the roof I'd worked on had caved in. Rumor had it the building was infested with raccoons.

I drove on. But I kept thinking about that cottage and how it would soon disappear. I thought about that faceless couple too, holding hands on their way to the shore. I tried to imagine myself where they were, except a century in the past, when this whole land was wild. Carrie was holding my hand. We broke through the last stand of poplars and beheld that impossible expanse of deep blue water, the first people since the Ojibwe to witness it from there. We smiled at one another, because we knew we would live there together and be happy for the rest of our lives. I tried so hard cling to that vision, but I kept drifting away from it. The current of truth was too strong.

Cam had gotten word from Chloe about my trip to Holyrood by the time I called to get after him. "What did you want me to do?" he argued. "Someone you care for says they're in trouble, you try to help them."

An excuse: I'd been down this road with Cam before; brazenly bullshitting me to get his way. He'd said he was changing, working to become a better person. Really? "Maybe if you'd told us straight up what the problem was."

"Chloe didn't want anyone to know. She didn't want to have to talk about it, especially with her dad. She was worried he might not even believe Mr. Rose would attack her."

"From what I heard, it wasn't an attack."

"Call it what you want."

"You know how Mr. Rose was," I reminded him. "He liked to put his arm around you. He liked to slap you on the back. Anyone who knew him knows that."

"I just wish she hadn't agreed to go," Cam said. "She should've been more suspicious of that. What pastor asks a follower to meet him alone at night?" That wasn't the story I got. She told Newf and me she went to the gazebo to meet friends. "Dad?"

"Yeah, I'm here."

"Chloe says her dad's thinking of getting her to the States. She has an aunt in Florida. Did you know that?"

"I did."

"Well, if there's anything I can do…"

"So, you really didn't want to see me." I don't know why I blurted it out. I didn't even know it had been on my mind.

"Come on, Dad," was all the reply he could muster.

"Sorry." I hung up before I said something else I'd regret.

After the flood, the gully didn't stop needing to be dug out. It had been a rainy week; that was part of the problem. The new culvert may have had something to do with it, too. I'd gone out to see the huge metal pipe, and it was draining more smoothly than the old gummed-up cement tunnel. But neither the rain nor the pipe could fully explain the runoff's persistence. Only one phenomenon could cause that: Rob was still draining the retention pond. Even if Newf built a new pond for his land across the road, there would always be water on the property Rob owned, probably more with sprinkler systems to keep the grounds lush. I didn't remember seeing any ponds on the resort drawing that graced the Mariner's Vista signs. Where would the water go? It didn't take a genius to figure out.

The only good thing about the flood was that people stopped accosting me when I dug out the gully. They'd seen how the waters had taken my deck steps. So, there was more sympathy, or at least less outright hostility. They knew I was fighting an existential battle, and even if some were privately hoping I'd lose, at least they had the decency not to make that known to my face anymore.

Still, my routine was to dig in the morning, and I kept that up. There was something about the solitude of it; the lake, calm and glassy, the soft hush of the surf it pushed ashore, the beach's alluring emptiness. I liked thinking I was the only one there, not just on the shore, but in this world, which wasn't really the world we know, the one of desire and obligation, despair and love. Not that world, but an exile from it; a peaceful, desolate place where I served out my penance, where I dug and kept digging, with no hope of reaching anywhere new or bending the currents that swept me along, except the dim remembrance of that other world and the resignation that there was no other way to get back there than through work, the constant subjection of myself to this unrewarding labor.

The runoff followed me obediently, gouge by gouge of sand. It was just a few shovels away from racing into the lake. That's when I saw Sharon coming toward me from my cottage, bounding down the dune. "There you are," she said, with her usual sunny disposition, as though the fact of my presence was a wonder.

"Here I am."

"I left something inside your back door." She came all the way down to the edge of the waves and splashed over to stand right in front of me. "I think you'll be happy."

I hadn't been that close to Sharon in years, actually since we'd broken up. She had those same lively eyes, that same quick grin. Yet in the clarity of the soft, unbroken morning light, you could see the toll time had taken—in the wrinkles that squeezed out the corner of her eyes; in the grey hair overtaking her ashy blonde bob; in the furrows that smoking had carved around her lips.

"You think so?" I put my head down to stop from staring and finished off the end of the channel. The gully started draining. We watched the water rush out together.

"It's the invite to Carrie's dedication."

I raised my eyebrows. "That's pretty bold of you there, Sharon. I don't want you incurring Rob's wrath for my sake."

"He's the one who told me to bring you the invite."

I tried to wrap my head around the news. "I can't figure him out lately"

"Welcome to *my* life."

I didn't know whether she expected a laugh, but I couldn't help myself. "One minute, he's flooding me out of my cottage; the next, he's welcoming me into his house. For the first time in—I can't remember."

"Never," Sharon clarified.

"What the hell's going on?"

"I don't—I don't know."

The catch in her voice said differently. "You know about the boiler, right?"

Sharon gave a quiet answer. "I think that's why he invited you."

It wasn't enough. "Sharon, what else do you know? I'm dying here. You can't just keep these things to yourself."

"I can't?" she snapped fiercely, as angry as I'd ever seen her.

"Sorry—"

"I can keep anything I want to myself. Everyone else does. I'm dying too. You don't even know!" She walked away, striding south.

"Sharon, come on." I hustled to catch up. "I didn't mean to get you mad. You have nothing to do with it."

Sharon stopped. "We all have *something* to do with this."

"I'll keep my mouth shut from now on. Hell, I'll just sell off. I've put too many people through too much already."

She was quiet for a moment, seething. Then she said, "Don't you dare. Don't give in. You don't want to do that."

Strange. Here was Sharon, urging me to dig in against her husband. "I don't know what I want anymore. Maybe it *would* just be easier to go with the flow."

"No matter what you do, this won't be easy. For anybody."

A resort looming over the beach would hurt a lot of cottagers. But it was going in whether I sold or not. "I guess you're right," I said, more to agree than because I understood.

Sharon didn't seem to be listening. "Rob says you're putting Joan's son to work."

"That's all Joan."

"You don't want to get mixed up in that. Joan and Bryan are having serious problems."

We were near the red cottage now, where Audie's family rented ages ago and Sharon and I first fell for each other. We both went quiet and looked at the dune that rose up to Audie's old porch. Back then, it was all sand, and we laid together on it, tanning and listening to CKLW on Audie's transistor radio; today, there was just a narrow winding path through a hill of beach grass.

"Audie's looking for a place on the beach," Sharon said.

"I know."

"I bet she'd love being close to here, where she grew up."

"I'm sure she would."

"Maybe you could use the company."

I stopped walking. "You want me to take in Audie?"

"It was a thought…"

"Audie—with all her quirks and phobias."

"Who knows how to handle them better than you?"

Where was *this* coming from? Before I could mount an objection, Sharon pressed further. "No matter where she winds up, she'll be calling on you every day."

"Why can't you help? You have a zillion rooms in your place."

"She couldn't live with us. You know that. Too much commotion. She needs the solitude."

"So, stick her with the hermit," I grumbled.

"Think about it," Sharon said. "Wherever she goes, people will do everything they can to make sure she's safe and happy. We all have a soft spot for Audie. Everyone—you, me, Newf…" then she paused, as if I was supposed to fill in the rest. When I didn't, she added, "Rob. Especially."

"Okay…" She was driving at something.

Sharon reached out and tugged my arm. "As long as Audie's under your roof, nothing bad is going to happen to your cottage."

Now I got it. If Audie was living with me, Rob would stop sabotaging my place. "Maybe I *could* clear out the back bedroom."

Sharon gave me a sad, relieved smile. "I have to get back. I'm not ready for the party."

"You and me both."

A moment after parting, Sharon shouted out above the surf. "About the boiler. You don't have what you think you have."

I didn't have what I thought I had. What did that mean? Had someone taken the plate from under my washer? That guy reading the newspaper at the Wondermat. Had he been spying on me? I hurried back and was on my way into town within minutes.

On the drive, I called Audie. She was surprised to hear my voice so early. "Is everything alright?"

"It's great," I lied.

"You sound upset."

"No. It's just...you said you wanted to move back to the beach. It may be a good idea to test whether you'd really like that."

"What do you mean?"

"How about if you spend a few days with me, see how it feels."

Audie didn't say anything. I drove down the shore road to the distant heaving of the lake. Finally: "You could stand a woman's touch in there."

"Right." She was probably staring through that telescope into my mess as we spoke. "So...what do you think?"

"I can be packed in half an hour."

"I didn't mean now. I was thinking tomorrow at maybe—"

"I can't wait," Audie cut me off. "I might change my mind."

D A NEW TOMMY STORM!
For the love of God. I had a better chance of stopping Rob from flooding me out than of finding this sign vandal. For the second time, I didn't bother fixing the sign. Thankfully, hardly anyone was in the store, just an older couple waiting by a dryer. I made a beeline for the cockeyed washing machine. To my relief, the metal plate was still there. I debated going through the effort of taking it out, but I couldn't think of a better place to hide it.

I slid the washer back in place and felt it slip off the plate. It didn't matter now. I'd made up my mind; I was closing down for a week. Too much was going on. I couldn't be tethered to the Wondermat. It didn't take long before the couple's dryer stopped rumbling, but it took forever for them to fold their clothes. As luck would have it, a guy came in right as the couple was leaving, one of those yachter types. "Sorry. Gotta close. Personal emergency."

The guy froze in the middle of the room. "I need books. I've been on the water for a week. I'll take anything."

I went back into the book room. There was a spinner where I put all the bestsellers. I grabbed two handfuls. There were some good reads there—a couple Kings, a Cussler, Patterson, Grisham, even two *Game of Thrones*.

"Go ahead, take them." It was 10, 15 books; 40 bucks tops, not enough to argue over. I just wanted the guy out of the store before someone else waltzed in.

He cocked his head at the spines and frowned. "No literature?"

"Literature?"

"You know, Hemingway, Melville. The great American novel."

"These are free. And we're in Canada."

The guy filled his cheeks full of air and slowly blew it out.

"Fuck it." I pulled the stacks back behind the window.

"N-n-no, wait! I'll take them."

I packaged up the paperbacks. "Is there even such a thing as the great Canadian novel?" he tried joking with me.

"I doubt it." I pushed the bag over to him. "Canadians aren't such pretentious pricks."

A udie's door opened to my rap. Two suitcases and a duffel bag were in her entryway. Audie wasn't there, but I knew where she was. I walked in, made a show of looking around, scratched my head, and turned. "Boo," she said from behind the door, with barely any of her usual gusto. I clutched my chest and gasped, slightly less theatrically than I usually did. "You knew where I was."

"Yeah." And that was that. The game we'd played at her door for nine years was over. The suitcases were the old types without wheels. They were so heavy my shoulders immediately hurt. "This is more than I have in my entire closet."

Audie hitched the strap of the duffel bag up on her shoulder. She took a few side steps to steady herself. "You said a few days. I didn't know whether you meant a week or a month." A week? A *month*?! I hung my head and tottered out. I didn't want her to see the shock on my face.

Audie insisted we take the shore road. It was the slowest way to go. There was always a caravan of rubberneckers putzing along, peering through the thin strand of trees that separated the road and shore. I'd gone back and forth that way so many times the view no longer held allure. Not so for Audie. She hadn't been that way in years, yet she remembered details I'd long since forgotten. "Wasn't the town's first roller rink up there?" she pointed to a road leading up the bluff.

"I guess you're right. Now it's just a big subdivision."

A little further on, Audie pointed lakeside to an overgrown path through the pines. "Where are those tiny bungalows that used to be down there on the beach?"

"Washed away about five years ago."

Audie went silent for a long stretch. Then, suddenly, she cried out, "Stop!"

I hit the brakes. "What—what?!"

Audie pointed out my side window. "Kozee Korners!" she gushed with a big grin. "You never told me that was still around."

Who was I? The beach historian? "Honestly, I never noticed."

"Let's pull over!"

I couldn't say no. We parked across from the entry. Audie was out of the car before I came to a stop. She ran across the road into Kozee Korners, a 52-year-old recluse running like a giddy teen, like she would've years ago, consumed with the urgency of sketching out a new idea. When I caught up with her, she was standing where Grant used to park the Chief. In those days, Kozee Korners was never anything but packed. Now, the lot wasn't even half full. And as old as everyone seemed 34 years before, the few watching us now looked older, more broken down, like they weren't vacationing so much as suffering purgatory.

Audie was making a picture frame out of her thumbs and forefingers, swinging it from side to side, like she was about to show the meager audience how to play eensy-weensy spider. "I should paint something here," she announced.

An old guy in nothing but swim trunks, tanned and leathery, skin and bones except for a bulging rock of a gut, eyed us from his RV a few slots away, smoking a cigarette and swirling a beer by the neck. It was Dean.

"I remember you." He pointed at Audie. "You were with that hippie way back long ago, the one who always gave me the devil."

Audie dropped her hands. Her eyes darted away. Her shoulders shrank. "We'll be out of your hair in a minute," I said.

"It won't take that long," he cackled, running his hand over his nearly bald eggshell of a skull. "Say…whatever happened to that fella? Grant. He was up to a lot of no good, that one."

"He's dead," Audie said before I could. She was staring straight out at the lake. "He's a man of God."

The grin drained off the man's face. He glanced from me to her and back, slack-jawed. "Shit, I'm sorry to hear that. He wasn't such a bad kid, really."

Audie's head started shaking, yet her expression was stone still. I had to get her out of there. I took her by the elbow. "Let's go."

"Aw, come on," Dean said. "No hard feelings. Let's have a beer. We'll drink to Grant."

We were halfway across the lot, and he was still calling after us. "I know where I seen *you*. You're that Wondermat guy with the bookstore. Is that *ever* open?"

Audie wheeled out of my grasp and shouted, *"Fuck you!"*

I was more shocked than the old man. Audie never swore. She stomped across the road. The old man's head had rocked back from the jolt and stuck. I couldn't help but smile. When I got in the car, Audie didn't say anything. She had her arms folded and hands at her shoulders, like she always did when she fretted over something. It wasn't until we passed Carrie's old cottage that she spoke. "That's what it's going to be like, isn't it?"

"Like what?"

"People remembering. Not letting you forget."

She could've been talking about Grant, but I knew she wasn't. "Fuck people." I gave her knee a pat. "In the immortal words of Audie Bell." She didn't stop rubbing her shoulders, but she did manage a little grin.

I still had to park out in Rob's field, but there was a new obstacle. He'd built a chain-link fence along Newf's property line, the same fencing he used to close off his resort. We couldn't get to my cottage without either traipsing through the thick brush near the culvert or going down to the beach. I pulled the suitcases out of the backseat and got the shoulder bag for Audie to take.

"Beach or woods?"

"Woods." The secluded way. Of course. We walked back to where the road had flooded and started trampling down a new path through the woods. It was a chore lugging those suitcases through the bushes. I had to stop a couple times to relieve the ache in my shoulders. Audie was following so closely that both times she bumped into me. After we broke out into the big field that was still my backyard, I went a little way before I realized Audie wasn't behind me anymore. She'd stopped just inside the brush, concealed up to her waist in wild grass, with this lost and frightened look I hadn't seen in years.

"It's okay, Audie. No one's around. It's just you and me."

When I was in the hospital, the only one in our gang who came to see me was the last person I would've expected. I woke up from a nap, rolled my head, and there, sitting beside me, was Joan.

"You look like shit," she said in her blunt Joan way.

"I feel worse than I look."

"I'm leaving tomorrow." I assumed she meant for home. After what had happened, the allure of a road trip seemed like a child's fantasy. "Grant and I are going to Vancouver."

There was an edge of defiance in her voice. I shut my eyes and took mental inventory. Carrie, dead. Newf and I, laid up. Rob and Sharon, against the trip from the start. Audie... "So, Audie came to her senses?"

"Are you kidding?" She pierced me with an outraged glare.

"She never should've gone in the first place. She has a chance to do something special. We shouldn't have gotten in the way of her art."

Joan's scowl dissolved into stupefied shock. It felt good to hurt her like that, after all she'd done. "Aw, Christ. You don't know what happened."

"To who?"

"Audie."

That's when I learned, three days after the accident. Joan told me everything—not because she'd witnessed it, but because Grant had.

After Carrie and I drove off, Joan, Grant, and Audie kept partying. Their only rides to Holyrood were the two cars that had just left. It didn't dawn on them that they'd been abandoned, not at first. By her own admission, Joan was angry, mostly with me, but with Newf and Carrie too. She railed on about how we were already violating the spirit of the trip. Grant insisted that they shouldn't let that get in the way of their good time. So, he did more mushrooms and got Audie to go along. They'd already done more than anyone else, and Audie had been spaced out from the moment I got to the gazebo. I can only imagine what another dose of psychedelics had done to her.

An hour went by. Neither car circled back. Joan started to worry, but she was the only one. Grant and Audie weren't in any shape to be reasoned with. All they wanted to do was wander out into the pasture, lie down, and watch the stars, like we had the night we made that human circle. Eventually, Joan got fed up with babysitting them. She figured the trip was off, or at best delayed. She told Grant she was going home. If someone came back, they could drive down and knock on her bedroom window.

By Grant's account, he and Audie didn't start wondering what was going on until they realized they were hot. Whether it was an hour after Joan left or three, Grant had no idea. But they suddenly decided they had to go somewhere else. Audie was too freaked out to cut through the woods, so they walked out to Lake Range and went along the ditch to the Eighth. Grant told Joan it was hard enough keeping it together himself, but trying to control Audie at the same time was driving him mad. Whenever a car approached, she bolted into the cornstalks. Once, she emerged with a cut across her forehead that looked like a black gash in the moonlight. As they bounded down the hill, Audie got the sudden notion she was about to take flight. She begged Grant to hold her down, so she wouldn't blow away and float over the lake.

At the bottom of the hill, a group of kids called out to Grant and Audie. That was enough to spook her. She bolted down the sideroad that went south behind the cottages. Grant didn't catch up to her until she reached the little path we took to get to the ballpark. It traversed a long stretch of rolling dunes that had been left to grow wild. By day, it was easy to follow. At night, even in moonlight, with blotchy shadows dappling the terrain, you could lose your way. Somewhere in those dunes, Grant decided they were going the wrong way. They wandered around for longer than they needed to—20 minutes, an hour; he wasn't sure. All he knew was that he was afraid—and his panic was rising.

Then came the hoard of mosquitoes. Or so Grant thought. Suddenly, they were all around him, too thick to wave away. He charged through the wild grass and funhouse shadows, in one direction, then another. He was screaming and flailing his arms, falling into the sand, spitting it out of his mouth. Then

Audie was beside him. She said he needed to be still and look at the moon. She sat and put his head in her lap, and she whispered to him, "We'll find the way. We'll find the way." Grant's heart stopped racing and his breathing settled, and the night was clear, and the bugs were gone.

Audie led him out of the dunes into the open lawn of the softball field, way out in the misshapen alley of left field. To Grant, their deliverance was nothing short of a miracle. When they got to the middle of the infield, near the pitcher's mound, the same mound where Audie had once placed a red monolithic Stratego bomb, Grant fell to his knees in front of her, clutched at her waist, and began sobbing. He was certain Audie had saved him, and he could think of no other way to express his gratitude than by loving her.

For her part, Audie was enigmatic. That was how Grant described her to Joan. She stood there as he clung to her in the moonlight-flooded ballfield with her eyes closed and this big beatific smile, and she seemed, as Grant said, a thousand miles away, out of her body, neither resisting nor embracing him. They made love in the middle of the diamond. Audie's eyes swirled with stars and her mouth opened in wonder to a black void that Grant, in his ecstasy, imagined her forever inhaling. And only when they were done and lying beside each other, bodies heaving under that vast, luminous sky, did Audie speak. "That never happened before," she said. "Where were we?"

They would've fallen asleep out in the open, and everything might have turned out differently. They were already dozing off. But as fate would have it, a car came rolling down the lane toward the ballfield. Its headlights swept through the stand of trees along the first-base line and spattered Grant and Audie. As it got stronger, Grant realized the car wasn't going to turn down one of the side drives; it was coming across the bridge, out in right field.

He rousted Audie. They grabbed their clothes and bolted behind the backstop, where the woods had been cleared to make it easier to find foul balls that lofted over the screen. The grass back there was uncut, so Grant and Audie could lie down unseen and still gaze up past the canopy of trees at the stars. And there they finally did fall asleep.

At some point, Audie rolled away from Grant, got up, and wandered into the hazy darkness. He assumed she went to relieve herself, and he drifted off again. When he woke later, in the dim misty light before dawn, Audie wasn't there. He figured she'd walked home and decided he better do likewise before someone came to line the ball diamond. After all, it was Sunday, and that's when everyone gathered in the morning to play. And this wasn't just any Sunday. It was the Sunday of the August civic holiday, the day after the Boiler Beach barbecue. And the game was the most important of the summer; the annual battle of the cottagers north and south of the Eighth.

Joan told me the rest of the story didn't come from Grant. She heard it from Rob, though any of a hundred different cottagers could've recounted a similar version. That's at least how many people the game had attracted that year. It was the fiftieth anniversary of beach softball. The organizers had pulled out all the stops. For the first time, the teams had their own jerseys—the North with green t-shirts and white lettering; the south with the reverse. The ballpark itself had been decorated like never before. Bunting hung from the top of the chain link fence that ran along the first base line to protect spectators. They'd mowed the words "NORTH" and "SOUTH" into left and right field. There was a picnic table set up behind the backstop with a circle of individual trophies surrounding a team trophy as tall as a child. The ceremony planned for after the game was over the top as well. A few old-timers who played in the very first game were on hand; the Aurora Quest was catering a lunch; tubs of beer were icing down by the trophy table.

On most Sundays, the only people who showed up for the early game were players. Not that day. The bleachers behind the backstop were crammed, and beach chairs were lined up arm to arm down both foul lines, three rows deep. The smattering of kids who usually came to watch their dads play had swelled into a pack, and they swarmed after every foul ball. One of those foul balls barely cleared the backstop, hurtled over the heads of the spectators, and disappeared into the woods behind that grassy clearing. Only a handful of kids were brave enough to wade into the prickery underbrush.

Then came the shrieking, a chorus of it, so loud everyone stopped and looked back where the children were racing out of the woods. Behind them, staggering through the brush, naked and pale, scratched so badly that bloody lines crisscrossed her entire body, came Audie. A collective gasp rippled through the crowd. Rob and a couple other players grabbed some towels and ran to her aid. It wasn't until he was within reach of Audie that he recognized who she was. Her face was scratched and swollen, her body covered with welts from mosquito bites. Her dark hair was a tangled mess, and her eyes—those bright eyes that were always flickering—gazed off, bulging and bloodshot, at some unknown horror.

As they wrapped a towel around her waist and draped a jacket on her shoulders, Rob talked to her, offered words of comfort. She didn't know who he was, and never broke her gaze from whatever unfathomable demon stared her down. She was in shock, and as they hurried through the crowd, past the bleachers and along the rows of beach chairs, every face that looked upon hers got stricken with a jolt of that same shock.

They walked Audie out of the ballpark, over the bridge, and up to the open door of a waiting car. When they tried to get her into the back seat, she fought them with a ferocity Rob had never seen from her—from anyone, he told Joan later. It took four people everything they had to force her into that car. And all that while, Rob whispered to her, "Audie. It's okay. We want to help. Let us help." Never once did she react like he was anything but a stranger. Never once did Audie utter a word, though she was louder than Rob had ever heard her, grunting and growling and spluttering.

He sat beside her in the back seat as they drove to the hospital. She was in the middle, with the beach pastor's wife on the other side. As they pulled out, Rob noticed that a crowd had followed them over the bridge and out to the parking lot. Audie stared at the gawkers, numbed and stupefied, her face still smeared with blood. That's when she said the only words Rob heard from her through the entire episode. "I'm not here," she muttered so softly Rob couldn't make it out at first. "I'm not here anymore," she insisted, slightly louder, with a kind of resigned sadness. Rob told Joan he would never forget it. Ever.

Audie stayed out on the deck long after the last sliver of sun slipped beneath the horizon. I was inside, watching her from across the great room. I didn't want her to see that I was watching. She stood straight and still, arms wrapped tight to her shoulders, straitjacketing herself as the dimming light drained the features from her silhouette. South of where the sun had set and just inside my window frame, Venus sparkled through the crimson wash. Soon, more stars would appear. When I finally went out to her, she didn't say anything. I was going to keep quiet too, just stand there with her and take in the coming of the night. But I could see she'd been crying. "You okay?"

"Isn't it beautiful?" she said.

"It is."

"So beautiful you wonder why anything else matters."

"Every day we find new reasons. Or the same ones."

"I forgot my pillows," Audie suddenly sobbed out.

"Audie, I've got plenty of pillows."

"Isn't that silly? I'm standing here before this enormous beauty, and I can't stop thinking about my effing pillows."

Audie. Nearly swearing again. "It's not a problem, honestly."

"I need six. The one between my legs has to be flat. The one for my stomach, gooshy. The one that goes under my head has to be firm enough to keep my neck aligned, but soft too. And I need one I can wrap over my head to keep the sound out. Then there are the two big ones I mold up against my back."

All that came out in a fevered rush. "I can drive back to town and get them."

"No!" she cried. "Don't leave me alone."

Wasn't she always alone? That was in her place, though, high above the harbor. She was here now, right on the beach, in this mossy old cottage of mine, days after it had been broken into, then nearly washed away. "Tell you what. I'll pull out all the pillows I own. You take the six you want."

"I'm sorry about this, Tommy."

"It's alright."

Audie looked up at the swelling bruise of a sky. "I can't help it. I need those pillows. I just—I don't feel safe without them."

I thought of Audie, naked and disoriented, fighting the brambles behind the ballfield, ravaged by prickers and bugs. "I get it."

"Maybe we shouldn't do this. I don't think I'm ready."

I shook my head. "We're not going to let six pillows stop us."

Audie took her eyes off the sky and met mine. She laughed. Then she took a deep breath. "Okay. I'll keep trying. But you have to promise me you'll keep trying too."

"Fair enough." I agreed. I didn't know quite what Audie meant, but I had the suspicion that it was more than I bargained for.

I left the hospital two days before Carrie's funeral. It was suggested by my dad, actually through him by others—the police, the mayor of Ripley, close friends of the Sinclairs—that I not make a spectacle of attending. With Carrie's fame, they were expecting hundreds of people to cram into Ripley's tiny church, and more surrounding the cemetery. Media outlets across Ontario, including the CBC, local TV and radio stations, and several newspapers, had called to ask about logistics for setting up and conducting interviews. The last thing I wanted to do, my dad advised, was walk into that hornet's nest.

The police had already exonerated me of charges in the accident. But in the court of public opinion, I was anything but innocent. I was the guy who let Carrie get behind the wheel, roar through town at 80 miles an hour, and didn't try to stop her; the American who led a national hero astray. Speculation was still rife about the circumstances of the chase. Why was Newf trying to get away from Carrie—and why was she so desperate to catch up with him? If that question had been put to me, I couldn't have answered it. Newf left the gazebo out of shame or heartlessness? Carrie chased him for her belongings or answers? And I sat by and let it happen out of spite or love?

Still, I told my dad I was going to go. If I skipped Carrie's funeral, not only was it giving credence to rumors I was somehow to blame; it was dishonoring Carrie's memory. How could I not be there for the girl I loved as she left this world? It was only the day before that I changed my mind. Sharon and Rob came to see me. It was a brief, awkward visit. Sharon wanted to know how I was and told me how terrible she felt about everything. Neither of them wanted to hear my side of the story. When they were walking out, Rob let Sharon go ahead. "Mr. Sinclair doesn't want you at the funeral," he said, without a trace of compassion.

"I'm going."

"No. You're not. He doesn't want you there. Ever. That's what he said. You've got to respect that."

That day, I told my dad I wanted to go home to Michigan. He said the doctors had advised that I not travel for a week to let the skin graft heal. I told him I didn't care; it was causing me more anguish to be cooped up like some prisoner, surrounded by so many who hated me for what happened. I threw a fit. That night, my dad bustled around with more energy than I'd seen him exert in years. He stripped the beds, laundered the sheets, swept the cottage, and packed the car, all while I rested on the couch and stared out at the lake.

The next morning, hours before Carrie's service was to begin, we took off for home. When we got south of Goderich, I raised my head from the passenger window. The high, arcing wooden TROONORTH *sign came upon us sooner than expected. I held my breath. A line of cars was in the driveway. But I didn't see any people. Then we were passing the pond, with the island that housed that gingerbread chalet. There, standing alone, was Mr. Sinclair. His head was bowed, and his stunted, flipper-like hands were pressed together, tight across his chest, straining to signal a prayer. I kept holding my breath, even as I turned to watch out the rear window. I didn't breathe again until I couldn't see Mr. Sinclair anymore. When I finally did, it burst out in a convulsive gasp.*

Three weeks later, I was sitting on the bottom bunk of my dorm room in Ann Arbor. I didn't know my roommate before he barged through the door. The first question he asked was if I had a good summer. I said I did. The second was if I liked to get high. I said I did to that as well. And that's how I spent most of my freshman year; stoned and trying to forget.

Audie was waiting outside my bedroom door when I opened it the next morning. There was no room to squeeze past. She had this gritting grin that twitched like she'd been holding it awhile. And her whole body was shivering with that manic anticipation she got when she was excited. "Good morning!" she chirped.

"Morning…"

"Can I get you some breakfast?"

I'd gotten up to pee. My plan was to catch another hour of sleep. "What time is it?"

"Five-thirty or so."

I let out a raspy yawn. "Alright. I'll have some breakfast."

"Good." She slapped her thigh and marched off to the kitchen.

My table was already set with placemats that hadn't seen the light of day since the Nineties. Orange juice was poured in glasses I'd never seen before. Scrambled eggs had been mixed. Bacon was waiting in a pan. Audie was a whirling dervish of activity. I tried to cross the kitchen to the coffee, but she spun in front of me.

"What do you need?"

"Just—just a cup of coffee," I stuttered.

"Sit. Relax. I'll get it."

I retreated to my lounger. After Audie hustled my coffee out to me, I started noticing things out of place. There were new throw pillows on the couches, but looking twice, I saw they were the same ones as always, just fluffed and positioned more invitingly. Strange blankets were draped over the furniture. A vase of flowers was on the fireplace mantel. That was also where Audie had balanced stacks of the books I'd been kicking around since Bogue broke in.

"What time did you wake up?" I asked when I came to eat.

"I slept fine," was all she said.

"So, the pillows worked out?"

Audie ignored the question. "There's a lot for me to do here."

"Pardon?"

"I don't want to ruin your meal. We can talk after."

"No, it's alright. Go on."

"Well…" She held out a folded paper towel. "It happens to be quite dusty in here." She opened it to expose a black smudge the shape of her hand. "This was one pass across the top of the fridge."

"Yikes."

Audie sensed my embarrassment. "The good news is that dust is 75 percent dead skin."

"That *is* a relief," I replied. Bless her heart, Audie couldn't have picked a more humiliating way to come to my defense. What could be worse than suggesting someone was confined in a fog of their own shuffled-off casing?

"That being said, a good dusting would improve the atmosphere in here, don't you think?"

I put my fork down. There wasn't going to be any eating until this was over. "I do." I felt like I was agreeing to something every bit as momentous as marriage.

Audie cleared her throat. "And that one towel swipe got me thinking." She pointed to the kitchen floor. A patch of linoleum was whiter than the rest. "I mixed a little vinegar and soap, took a rag, and wiped that clean in less than a minute."

I didn't even know I had vinegar. "You don't say…"

"And I'm hesitant to bring up the condition of the washroom."

"Alright." I threw up my hands. "What's your point, Audie, before I lose my appetite? Would it make you happy if we had a cleaning day?"

"Heavens, no. I wouldn't ask you to do that."

"That's a relief."

"I'll do it myself."

"Audie. Come on. You're here to relax, sit on the beach, put your toes in the water. You don't want to be doing this."

"This is exactly what I want to do. This would make me happier than anything."

"Cleaning my washroom?"

"Yes."

"Fine." I stabbed my eggs.

"And you get to go about your day," Audie kept selling. "Isn't this just perfect?"

"Perfect."

"And, maybe," she added, tentatively, "if you have time, you can get those pillows."

I broke out laughing. "Not a fan of my pillows, eh?"

"Heavens, no. How do you get any sleep on those?"

As humbling as it was to let Audie root out the grubbiness of my life, it was liberating. Forced from the cottage, with the Wondermat closed, no one left to confront, and no hidden booze, I had nothing but time. I'd been meaning to fix the deck steps; today was the day for it. After I dug out the gully, I found a YouTube video on how to build a staircase, wrote down what I needed, and headed for town. When I swung open the back door, Bruce was standing there, the second person blocking my way that morning.

"My mom told me to come down."

"Well, if it isn't Bruce!" Audie had snuck up behind me.

Great. Trapped between these two. "Yes, and he's coming shopping with me."

"I could use some help," Audie said.

I turned to her, flabbergasted. "You just said you wanted to do this by yourself."

"It's more than I thought. There's the mopping and sweeping, and rugs and windows. I can't get this done by the party tonight."

Incredibly, Bruce had a hopeful look on his face. To do housework. With a strange lady he met once at Grant's funeral. That's how bad things must've been in the Duncan cottage…or how unappealing the thought of shopping with me was.

"If you want to help clean my cottage, then I'm not going to argue. This is Audie." I stepped aside. "I think she mentioned at the funeral, she's an old friend of your mom's."

"My mom told me about you," Bruce muttered.

Audie's smile fell. Not a good start. "Well, she's in charge." Bruce crept past like I might change my mind and toss him out.

"You okay?" I asked Audie.

She rallied, puffing her chest, breaking out a big grin. "Bruce and I are going to make a great team. Aren't we, Bruce?"

Audie never did go to the Rhode Island School of Design. After she recovered physically from her nightmare in the ballfield, her parents drove her home and started getting her professional help to heal mentally. She was diagnosed as manic depressive with a schizophrenic episode brought on by psychoactive drugs. But there had been some debate among doctors as to whether she should be treated for schizophrenia. Years after the fact, it was agreed that Audie had something called schizoaffective disorder, a combination between schizophrenia and bi-polar symptoms. Whatever you want to call it, Audie was not in a good way. The family got her on a regimen of medication and psychotherapy and kept her at home for over a year.

She didn't come back to the beach the next summer. Neither did I. But a few days into my second year at Michigan, I got a call from her. She had gotten a hold of my dad, and he gave her my number. She told me she was feeling better, taking her meds, doing her therapy. Her dad had gotten her a job as a bank teller, and if all went well, she'd get her own apartment. I asked Audie if she still planned to go to art school. She said she hoped so, then asked how I was doing. I talked about my decision whether to go to business school, like my parents had been urging, or switch to English, like I wanted. Audie interrupted me. She meant how was I handling what happened the summer before? I told her I never thought about it. Then I said I had to go.

The next time I heard about Audie was four years later, when Grant came to visit me. I was teaching freshman comp at the time and working on my master's thesis. Faulkner. Absolom, Absolom! *We went to the Del Rio, an old hippie bar in Ann Arbor, and got roaring drunk. He waited until we staggered back for my apartment and made a detour into the big cemetery near campus before he brought up the subject of Audie.*

He'd learned that her mother had died of bone cancer, and that Audie had spiraled again. She lost her job at the bank, tried another job at a video rental store, got fired there too, and had to move back in with her dad. He was never really the nurturing sort, and his overbearing efforts to help her only made matters worse. He wanted to put Audie in a treatment facility, but her sister Allie would have none of it. She had married a power plant worker from Owen Sound, and she stepped in and agreed to take care of Audie on a trial basis. That had been going on for over a year.

"I saw Allie once at the piper's parade, and she told me Audie would love for a friend to come visit," Grant said. "So, one day I drove up to Owen Sound, and knocked on their door. Allie went to get Audie and I heard a scream. Then Allie came back and told me Audie wouldn't see me, and she was sorry, but I shouldn't try again."

We stumbled on in silence through the moonlit cemetery. "I wonder…" Grant let hang in the chilly air.

"You wonder what?"

"Is it all of us she doesn't want to see, or just me?"

That was the first time Grant asked me to plead with Audie for a chance at redemption. The next summer, I drove to Owen Sound. When Allie answered the door, she knew immediately who I was—that kid whose football she used to steal. There was no argument from Audie about letting me in. I was surprised. Of the guys in our gang, I was the least close to her. Newf had saved her from the offshore breeze. Rob had gone out with her. And she'd lost her virginity to Grant. Our meeting was quick, 15 minutes tops. She asked what I was doing; I told her about my efforts to become a professor. I asked how she was doing; Audie started with a shallow answer, and when I didn't change the subject, went deeper. The drugs she was taking. The dreams she had. Her thoughts of suicide. All very casually imparted, like she was talking about the weather.

Thank God Allie was there. She steered the conversation into safer waters. Then I found a moment to say I had to be somewhere. Later that summer, conscience got the better of me, and I drove out to visit again. That time wasn't much longer than the first, though I did make a point of telling her that Grant asked if he could visit. She said no and offered no further explanation.

Thus began a ritual I kept for nearly 20 years, through my marriage, after my divorce, even into my darkest drinking days. Every summer, once at the start and again near the end, I'd drive up and sit with Audie. I told her my troubles, but never went too deeply into them. And she'd share her struggles with me, in more detail than I needed. And even though I pleaded Grant's case once a summer, I was quick to back off when she declined to see him.

This ritual went on until I quit teaching at age 43—after Barb Bowen convinced me to resign—moved to Boiler Beach, and bought the Wondermat. That summer, before I had a chance to visit Audie, Allie showed up at my back door. She warned me that Audie was going to suck me into a fantasy she was having of getting her own place closer to Boiler Beach. Allie didn't think Audie was well enough to go it alone. She said all I had to do was say no and her sister would give up the whole pipe dream. "Gladly," I told her.

By the time I showed up in Owen Sound, I was ready for Audie to raise the subject. I had my reasons marshalled and my performance down pat. I nodded thoughtfully, brow furled, mouth twisted, as she laid out her plan to find a place in Kincardine by the harbor. And when she asked if I'd help get groceries and check on her once a week, I tapped at my chin, looking for all the world like I was giving it due consideration. I told her this was a serious decision, and she needed someone she could depend on. I said I was so preoccupied getting my business off the ground I wasn't the most reliable person.

Audie pushed back. "You and Allie can alternate weeks."

Excuse number two: "I don't even know my legal status in the country. I might have to go back to the States for the winter."

"I'm okay living in Owen Sound for the winter," she said.

I finally leveled with her. "Audie." I put my hand on her jittering leg. "I'm in no condition to take on a responsibility like this. I've been having my own troubles with drinking."

Audie sagged into the couch. I was sure I'd gotten through to her. Then she roused back up, leaned in close, and said, "We can help each other!" She offered me a shaky smile of reassurance. Of comfort. Audie: comforting me.

I don't know what it was—the despair of being cornered, the fragility of confessing, the sincerity of Audie's offer—but I broke into tears. Like I hadn't since I was a child. I hid my face, my body wracked by the sobbing. Audie put a hand on my heaving shoulder. "We'll get through this, Tommy. Together."

"Okay," I finally surrendered. "Okay. I'll do it."

After I picked up Audie's pillows, I went to Timber Mart and got everything I needed to rebuild my deck stairs. Audie barred my entry to the cottage when I got back, proclaiming the results of the clean-up effort were a surprise. I was able to pry Bruce away to help me carry the supplies to the deck, but he lingered too long. Audie came out, stood over us, and told Bruce the floors needed mopping.

"But Mr. McTavish needs help out here."

"No, I don't."

"Two more hours," Audie demanded. Bruce scowled at me like I was a traitor.

I made more progress on the stairs than I expected, laying the concrete landing, scabbing a new board to the bottom of the frame, doing the math for the stringers, and cutting them out. It had been years since I'd bothered with a home improvement project. I didn't think I still had it in me. I would've gone further too, but Audie came outside with Bruce, announced they were finished, and reminded me that we needed to be at the party in an hour.

I followed them inside. The first thing I noticed was the smell. It was mostly cleaning products, but there was a floral scent, too. Sure enough, I saw flowers throughout the cottage. And there were candles too. Candles! More than that, everything sparkled—the windows, the furniture, the floors. Them most of all. The planks in the great room looked like they'd been replaced by lighter, younger wood. The kitchen floor gleamed so clearly it mirrored the cabinets above it. The whole place felt brighter, more cheerful. I was delighted that Audie and Bruce had transformed the place so quickly—and ashamed I'd let it lapse into such dreariness.

"Wow," was all I kept saying as I walked to the back door. When I turned there, Audie was waiting in the kitchen, a big, expectant smile. Even Bruce, hanging back, had this eager grin I'd never seen. "This doesn't even look like it belongs to me."

Audie closed her eyes as if in contented meditation.

"Look at the floor," Bruce said. "Look how bright it is!"

"You can't believe how hard he worked on that." Audie put her hand on his shoulder.

"Hardest job I've done here." It was strange to watch them, standing so closely together, both beaming with satisfaction. And only hours ago, the two were virtual strangers.

After Bruce left, Audie took me on a tour of the less apparent results of their handiwork. The washroom glistened like everything had just been installed. The light bulbs had been changed too, so the room seemed bigger, glossier. Before we left, she filled the sink, then drained it. The water swirled right out; it usually seeped down the pipes. "You don't want to see what I yanked out of there," Audie said, as if she would like nothing more than to show me.

We ended the tour in my room. Like everywhere else, it was brighter, more polished. The curtains were open. I went over and closed the ones that looked out on Bogue's cottage. "Funny," Audie said, pointing out the slit I couldn't manage to cover. "Somewhere across the water, my telescope is looking right at us."

Any other time, knowing her view was locked onto my window would've bothered me. "It's not looking if there's no one behind it." She started to laugh, then stopped herself and gazed off, like I'd posed a riddle.

There were clothes set out on my bed. Audie had pulled out an old pair of white draw-string linen beach pants and a blue-and-white striped seersucker shirt. I couldn't remember the last time I wore them, or what possessed me to buy them in the first place. They were the sort of clothes you'd see on the beach's cocktail set. Was there a time when I wanted to be among them? "Oh no," I groaned, realizing suddenly why they were laid out.

"Please? You look so handsome when you clean up."

"And when the hell was that exactly?"

"You wore this once to Owen Sound. It was like you'd sailed in on a boat to find me."

"Audie, I doubt I can even fit into these."

"They're loose fitting. It's a drawstring."

Here I was again. Trapped. "Okay," I said. "Okay, I'll do it."

Audie didn't realize parking for the party was in the ballpark until I turned that way from Tout's Grove. She squirmed in her seat. I hadn't considered that she might not want to revisit the site of her public shame. "We can park in the church grove."

"No," Audie was adamant. "We're going to the ballfield."

I had no intention of arguing with her. Still, as we crossed the little bridge that carried the road into right field, Audie got more agitated. Head thrown back, eyes closed, she was struggling to get control of her breathing. Then she began mumbling an anxious, stuttering chant: "*Oh-God-oh-God-oh-God-oh-God.*"

"It's going to be fine. We'll park way out in left field."

"No." She pointed out an open spot near second base.

We got out of the car. Audie walked to the pitcher's mound and stopped. She peered in toward home plate, staring down a phantom batter. The backstop looked like the gate to a tunnel that burrowed into those woods where she'd lost herself. Then Audie straightened up and gave a shiver. With that, she stalked off the mound and headed for the footpath to the Gartons.

I caught up to her in the clearing behind the vaulting glass palace. Through the smoky aqua glass, partiers milled about on all four floors. There was a crowd outside too, on the huge deck that surrounded the giant shimmering cube. The two people we came upon first, at the back edge of the yard, were Rob and Newf. Audie headed toward them. I grabbed her by the wrist.

"Not now." They were arguing. We couldn't hear about what, but Newf was jabbing his finger at Rob, and Rob was shaking his head. My guess: the retention pond. Much as I would've loved to hear, I didn't want to get into it before we even made it to the party. I steered Audie toward the deck.

Not fast enough. "Tommy!" Rob called out. He was striding our way. If the run-in with Newf had rattled him, you wouldn't know it. And you wouldn't think, only days before, I was *persona non grata*. Rob approached Audie and me with arms outstretched. I backed away. Audie stepped into his embrace. "Look who's here!" Rob gushed. "My favorite person."

While he fawned over Audie, Newf and I exchanged glances. He was still simmering from his words with Rob.

"And look at Tommy!" Rob was saying now. "Mr. Beach Boy!"

Damn these stupid duds. "I put him up to it," Audie said.

"My original plan was to come as my bedraggled old self, get rip-roaring drunk, and embarrass the shit out of you," I deadpanned. "Audie talked me out of it."

Newf coughed out a laugh. Rob stared at me flatly, deciding whether or not to get angry. He broke into a lopsided grin. "I knew you'd do the right thing, Tommy. You always rise to the occasion."

There was some deeper meaning in there, no doubt. But I let it go. Audie was getting anxious. I could tell by the way her eyes traced all the people circulating in the glass monolith. This would be her big moment, stepping across that threshold back into the world of the beach.

"So...we just head on inside?" I asked awkwardly to break free.

"Actually," Rob said. "I've got something I want to show you."

Audie had already taken a step away. "I should really—"

"Newf can help with that," Rob interrupted. "You can show Audie around, right?"

"Sure. I could use a pretty girl at my side." Audie blushed and hid a smile under her hand. Bless his heart, Newf could still charm her when he needed to. I watched them walk toward the crowded deck and thought of all those times when we were kids, and they walked together down the beach, ahead of Sharon and me.

"Gotta be honest," Rob said. "I didn't think you'd show."

"If it weren't for Audie, I wouldn't have. Now, what's so damn important you'd actually invite me to this party?"

I could tell by how he propped up that half-grin that he'd made another decision not to take the bait. "Come on," he said with a chipper lilt. "I think you'll find this interesting."

I knew it had to do with the boiler even before Rob flicked on his woodshed lights and shut us in. From a slot between the workbench and the far wall, he pulled out a rusty slab, big as a sidewalk block. Rob strained to get it up onto the counter. I could've helped, but I knew he was about to reveal something that wasn't going to be any help to me. Once he got one end resting on the edge of the workbench, Rob slid the metal onto the counter. Right away, I saw the hole where my part fit near the jagged flap. Rob stood back and motioned to the slab with one hand, presenting it like it was about to speak for him. So, he'd cut a bigger chunk out of the boiler. So what?

"I was worried there for a while. Bogue was getting all kinds of crazy ideas. I'm glad the answer turned out to be so easy."

"Burning more off the boiler? You don't think people are going to notice that?"

"And if they do?"

"They'll know someone's messed with it. Now, it's obvious."

"That it is," Rob agreed. "It's a lot more obvious that souvenir hunters scavenged the boiler. It's also much less obvious why."

Something wasn't clicking for me. And Rob seemed amused by that. "But I still have the piece with the tractor logo."

"You mean this piece?" Rob poked his finger in the hole his slab contained. "The one that fits right here...but nowhere on the boiler anymore?"

He waited. Finally, I got it. If I couldn't show that my piece fit on the boiler, then who was going to believe a story that it had been blow-torched off to hide the fact that it came from a tractor?

Rob had me. That's why he'd been so cocky about it at the gate to his resort. I'd lost the only thing that made me a threat. Sure, my cottage was still standing in the way of completing his dream. But time or money would take care of that.

"It was a crummy thing Great Grampa Bud did," Rob said. "I always thought that. But when a lie goes on so long, and so much good comes of it, why ruin it with the truth?"

"Because it's the truth?"

Rob huffed like that was a preposterous guess. "You don't want to be the one telling everybody Boiler Beach isn't real. You know more than anyone how crazy people get when you kill their legends." It was a low blow. I was stunned he even had the gall to go there. On this of all days. Rob must've realized how it came across. "Shit, I didn't mean it that way. Honestly."

"I get why strangers blame me for Carrie, but you—"

"I never blamed you," he was quick to correct me. "I feel sorry you had to take on that whole burden. I do."

"Who do you think you're talking to? You didn't even want me here at this party."

"That's got nothing to do with Carrie. What I don't like—what I've never liked—is what you've let that accident do to you."

"What I've let it *do* to me?"

"You've made it your grand excuse. For drinking. For acting out and getting in fights. For holing up in that hovel of yours and pushing away anyone who tries to reach out to you."

"That hovel of mine. That's what this is really about."

"Oh, for God's sake." He grumbled out his exasperation. "You know what, Tommy? Keep your cottage. I don't give a shit. Sit there feeling sorry for yourself and let it cave in on top of you. I'm done giving you a way out. I'll just let time take care of things."

"Meanwhile, you'll keep helping it along, draining that pond."

"I'm going to do what I have to do. Sorry you're in the way." He started tugging the metal slab off the counter.

"That includes ruining the boiler," I said.

Rob stepped back and flexed his hand. The counter had a lip, and he was having trouble getting the slab over it. "I wish it hadn't come to this."

"Blame it on the low tide," I joked, stepping in to help. What was the point in fighting anymore? I'd lost any leverage I'd had. And Rob was who he was. His biggest beef with me was that I was an asshole. Guilty as charged.

I was drifting through a dream. Wandering from room to room, everyone I passed was familiar, some by contact, others by reputation, most from memory. It was those people, those transfigured apparitions, who were most unnerving. There was Bill Murray, who I hadn't seen since I was eight, hale and hearty as his father had been, still with a shock of floppy red hair, still with that elastic smile. And there Gord Jeffrey, a friend of my father's, with that same smirk and swooping pompadour, no longer jet-black but bone white. And there Donnie Sibbald, wide-eyed as ever, whose black lab Snort chased tennis balls so incessantly the vet had to pump sand out of his stomach. And Nancy Honeyman, the little girl I used to play hide-and-seek with from behind the corners of our two adjoining cottages. All these people, so fixed in my memory, suddenly passing before me, all but strangers.

I promised myself I wouldn't drink, but the longer I went without finding Audie—the more drinks I saw in peoples' hands, the more waiters I passed with trays of champagne glasses—the thirstier I got. Had I not spotted Audie when I did, silhouetted in sunlight across the open room on the fourth floor, I would've grabbed the next flute of champagne thrust in my face. She was talking to the Fergusons. Loudly. I could hear her over packs of other people. She had a glass of wine and she seemed to be enjoying herself. I didn't want to hover, so I took a seat behind her on the big hearth that surrounded the central, four-sided fireplace.

"It was very disorienting," she was saying. "People tell me I was naked. I can't imagine. But you were there, eh?" Sid Ferguson was much more discreet in the exchange. I could barely hear him acknowledge her. By the sounds of it, they'd been on the topic a while. "Anyway, I've been on medications ever since. It's what they call schizoaffective disorder, somewhere between schizophrenia and bipolar. Crazy and moody, that's me." I got up off the hearth and came up beside Audie. "Ah, and here's my keeper. Do you know Tommy McTavish?"

Bernice Ferguson warded me off with a brittle smile. Sid squeezed her elbow. "We know Tommy." He guided her away. "It was nice to see you, Audie. Glad you're doing better." With that, they hurried through the crowd.

"Audie, you can't be announcing your problems to everyone."

"I'm not announcing my problems. I'm opening up. You should be happy I'm willing to talk about things."

"Not so the whole room can hear."

"The whole room," Audie scoffed. "Look around. Nobody's listening. Nobody cares."

"I heard you from over there." I pointed to the center fireplace.

"That's because you were snooping. Bernice was very interested in my condition. She's a psychologist. She's writing a book."

"Oh, a book. Well, then."

"For your information, they didn't walk off because of me."

Like I didn't know that. Still, it hurt to hear Audie voice it. "I'm well aware. You don't think I see the way people look at me?"

I didn't point it out for Audie's pity, but that's what she gave me. "I'm sorry." She put her hand on my wrist. "Would you feel better if we walked around together?"

I laughed. "The Outcast Squad on the prowl."

"You don't have to mock everything."

"I'm sorry. I'm just not very good at parties anymore. Go on. Enjoy yourself."

I started to leave. "Promise you won't drink," Audie shouted over the crowd. I threw my hands up. "I'm sorry!" Again, with the shouting. "Go have fun."

Have fun. I wended my way back through the partiers. *Have fun.* How exactly did that work in a roomful of people without a drink in hand? The doors to the Garton's elevator opened. I hit the button for the first floor. I could find a seat on the beach deck away from everyone and turn my attention to the lake. The elevator had three glass sides to watch the stacks of partiers as I descended. The fourth side, where the buttons were, was mirrored. There I was—or was it me?—long hair shorn, clean-shaven, bright, loose flowing clothes. Who was I trying to be? The doors split my reflection in two. Wendy was standing before me, holding a tray of champagne flutes. I hadn't seen her since she biked past me in Holyrood.

"I thought you said you wouldn't be here," she said. The doors started closing. I stepped out. Wendy let the elevator go. The champagne sprayed prisms of light across the side of her face.

"I got a late invite," I told her, voice lowered. Sharon wasn't too far away from us, bustling around her big open kitchen.

"About Ripley. I don't want you to get the wrong idea."

"It's none of my business."

"Is that *really* how you feel?"

The doors opened behind me. A couple ambled past us. The woman grabbed a flute as an afterthought. Oh, to make that decision so easily. "Well," I said, stepping aside, "I won't keep you."

Wendy got on the elevator, eyeing me the whole way, even when she was inside, and the doors started closing. I couldn't read her face. Angry? Disappointed?

"Look who cleaned up," Sharon called out from her kitchen.

"Audie put me up to this."

"Apparently she's a good influence." Sharon took a pan of cookies out of the oven. "You remind me of that innocent boy who came calling on me so long ago."

"Hardly."

She took off her oven mitts and found a glass of wine. "What were you and Rob doing in the woodshed?"

"You don't want to know."

"I've heard a lot of that lately."

"Well, do you?"

There was another pan of cookies cooling. Sharon started taking them off, arranging them on a tray. "I could probably guess."

"Why are you hiding in the kitchen?" I changed subjects. "This is your party."

"It's never my party."

"Okay. Carrie's party."

"It's Rob's party," Sharon clarified. "It's *always* Rob's party."

With the pan of cookies cleared, Sharon started making new balls of dough. I would've asked if she needed help, but I knew the answer. I looked back before heading out on the deck. She was refilling her wine with the kind of hefty pour I'd give myself.

To my disappointment, the front deck was more crowded than inside. Couples everywhere; by themselves, clustered together. I started around the perimeter of the huge platform, its railings and benches glass like the house, so you had that infinity mirage of walking on the lake. It was still a good hour away from sunset. There was no excuse for me to be turning my back on the party.

I wasn't ready to be around so many people. But it was more than that. It was the presence of that draped figure that I couldn't bear to see. Carrie's statue loomed over the crowd, hidden under a red velvet blanket, rolled out on a cart in the middle of the deck, bigger, it seemed, than she was in life. Part of what made it so tall,

I could tell, was the golf club angling up in its follow through. I'd heard they were planning to put her statue near the first tee at the golf course, but they were unveiling it here. I couldn't watch that happen, not in front of so many people. I hurried to go back inside and find a place to be alone.

"Tommy!" A hand tugged at my arm.

It was Joan, and she was with her husband Bryan. Just the happy couple I wanted to run into. By the looks of it, they'd had their share of drinks. Bryan was double-fisting it, martini in one hand, flute in the other.

"Well, if it isn't my boy's warden," he said with a sneer.

"Bryan, you promised to be nice."

What had Sharon told me? Stay away from the Duncans. I pointed inside. "I have to…"

"Stay!" Joan insisted before I could invent an excuse. "Bryan's just being an asshole. Aren't you, darling?"

"I'm being an asshole." He slurped his martini.

"Honestly, we appreciate your taking Bruce. We needed time to sort a few things out."

"More than a few." Bryan raised his flute, toasting to that.

"Well, I think he's done his time," I said. Maybe now I could put an end to Bruce's visits.

"We'll see," Bryan said. And he slid a glance over to Joan.

"You're such an adorable shit!" Joan laughed a little harder than the moment warranted. And she gave him more than a playful shove. A slosh of champagne leaped from his flute to the back of a woman's dress. He mocked a horrified face. Joan laughed again. "Isn't he an adorable shit?"

Bryan and I eyeballed each other. "He's an adorable shit," I agreed, then hustled away.

I couldn't get inside fast enough. A wave of people rushed out the double doors and pushed me back. Suddenly, there was a hush, and Rob was speaking. I wedged into a spot up against the house, Carrie's statue shielding me from Rob's view. He said Carrie had been taken too soon. He lamented that we never got the chance to see what she'd become. He spoke about how the country viewed her as a legend, but beachers loved her for who she was. He told everyone that, thanks to our charity, Carrie's statue would be a permanent reminder of her impact on our lives. He hoped that every time we walked across the new greens they were installing to replace the bumpy "browns," they'd think of Carrie. And he invited everyone to the first annual Carrie Open charity tournament.

I couldn't listen anymore. I squeezed through the packed congregation and made it to the doorway. Just inside, a collective gasp rose. Rob had pulled the red covering off the statue. And there was Carrie, sculpted in a rough painterly style, with finger-smeared dabs of bronze. It had the feel of an impressionist rendering, but the way her hair flowed as she followed through on her golf swing, the molding of her cheeks and lips, her hollow, distant gaze at the drive that would forever rise in the sky, it was quintessentially Carrie, more true than if the sculptor had adhered to reality.

I looked away. Seeing her there, as if hewn out of my memory, it was too painful. I retreated into the house. Sharon wasn't in the kitchen anymore. No one was. Next to a tray of cookies was a half-filled bottle of vodka, the top already off. One more glance around. I grabbed the bottle, downed a quick swig, caught my breath, and took a longer pull.

"Jesus, Tommy!"

Wendy was behind me. "Aw, shit." I put the bottle down.

A hail of chanting came from outside. The clinking of glasses made as much noise as the voices. Wendy came forward, head down, and went straight to the fridge. "It must have been upsetting to hear that," she said, granting me that much as she pulled out another bottle of champagne.

"There's no excuse."

She stared at me as she unscrewed the cork's wire cage. "Bo is giving me a chance to manage that restaurant in Ripley."

We were going back to that. "It surprised me. That's all."

"Am I not supposed to look out for myself?"

"I'm happy for you. What do you want me to say?"

"There's nothing more to it than that."

Then why the protesting? Why go biking with Bogue? "Okay."

She put the bottle down and rubbed her forehead. Then she said, "The price for the raise was my grandma's butter tarts."

"Fucking-A," I let slip. "That son of a bitch got the recipe."

"Not yet. Only if I don't make 15 dozen a week. That's the deal. And for that, I get the run of the place in Ripley."

"You sure you can keep up?"

"I'll have to." I didn't realize how close she'd come to me until then, so close I must've been leaning in myself. I kissed her. She shuddered and backed away. "What are you doing?!"

"I don't—I don't know."

"You kiss me now?" Wendy looked hurt. "*Now?*"

People were flooding into the cottage. We backed away from each other. Wendy went to intercept them with more champagne. I went to find Audie. We'd made our appearance. We'd witnessed the ceremony. Time to go. Just my luck: she was sitting at a side table with Newf, and Joan and Bryan were across from them. I had half a mind to turn around, leave her, and head for the car. She'd get a ride back. I'd catch hell from everyone, but that was better than staying and doing something worse.

"There he is!" Joan slurred. "Sit down, Terrible Tommy. Have a drink."

"That's probably not a good idea." By the mortified look on Newf's face, he didn't think so either. "You ready to go, Audie?"

"Go?" She laughed. "The party's just starting. You haven't even had anything to eat."

I hadn't noticed that people were eating. They all had fancy paper plates in front of them with pulled pork sandwiches, potato salad, corn on the cob. "I'm not hungry."

There was a slap on my back. "What'd you think?" It was Rob. He left his hand on my shoulder, but he was talking to the table.

"That statue," Audie said. "It's like Carrie's here with us."

"Well, if she was," Joan said, getting up from the table, "she wouldn't want our glasses empty. Can I get anyone else another?"

"Long as you're going," Bryan said.

"I'll have one more," Audie chimed in.

"Audie…"

"Two glasses of wine. I think I can handle that."

"Don't be such a downer, McTaffy," Bryan joked.

"You'd be amazed how much that statue set us back." Rob finally took his hand off my shoulder and sat. "The material, the artist. Big name, too. You could buy yourself a Porsche for that." Newf turned away and looked out over the lake. I bit my tongue. "I'm just saying." Rob realized, maybe, how he'd come off.

"I'll take the Porsche," Bryan said, with a big, stagey laugh.

That tore it. "Who the fuck asked *you*?"

Sudden silence. Bryan's grin took a while to fall. When it did, his face settled into menace.

"Hey, come on," Rob tried to make peace. "It was a joke."

"I don't get it." Newf shifted in his seat to face Bryan. He was calmer than I was. But I knew Newf, how he held his emotions in. I could tell; he was just as mad as I was.

Bryan held that hard squint another second—who knows why? to show us he wasn't backing down?—then he wobbled his head and sputtered like a deflating balloon. "*Shiiiitttt.*" He stretched the word out. "I'm sorry. Don't listen to me. I'm drunk."

I'd used that same excuse more than a few times myself. Now I realized how flimsy it was.

Joan was coming back with drinks. And Sharon was beside her, holding a bottle of champagne in both hands. "When's the last time this ever happened?" Joan gushed. "Everyone's all together!"

If by "everyone" she meant the old gang, well, two of us were missing now, and always would be. Still, Audie and Rob, and even Newf, celebrated Joan's spirit with a rousing cheer. Who was I to deny the significance of the moment?

Wendy came up beside Sharon with a tray of champagne flutes and set it on the picnic table. Bogue lingered behind her. He was never part of the group, and had no real claim to be there, but I wanted Wendy to stay.

"Let's have a toast," I said. "Bogue, get in here. You too, Wendy." I snatched up one of the champagne bottles and started pouring. Audie looked like I was waving a gun around. Rob folded his arms and stared me down.

"Oh, for Christ's sake," Joan said. "Give him a break. It's one lousy glass of champagne."

"How many times will we get a chance to do this?" I lobbied everyone. Wendy thrust her flute in front of me. I looked up at her. It was just a quick glance between us, but I could see her concern.

"To Carrie and Grant," I said, when everyone had their fill. We clinked glasses and drank.

"To being here with all of you," Audie added.

I was done with my glass and ready for another.

"The last supper," Joan mused as I refilled glasses.

"I sure hope not," Sharon said.

"To betrayal!" Bryan blurted out. He thrust his glass into the circle. No one touched it.

"What's your point?" Newf challenged him.

"The last supper," he said, spreading his arm's wide. " 'One of you will betray me.' "

"Does that make you Jesus in this analogy?" I jumped in. Two swigs of vodka, a quick glass of the bubbly. It was already getting to me. I could feel myself loosening, getting bolder.

"Hell, I'm not sure who Jesus is, or Judas," Bryan backpedaled.

"You have to remember the Central Principle of Bryan," Joan broke in. "My husband is an asshole."

Bryan raised his hand. "Here, here!"

I downed glass number two and poured another. *Fuck it.*

"Weren't you going easy?" Sharon was the one to speak up.

"I was," I said, getting up from the table. "But now that it's okay to be an asshole…" It was the best I could do for such a quick getaway. I headed to the front deck. Maybe now, with everyone eating, I could take in Carrie's statue without attracting attention.

Rob caught up with me. "Tommy." He grabbed my arm and spun me around. *Here it comes. He's kicking me out.* "You want to see what's hiding behind that fence on the bluff?"

"I already saw on the billboard. Shiny, happy people lounging around and making pilgrimages to scrap metal."

Rob ignored the jab. "I've got a scale model in the bunkhouse. I'm showing it to a few investors right now. Want to have a look?"

He motioned to the stairway that went from the side deck to the bunkhouse, that relic of his dad's cottage where Grant stayed during the winters. Bogue was already leading Newf down there, and Bryan was tagging along. Audie and Joan were getting up from the table, laughing together and following Sharon to the back patio. Wendy was clearing our mess. I caught her eye. She straightened up. Again, I couldn't tell if she was angry, sad, worried, or what. But she kept on staring.

"What do you say, Tommy?"

I followed Rob to the stairway.

"This is it!" Rob proclaimed, sweeping his arms out wide. "The entire view of Mariner's Vista, in one fifteen-by-nine-foot model." We were standing where the lake would be, the model resting on a makeshift platform that lifted it to our bellies. We were like Audie's giant Sorry aliens storming Boiler Beach. There were seven of us pressing against the edge of the sprawling diorama. Paul Ackert, the tractor collector, and Hugh McLean, owner of the Spider's Web, were on either side of Rob. Bogue was with some banker on the model's south end. Newf and I were shoulder to shoulder on the north side, me within arm's length of a dark red nub no bigger than a Monopoly house: the boiler. Bryan stood away from the diorama, head swiveling around, taking in everything but the resort model.

It was an impressive work of art; I'll give it that. The model took in a swath of Boiler Beach from the Eighth to cottage 145, near Carrie's old place, and it went inland from the second sandbar, up the bluff, past Lake Range, into Newf's pasture to the east. Rob said the scale was 200 to one, so the 15-foot stretch depicted over half a mile. The part of the model representing Mariner's Vista formed a sort of tipped-over H, the run of land Rob had bought from Newf, the same stretch of shoreline, then a wide belt connecting the two, including the area around the gazebo, the ravine down the bluff, and the Garton stretch of cottages. My cottage was smack dab in the middle of that. The property that didn't belong to the resort was made of bone-colored balsa with a minimalist style. By contrast, the resort property was frighteningly realistic. The water we were leaning against glistened and rippled like a breezy Huron day.

The resort itself was a marvel. Perched on a ledge nearly a foot higher than the base platform, dozens of bungalows, each glittering on the inside as if their owners turned the lights on against this early evening, spanned the entire length before us. And each one was so meticulously constructed, you could see the woodwork of the deck railings, the shimmering glass on every window, the burnished glow of the copper metal roofs, the detail of the tiny three-eighths inch occupants. In the middle of these bungalows, a gigantic swerving, free-form pool with tentacles of gleaming water enveloped the complex. All around the pool, there was a sandstone walkway with beach umbrellas, lounge chairs, vacationers, even the occasional tiki bar, staffed with miniature bartenders.

The vegetation looked as real as if you were seeing it out the window of a low-flying plane. The trees, bushes, and boulders in the landscaping and the lodgepole pines sloping from the bluff all had unique character. The banks along the ravine were especially impressive. Rob envisioned two walking paths with winding steps made of granite slabs following the pristinely aqua stream down a succession of waterfalls until it emptied into the lake. At the mouth of the stream, which would be at least 10 yards wide if the scale was right, kayakers and canoeists were coming out and going in. My gully; now an inviting river.

How far they could actually paddle upstream was one of the few details of the resort that was unclear. That's because the whole area around my cottage, from the high dunes to the open oval of my backyard, had been stripped of model elements—no buildings, no trees, no landscaping, nothing except the base paint. It was a different effect than the bone-colored sections that weren't part of the resort. At one point, something had been there—that was obvious—but it had been denuded, and now looked as though it was covered with a huge grey tarp. What point was Rob trying to make by doing that? What message was he sending me? Why even invite me here to witness the magnitude of what would someday be surrounding me? That, I suddenly realized, was the answer to my questions. Rob wanted me to see exactly what I would be up against, to envision what life would be like in the midst of the resort crowd, cut off from the rest of the cottagers.

"Holy shit," Hugh, the Spider's Web owner, exclaimed. "It's a goddamn Ritz-Carlton. No wonder you need so much money."

"It's an investment," Rob corrected him. "An investment."

"How many units?"

"Ninety-eight."

"And not a restaurant on the property."

"That was the deal, Hugh. They're all coming into town."

"Then those tiki huts are going to have to go."

"Or you can run them."

"I like the sound of that," Hugh said, rubbing his hands.

"And the landing strip's still going in over here?" Paul Ackert piped up. He motioned to the far-right side of the model, where Concession 8 and Lake Range crossed at the top of the hill. All the property south and east of there, just a six-inch square of which was represented in the model's corner, was owned by Ackert.

"Nothing's changed with the air strip," Rob told him. "I still want to buy that land."

"What's with the armada?" Newf broke in, waving his hand over the kayaks and canoes at the mouth of the gully and further out into the lake, close to where we were standing. There, miniature sailboats leaned away from a phantom wind.

"It's a resort. You've got to have some boats to rent."

Newf reached over near the plate-sized oval where my back field should have been. He picked up a stray canoe tipped on its side. It was about an inch long, and there was a tiny man at the stern with a woman at the bow. "Looks like someone capsized in the gully," he said, displaying the canoe in his open palm.

"I guess that broke off." Rob went to take it.

Newf pulled his hand away and showed it to me. I could see it just fine from where I was. But Newf eyed me like there was something more to the piece that I was missing. "What's with the steamroller treatment to my place?" I decided to press Rob.

"It's what it looks like, McTavish," Bogue blustered. "A giant parking lot."

"They paved paradise…" Bryan weighed in. He was still craning his neck to take in the rest of the bunkhouse.

"I didn't have them model up your property," Rob explained. "You told me you're not going to sell, so I wasn't going to get ahead of myself."

"What a guy you are."

"Not counting the chickens…" Bryan chimed in again. He'd gone around to the other side of the model, where the two bedrooms were, and was peering into a half-open door.

"Looking for something?" Rob raised his voice.

"This is not your average bunkhouse," Bryan answered.

"What do you think?" Bogue asked the banker. "More or less than you expected?"

"I'd have to see numbers," he said noncommittally.

Bryan hadn't taken Rob's hint. He pushed open the door of the second room, glanced back—Rob and the banker were talking money at this point—then took a half-step inside. What was he doing? The answer came a moment later, when he took his phone out, shielded it at his side, then started poking buttons. Seconds after he finished, there was ringing in that bedroom.

Bryan had found the owner of his mystery number. "Phone," he announced, as if it wasn't clear how the sound was made.

"Don't worry about that," Rob said. "It's telemarketers. No one knows that number."

"Somebody does," Bryan muttered.

Bogue and the banker were on their way out. Paul Ackert said he better get back to his wife. Rob was disappointed to see everyone go. "I stocked the fridge full of beer. We can stick around." The land line rang again. Rob looked past Bryan, dumbfounded. "That never rings."

"Someone's anxious to find you," Bryan innocently suggested.

This—was—not—*good*. Rob and Joan together? I couldn't believe it. They were so unlike each other, both when we were young and now, in our fifties. Joan was this free-spirited dreamer who had no time for the dreary practicalities of life. Rob was a hard-bitten, bottom-line businessman who wouldn't do anything unless there was an angle to it. *And yet.* And yet Rob *was* the one who got Joan her first gig at the Windsor so many years ago. And he'd paid a lot of money under the table to keep her there. She wasn't grateful at the time—far from it—but maybe over the years, she'd come to appreciate the power of a man who could get things done.

Just as I backed away from the model, Bryan came up against the other side, along the ghostly strip of Newf's land. He had his phone out in front of his face. He gave it one poke, then held it up, screen side out, and waved it like he was saying goodbye. The bunkhouse phone rang again. This time, Rob didn't say anything. He seemed frozen, staring at Bryan across the replica of his dream.

"*I* know this number," Bryan glared back, his voice trembling with restrained rage. "I've had it on my phone bill for 18 years."

Whether Newf gathered the import of this moment, I couldn't say. But when I headed for the door, he followed. Bryan didn't let me leave unnoticed. "Where are you going, Wonderman?"

"I've seen what I needed." I threw my hands out at the model. "If the idea was to impress on me how fucked I was, it worked."

I left without waiting for a reaction. I was halfway up the stairs, when Newf called out, "What the hell was *that* all about?"

"Trouble for Rob," I said, not bothering to stop. "And Joan." That's where I was going: to warn Joan. As long as Bryan had been obsessed over this and as drunk as he was, there was bound to be a clash. By the time I got up the stairs, I heard shouting at the bunkhouse. Off the deck, there was enough cover from the trees overhanging the stairway that they couldn't spot me, but not so much I couldn't see them. Newf leaned over the railing with me.

"Do you think I'm stupid?" Bryan bellowed, following Rob along the bunkhouse path.

Hugh put a hand on Bryan's chest. "You need to calm down."

I thought fists were going to fly, but Rob got between them. "I'm telling you, I don't come up here in the winter. If you have calls from that number between November and May, they aren't mine. I've rented this place in the offseason to Grant for ages."

"The dead guy," Bryan huffed in disbelief.

Newf straightened. He started back for the stairs. I grabbed his arm. "Don't make this worse." He pulled out of my grasp but settled back on the railing.

"Ask anyone," Rob said. "Grant's stayed here every winter for 20 years." There was some muttering we couldn't hear, then the men backed away from each other. Bryan had his head bowed, and he was shaking it, maybe crying. Rob was patting his shoulder.

"We have to find Joan," I told Newf. "Get her out of here, down the beach, back in the woods, anywhere but near him."

Newf nodded and hobbled off to the back of the house. I hurried to the front deck. Joan was in the far corner, holding court with a circle of men. "In a week, I'll be in Vancouver," she was saying as I rushed over. "A week later, Alaska. Then in a month, Japan." I waved at her over the huddle. She ignored me. "Six weeks of singing and dancing. I don't know if I'm ready for it."

"Joan!" I barked out. All the faces turned my way. "I need to talk to you." She was peeved to have her audience distracted. "It's about Bruce," I lied.

She gave a big dramatic huff. "Teenagers..." I hurried down the main stairway to the lake and ducked under the deck. Joan straggled behind, breathless, exasperated, and very drunk.

"What's the li'l shit done now?"

"It's not Bruce. It's Bryan. He found his mystery phone number." She screwed up her face. "We were in the bunkhouse. Bryan, me, Newf, and Rob."

Her mouth dropped open. She started looking all around, as if Bryan might pop out of the shadows.

"He's angry. And drunk. And he's looking for you."

"What happened?" She burst out a flurry of questions. "How do you know? What did he say? What did Rob say?"

There wasn't time for this, but I had to tell Joan enough to get her moving. "We were in the bunkhouse. Rob was showing us his resort model. Bryan saw the phone in the bedroom and called his number. It rang, Rob dismissed it, and he called it again. At that point, I knew there was going to be trouble. Newf and I left—"

"Newf knows?"

"Just listen. We left. Then they came out and we heard them arguing. Rob told Bryan it was Grant who lived there in the winters. That settled things down, but I'm worried Bryan's going to come after you and make a scene."

"Oh, he'll make a scene, all right."

"You can sneak down the beach. Or head back to the ballpark. Hide out in the dunes until things blow over."

"Things won't blow over." Joan was rubbing her temples now.

I had to prod her. "But we don't want a scene here, right?"

"No." Joan leveled me with a grim, calculating stare. I'd never seen that look before. "I'll wait it out in the dunes. You know the old swingset back by the woods?"

"Yeah."

"I'll be there. I can't go home tonight. I can't."

I knew what she was implying. "I'll come find you when we're ready to leave. What's your number? I'll text you."

After Joan disappeared around the side of the cube, I went back up on the deck. It was the sort of night that promises a sunset right to the last minute, only to disappoint. A haze of deep blue clouds smothered the sunlight. I found myself standing in front of Carrie's statue. Lifted up on the cart, she towered over me. Ten minutes ago, I was taking in a resort 200 times smaller than real. Now, I beheld Carrie's avatar, forever cast in that split-second of fluid majesty, peering with hollowed eyes at her distant, rising perfection. Without the sun to burnish the bronze, Carrie's face actually looked more authentic, even though I could see more plainly where the sculptor had smeared the impressionistic dabs. There was a vulnerability to the permanence, as though her immortality hadn't come without a struggle, and whatever the opposing forces were, however futile their attempts, they would always be reaching for, stroking, smudging that unassailable beauty.

I was tempted myself to reach up and touch her cheek. Her face wasn't so high above me. I even held my hand out, just to get a feel for the bronze. As my fingers made contact, I pulled back. What was I doing? Was that opposing force inside me? Was that who I was—an unwitting adversary to Carrie, clinging to her memory and defacing it at the same time?

"Where the *hell* is my wife?" Bryan was lurching through the living room, inside the doors to the deck. "Where is my wife?" he thundered. "Where is my *fucking* wife?!"

He was knocking into furniture, spilling drinks, careening toward me. Could he see me through the screen? I backed away from Carrie's statue. If there was going to be a fight, I didn't want the statue to get knocked over. Before Bryan could get outside, Newf and Rob rushed up and grabbed him. I hurried to the side deck, went around back, and looked through the glass walls for Audie. She and Sharon were in the kitchen, oblivious to the clash across the cube.

"Time to go, Audie," I demanded this time. She and Sharon gaped up at me. "*Now.*"

Audie's face flushed. "Well, I don't want to. We're having a perfectly pleasant—"

"You know what's going on in the other room?" I cut her off. "Hear that?" In fairness, you *did* have to stop and listen to discern the noise from the usual party hum. "Joan's husband is out of control. He thinks she's having an affair and he's making a scene."

Sharon knocked over her chair getting up. "Rob and Newf have it handled. But I don't want to get in the middle of this."

Audie gasped. "What did you do?"

"Nothing!" I couldn't very well say that Bryan accused Rob, or that it had come out that Grant was the culprit. Not in front of Sharon. "It's just—he's drunk and lashing out. He came into my store the other day and all but accused me."

"Where's Joan?" Sharon wondered.

This wasn't going well. "I don't know. Let's go."

"Shouldn't we stay and help calm things?" Audie countered.

If I only could've pulled her aside, told her what was happening, how we were helping Joan get away. But Sharon was standing between us, eyes working back and forth, trying to put everything together.

"We just have to go," I insisted again. "Trust me."

"Well…" was the sum total of Audie's response.

"I can take her home." It was Wendy. She was standing at the sink behind me. How long had she been there?

"Oh no. You have to stay and clean up." Bogue ambled into the conversation. "That's our deal."

I should've known this was why Wendy was working the party. "It's a fifteen-minute break," I jumped in to defend her.

"Funny. I didn't know *you* got to decide when my employee took a break."

"For God's sake, Bo," Sharon muttered.

If it hadn't been so long since my last drink, I would've taken a swing at him. Instead, I said, "Be a little decent, Bogue. Just for once in your goddamn life." I might as well have taken a swing. He came toward me. Wendy got in his way.

"I can wait until the party's over," Audie offered.

Bogue waggled a finger at me, then stomped away.

"Thank you," I said to Audie. Then I turned to Wendy and bowed my head. She managed a brittle smile. This time, I knew exactly what was going through her mind. She was ashamed. Maybe of me. Maybe of Bogue. But more than likely, Wendy was ashamed of herself, that she was in this position of having to take orders, of losing the freedom to do as she chose.

I left without another word, dodged partiers on the back deck, then headed up Rob's drive. Just before it opened into the outfield down the third-base line, I heard thrashing in the bushes, muttering and swearing. It was Bryan. Rob and Newf must've walked him out while I was trying to get Audie to leave. Now, I was glad I hadn't convinced her. I tried to hurry by unseen. No such luck.

"Where the fuck *you* goin'?" he spluttered when I passed.

"Leaving." I kept moving. I heard him tromping through the underbrush, then kicking up stones behind me on the ballpark lane.

"Hey! I'm talking to you!"

Against my better judgment, I turned. We were out in the open now, on what the softballers called the warning track. Cars were parked on either side of the lane. I couldn't get Joan until I got rid of Bryan. "It's been a long night. Why don't you go sleep it off?"

"Why'n't you go fuck yourself?"

Getting rid of Bryan… I have to admit: in the moment, the thought of coldcocking him and dragging his body into the woods crossed my mind. "Whatever the hell's going on, I've got nothing to do with it."

"Yeah? Where's Joan? Someone said you were talking to her."

Whether he was bluffing or not, I wasn't about to admit any-thing. "I have no idea what you're talking about. Now, I'm going to get in my car, drive home, and go to bed. Or, we can settle this another way. But you're drunk, and I'm not. So…" I let it hang.

"I wanna check your car." He swept his arms in big, cockeyed loops across the sea of metal surrounding us. The force of his swinging sent him careening into the trunk of a car.

"You want to check my car? Fine. Let's go."

"Fine," he mumbled, regaining his footing. He took a couple unsteady steps my way, wobbled, then fell back on the seat of his pants. "You guys. All of you! You're all in it, covering for each other, protecting a dead man. Oughta be ashamed of yourself." I left him there, sitting in the outfield ranting. "This beach is evil. You hear me? It's *evil*!"

I got in my Lincoln, drove over the bridge and down to the base of Tout's Grove Hill. There, I pulled over and gave Joan a call. No answer. There's another hill between Tout's Grove and the Eighth called Davey Hill. I drove down there and wound back south along the private lane by the dunes. This was the place where Grant got lost the night he slept with Audie in the ballfield.

I thought about that as I parked the car in the high grass beside the private lane. Joan still wasn't answering her phone. I headed for the old swingset where we'd agreed to meet. It was more over-grown by the base of the bluff than I expected—prickers and creepers and who knows how much poison ivy. I started to worry. It was hard to even find the swingset. I called again. A ringing rose up in the high grass. I followed it and got close enough to see the light from Joan's phone go black. Then, I stumbled over a log, or so I thought. It was Joan. I shook her. Nothing. Harder. She groaned. Thank God. She'd only passed out. The booze was just part of the problem, I realized as I propped her up against one of the swingset poles. She reeked of weed, too.

"What are you doing?" she asked, her voice slow and thick.

"We were meeting here, remember? To get away from Bryan."

"You took so long…" Joan started listing. I got to her before she hit the ground.

"We've got to get you up and in bed. Can you stand?"

"Sure as hell give it a shot."

It took twice as long to get out of the dunes as it did to wade into them. Joan wasn't exactly cooperative. She'd go a few steps, then stop shuffling so I had to drag her. Sometimes she'd even dig her heels in and refuse to go, wondering what we were doing. When we got to the car, I was congratulating myself for keeping her from falling. Then, as I went to open the door, she spun out of my grasp, did a clumsy pirouette, and banged her head against my hood on the way to the ground. Luckily, there wasn't a cut. But a purple knot rose out of her forehead as I got her in the car.

At my cottage, there was a whole other struggle getting Joan from where I parked in Rob's field, along the new path through my woods, and across my backyard. I thought of the diorama as I lugged Joan along; if only this field was as bald as that model suggested. When I finally deposited Joan in my lounger, I was more out of it than she was. I plunked down on the couch across from her and started dozing off.

"Got anything to drink?" Joan woke me.

"Anything *to drink*? No. I got rid of it all."

"Bullshit."

"I did."

Joan wriggled up out of her slouch and tried to stare me down. Her eyes kept floating off. "So, what the hell did Bryan do now?"

"I told you. He was in Rob's bunkhouse. He saw a phone. He tried that number."

"Then what?"

"I didn't hear everything. Bryan accused Rob of having an affair with you. But Rob managed to talk sense into him. He said he let Grant stay there in the off-months."

Joan's chin dropped to her chest. She closed her eyes. I thought she was going to drift off again. Then she gave a sudden snort and her head jolted back. "Poor Grant."

"So, what's going to happen? He already knew you were having an affair. How does knowing who it is make things worse, especially when the guy's dead?"

"You're using logic," Joan said. "That's your first mistake."

"So, then…what?"

Joan took a long rumbling breath. "There will be yelling. He'll push me around. Slap me. Then comes the guilt. Then the self-pity. Then begging. And then," she threw out her hands, "we make up."

"And it's not going to be different this time?"

"We have a lot of fights, Tommy."

I wasn't going to press the matter. The best thing for Joan was to get to bed. I helped her to the washroom. Then, while she was cleaning up, I got my bedroom ready for her. Thanks to Audie, there wasn't much to do. Joan even noticed that much. "Why's your place so clean?"

"This is what happens when you leave Audie alone for four hours." Then I remembered: "Your son had something to do with it too. He mopped the floors."

Joan fell on the bed as if the news knocked her off her feet. "My Bruce, mopping floors."

"He was damn proud of it, too."

"He really does have a good…a good…" Joan's face was suddenly overcast with worry. "You know, deep down," she added, long after she'd trailed off.

"He's a good kid," I translated for her.

Joan wobbled her head. Then, as if it was too unwieldy, she toppled onto the pillow. I'd turned down the covers, but Joan struggled to get under them. She kept kicking at the blankets, even as I tried to settle them over her.

"I'm scared to death what's going to happen next week, when he's all by himself."

"All by himself?"

"I'm leaving to work that cruise."

I didn't recall her telling me a date. I thought it would be closer to the end of summer. Anyway, wouldn't Bryan be there to look after the boy? When I asked her, Joan shook with wheezy laughter. "That's what I'm afraid of. At his best, Bryan is negligent. At his worst and most vindictive…" She let it hang.

I didn't know how to comfort her. So, I just sat on the bed, in the crook of her near-fetal constriction. She tightened around me and closed her eyes, deflating with a long sigh. I waited for her breathing to steady, then carefully slipped out from under her arm.

I would've liked to sleep too, but I'd relegated myself to the couch, and had to keep the lights on for Audie. At eleven, I started to worry. Maybe Audie wanted to leave, and Bogue was making it hard on Wendy. I called her. When it started ringing, I heard a faint echo. Then it got stronger. Then, as if the act of calling had served as a summons, Audie poked her head in the door. Wendy followed her in, holding her ringing phone like a police badge.

"Sorry we're late, Dad." Audie giggled.

"I, for one, am touched you were worried enough to call," Wendy added.

"It's not like Rob to go this late," I offered as an excuse.

"Oh, the party's still raging," Audie said. She was tipsy, I could tell by the lilt in her voice. Not drunk, but definitely buzzing.

"So, how did you get away?"

"She just told Bogue she was leaving," Audie answered. "You should've heard her."

"Probably get fired." She retreated to the back door.

"He's not going to fire you," Audie told her. "He wants your tarts. You've got nice tarts."

Wendy laughed. "Yeah, I hold the power. The power of a slave. I can do what I please, as long as what I do is make tarts."

Had Wendy been drinking? "You two alright?" I was between them now, Wendy at the door, Audie in the middle of the kitchen.

They each glanced past me to the other. "We had a joint in the ballpark," Audie confessed.

Audie. Taking drugs. On the ball diamond. At night. "Whose bright idea was this?"

"Aw, come on, Tommy." Audie sensed my anger. "We took a couple hits. I told Wendy what happened to me there. And we just talked. We figured a lot of things out, didn't we?"

"Yes, we did. Yes—we—did." Great. The two in cahoots. "I need to get back," Wendy said.

"You should walk her," Audie said. "It's dark out there."

Wendy and I stared each other down. "I can do that."

"There's really no need."

"Okay." I wasn't going to push it.

"Well, then," Wendy hesitated. Then she was out the door.

When I turned to Audie, she was glaring at me. "What?"

"Don't let her wander into the dark like that!"

"You heard what she said. There's no need."

Audie shook her head. "You really *are* a lost cause."

I hurried out the back door and ran until the light from the bare bulb on the back of my cottage faded out. It really was dark. When there are no stars out up here and the trees wall you in, you can barely see your hand in front of your face.

"Wendy," I called out. No answer. "Wendy?"

"What?" She was well off to my side, over by the gully.

"What are you doing over there?"

"I can't believe you don't have lights out here."

I finally spotted her shadow shifting against the varied dark of the trees. She was way off course. "I never had to walk out here until Rob closed my driveway." I was close enough now to put a hand on her shoulder and turn her the right way. "See the grey gap in those trees? Follow that."

We started off together. Halfway across the field, Wendy said, "I've got my bearings." I just kept walking alongside her. We came to the edge of the woods, where I'd worn that path out to the road. "You can go back now," she added.

The hardest part was ahead of us; getting through the woods. But Wendy seemed so adamant about my leaving, almost angry. "If you'd rather I left..."

She stopped abruptly. "You know what I'd rather?" She was on me before I could react, taking my face in her hands, pulling herself near. And then. The kiss. Hard. Hungry. I barely had a chance to kiss back. Then, as forcefully as she locked onto me, she disengaged.

"If you're going to kiss me after all these years, do it like you mean it."

"I'm sorry."

"You're sorry. *You're sorry.* You're always sorry."

"I know. "I'm—" I caught myself.

"And you're old. And you're a drunk. And you're angry and sad. And you should've never gotten me into this."

"Into what?"

"Oh, for God's sake." She stomped into the woods.

"That's not the path," I called after her.

"It's not a jungle," she said, thrashing off course again.

No, but there was poison ivy. "Here. Let me—"

"I can find a road. I'm not helpless."

I stood there, listening to Wendy thrash. Then I went into the woods myself, creeping quietly along the path she should've taken. When I got to the back, she was still flailing in the brush, heading toward the culvert. The vision of Grant lodged there in that tangle of branches, doll-eyed, ghostly pale, flashed in my mind.

"You alright?"

She stopped flailing. "Where are you?"

"On the road."

"Keep talking."

"I'm here," I said, waving my arms in the near pitch-black.

She popped out of the woods right in front of me. Her breathing was hard and shaky. "Wendy…"

"Don't." She hurried past, silhouette receding on the road. Her car door opened. The headlights went on. Then they swung my way, hit me full force. I was blinded. I didn't see them swing away. For a second, I didn't see anything at all. Then, when my sight came back, Wendy was driving away.

The walls were rumbling before I even realized the night was over. Dim light leaked through the front window. How early?

The clock on the fireplace mantel said just after six. More thumping. This was the third time I had to wake to this crap. I hustled out to the kitchen to stop it before anyone else woke up. I knew who it was before even opening the back door.

"Where is she?" Bryan hadn't changed from the night before. He rocked on his feet and wouldn't look me in the eye.

"Where is who?"

"Cut the shit. I know she's here."

It was worth a try. "She's sleeping, like everyone else."

He stopped rocking and scowled at me. "Wake her up."

I'm not my friendliest in the morning. That's what comes from all my digging disputes. "Why don't you get the hell off my property and wait for her to come home when she's ready?"

He stepped closer. There was just a flimsy screen between us. We were face to face, inches away. He pointed his finger at me. "I'm not leaving until I talk to my wife." He jabbed the screen in front of my nose to punctuate the threat.

"Suit yourself," I went to close the door I could dead-bolt.

"Wait." Joan was there behind me. "What's your problem?"

"I'm leaving," he said. "Right now."

"Where to?"

"Home. Chicago."

"Now?"

"As soon as I walk away. And for good."

"Where's Bruce?" Joan was suddenly alarmed.

"Back at the cottage."

"No-no-no-no!" She rushed past me and banged open the screen door. "You can't do that," she said, facing him now. "You know I'm headed to Alaska in four days."

"That's *your* problem." Bryan backed away.

Not fast enough. Joan gave him a two-handed shove. "You son of a bitch. You never did want me to go. Now, you pull *this* shit?"

He fended her off. "I think I've got a pretty good reason."

"Spare me your outrage. You always knew. I never denied it."

"But you never told me who."

"What's the difference?" she thundered. "And...he's dead."

Bryan hung his head. "I can't do it anymore," he said, so quietly I could barely hear. Then he turned and walked away.

Audie came up beside me. Joan ran after Bryan. "Take Bruce. Just for my trip. We'll figure things out when I'm back."

They were out in my backyard now. I stepped outside. Audie came out with me. "Should we do something?" she whispered.

"There's nothing to figure out." Bryan's voice was calm, cold.

"What am I going to do with Bruce?" Joan bawled. "What am I going to tell him?"

"Tell him the truth." Bryan stalked off. Joan kept calling after him, but he put up his hand and hung his head. He'd heard enough.

Joan shuffled back toward us, wiping away tears. Audie whispered, "What *is* she going to do?"

What did Sharon say? Don't get mixed up with the Duncans. And who'd be the worst person to drag into that mix? Here they were, parked now at my dining table, Joan spilling out her heart, Audie drinking it in. I kept my mouth shut and made coffee.

I got enough of the gist: Bryan knew Bruce wasn't his. And he punished the boy for it, mostly with coldness, sometimes cruelty. Still, as long as he didn't know the father, he didn't disavow Bruce. Then, over the winter, when Joan claimed to have a meeting with the cruise line in Detroit, Bryan got suspicious. He dug through phone records. That's when everything changed. He confronted her. She denied having an affair at first, then admitted it, then refused to tell him who her lover was. He withdrew from her, got harder on Bruce. In the spring, he insisted they attend the Duncan reunion. Joan knew that Bryan would be looking for the source of that number, but she was sure he wouldn't find it. When would he ever be in the Garton bunkhouse? And here we were; everything out in the open. Bryan knew it was Grant that Joan had been seeing for 18 years. He knew who Bruce's father was, so he no longer felt obligated to pretend. It didn't matter that Grant was dead. "That's how little love he invested in Bruce," Joan told Audie.

When they came to the question of what to do with Bruce, I told them I had to dig out the gully. Morning ritual, I said. They waved me away without so much as a glance.

No rain and a full gully. Again. How long would I have to endure this? Was I one bad storm away from disaster? I told Newf I'd help him with Chloe. What if I had to drive her to the States? That's one thing Bruce could do: keep an eye on the gully when I was gone. But with Joan leaving, would he even be around? Besides, what claim did I have to his time? He'd long since worked off his beer stealing lie. If anything, *I* owed *him*. If only there was a way…a way to what? Fix the gully? Stop the runoff? Kill the resort? Make peace? What? *Let it go…just be done with it.*

I was trying to think. *Trying to think. Think, McTavish. Think.*

"Tommy! Are you alright?"

It was Sharon. She was gazing at me with relief. "You scared me. I kept calling your name and you just kept standing there."

I shook my head clear. "Sorry. I was somewhere else."

She laughed wistfully. "And how was it there?"

"Not great."

"That makes two of us."

I had a pretty good idea what she was talking about. "What's a party without someone making a scene?"

"What happened?" She asked like that's why she came.

"What did Rob say?"

"You know Rob. Everything's no big deal."

I snuck a glance up at the cottage. The last thing I needed was for Joan and Audie to see us and get the bright idea of coming down. If someone had been conducting an affair in my place, I wouldn't be too eager to chat with them. I stabbed the shovel into the sand. "Want to take a walk?" Sharon nodded warily. "Think of it as a beach glass hunting reunion," I joked.

She fished in her jacket and pulled out a handful of pieces. "A pretty good haul for these days. No greenies, but a chunky."

"No sapphires, either."

Sharon laughed. We walked north. She came back around to her question. "I take it there's more than what you said last night."

"I told you about how Bryan figured things out, right?"

"Newf did; from the phone in the bunkhouse."

"And you know it had been going on for 18 years?"

She bent down for a piece, came up with a shell, and discarded it. "No, I didn't."

"All the way up until last winter, I guess. That's when Bryan got suspicious and started checking phone records."

"Last winter?"

I'd gone too far. Did Joan just tell us that this morning? "I thought that's what he said." I shrugged and went on, eyes on the strip of stones at the edge of the shore. Fat chance of finding any glass with my eyesight.

"And he accused Rob." Sharon prompted me.

"At first, yeah. Until Rob explained the Grant arrangement."

"What on earth are they going to do now?"

Should I tell her what I knew? How Bryan had left and what a predicament that put Joan in? While I debated, as luck would have it, I saw a green sparkle in front of Sharon. "Ha!" I roared in triumph, bending to retrieve the greenie after she stepped over it.

"Did I miss that?"

"You did," I crowed, handing Sharon the piece, like always.

"I just can't imagine what they're going through."

"Bryan left this morning." Why not tell her? She'd find out soon enough.

"Left? For where?"

"Home. That's not the worst of it. He took off without Bruce. And Joan's flying out to work that cruise this Wednesday."

"Who told you that?"

"Joan stayed with us last night. I guess Bryan can be violent when he's angry and drunk."

"When did all this happen?"

"About 20 minutes ago. He came banging on my door, had it out with Joan, told her Bruce was her problem, and left."

Sharon shook her head, trying to take it all in. I started looking for beach glass again. I'd said enough. Sharon caught up with me, and we walked side by side, again in silence.

"Who would do that to their son?" she finally said.

I realized that I'd left out the most important thing. "That's just it. Bruce isn't his son. Not by blood anyway."

Sharon wouldn't look away from me, so I didn't from her. We kept walking. And I waited. She was bothered. I could see that. There was a lot to be bothered about. She tried a couple times before she found words. "How would he know that?"

"Joan said he's known for a long time."

"Then why now? Why after raising him his whole life?"

I shook my head. "Who knows? He's upset. Maybe he drives a while, realizes what he's doing, and has a change of heart."

"And maybe he doesn't."

She'd stopped. I had to turn and face her. "Maybe not. What I don't get is, okay, Joan was having an affair. He already knew that. And he knew Bruce wasn't his. All he really learned is that the guy she was seeing is dead. Grant is dead. It's over."

Sharon squinted like she'd spotted a piece at my feet. I was convinced enough to look down myself. "It was like knowing, really finally knowing, severed the last strand of his love," she mused. "The second there was nothing more to know…anger, suspicion, jealousy…they were no longer useful. There was only forgiving. And he couldn't do it." Sharon stepped forward, reached down, and actually did extract a white wafer of glass from the bed of stones in front of me. Then she hurried ahead.

"What kind of love is that?" I scrambled to catch up. "Leaving when you can't be angry anymore, when love is the only thing left that will save you?"

"An imperfect one." Sharon gazed straight ahead, to somewhere along the winding shoreline. "Is there any other kind?"

Why did I feel like we were arguing? I knew there wasn't any such thing as perfect love, at least not a human kind. So, what was Sharon driving at? She knew my marriage had fallen apart, that I was to blame for it. She also knew about my love for Carrie, how I wouldn't let it go, even without hope of forgiveness. "Maybe it's Joan. Maybe she never asked to be forgiven. You know Joan."

"You can't love alone," Sharon said finally. I couldn't tell if she was agreeing with me or not. Either way, it was her final word on the subject. She veered off the rocky strip we were following and went to the lake's edge, where the water made the stones gleam.

We kept walking; for what reason, I didn't know anymore. I didn't mind it at first, but then we rounded the little point at 130 and I saw the boiler in the distance. I was about to say I needed to get back when a flash of blue caught my eye. It couldn't be. A piece that big was always plastic. But there it was: a sapphire, as big as an eyeglass lens and thicker. A chunky, sitting, unobserved on the hard sand in the middle of a stream of footprints. Just waiting there. I picked it up. There was etching: part of what looked like a shield, two concentric arcs spanning the diamond-shaped glass, and under them faint lettering: MAGN.

I took it down to the water, dipped it in so the glass glistened. "Look at this." I caught up to Sharon. She brought it close to her face. It was only then that I noticed she'd been crying.

"It's incredible." She stifled a sob.

I pretended not to notice. "M-A-G-N," I spelled out the faded letters. "Milk of Magnesia. You think it's from the same bottle?"

I didn't have to remind her of the piece we found as kids. The one with MILK on it. The one I lost. "How *could* it be?" Sharon started crying in earnest. "Remember then?" she smiled gamely.

"I still go to that dune and kick around for it."

"What I mean is, remember that time? Remember *us*?"

"Oh."

"It was so sweet, Tommy. We were so innocent, so vulnerable, so...so alive."

"We were, weren't we?" I smiled back, but I could have just as easily cried too. I was touched that she hadn't forgotten what we once had, that as young as we were and as fleeting as that time was, it still held a place in her heart. Like it did for me.

She held out the piece. "Oh no. That's yours. The gods placed that in the open for a reason. They're giving me a second chance."

"The gods..." Sharon held the sapphire up to catch the light. She pocketed the glass and continued on.

"I better get back." Sharon just kept walking. Was she disappointed I was breaking off? "I'm going to clean out Grant's RV," I called out, as if that would cheer her up.

J oan was gone when I got back, and Audie was on the deck, setting up her easel. "I'm going to try waves, like my mother used
to do," she said, squeezing paint onto her palette.

"I have to go to the Chief and box up Grant's belongings."

Audie set the palette down. I was sure she was going to ask to
come along. I needed a reason why she couldn't. "We should take
him in." She eyed me, nodding with a tight mouth.

It took a second to catch her meaning. "Bruce? No—"

"She's really in a bind, Tommy. And we have the space."

"Who's this *we* you keep talking about?"

"Well...I just knew you wouldn't want to do it alone."

Was she suggesting what I thought she was? "Audie, if Bruce
is staying here with me, you can't help unless you're here as well."

She smiled. "I'll stay for as long as you need."

"I wasn't asking you."

"Well," she said, arching that one brow at me. "I'm just saying,
I'm available to help."

Bruce and Audie, here all summer; it was preposterous. "Think
of everyone you'll be helping," she called out before I got inside.

G rant's RV looked like he'd just stepped out to run an errand.
It didn't smell that way. The first order of business: dump
the black water in the toilet and grey water from the sink. That
meant driving the Chief out of the dunes and down to the RV park
off the highway. The beast rumbled to life on the third try, stuttered, coughed, then revved up when I laid on the gas. Getting out
of the dunes was treacherous enough, but not nearly as nerve-
wracking as emptying the tanks. I'd done it before with Grant, but
that was 34 years ago. Luckily, there was a guy at the park who took
pity and showed me how to do it.

"This is Grant Rose's RV," he observed, as we waited for the
black water to drain out. "I was damn sorry to hear of his passing."
My God. Did Grant know everybody? "Couldn't have been more
than two weeks ago I saw him right here with his girlfriend."

"His girlfriend?"

"Sure seemed like it, the way she was clinging to him."

"What did she look like?"

"You been out to Holyrood for ice cream?"

"Yeah…"

"The gal that makes the scoops."

I don't know how long I stood there taking that in, but the guy had to nudge me and point out that we were done.

The whole ride back to the beach and long after I'd reparked and started in on the cleaning, I was dazed at what I'd heard. Grant and Chloe. *Her* clinging to *him*. An 18-year-old girl and a 52-year-old man. What in the world was he thinking? Having an affair with Joan was bad enough, but given their history, I wasn't surprised by it. This was unconscionable.

And how did it square with the story Chloe told about Grant making advances on her at the gazebo? As I suspected, there was more to it. A lot more. Here I was, days away, maybe, from driving Chloe to America. Was I abetting in a crime? Would more evidence come out? If some old guy at an RV park had seen Grant and Chloe behaving like more than pastor and disciple, others had too. Probably some of Chloe's friends. All it would take is one of them to walk into the OPP station, and everything would change.

There was more work to do in the Chief than I'd bargained for; vacuuming, emptying the fridge, wiping down everything, boxing up Grant's clothes. I went late into the afternoon, propelled by adrenaline alone. As I was cleaning the windshield, I noticed a blue sheet of paper crumpled up against the dashboard and glass. I pulled it out and opened it up: "STONY POINT FIRST NA-TION PARKING, WINTER 2017-18." I was about to toss it in the trash. Then I froze.

Last winter. That's where Grant had lived. Hadn't he told me that a few weeks back when we sat around his firepit? And it wasn't just one winter, either. What did he say? Rob kicked him out of the bunkhouse two, three years ago. So…

I folded up the parking pass and put it in my pocket. The discovery about Chloe, and now this. Grant may have been having a secret romance, but it wasn't with Joan. And that meant…something so much worse.

It was almost six by the time I loaded the boxes from the Chief into my car. I called Audie to tell her I was going to skip dinner, take the books to the Wondermat, and clean Grant's clothes before I sold them to Victoria's Vintage Threads. I expected her to be disappointed, but she sounded relieved. Just as I was about to hang up, she said, "Did you give any more thought to taking in Bruce?"

I told her I hadn't and hung up. In truth, I couldn't *stop* thinking about him. There was a lot to take in—Chloe's lying and how that played into Grant's fall, Rob's secret and how much Sharon suspected. I'd told her Bryan had phone records from the most recent winter. Did she put together what was going on? What if I *did* take Bruce in? I couldn't watch after him all the time or make his meals. I didn't even do that for myself. So, if I asked Audie for help, what would that mean? Her staying with me for the whole summer? Where would I sleep? The third bedroom was crammed with junk. And that couch…three, four days; fine. Any more than that and I'd be walking like a question mark.

And how would Rob take all this? If Bruce really was his son, what would he think of me looking after him? Nothing good. Having Audie there might ease tensions. But would Rob really want Bruce staying in a place that might topple over?

MOST WARNED TOMMY! Yeah, yeah. Whatever. It sounded ominous, like I'd already suffered a catastrophe others saw coming. Who were these people who came with warnings, anyway?

I lugged the box of books into the store and was about to bring in Grant's clothes, but someone came wandering over and asked if I was open. I couldn't very well say no, then sit inside and do my own laundry. I told him I was still closed and drove to Sparkles on Queen Street. I couldn't get over how futuristic it was. Two walls of shiny front-loading washers and dryers, facing each other down a corridor with a long folding table book-ended by two slick stations of rolling carts for transferring clothes.

I was the only one in the place. It didn't break my heart. Sparkles was doing the same business as the Wondermat, excluding me.

Halfway through the wash cycle, I figured out why. Parking spaces were filling up, people were setting out folding chairs along the curbs, crowds started clogging the sidewalks. The Saturday pipe band. How had I forgotten? I ran out to move my car before they put up the barricades. The last thing I needed was to be stuck in town, trapped by the parade, past sunset. I drove down Harbour Street to the municipal lot behind the Aurora. By the time I got back, I could hear the distant caterwauling of bagpipes. The band was assembling in the park. I checked my phone: 6:30. No way I'd get the laundry done before they started at the top of the hour.

My loads were done washing, at least, when I got back. I was transferring them to the dryer when my phone rang. It was Newf. What would I tell him? I hit the red button to hang up on the call. Then I thought about it. I didn't know for sure what had been going on with Grant and Chloe. Why upset him?

"I saw you called. I'm in town washing Grant's clothes."

"Why the hell are you doing that?" I told him I'd cleaned out the Chief. Newf laughed. "That may be the first cleaning it's had in 30 years. Did you dump the tanks?"

"Yep."

"That's more than I would've done." This from a man well acquainted with pig slop. It wasn't that he wouldn't have dumped the tanks; he just wouldn't have done it for Grant. "You there?"

"Sorry, the pipers are starting."

"Chloe's there tonight." I looked out the window of the laundromat, as if she might appear at any moment. "Hello?"

"I'm here."

"I think we have a bad connection. Let me call you back."

"No, it's okay." *Focus, McTavish.* "My reception's not great here. I can go outside."

I walked up front, my view of the street widening. Should I go looking for Chloe? Take this chance to confront her?

"I talked to my sister Bryne in Vero Beach. She's agreed to take Chloe until the end of August, longer if it works out."

"So, Chloe needs to get to Florida. When?"

"Next week. If you're up for it."

Me, in the car with Chloe. For hours. Knowing what I knew. "Fine. What airport is she going out of, Detroit or Toronto?" Now the silence was on the other end. "Newf?"

"Chloe won't fly. She's scared to death of it."

"Are you asking me to drive her all the way to Florida?"

"Maybe Bryne could meet you in Atlanta."

"I've got to think about this," I said—for all sorts of reasons I couldn't share with Newf.

"Well, just so you know, I'm about to do *you* a favor."

"Oh yeah?"

"I'm going to see how many wind turbines I can put up across from Rob's resort."

"Holy shit, Newf. That's war."

"He pissed me off with that pond."

"But that's not just hurting Rob. A lot of cottagers are going to be up in arms, too."

"What would you rather have? A big resort ruining the beach, or a bunch of windmills out of harm's way on the bluff?"

"Neither?"

"That's what I hope it comes to. Anyway, think about Florida."

Before I could answer, he hung up. What in God's name was happening? Rob trying to flood me out. Grant mixed up with Newf's daughter, dying from what may not have been an accident. Joan with Rob. Sharon in despair. Poor Bruce caught in the middle. Audie pressuring me to step in and help. Now Newf, going to war with Rob. Where was a drink when you needed one?

By the time the band started marching, I couldn't even see out the window. It was lined with people leaning against it to watch the parade pass. Then came the rattle of drums, the humming of a hundred pipes, one plaintive sigh, and now that familiar skirl, sad and shrill. Impossibly beautiful. I went to the door. The three leaders strode past, twirling their spear-like maces. Now the pipers, men and women, some so old it was a struggle to march, others teenagers, giving up their Saturday night for this, and a few children, striding as far as they could to stay in formation, blowing their pipes as solemnly as everyone else. It was momentous work,

raising that mournful cry between the buildings and into the
burnished sky. As if to pump energy into them, here was a row of
bass drummers from Kincardine and Clinton and Teeswater,
drums as big as truck tires strapped on their bellies, banging away
with their mallets. Then, the tenor drummers, and finally the prod-
ding snap of the snares. After that, a sea of people, cottagers and
townies alike, kids on their fathers' shoulders, babies in strollers,
the old and disabled in wheelchairs. The happy, the drunk, the
devoted. A great procession of humanity, two blocks deep,
shuffling along to the siren call of the pipes.

The parade passed. The crowds thinned. Cars pulled out. It
wasn't over. They'd come back the other way in a half hour. Then
they'd have a concert in the park until dark. But for now, in this
block in front of Sparkles, Kincardine was its sleepy self again.

I boxed up Grant's clothes and hurried to Victoria's. I didn't
want to go into protracted negotiations over the items. If Vicky
gave me 20 bucks for the whole shebang, I'd be happy. Still, even
after I plopped the box on her counter and said, "Whatever you
offer is fine," she picked through them piece by piece. As it turned
out, Grant's wardrobe was gold for a retro clothier like Vicky.
"Wow, Grubb bell bottoms," she fawned, holding up a pair of
paisley-swirled pants. Then to the blue poncho hoodie I told Grant
looked like a wizard's robe, she said, "This is a classic." Every arti-
cle of clothing earned a comment. The drone of the bagpipes was
growing off in the distance.

"I'll take a hundred bucks for all of it."

"Oh, I couldn't short-change you."

Before long, the pipers were back again, returning to the park.
Vicky stopped picking through Grant's clothes and went outside
to take in the parade. There was nothing for me to do but watch
the procession again. The rows of pipers were just ending, and a
gap opened before the bass drummers. There was Chloe, on the
other side of the street, weaving against the grain of the crowd, at
the back of a snaking line of her rag-tag friends.

"I've got to go," I told Vicky.

"I'm almost done."

"Just keep it all."

I caught up to Chloe by the boarded-up Aztec theatre, but I stayed on my side of the street and hung back, waiting for a chance to get her alone. I didn't want to drag her friends into things. One of them was that Derek kid who gave Grant such a hard time at youth night. As luck would have it, they crossed over to my side to get to the Tim Horton's on the road out of town.

I let Chloe see me first. "Mr. McTavish!" She broke away from her pack, and they went on into the store. "Did my dad call you?"

"He did."

"Florida. Right on the beach. Can you imagine?"

"I told your dad I'd think about it."

A slight ripple of worry disturbed Chloe's face. She shook it away. "Did you talk to Cam? He wants to meet us for lunch at the border. He says it's time you got together, patched things up."

That was a surprise. I looked down Queen Street, where the parade had gone. Boys on their father's shoulders. And once, long ago, Cam on mine. I must've softened my expression; Chloe said, "He knew you'd like that." I nodded, still half-lost in that old parade, holding his little legs around my neck, bouncing to the drums. "Anyway, I hope we can go." Chloe started walking away.

"Wait." When she turned, Chloe's face had changed. Gone was the cheery mask she wore a moment before. It was like she knew what was coming. "I cleaned out Grant's RV today."

No reaction. "I had to empty the tanks. Up at the RV park. The guy there said he'd just seen Grant a couple weeks back..." Chloe's mouth dropped open slowly. "Him and his girlfriend. The gal who scoops ice cream in Holyrood."

Chloe's eyes started darting everywhere. "I went up there with him that one time, yeah."

"He seemed to think you were more than just friends."

"Well, he's wrong."

"If I'm going to take you out of Canada, I need to know everything."

She turned away, facing the crossroads of Queen and Broadway. Kitty corner from us, there was a stately old house, converted into an accountant's office. Back in the day, it had been the Windsor, where Joan played guitar naked, where Chloe's dad cheated on Carrie, where Grant and I sat on that curb, arguing over love, possession, and betrayal. Time folding in on itself: Here I was, reeling again from faithlessness and deception, having to decide about a girl. Chloe paced in front of me. Would she tell me the truth, a lie, or just enough to appease me? "What do your friends know?" I pressed. "What if one said something they shouldn't?"

"Okay!" Chloe shouted over the rumble of traffic. "We were close. But not how you think. We held hands. He hugged me. We never even kissed. But he *did* want to take me away, from all my troubles here. He wanted to go on the road. In search of God. 'To find a brand-new day,' he said."

A brand-new day: the goal of our aborted road trip so many years ago. Chloe waited for me to say something. I was waiting for her to tell me more. She seemed to recognize that. "That night at the gazebo," she went on, "we met to talk about it. It was my idea to meet there. I knew if I went to his RV, he'd talk me into leaving. And I didn't want to. I was changing my mind. The day before, I texted him that I would go. Then…I realized it was a mistake.

"When I told him that at the gazebo, he got upset. He begged me to leave with him. He said I needed to escape the temptations here. He put his hand on my leg. I pushed it away. He leaned in close to me…and I swung." Chloe's arm froze, outstretched.

"Then what?"

"Then he started falling back. And there was a crack."

"Then?"

"What do you want me to say?" Chloe bawled. Her fists were clenched, pumping at her sides. "Then his arms were waving. I knew he was going over. And I didn't—I didn't reach out! There was a second. And I could have. But I didn't. I thought he'd hit the ground, and it would serve him right. I didn't know we were so close to the edge."

People were eyeing us out of passing cars. "Okay," I said, moving to calm her. "It's okay."

Chloe backed away to the curb. "I swear!" She was crying now. "I didn't know how far he'd fall. And I tried! I tried to find him. I called and called. I felt through the dark. I crawled in the mud. I went to the edge!"

"Chloe. It's alright. I believe you."

Cars honking. People shouting out of windows. Chloe's friends rushing up on us. "What the fuck?" Derek barked.

"Back off, eh?" another shouted.

"She's alright," I told them. "You're alright. Right, Chloe?"

She was wide-eyed, whimpering, gazing around in terror, like she didn't know where she was. I inched forward, whispering her name. Her friends kept yelling. And then she was in my arms. "It's okay. It's not your fault. We'll go to Florida. We'll get out of here." She let me walk her over to a half-wall of cement that ran alongside Tim Horton's. It was short enough to sit on. Her friends started to come our way. I held up my hand. Thankfully, they understood.

"You don't have to talk about it anymore." Chloe was staring down at the sidewalk, gazing though the cement, it seemed, by the vacant intensity of her eyes.

"He was just trying to lead me to God," she said. "I lost my way." She leaned into me. Her breath rattled like she'd come out of cold water. I put my arm around her. There was a break in the traffic leaving the parade. As the last car passed the old Windsor, the curb across the street came into view. I felt a pang of anticipation, as if Grant and I would actually still be over there, debating.

By the time I got back to my car, the pipers were done playing. The Aurora was packed with late-night revelers, its outdoor deck lights outshining everything but the beacon that swirled from the lighthouse across the bridge road.

A beer would've been nice. I stood in the parking lot considering it. A car beeped. I was blocking his way. The driver got fed up and started swerving around me just as I moved off in his direction. He hit his brakes. I waved to signal I was sorry. "What the hell's your problem?" he thundered out his window. It was only as he roared away that I realized it was Wendy's ex-boyfriend Ray.

I got in my car, started it up, put it in reverse. Then I threw it back in park. I fished my phone out of my pocket.

Newf answered on the first ring. "This is late."

"I'll do it," I said.

"Do what?"

"Drive Chloe to Florida."

A pause. Then: "Thank you."

"How soon can she be ready?"

"How soon can you go?"

I came up on the back of my cottage into a flood of light. I'd never seen it so bright. Audie must've turned on every switch in the place. The glow inflated against the darkness in a way that made the cottage seem more substantial. *Not mine.* I snuck up to the back door and peered through the panes. Audie was all the way on the other side of the cottage, through the kitchen and across the great room, sitting in my lounger, bundled up in a blanket, reading. The contented owner, and I, the bygone drifter. The ghost.

How did Grant put it when we stopped on the bridge after the Windsor brawl and he told me that he'd thought of leaping into the harbor channel? He said it was like he wasn't there. That's how I felt looking at Audie in my cottage. Grant said he could disappear, and no one would care. If I disappeared, everyone would be better off. What did Audie say? *Think of everyone you'll be helping.* She'd have a safe place to stay. Rob wouldn't sabotage her; Sharon said as much. He'd probably stop feeding runoff into the gully, even shore up the banks. And with me gone and the cottage fortified, it would actually be helpful for Bruce to stay with Audie. That would be better for the kid and Joan. Hell, it would help all the cottagers around me. No runoff in the gully; no need to dig it out; no fertilizer in the lake; no reason for anger.

Vanishing would be good for Chloe and Newf, too. Any suspicion over Grant's death would fall on me. Why else would I leave? And what about Wendy? Hadn't I tortured her enough? What did she say? *You should've never gotten me into this.* The best she could hope for was my broken, feeble love. She deserved so much more. *Just disappear.* Hadn't this been in the back of my mind ever since I let Carrie die? It was always for selfish reasons, though; penance, punishment, putting myself out of misery. But now, it could be something helpful, a selfless act, steering others away from dangers, like Carrie steered me away from death.

Was I really thinking of doing this? Like my dad did on that lonely road in Michigan? Like Grant contemplated when he first came to town? What was it that prompted him? *I don't have blood relations.* That wasn't true for me. I still had Cam. Poor kid; so many strikes against him already. Dropping out of college…getting that DUI…no job prospects…nowhere of his own to live. I remember how I felt when my dad did it—ashamed, abandoned, vulnerable. And Cam was so much younger, so much more exposed. I thought again of how he used to sit on my shoulders, surfing atop the rolling parade. I even put my hands up and squeezed his phantom legs. I couldn't leave the way my dad did, the way Bryan left Bruce. I needed to be there for him, closer…and away from here.

Vacation is over.

I walked into the flat, dark expanse of my backyard. It seemed as vacant as Rob had made it on his diorama. I took my phone out. "Barb, this is Tommy McTavish. Am I calling too late?"

"No. You know me," she said. "I'm a night owl."

"I was wondering if that job offer was still on the table."

"It is. " She paused then added, "If you're serious about it."

"I am. What do you need from me?"

"We'd have to get you in here for the department interview. But that's a formality. I'm making the decision." Barb went quiet. And then: "And I'd need your assurance, you know, that—"

"I know: that I'm cleaned up. You can count on that."

"Can you get into town in the next couple weeks?"

"I think so." Newf and I hadn't settled on when I'd be driving Chloe to Florida, but I'd go straight to Ann Arbor afterwards— and for good. "I'll call you as soon as I know when I'm coming into town."

"If you don't mind my asking, what changed your mind?"

I thought about it a moment. "Family."

I pushed open the back door as quietly as I could, like sound alone would betray my presence. Audie was smiling up at me before I even shut the door.

"So, it's all cleared out. The Chief is no more," she said as I came closer then sat on the foot stool in front of her.

"That's right."

"So many memories. Whose is it now?"

"I don't know. It's not my decision."

"Whose else would it be?' she laughed, bringing her feet up to sit cross-legged.

She was eager to talk. For once, I was too. "I think we should take in Bruce."

"Oh!" She was surprised. "Good. *Good!*"

"But I *am* going to need your help."

"I'll help as much as you need."

"It may be more than you thought. Newf asked if I'd drive Chloe to his sister's in Florida."

Audie's smile crumbled. "Florida? That would take days."

"Maybe a week. Maybe more."

"I—can't. I can't do this alone. You never said Bruce and I would be *alone.*"

"You can do it," I reassured her.

"Why more than a week? It wouldn't take that long to drive down and back."

I took a deep breath and let it seep out. I already resolved that when I left the beach, it would be for good, like Joan did after the accident. It was time to get on with my life, to stop "vacating" and change. Audie was conducting her life now like she'd forgiven Grant. I needed to start behaving like Carrie had forgiven me. Move on. Salvage my family. But I couldn't tell Audie that now. There would be time later, after she settled into her routine as the cottage's new occupant.

"I need some time away, Audie. From here. From Boiler Beach. I'm afraid if I just stay here, doing the same thing, fighting the same demons, I'll never make anything of my life."

She gasped. "You're leaving *for good?*"

"No!" I insisted. "No…"

"Then how long?"

"A few months. So I don't have to watch this resort go in."

"They'll be building that for years."

"Look, Audie," I tried a new tack. "You need a place to stay, and I want to rent you my cottage. July and August. A dollar a month. Do you want it or not?"

Her gaze floated up to the ceiling. "What if it floods again?"

"It won't," I said, with completely unwarranted certainty.

Audie's eyes swam with unfallen tears. "I was just supposed to help you. Who's supposed to help *me*?"

"Everybody," I promised, again with no authority. "Sharon will. Rob. I'll make sure Newf checks in too. And Bruce is a good kid. You said so yourself. I can tell he likes you."

Audie blushed. "You think?"

"I've never seen a teenager so happy to mop a floor. You've got a way with him." She pulled at her lip, squeezed it, let it go, over and over. "I'll never be more than three days away. If you need me to come back, I'll be here." She nodded, taking it in. "And if you don't, stay as long as you like. A dollar a month."

"I don't want to get stuck here in the winter."

"I'll be back by then," I vowed. Even as I did so, I knew I wouldn't. Her sister Allie would have to take her in.

Audie sighed. Then she unfolded her legs, popped out of the chair, and hurried off to her bedroom. I figured she'd need time to think it over. But before I could get up, she came hustling back to me. "Here." She thrust out her hand. It was two dollars. "Rent for the summer." I took it, doing my best to keep a straight face. "As long as I'm staying here, am I allowed to change things around?"

"Okay…" I braced for what was coming next.

"Tommy, I can't live with that outhouse poster you put up inside the washroom door."

I laughed. "You can take it down. I'm not crazy about it either. But Grant did it, and I…" Suddenly, I couldn't find the words. Then I thought I might choke up.

"I guess it's not so bad," Audie said, her voice cracking, too.

The next day, I went to see Wendy. It had been so long since I'd gone to Point Clark, I got lost. Finally, I turned a corner and the lighthouse was there, higher and more isolated than I remembered, a slender stone tower, nearly 100 feet tall, painted white and topped with a circle of windows and a red domed roof. It occurred to me, as I took the road beside the lighthouse's austere grounds, that my impression of Point Clark was skewed by Audie's picture of the Sorry pieces marching ashore. They loomed so high over the lighthouse I'd come to believe it was unimposing, a tourists' curiosity. I was wrong. There was a simplicity to the soaring column, a strength and sanctity. And to think, it was nearly in Wendy's front yard. Her place faced the old lightkeeper's house and an open field that ended at the shore of Lake Huron.

Before I even got to Wendy's door, I could smell the goodness of her pecan butter tarts. "I told you I wouldn't be done until three," she greeted me with a pitcher of amber syrup. I'd never been inside Wendy's place. It was smaller than Rob's bunkhouse. Half its width, the part that faced the lighthouse, was a kitchen suitable for a high-class restaurant—with an industrial-sized fridge, a double-stacked oven, a wall of pots, pans, and utensils, and a long countertop island where she was working.

"This is what I've been waiting to see," I said, sitting down on a stool at the island. "Wendy making her magic tarts."

"You're a privileged man."

She was pouring the syrup into shells of dough on two cupcake tins. I peeked inside the shells. "That's all the pecans you use?"

Wendy stopped pouring. "Do you have a better way?"

I threw my hands up. Point taken: don't mess with perfection. She put the tins on one of the racks in the oven, then checked two tins on another rack. "How many dozen are you making?"

"When I'm in rhythm, I can do four dozen an hour."

While she mixed more syrup, I did some math in my head. "So, you're talking about nearly 400 tarts in an eight-hour day."

"Then I shoot myself," Wendy deadpanned.

"Times five days." I took it further. "That's 2,000 a week. Times 50 weeks. Holy hell, that's 100,000 tarts a year."

Wendy scraped a big chunk of butter into a pan on the stove, then packed a cup of brown sugar in a scoop, and dropped that in.

"Ah, the secret recipe."

"Everyone uses brown sugar and butter in butter tart filling." I shrugged, like, who didn't know that? Wendy stopped and stared me down. "Do you want to help?"

My only standard for cooking was whether you could eat the dish over the sink. "I better not. I don't want to—"

"Nonsense. You're not going to ruin anything." Wendy went to her extra-wide fridge and took out two rolls of dough. "You can do the shells." She showed me how to cut the log into puck-sized disks, flatten one with a roller, punch out a circle with a cookie cutter, then press it into the jumbo cupcake tin. I showed her the first couple I did. She was amused by the care I was taking.

As we worked. I got back to the numbers. "How much does it cost you to make a dozen?"

"A batch is two dozen."

"Okay, then. A batch."

"I don't know. Three dollars a batch."

"Twenty-five cents for two tarts?"

"Yeah, I guess so."

Wendy used to sell the tarts at O'Shea's for two bucks apiece. So…with at least a buck eighty profit per tart… "Wow. You could make 180 grand a year on tarts alone."

"You've just described Hell to me—chained to my own oven." She was pouring maple syrup into a glass bowl of cracked eggs. Then she started pouring lemon juice into a tablespoon.

"Is *that* the secret?" I pointed to the glass bowl.

"Are you spying on me, Tommy?"

"Just curious."

"There's no secret. It's how you do everything." Wendy pulled a fifth of Jack Daniels out of the cabinet. "But I don't know anyone else who does this." She poured two capfuls of Jack into the bowl.

"No wonder I like these tarts so much."

"You'd have to eat a lot of tarts to get your buzz on. You'd probably die first." Wendy bustled over to the oven. She pulled out two tins and set them in front of me. The tart concoction was still bubbling. The sweet smell overtook me.

"What a way to go." I reached for one. She slapped my hand.

"I've done the numbers you just did." Wendy was suddenly serious. "It's 99,840 a year to be exact; 8,320 dozen. Problem is, somebody's got to buy them all."

"I thought this was your Hell."

"I did the math when my mom did the baking."

"You could always hire someone."

"And there go the profits," Wendy said.

We made more tarts over the next hour, and Wendy let me try my hand at every step. Sift the flour. Slice in the butter cubes. Roll the dough. Mix the syrup—even the capfuls of Jack. Whisk it. Pour it into the shells. Bake. We didn't talk much. We just threw ourselves into the work. For a while, I was even able to forget the real reason I'd come to visit.

After we'd taken the last tin out of the oven, I asked Wendy if she wanted to get some fresh air. The day was blustery, but the clouds were breaking, and the sun was spilling out everywhere. We walked through the lightkeeper's yard, down into the wild brush of the dune. There was a faint path that only locals could've made, likely just Wendy and her neighbors. It opened onto a tongue of rocky shore that jutted out in front of the lighthouse a good 30 yards, tapering to a sandy point. Beyond that, there was a small island of sand you could've waded to. Was this the start of that ancient land bridge that once cut Lake Huron in half?

"I'm going to be leaving for a while," I told Wendy as we walked that rocky tongue.

"Oh," she said. "How long is a while?"

"I don't know. Maybe a long time."

"Maybe forever?" She turned to me.

"Maybe." There was no reason to lie to Wendy.

"Where will you go?"

"I'm doing a favor for Newf. Then…I have to help my son."

Wendy squinted into my eyes. Then she walked off toward the tiny marina beside the parking lot—boat dock is more like it; a concrete ramp into the water, six small berths, with one old skiff and a rowboat. There was a narrow breaker wall, no more than a rocky berm. It hooked out into the lake to shield the marina from the waves. Wendy rambled off ahead of me. I was slow to catch up, giving her time. When I did finally come beside her, we were at the end of the breaker. A hard wind lashed at her hair and fluttered through her blouse.

"We really screwed this up," she said, refusing to look at me.

"This isn't your fault."

Wendy's head snapped around. "No. It isn't." With that, she edged past me and hurried back along the berm to the parking lot.

I had to run to catch up. There was a handful of cars in the lot, tourists come to climb the lighthouse. "You said it yourself," I lowered my voice around the milling people, "I'm just an old drunk. And I hurt everybody I love." She kept walking up the lane, ignoring me. "It's better this way," I tried again, after we passed the line to buy tickets. "You don't want to be with someone like me."

Wendy crossed her front yard, tromped up onto her deck, opened her door, and only then turned to me. Her eyes were ablaze with fury. "You don't get to tell me who to love. You love a dead girl you barely knew. That makes everything very easy for you."

She went inside and slammed the door, leaving me on her deck, stunned, wounded…then, the longer I listened to the clattering of pans, outraged myself.

"Easy?" I pounded on the door. "Easy?!" I went to the kitchen window. I could see her outline through the screen, head down, packing up tarts. "I *killed* her. Try living with that. All you have to worry about is making your fucking tarts."

It was mean to say, but she'd hurt me. If my words struck a nerve, Wendy didn't show it. She kept on working, separating tarts from the tin. The hell with it. I'd come to tell her I was leaving, and I'd done it. I hadn't expected it to go well. This was worse than I imagined, but maybe we needed a harsh break for the sake of finality. I bounded off the deck and started for my car.

"You're just going to leave?" Wendy was standing in her open doorway, holding a wrapped plate of tarts.

I came back to the steps. "I don't want to hurt you, Wendy. We shouldn't have to do that to say goodbye."

Wendy managed a faint smile. She'd been crying. "These are for you and Audie." She held out the plate. I came up the steps. We were in front of each other now, looking down at the plate between us. I went to take it, then looked up for Wendy's eyes. I leaned in to kiss her. She stepped back. I thought I'd overstepped my bounds again. She set the plate of tarts on a deck chair. Then came toward me. This time, we both kissed each other. Then we were embracing, and you could feel the energy coursing through us. Her mouth was soft and tingled, warm and sweet. It was Wendy who finally stopped. When I opened my eyes, she was gazing into them. My breath got stuck. Wendy took me by the hand and led me inside.

It's been a while," I told her afterward. We were nestled on the couch in a blanket, watching broken clouds scud over the lighthouse and shafts of sunlight pulse across the lake.

"You seemed to get the hang of it pretty quick."

"Too quick?"

Wendy backhanded me in the chest. "You were there. What do you think?"

"It seemed adequate," I deadpanned.

"There you go." Wendy ran her hand across my cheek.

I started wondering about the wisdom of what we'd done. "I just…I just hope—"

"Don't." She put a finger on my lips. "I know what you're thinking. And don't."

I tried to laugh. It quickly lapsed. "Fair enough. So, this doesn't have to be—"

Wendy sprung up off the couch. The blanket fell to the floor. "I'm not listening," she announced, gliding away from me. I lost my train of thought. The purity of that skin. The miracle of her beauty… She stood at the sink naked, looking out the window at the lighthouse.

"The tourists are getting quite a show."

"They can't see anything from up there." Wendy looked over her shoulder and swept her cinnamon hair out of her face. "You're the only one who can see me."

I took a deep breath. Lucky me. *My cinnamon girl.* Wendy came back carrying two butter tarts. She settled back down and snuggled up next to me without her blanket.

The tarts were even better than when I had them at O'Shea's. Warmer. Crispier. Gooier. And when I spilled some filling on my chest, Wendy licked it off. I never got that service at the bar.

"You ever go there anymore?" I asked. "Up in the lighthouse?"

"No. It would make me too sad."

We grew quiet then. What had Wendy's father told her? Small steps to reach big dreams... Suddenly, the day felt late, our time together scarce. Wendy must've sensed the same thing: "When do you leave?"

"Friday."

"Four days." I could feel her squirm beside me. I put my hand on her thigh to calm her. "You're going to miss the O'Shea's closing party," she said.

Shit. I'd forgotten that. It couldn't be helped now. "I'm sorry. I have to go that morning. It's all been planned."

"I shouldn't have said anything." Then she was crying.

"I thought we weren't going to feel bad about this."

"I can't help it."

"Look, I don't know what'll happen." That much was true. "I may be back in a few months."

"You won't be." She got up and went into her bedroom.

After we dressed, Wendy went out on the deck, brought the plate of butter tarts inside, and handed it to me. "Can you add a few more?" I asked. "Joan's son Bruce is staying with us."

"Oh?"

"Long story."

She stacked a couple tarts on the pile. "But if you're leaving..."

"He's staying with Audie."

"And that's a good idea?"

"She'll be fine. I'm giving her my place for free."

"It's not the money I'm wondering about."

"It's already decided, Wendy." I got a little testy. "Sharon's going to be there for her. Newf. You don't have to worry."

Wendy could see she'd upset me. "I can look in on her, too."

"Thank you." It was more of a relief than I let on. Every feeling at this point was more than I was letting on. I made my way to the door. Wendy followed with the tarts.

"Well, Tommy McTavish…" she said, handing me the plate.

I took it from her. "Well, Wendy O'Shea…"

Neither of us were going to say goodbye. Wendy leaned in, kissed my cheek, thought about it. Then one last soft kiss on the lips. "Take care of yourself," she said.

"I will."

"Promise me," Wendy insisted. "Promise me you'll take care of yourself."

"I promise."

When I pulled out of Wendy's place, she was standing in her kitchen window. The sun was low enough to be slanting in on her, but the screen gave her a gauzy glow, like she was dissolving.

A udie had eaten two tarts before I got back from my swim. "Some of those were for Bruce. Wendy gave us three apiece."

"Oh my!" Audie gaped down at the plate, like how would she ever be able to get through the next few days with only one tart?

"You can have one of mine."

Anyone else, and you would've said she was exaggerating her relief. Audie was genuinely grateful. "Joan's dropping Bruce off Tuesday," she said then.

"You told her we'd take him in?" I wanted to do that.

"She came down and asked for an answer."

"Did you tell her about…the arrangement?"

"I told her not to worry. I could do it. Joan seemed fine." She had no other choice. "What about Wendy?" Audie asked out of the blue. "How did she take the news?"

"Fine."

Audie arched that eyebrow of hers. "She wasn't upset?"

"No."

"You're going to miss her. You don't even know how much."

"Probably not," I lied. Then I thought about it. Maybe it wasn't such a lie. "Probably not."

I drove the Lincoln into town to gas it up for Florida, then took Lake Range home, past the resort. The fence now ran the whole stretch of Rob's land. You still couldn't see what they were doing behind the screens. But the fanged heads of excavators swung over the fields. The clatter was so loud, it had to be carrying down to the beach. At the entry gate, a couple dozen protestors paced in front of a new security tent. Two guys in what looked like police uniforms stood guard as protestors paced nearby, shaking signs that read "STOP GARTON GREED." This was the first of what would be many protests. They wouldn't all be so peaceful.

As I eased up to the stop sign, I saw Newf and Rob, not too far around the corner, on the way to the highway. Two white vans were parked in an access drive to the field that faced Rob's resort. They had blue, red, and yellow Windcor Energy logos on their sides. The wind turbines; Newf hadn't been kidding. I parked on the shoulder and got out of my car. In the field behind them, Windcor workers surveyed the land butting up to Lake Range. Two other guys kneeled beside one of the vans, getting ready to launch a drone. Newf and Rob were toe to toe, just on the other side of a line of orange cones arcing partway into the road.

"It's not personal?" Rob thundered. "Not *personal*?! You've got all this land, and you start in with the windmills *here*?!"

"What was it you said about the pond?" Newf eyed me as he countered. "You could do what you wanted with your land? Well, this is what I want to do with mine."

Rob followed the drift of Newf's glance. "Oh, him! I get it now. He comes whining to you about his gully, and suddenly you want to put windmills next to my resort."

"He has nothing to do with it. This is about our agreement."

"Bullshit!" Rob snapped. I'd never seen him so unhinged; face bloated, eyes swollen, beads of sweat rolling off his forehead. "You knew I was going to drain that pond." He was pointing his finger in Newf's face now, twisting—not jabbing—like he was boring it into him. "He knew it." He suddenly appealed to me.

"Don't bring him into this. You know what you said. You said, 'I won't drain that pond until you build your new one across the road.' That's what you promised."

"That isn't in the contract."

"Nothing in the contract about wind turbines either."

Rob worked his mouth, but nothing came out. He snapped his glare toward me and back to Newf. Then he let out a savage sort of howl and went stomping off. He kicked one orange cone, then another, swept at a third, whiffed, and staggered into the road.

"You two!" he screamed. The drone guys stopped their work and were watching now. "You never fucking liked me. *Never!*" This was a full-blown meltdown. "You!" he jabbed his finger at Newf. "You will never forgive me for your raft disaster. Never mind that I brought that business to you. Never mind that you fucked it up, and I took a bath! And you!" He swung his arm wildly at me, stumbling further into the road. "I gave you work, making five times more than that shitty golf job, and what do you do? Stab me in the back!"

I don't know why, but that set me off. "Yeah? Who stabbed who in the back?" I started toward him. "You took my girlfriend. And now you're treating her like shit. Don't think I don't know."

Newf lurched in front of me, hopping on his bad leg to hold me back. If I could've broken free, I do believe I would've come to blows with Rob. And that wasn't like me, not sober anyway. When Newf finally got me cooled down, all three of us were in the middle of the Eighth. A car cruised by slowly, the driver rubbernecking. It was old man Moore, our beach president, the guy whose property Rob had peed on during his legendary French bread run. A whirring started up. The drone. It hovered above us for a second, then raced off down Lake Range.

That triggered Rob's rage all over again. "What the *fuck* is that? What the *hell* are you doing?" He bolted after the operator, who scurried off behind the van. His partner, a hulking man, no more than 30, blocked Rob's way. Rob tried to fake and dodge past the bigger, quicker man. It would've been comical if he wasn't so unglued. Finally, he threw up his hands and stomped away. But before he got too far, he whirled back to confront us one last time.

"You're going to regret this, Newfield. A lot of people will fight you on this, people who don't lose."

With that, he strutted away toward the top of the hill, right down the middle of the road, his figure framed by the high pines on either side, exposing a slot of the lake's horizon. He looked so lonely, so lost, head down, trudging toward that divide, the same opening his great grandfather had cut into the woods over a hundred years before to lay claim to the beach.

As we watched Rob leave, Newf said, "He's right. A lot of people around here can't afford to have Rob fail."

"So why do it?"

Newf thought about it a moment. "A deal's a deal."

"That's it?"

He gave me an icy glance. "What else were you expecting?"

No matter how many times I told Audie I had it under control, she kept peeking in as I packed. Did I have sunscreen? What sort of shoes was I taking? What about food? Should she pack a cooler? Did I want her to bake something? What might Chloe like? Even though I was leaving for good, I didn't want to take all my clothes. Audie needed to think this was temporary. Still, with everything she was suggesting, I could've been gone for years. What about boots? And a heavy coat and gloves?

"I guess it all depends on where you plan to go," she said, fishing for my plans.

I didn't take the bait. "After Florida, it's wide open."

"Well, don't forget pillows and sheets." She backed away. "Who knows what the story is with Grant's bedding?"

"I'm not taking the Chief. I'm driving *my* car."

"What'll *I* drive? I still have to move out of my apartment."

I hadn't thought of that. "Can't Sharon help?"

"I can't impose on people for two months. I need a car."

This was a problem. Could a 40-year-old Winnebago make it all the way to Florida and back? And would I be stuck with it when I settled finally in Ann Arbor?

"Take the Lincoln," I told Audie. What choice did I have?

Audie never told me Joan was coming so early to drop off Bruce. I was in the washroom when I heard Audie greet them. By the time I threw on some clothes, Bruce was shuffling toward me, lugging a duffel bag. Joan was leaving. I told Bruce to take my room and raced after her.

"You weren't even going to say goodbye?"

Joan looked over her shoulder, but never stopped. "I have a one o'clock out of Toronto."

I didn't catch up with her until I was halfway across my back-yard. She was buttoned up like a businesswoman bustling off to a meeting, right down to her high-heeled wedges. There was still a faint bruise in the middle of her forehead from the night she fell against my car, a near-perfect purple circle. Her version of a scarlet letter. "O"—for what? Outcast? Open? Original?

"You can't take two minutes to talk?" I was hurt, more than I would've been under normal circumstances. This was likely the last time we'd ever see each other. Joan didn't know that. But still; she was leaving her child at my place for weeks. And the last time we said goodbye, decades passed.

"What do you want, Tommy?" Joan swung around. "I've got a lot of shit going on right now. I don't need any more from you."

"A simple thanks would've been nice. After all—"

"After all, what? You're leaving. What am I thanking *you* for?"

"I guess you had a lot of other places Bruce could've stayed."

Joan closed her eyes and sighed. "I'm sorry. What is it?"

"It isn't anything, Joan. Just…good luck."

"Oh." She seemed baffled by the sentiment. "Well, thank you."

"You'll be great." I mustered a smile. "You always are."

Joan had no reason to suspect this was anything but a momentary parting. But she seemed to sense there was a greater gravity for me. "Not always," she acknowledged sadly.

"Everything'll work out. You know what they say about time."

"Right," Joan said, gazing absently up into the trees. I doubted she had much faith in a month's ability to heal. I didn't either.

She turned to go. I stepped forward and hugged her. It took a while before she hugged back, but when she did, Joan clung to me like I was the one about to leave. Then she broke away and went striding off in her high heels, on her way for brand-new day in Vancouver.

"You know how to drive?" I asked Bruce, after we'd finished the pancake breakfast Audie made.

"I have my driver's permit," he said.

"Let's take the old Town Car for a spin." I tossed the keys at him. I'd been digging out the gully, thinking about all the things I needed to do before I left. Getting the Chief in shape for the long drive was at the top of the list.

"Does your mother let you drive?" Audie asked. I was glad to hear her consider his safety.

"My dad used to take me," Bruce said. Audie and I glanced at each other. We both caught how he'd referred to him in the past.

I backed the car out of Rob's field and onto the beach road. No sense giving the kid a tough challenge right off the bat. He did fine going along the short straightaway to the Eighth, but when we started climbing the hill, he went so slowly, I had that precarious sense we could roll back down any second.

"Speed up a touch," I suggested. Bruce lurched ahead, tapped the brakes, lurched again.

"Where are we going?"

"Just concentrate on driving."

"I mean, do you want me to turn?"

We were cresting the hill. "Shit. Yes. Turn right." I should've given Bruce more warning. The intersection came up on him too fast. He understeered. We veered across Lake Range and were headed for Ackert's old hay barn on the corner, where Rob was planning an airplane landing strip. Still, plenty of time to correct.

"Brake…brake…" I tried to keep my cool for the kid's sake.

He hit the gas. We hurtled over the road and headed straight for the barn. I reached over, wrenched the steering wheel. Bruce finally figured out which pedal was the brake. We fish-tailed past the barn, the back end of my Lincoln just missing its stone base. The car came to a stop well into the field. We'd slipped right through a row of sapling pines, missed a boulder, and put just a single tire into a newly planted vegetable garden. Bruce gaped out the front window. I blew a big gasp of air.

"I pressed the accelerator by mistake."

"Yes, you did." He opened the door and unlocked his seatbelt. "Where are you going?"

Bruce swung a frightened glance my way. "I can't drive."

I shrugged him off. "You put us in here. You get us out."

It took a lot of coaching, but Bruce managed to steer his way out of the field and onto the shoulder of the road. Even there, he tried again to relinquish his duty. "I don't want to wreck your car."

"I don't want you to wreck my car either. But you've got to get back on the horse."

If it hadn't been a straight shot to Concession 6, I might not have been so fatherly with the kid. As we approached the turn at the hill road, though, I started to regret my decision. To have him pull over now, so he didn't have to handle the hill to Grant's camp, would undo all the confidence he'd built. "Okay, we're going to turn right up here." I gave him plenty of warning. "Get ready with the brake. Go as slow as you need."

Bruce nodded without so much as a glance my way. We crept around the turn slower than I could've walked it. Bruce rode the brakes all the way down the incline. I had him turn around and park where the road dead-ended, so he was pointed back up the hill. Then I opened my door. "Where are you going?"

"I've got to drive the RV. Didn't I mention that?"

"So, I have to drive home alone?" You would've thought I was asking him to fly a jet.

"I trust you."

His eyes swam. He puffed his cheeks and blew out a big, nervous breath. "O-kay…"

I headed for the woods. It was a few seconds before I heard the Lincoln rumble over the gravel. I snuck back out to watch his progress. He was taking the hill a little faster than I would've liked. Nothing I could do about it now.

I had two errands to run in town. One was to get a checkup on the Chief at Pierson Motors. The mechanic told me he'd need the RV for a couple hours. That gave me time to take care of my other to-do: closing the Wondermat for good, or at least until I could persuade Cam to run the business.

MAD TOMMY. That's all my sign said. The other letters were scattered in the dirt below it. Had they run out of ideas? I tried to think of a couple myself. Nothing came to mind.

Inside, there wasn't much to do. I double-checked that no clothes had been left in the washers or dryers, then I unplugged every machine. My biggest decision was what to do with the tractor scrap. There was something fitting about leaving it hidden away, propping up a rickety washer in this shuttered dump—the great secret of Boiler Beach's spurious origins never to be revealed. Then I thought, why not yank the thing out, take it to the *Kincardine Record*, drop it on some eager reporter's desk, tell them what I knew, and let them unravel the mystery?

In the end, I took the piece, but I couldn't let my fellow cottagers know the shipwreck that gave their beach its name was a hoax. On the bridge over the channel, I stopped and leaned over the railing, like Grant and I had after the Windsor brawl. This was where he contemplated ending things before he met Sharon's dad, then made a family of our gang. I gazed down into the murky waters. What was it he said in his despair? That he would dive in and will himself not to resurface. Was that even possible? Wouldn't the instinct to live overwhelm the conviction to die?

Below me, a truck with a trailer and skiff was backing down the road that ran by the harbormaster's hut and ended at the boat ramp. The last time I'd been down there, Wendy was lamenting her wasted years. The driver was having trouble guiding his boat onto the ramp. The trailer jack-knifed away from it and was inching toward the ledge that dropped into the channel. The driver craned his neck out the side window as he tried to straighten out. I was about to shout a warning, but he finally stopped, got out of the truck, and went back for a better look at his predicament.

I moved on. What would've happened had the boat and trailer gone over that ledge? Would they have pulled the truck down with them? What would it feel like to be in the driver's seat as that truck sunk? How fast would it go under? How deep? When I dove off this bridge that fateful summer, I never did touch bottom.

I imagined myself, strapped into my seat, resting at the bottom of the dredged channel, gazing lifelessly into that subterranean void, fish skittering across my windshield. It gave me the shivers. I thought of the dream I had after Newf knocked me out in the Aurora, floating helplessly in my capsized cottage to that otherworldly border, facing the judgment of that fearsome serpent…the resemblance to Carrie's father…

I hurried away from the bridge. As I approached the Aurora, I saw Bogue out on his deck regaling patrons. When we made eye contact, I shook the slab at him. For a second, Bogue didn't get what it was. Then he came to the railing and started following above me along the length of his deck. If he leaped off it, he would have landed on me. Neither of us said a word, just stared at each other. It wasn't until he had to stop at the deck's edge that he called out. "That's worthless now." When I reached Queen Street, for the briefest moment, I considered changing my mind, heading for the *Record*, turning in the piece. But what was the point anymore?

The mechanic at Pierson's said he'd changed the oil, changed the filters, flushed the carburetor and fuel system, replaced hoses, rotated tires, the works. I asked: could it get to Florida and back? "I wouldn't guarantee it could get to Bayfield." he said.

When I got back to the cottage, I found Audie and Bruce out on the deck. She was showing him how to paint. Two easels were side by side, and the same stretch of shoreline was rendered on each canvas. Of course, Audie's painting was more accomplished, but the kid had done a pretty damn good job.

"Where'd you learn to paint?"

"This is his first time," Audie said.

Bruce never took his eyes off the canvas. I'd seen that grim look of determination before—yes, when he was driving along Lake Range, but also in his father's face, back when Rob was nailing down boards on Carrie's barn. "He's a natural." I said.

"His biggest problem is keeping paint off his clothes." Audie pointed out a smattering of dabs on Bruce's shirt. "We're going to have to get him a smock."

As soon as the idea came to me, I spewed out a laugh. "I have something." They were buried in the bottom drawer of my dresser. I held the coveralls up by the shoulders. Wrinkled and slumped as they were, I felt like I was consoling a despondent ghost.

"No…" Audie groaned when I came out and presented them.

"Why not?" I shook the coveralls at Bruce like a bullfighter.

Audie was aghast. "He can't wear those! Not around here."

"Nobody cares anymore." Bruce took them from me. He held it close to his body, enthralled.

Audie watched him. "Okay, but not around Rob."

"What does B-N-D-R-T stand for?"

I considered telling him—at least that the B was for Bruce. Then I noticed there was a D that could be for Duncan in there too. "What do you want it to stand for?"

He stared at the letters, mulling it over.

"Does your middle name start with an N?" Audie asked.

He shook his head and shuddered. "No. With a U."

I could tell by the way he mumbled, he didn't want to tell us. That didn't stop Audie from guessing. "Uri? Uriah? Ulrich?"

"Let it go, Audie."

"Ulysses," the kid spoke up.

"B-U-D," Audie spelled out. "We could always paint over the N and replace it."

"Naw," Bruce said, stepping into one leg of the coveralls.

It was only when I was back in the cottage that it came to me: Bud. Like the great, great, grandfather the kid would never know. Had Joan named him that on purpose?

Wednesday. A day of last things. On this, of all days, July Fourth, America's Independence Day.

I woke up Bruce before six and told him this was wake-up time for the rest of the summer. It was earlier than I'd start digging, but I didn't want there to be any chance he'd encounter an angry neighbor. I showed him the fastest way to dig the trench, how to angle it against the waves, where to throw sand so the channel wouldn't collapse. As with everything else, the kid took it seriously, listened intently, worked doggedly.

We were nearly done when Marc came out from behind the bushes on the Garton side. He might've just been getting home from the night before for how rough he looked. I saw him before Bruce did. But even after the kid knew his oppressor was there, he didn't acknowledge him.

"He's still got you slaving for him, eh?" Marc said. Bruce didn't answer. "For stealing beers you never stole."

Again, no reaction. "Maybe I should tell your dad what really happened," I said.

Marc ignored me. "You never come around anymore, Brewski. What's with that?" Still, no response. Not even the slightest hesitation in his digging. "Molly even asked about you. Don't you like us anymore?"

Finally, Bruce stabbed the shovel into the sand and glared up at Marc. He was a whole head shorter, two years younger, wirier. "I never *did* like you," the kid said flatly.

Marc glared at Bruce, then stomped away. This was a problem I hadn't considered. Who was going to protect the kid when the bully was right next door? "He's not going to stop riding you."

"No."

"You worried about that?"

"He doesn't scare me," Bruce said. He was a brave little shit; I'll give him that.

I went north for my last beach walk. It was so early I had the shore to myself. It reminded me of the end of summer, when the seasonal cottagers left, and hardly anyone was around. That's when you learned the true nature of these shores, its subtle rhythms, its quiet language of wind, waves, and sand.

I stopped in front of 112, the shabby cabin we started renting when I was three years old. It was nearly the same as I remembered; in need of a paint job and hidden more among the birches, but still with that sagging screened-in porch, still the widow's watch at the apex of the roof that was so tiny it could only fit one chair. I wondered: was that chair still there? This was the shore where my dad taught me to drip sand out of my fingers to form sandcastles. There was the patch of sand where I drove my Tonka trucks. And that was the dune I used to take a running leap off, towel around my neck like a cape, emulating the flight of superheroes.

I went around the false point at 130 and onto the stretch near Carrie's old place. More and more cabins were giving way to year-round homes. As soon as her path through the dune came into view, I looked for those steps we'd sat on, where I nearly confessed my love—*should've* confessed my love. They weren't there. Neither was the cottage; only the crooked yellow arm of a backhoe loader and the gaping mouth of a bulldozer bucket.

I went up the path to get a better look. A big pit had been dug. Carrie's golf barn was flattened too, hauled off and smoothed over so there was no sign it had ever been there. A perfect disappearance. Isn't that what was happening to the Boiler Beach I knew— buried as completely as that ancient land bridge that cut the lake in half? I turned to leave. Something knuckled the arch of my foot. I looked down. A yellowed golf ball was poking out of the sand. It was an old Spalding Top-Flite #8. How could it *not* be Carrie's? I put the ball in my pocket, then went back down to the beach.

I sloshed out through the ankle-deep water to assess the damage Rob's theft had done to the boiler. From the front, you could barely tell a square yard of metal was missing from the venerable relic. But around back, on the lake side, the cut was so clean, there was no mistaking that something unnatural had happened. As I splashed back to shore, a man and woman came bounding down from the boiler monument. I got out of the water about the same time they reached it.

"Excuse me," the man called out. "Would you mind taking a picture of us?" He was a young guy, and the woman was younger. They were the sorts you'd expect to be content with a selfie. But he had a big expensive camera around his neck.

"Sure." They galloped out into the water and posed on the front side of the boiler, where its mangled ribs stuck out. I snapped off a shot and figured that was that. But they moved to a couple other places beside the boiler.

When I handed the camera to the guy, he said, "This is quite a treasure you have."

"Yep."

He must've sensed an edge to my clipped answer, because he followed with: "I guess it can get aggravating to have all these sight-seers invading your beach."

"Not really."

"Did they ever find the rest of the boat?"

I mulled over the question so long the woman got anxious. "I bet it says on the plaque," she told her boyfriend.

"Tell you what," I answered finally, "If you want the real story of the wreck, go have breakfast at the Aurora Quest in town. The owner's name is Bo. He knows the whole story. Ask him why someone took a blowtorch to the back of the boiler. That's been the big mystery around here."

A moment down the beach, I turned back. The guy was behind the boiler, crouching in the water. The woman was taking pictures.

When I got back to the cottage, the sun was just climbing the high ridge of pines. The water was glass. All the stones at the lake's edge glistened with color. I hadn't swum to the second sandbar in years. I waded out to the end of the first sandbar. It was barely up to my belly. I dove in and started swimming. Bigger rocks were visible below me, their color and sheen slowly overtaken by the pervading gloom. I stopped and touched bottom; up to my neck. A few more strokes, and I'd be out on the second sandbar.

I didn't realize I was in trouble until the next time I stopped. I was suddenly out of breath. Treading water, I peered beneath me.

I couldn't see the bottom. I should've gone back. But I'd come all that way. The second sandbar had to be close. I carried on, this time taking it easier, breast-stroking, one pull and a long glide, then another pull. Still, in less than a minute, I was tired again. My body felt heavy. After another glide, I had trouble lifting my head out of the water and breathed in before I surfaced. The coughing took more out of me. I treaded again. This time, it was a struggle to stay afloat. It was then that I wondered, is this what distress feels like? People always imagine drowning coming in a fit of frantic thrashing. Truth is, most victims just quietly slip under.

Where the hell was the sandbar? It had to be close. Keep going or turn around? Could I even make it back? One more push. One more. I went back to the crawl, kicking harder, willing myself. And then the bottom of the lake came back into view, ripples of sand. Sand! I went to touch down and kept plunging. Over my head. Still. And now there *was* panic. But I was too exhausted to summon any reserves. I stopped again, treading, treading...

That's when I saw it, a pale shimmer off to my left. As I made my last push, I found myself praying, *please be high enough to stand. Please.* Then I touched down on it: Mammoth Rock. My head and shoulders were out of the water. I stood there, gasping for breath, looking down at the ghostly monolith. It was as clear and defined as I'd ever seen it. I looked back to the shore. I was a long way out, over 200 yards. But I always thought the rock was further. Thank God the lake was low. Thank God I'd caught that pearly glimmer out of the corner of my eye.

Up on the deck, barely recognizable so far away, were Audie and Bruce. Audie was holding something to her face. Binoculars. I waved. She waved—then gave Bruce a turn to see. I waved at him, too. He handed the binoculars back and went inside.

I waited on Mammoth Rock a while, building my strength to get back to shore. It wasn't as grueling as the swim out. I knew where I needed to go, and the waves had picked up a little to help push me along. When I finally touched down, neck deep, on the bed of stones between sandbars, I thought of the question I'd pondered on the bridge the day before. Does the urge to live hold dominion over a will to die? As much as I'd just panicked in that fleeting moment of peril, I had no doubt that it did.

"You were out there a ways," Audie said, as I climbed the steps to the deck.

"Last swim to the sandbar."

"You looked scared for a minute. I could see your face."

"I wasn't."

"Bruce was just about to throw his suit on and swim—"

"He doesn't swim out there," I cut her off. "Ever. Got that? I don't want him past the first sandbar." Audie's eyes bugged out. "When I'm away, you *have* to be safe."

She nodded, tightening her mouth. I hurried inside. As I put on my clothes for Ripley, I couldn't stop beating myself up. Audie didn't deserve my anger. I'd have to make it up to her.

On the way to Ripley, Cam called. "For lunch on Friday, I was thinking about the place in Marine City beside the ferry."

"Anita's?"

"No, the other one, with the long window that looks out on the river. You, me, and mom stopped there the last time—"

"The Riviera."

"That's it. The Riviera." He laughed. "Remember how funny we thought that was?"

You'd have to see that stretch of the St. Clair River to get the joke. The Riviera it was not; warehouses and gravel pits and tiny homes time had forgotten. "Your mother couldn't stop laughing," I reminisced along, but it came out more sad than joyful. How long ago had that been? Ten years? It seemed like a lifetime.

"So...noon?" Cam reeled me back into the moment.

"As long as the ferry in Sombra cooperates."

"Alright." Cam went quiet. "See you then." More silence. I thought he'd hung up. "Sorry about this."

"Sorry?"

"Just that I waited so long to do it. I hope—I hope—"

"Don't worry about it."

"I hope you don't think I don't love you."

That caught me off guard. All I could think to say was, "Okay." It didn't occur to me until a mile later that I hadn't told Cam *I* loved *him*. I'd have to make sure to tell him that on Friday. Then there would be plenty of opportunities to *show* him after I got the teaching job and settled down in Ann Arbor.

I wondered: should I tell Cam my plans for moving back when we met? It would come as a surprise, for sure, and maybe not a welcome one. No point in ruining lunch. The best thing to do was quietly slip back into my American life, give it time, keep working to heal the old wounds, then let Cam know I was in town—after I knew for sure I had my act together.

The Ripley Farmer's Market was going on when I cruised into town. I parked at the church where they'd held Carrie's service. Walking up to the crowd in the main intersection, I felt exposed, as if any moment, someone might call me out, a circle might tighten around me. This town was too small to forget its most public tragedy. As luck would have it, I was headed away from the drift of people drawn to the booths by the park.

I lingered at the crossroads, that intersection Carrie had blown through as I sat by, failing to stop her. I scanned down the row of vendors heading out of town. All the way at the end, nearly across from where we had veered into her father's buggy, Beth was at her booth. She may as well have been a statue for as still as she stood. No one was around her table.

There was a long line to get into Fig. I passed it and went inside. I didn't need a table. A quick goodbye; that was all I could bear. Wendy was at the far end of the bar, making drinks for a huddle of hipsters. She didn't see me, even as I came within a few chairs of the group. One of the young women said something, and Wendy laughed, throwing her head back, rolling her eyes so they flashed with light, radiating that infectious cheer. I wheeled around and walked away. What was the use of making an appearance to reinforce my disappearance? She laughed again, and as I slipped past the crush of customers waiting by the door, I heard Wendy say, "I'm sure there's more to *that* story!"

Then I was back on the street. Coming here, I worried I'd be recognized. Leaving, I didn't care. I gazed through people as I walked, down to the crossroads, across the intersection, past booth after booth, and finally to Beth. "Can I help you?" She hadn't seemed to move a muscle since I last saw her.

"No." When I glanced up, she was staring at me, not sternly like she had in times past, but almost mercifully. I just wanted to stand there with her. Just stand.

"Thank you," she said after a moment.

I was mystified. "What for?"

"For helping Chloe."

"I'm just taking her somewhere."

"Gordon believes you're saving the child."

Gordon? Ah, Newf. I hadn't heard him called that name since I was a kid. "Saving people is God's business, isn't it?"

"It's all God's business," Beth said. She shifted her eyes away from me, over to where we'd collided with her family years ago.

"I guess it is." I looked back over my shoulder, joining her.

"I once asked Gordon if he loved the girl who died."

"What did he say?"

"He said that, as much as he wished he could, he did not. He said that the person who truly loved Carrie Sinclair was you."

"I don't know what love is," I whispered. Then I buried my face in my hands. When I finally looked up, Beth was there. She took me by the shoulders, as close as she could come to a hug. Her hands trembled. Her smile did too.

I tried to buy flowers from her, but Beth refused to take my money. Instead, she gave me twice what I picked out for free. I had one last stop in town—a place I'd never visited: Carrie's grave. Her father had insisted I never go, and I always felt like it would be dishonoring him if I did. But since I was leaving for good, I figured there was a chance Carl might grant me this small concession. Word was he was still alive, living alone at Troonorth for the last few years since his wife died. Last time I drove past there, it was falling into a state of disrepair. I'd be driving by again in two days.

The Ripley-Huron Cemetery was down a long narrow lane in the middle of a fallow field on the outskirts of town. Less than half the land they'd allotted held graves, yet there must've been 500. It seemed impossible that so many had died in this forgotten hamlet, and that they planned for so many more. Audie told me once that Carrie's grave was just off the main road that snaked around the cemetery. I had to walk the loop twice before I found it.

IN LOVING MEMORY
CARRIE SINCLAIR
1966-1984
"They can no longer die;
for they are like the angels."
Luke 20:36

Like the angels. I didn't doubt it. Carrie was more of an angel than anyone I've known. Her aura, her power, her purity. And that final act, that intercession in my life, swinging the car away to avoid my hitting the tree. Sacrificing herself. She can no longer die. Did that mean she was dead forever, or eternally alive?

There were already flowers by her grave; two vases full on either side of the headstone, a bouquet on the ground above where she lay. They were all fresh, as if they'd been placed there this morning. Was this someone's daily ritual?

Ah, Carrie. You never did get to find yourself. And we barely knew you, the closest friends you had. If you were alive, how would you feel about what I've done with the gift you gave me—my life, these last 34 years, the mess I've made. Is going home, leaving the purgatory of Boiler Beach, trying to redeem myself enough? I'm sure you'd forgive me no matter what. But what if I couldn't forgive myself? What if I make everything right with Cam—and I still can't exorcise this pain?

I don't know what I was expecting. A voice to overtake me, an epiphany, a sudden rustling in the trees. There was nothing. It was me standing over the body of a long-dead girl I once loved, holding flowers that were too late to be of use, on a quiet patch of lawn in a huge, empty field.

I was going to lay the flowers on Carrie's grave anyway. I was going to whisper a goodbye. I was going to wait for the gravity of the moment to weigh on me. I did none of those things. I walked away, got in my Lincoln, and drove back to the beach.

"Such lovely flowers!" Audie gushed as I came through the kitchen door.

"I knew you'd like them."

"This isn't about the Bruce incident, is it?"

"No—"

"Because you were right. I have to have rules."

"I shouldn't have yelled at you."

"So, it *is* about that."

"No. I saw these flowers and thought you'd like them."

"I do," Audie said, taking them from me finally.

"I had another idea. Maybe we should have a bonfire tonight."

Audie's face lit up. "Yes! And we could invite some people! It's the Fourth of July, you know."

"Some people?" This wasn't in my plan.

"The gang! Sharon and Rob and Newf."

"I don't think that's such a good idea, Audie." She didn't know what I knew about Rob and Joan. And Bruce.

"Of course it is!" She was undeterred. "Why wouldn't it be?"

"For one thing, there's the whole business between Rob and me about the gully. And Rob is having troubles with Newf, too."

"All the more reason to get together."

"Newf and Sharon aren't even American. They don't care about our Fourth of July."

Audie gave me a flat, frosty glare. "Honestly, Tommy."

What could I say? "Fine. Invite them. We'll see what happens."

There was a knock on the door behind me. I turned. There, on the other side of the screen, was Blair Henry.

"We're taking another look at Grant's case," Blair said, once we were in my backyard.

"Really..."

"A couple things have come to light."

"Whatever I can do to help."

Blair looked up toward the bluff, like he could see that far. "When you were at the gazebo that morning, you didn't see any extra footprints anywhere, did you?"

"I would've told you if I did."

Blair screwed up his mouth. "That's what I thought. No tire tracks, either?"

"Tire tracks? No. What's going on?"

"Larry Moore came in yesterday. Told us there was something that's been eating at him ever since they found Grant. Said the night before, he drove by and thought he saw car lights out by the gazebo." He squinted into my eyes, weighing the effect of his words. I just lifted my eyebrows. "So, you can understand why we're taking another look."

"Absolutely. If something else…happened, we need to know."

Blair stared at me. I did my best to hold his gaze. "Of course, a lot of time has gone by," he broke the silence.

"Yeah."

"We were hoping we could find anything that might suggest someone else was there…"

I shook my head. "I wish I could help."

"Well, I had to ask." We stood there, nodding at each other. It seemed to be over. I took a step to go. "We were lucky nobody threw out the board that broke when he fell."

I froze. Blair was watching my reaction. "Oh, yeah?"

"We found a few threads of fabric snagged on a popped nail."

Now I was the one waiting. "And?"

"And they didn't come from Grant's clothes."

"Hmm." I made a show of thinking about it. "How can you tell it happened that night?"

"We can't. But with Larry's story, we have to dig deeper."

"Yeah." I scratched at my jaw. "For sure."

"So…" Blair let it hang for a good long moment. "You said you didn't walk up there until the morning after the storm."

Here it was. This is what he'd really come for. "That's right."

"But you'd seen Grant the night before."

"That's what I told you."

Blair frowned. "Okay."

"Do I have to remind you I was laid up after getting my clock cleaned in the Aurora?"

"No…" Blair was looking down at his feet now. "But you *were* okay enough to wake up early and walk up the hill."

Hearing him say it like that, I could understand his suspicion. "Yeah," I snapped, "because I was mildly interested in why my cottage flooded out."

Blair put up his hands. "Fair enough." Then he came right back at me. "So, if we happened to check your closet for light blue shirts and compared the fibers with what we found snagged to that nail, there wouldn't be a problem, eh?"

Light blue; like Chloe's Ice Cream Trail shirt. "Not at all. I burned that shirt right after I pushed Grant out of the gazebo. So, I'm good."

Blair glared at me. Then he laughed, in spite of himself. "I'm just doing my job, Tommy."

"I get that. I want to get to the bottom of what happened, too."

"It's all probably nothing," Blair finally relented. "I might have more questions later."

"Fine."

Blair walked away. I was nearly out of my backyard when he called out, "Know anything about a youth ministry Grant ran?"

"I know he had one."

Blair nodded and went on. I watched him go. There was no question anymore that Chloe had to leave. And that I had to take her. The only question was: could we do it soon enough?

Audie and Bruce were out on the deck, painting side by side again. He had the BNDRT suit on. The toy ark and all the carved animals I bought from Beth were lined up on the deck railing. Bruce was painting them into his seascape.

"Looks like something you might've done," I said to Audie.

"He wants to do a Sorry kind of abstract. The ark's perfect."

Bruce squinted at the animals like Audie used to when she was fitting game pieces into her scene. Audie seemed to be holding her breath, waiting for my reaction. I smiled. She exhaled. "I talked to Sharon. She'd love to come for a bonfire. But Rob can't make it."

"Too bad." It would've been a shock if he could.

"I've never been to a bonfire," Bruce muttered absently.

"You've never been to a bonfire?" Audie marveled. "Then you have to come."

"You don't *have* to."

"I'd like to," he decided. Bruce: sitting by the fire with Sharon staring across at him. Her husband's illegitimate child. Wonderful.

"I don't have Newf's number," Audie said then.

"I'll get a hold of Newf," I told her. We had a lot to talk about.

Newf didn't speak for a long time after I told him about Blair. He was still on the line, though. I could hear his ragged breathing. Finally: "He asked about the youth ministry?"

"That's what worries me most."

"I can have Chloe ready in two hours."

I was out in the Chief as we spoke, packing it up for the ride. We *could* leave now, but then I'd have to change plans with Cam, and he might not be able to get away on short notice. And there was no way I could get out of the bonfire. Besides, how would it look if we took off the very day Blair questioned me?

"Let's stick with Friday morning. We leave right away, and it looks bad. Wait a couple days, and we don't seem so suspicious."

"I guess." Newf didn't sound convinced.

We hung up. I got out of the Chief and headed back to the cottage. Halfway there, I called Newf back. "I almost forgot. Audie wants to have a bonfire tonight. July Fourth celebration."

"You're shitting me."

"You, me, Sharon, and her. Like old times."

"No Rob?"

"No Rob."

Another stuttering breath. "Aw, hell. I can't say no to Audie."

"Welcome to my world."

There was so much this kid didn't know how to do. Shuck corn. Make burger patties. Turn on a gas grill. Cook burgers. Butter corn on the cob. Doing the dishes was a whole other fiasco. He practically used up the entire bottle of detergent, giving every dish its own squirt of soap.

Audie would have her hands full with this one. I felt like I was helping Bruce cram for a test. It's hard to fathom that a 15-year-old kid had never been to a bonfire. Naturally, he didn't know the first thing about building one. But it didn't take a genius to figure out where to get wood. There was a thing called "the woods" in our backyard. Even after sending him off with explicit instructions on the kind of wood we needed, he screwed that up, dragging full-length lodgepoles down to the beach. He claimed there was nothing that fit my description for bonfire-worthy material.

Amazingly, the kid was right. I used to find smaller, thicker pieces of wood back when my dad gave me the chore. We found plenty of kindling, but nothing that would sustain a bonfire. Then I remembered the woodpile at Newf's old cottage. Rob had cleared most everything away from the outside of the place, but somehow, he left that. The wood was old. I worried it wouldn't burn. Still, I loaded Bruce up with an armful and took one myself. We were on our way back for another load when Sharon came walking down the path to the beach. She was on the other side of the fence her husband had erected.

"This must be Bruce Duncan. I've heard a lot about you. I'm Sharon Beam-Garton." She shifted the fold-up chair and tried to reach her hand over the fence. It was too high. Instead, she offered a bow, like she was meeting a Japanese dignitary. "I've known your mom for, oh, 35 years, isn't it, Tommy?"

"About that."

"She's a firecracker," Sharon said, with a smile Bruce would never recognize as forced. He just nodded. It occurred to me that I didn't know what the kid thought of his mother.

"Well," Sharon paused awkwardly, backing away.

"Audie's in the cottage," I said.

"Then I should go see if she needs help," Sharon announced, directing her words at Bruce. She twirled around theatrically and headed down to the beach.

"She's weird," Bruce said when Sharon was out of earshot.

"She's got a lot going on."

Newf showed up a little after that, in time for the sunset—and for dispensing advice on how to build a bonfire.

"That's not how you do it," he stated, after I'd given Bruce a long explanation on the proper formation of logs.

I glared at him. "This always works."

"Not with wet logs and beach grass. You'll smoke us out."

While we went back and forth, Bruce got up and walked away. "See what you did?" I said to Newf. "All that work trying to teach him something, and you undermine it in a minute."

"I can't help it if you can't make a bonfire."

I tried to think of a good comeback. But the silence wore on. Then the weight of our troubles pressed on us. "How's Chloe?"

"Scared. I didn't tell her about Blair. She's worried enough."

"It'll be over soon."

"I don't know. If he starts talking to all those kids that went to Grant's little revivals, it won't matter if Chloe's in Florida." He gave shudder. How would he react if I told him what the guy at the RV park had seen?

"Joan's boy is one shitty stone skipper." Newf pointed to the shore. Bruce was doing it all wrong—no wind-up, too upright, too much overhand. Probably the wrong stones, too. I started down to the water. Newf overtook me, even with his bad leg. I slowed to scan the beach for good skippers. By the time I came up beside them, Newf was already showing Bruce his form. It didn't go well. One throw made four skips. The rest managed a single hop, if that. Bad stones. Too anxious.

"He never could skip stones." I leaned over, took two hops, like a shortstop gathering himself, and side-armed a low toss over the water's surface. The stone skipped half a dozen times then curled in a long skittering tail. I threw my hands up in victory.

"Lucky toss," Newf grumbled.

"What you've got to do," I told Bruce, "is crouch down so your arm angle's level with the water. And you have to snap the wrist." Damned if the kid wasn't listening, much more intently than with the bonfire. He bent down, cocked his head sideways with the lake's surface, and took a few practice wind-ups. "Here," I gave him my stones. "You need good rocks, too."

"*That* was my problem," Newf muttered. "Anyone can skip a good stone."

Bruce galloped toward the surf and let it fly. The rock hooked into the water and never rose. Newf rolled his eyes at me. The kid tried again. This time, the rock took one big hop before plunking into the lake. "Flatter. You're still throwing down at the water." His next throw made two skips before hooking left. "Flatter…"

Then he tossed one just right. It must've taken eight skips. Newf even had time to roar his amazement. And it kept going, floating, it seemed, on a line of uncountable ripples. Bruce looked back at us with a big, proud grin. It was the happiest I'd seen him, happier, even, than when he mopped the floor.

"There you go," I said. Then I had to turn away. I was getting teary-eyed. What in the world? One lucky throw.

It was that kind of a night. The sunset nearly made me cry. I got emotional when the bonfire didn't smoke like Newf thought it would. When Audie broke out marshmallows, I gasped with giddy surprise.

Last things.

I could've had a last drink, too. Newf offered me a beer from his cooler. Sharon was drinking a boda of wine, and Audie said she could open a bottle if I wanted a glass. "One drink," they all said. I declined. Why tempt fate so close to leaving?

Sharon kept trying to connect with Bruce. She showed him how to bronze a marshmallow, made a S'more for him, tried to draw him out. "We all met when we were your age," she said as we reminisced. "Have you met any friends up here?"

"I don't like to do what other kids do," Bruce said. It was the most he'd talked since we sat down at the bonfire.

"What do *you* like to do?" Sharon asked.

"He's a hell of a painter," I jumped in. "Audie's teaching him."

"He's a very fast learner," Audie added.

"Well, I'd love to see your work," Sharon said.

Bruce didn't seem too thrilled with that idea. He just shrugged.

"You like sports?" Newf broke the silence.

"Not really."

"What about boating?" Sharon kept trying.

"I don't know…"

"We have kayaks and jet-skis and sailboats." She sounded like Rob. I'd never heard her shill their abundance so openly.

Bruce said, "We have a canoe."

"There you go! Kayaking is easier. And you'd love jet-skiing. Mr. Garton would be happy to teach you."

"Your mother was quite the jet-skier," Newf added. I never remembered her doing anything but holding tight to Rob's waist.

"That's right!" Audie agreed. "It's probably in the blood."

"My mom?" Bruce seemed as skeptical as I was.

"Then it's settled," Sharon insisted. "We'll figure out when to have you down. There happens to be a young lady who comes around to ride it, too. Do you know Molly Moore?"

"I know Molly," Bruce muttered.

"She's quite a looker."

"Alright," I broke in, "we don't have to matchmake for the poor kid." Molly was way out of Bruce's league.

And that's when we lost Bruce. "Well…" he got out of his chair, "I'm going to head up."

"Oh no!" Sharon lurched out of her slouch. "Don't! We'll be more fun. We promise."

"I have to read," Bruce said, withdrawing. "Audie gave me this book. *Catcher…Catcher…*"

"*In the Rye,*" Audie called out to him as he was walking away.

"*Catcher in the Rye?*" I was flabbergasted.

"It's a coming of age story," Audie said, getting up herself. "I'm going to see if he's okay."

"Why wouldn't he be okay?" Sharon wondered aloud. When Audie was out of earshot, she added, "Poor boy."

"Grant is such a shit," Newf muttered.

"*Grant's* a shit?" Sharon barked, her temper suddenly flaring. "You know…"

I knew what he meant, but he didn't know what I did—and Sharon, too, by the sound of it. "It's all shit," she declared. Then she took another long squeeze from her boda. I'd never seen her drinking so much, acting so unhinged. Of course, I knew why. But this wasn't the moment to dwell on that. This might be the only chance I'd have alone with Sharon and Newf.

"I was hoping you guys could help me," I said. "Bruce is going to be here the rest of the summer, and Audie will be taking care of him. On her own."

"Where are you going to be?" Sharon asked.

"I'm leaving for a while."

Her mouth dropped open. The orange glow of the fire fluttered across her bewildered face. "Where will you go?"

"First, to help Newf out and drive Chloe to his sister's in Florida. After that, a vacation."

"Like I told you, I'll look in every day," Newf assured me.

"Of course, we'll help," Sharon said.

"How's the gully?" Newf asked.

"Still filling up, but I showed Bruce how to dig it out."

"What I meant was, what if we have another big rain?"

It was a hard exchange to be having in front of Sharon. Most of the runoff problems had to do with Rob. "Just—if you—just keep an eye on the weather," I sputtered.

"Watch the weather?" Sharon fumed. "*That's* the plan?"

What else could I say? Stop your husband? "It's the same problem whether I'm here or not."

"What problem?" Audie broke into the bonfire's glow.

"The state of the gully," I recovered.

"We've already discussed that," Audie said, like I was the one who needed comforting. "If I have a problem, you'll be here within three days."

"We're going to take care of this." Sharon started stabbing her finger at the bonfire. "We are taking care of it. Don't you worry."

"I don't want to talk about bad things," Audie declared. "Look at us! Sitting around a bonfire again like teenagers."

It was a relief to hear Sharon laugh. "Remember how excited you and I would get for our evenings with the boys?" She leaned against Audie. "You two were so cute, with your long hair and your tans and your muscles."

"You were never cute," I let Newf know.

"You never had muscles."

So the night went. Audie reminded everyone of my "dumb-struck awe" after that first time I saw Sharon at the store. Newf dared to bring up Audie's treacherous swim across the Pine River. ("I had it all the way," Audie insisted, to our laughter.) Sharon brought up Newf's raft, the one he built for the four of us before we met Rob and Joan, and everything changed. "Ah, the Island." She recalled our nickname for it. "I wish we never got off that raft and took it down south."

"Me too," Newf said. "I lost my shirt on those damn things."

More laughing. More stories. And every one of them about the summers that *we* were together, just the four of us, before we ventured south of the Eighth, yearning for something more.

When we ran out of stories, we leaned back in our chairs and watched the multitude of stars sparkling above us. I couldn't remember the last time I'd gazed up at the night sky for that long, that sober, and with other people. There were shooting stars, and we called them out when their trails scraped the darkness. Most were small, but a handful seemed to span the entirety of the heavens, and we howled out our amazement and gratitude.

Sharon drank her entire boda of wine. Driving home was out of the question. It took Newf and I buttressing her on either side just to get her to the cottage. He said he'd drive her home, but she declined. "I like it here better," she slurred out dreamily.

We put her in Audie's bed, and Audie set up on the couch at a right angle to the one I'd been sleeping on since Bruce came. We were out within minutes. At some point, I woke to groaning. Audie was kicking at her blanket. And she was whimpering and muttering, mostly gibberish, but I did hear her repeat, "Leave me alone" a few times. I put a hand on her forehead and whispered everything was okay. She finally settled down. It took me some time then to get back to sleep. Every moan, every rustle had me on alert.

At some point, I succumbed. And I had a dream of my own. I was down by the shore. It was night, but the moonlight was bright enough that I could see people walking from a long way off, coming in both directions. As they neared me, I felt myself sinking. Finally, they started passing, from one side, then the next. They didn't seem to know I was there. But I recognized them. There was Jerry Sharp, juggling three Jarts; and Dave MacLennan, one of the older kids I looked up to, who died in a boating accident; and Sue Moulden, who babysat me once, told me ghost stories, and kissed me on the cheek goodnight. Everyone who passed was someone I knew, all of them had died, and not one acknowledged me.

That's when I realized I was buried up to my neck in sand, and the sand was wet and rising higher, nearly to my mouth now; so close, I was afraid to cry out. I felt dripping on my head, a constant drizzle. It ran down my face, burned my eyes. But it was pleasing on my tongue. I leaned my head back as far as the sand would allow and licked the elixir as it streamed over me. That's when I saw the giant hand, and beyond that, in a blur, my father's face. He was dribbling the liquid the way he taught me to make sandcastles. Then, as the pattering slowed, the blue stem of a bottle came into focus. Skyy vodka. My dad poured some in his hand and started drizzling the liquor over me again.

I gasped for it desperately, but my mouth wouldn't shut. My whole face was hardening, and I could taste the grit of rust. I was turning to metal. The barrel of the bottle above me no longer held vodka. It was a blowtorch, and the blue end was glowing orange. I tried to scream, but my jaw was locked open, rusty and solid as the boiler. No sound came out. Then the blowtorch wheezed, and everything was light...

And I was screaming.

"Tommy!" Audie was shaking me.

"What? What?!" I bolted up and sat gaping at her absently.

"You were having a dream."

I took a hard breath. My mouth was dry. I licked my lips, expecting the taste of that phantom liquor. There was only the salt of my sweat. "I guess I was."

"You kept saying, 'Let me go. Let me go.' What were you dreaming about?"

"I—I...don't remember."

"Dreams are windows into the soul, you know."

"They're something, alright." We both settled back onto our makeshift beds. It was light outside, but too early to wake up. I tried to fall back asleep, but I kept seeing that rusty monolith of my face on the shore, waves pooling in my unhinged mouth, the blowtorch rasping above, poised to dismantle the myth of me. I sat up on the couch. Audie was tucked in a ball, hands locked around her knees, watching me.

"I can't sleep," she said. "Did you think about your dream?"

"No." Then I decided to ask, "Did you have any dreams?"

"I never dream anymore," Audie claimed. I'm sure she thought she was telling me the truth. She didn't think her soul had a window. Having seen what I saw and heard what she said, I knew it did. But that window had been boarded up from Audie. And that was sadder than her belief that she didn't dream at all.

"Dreams aren't all they're cracked up to be. Living is better."

"Amen to that," Audie whispered, releasing her knees and rising up. "Might as well embrace the day."

I got up with her. "Might as well."

"Your last one at the beach," she added, arching that eyebrow.

I felt a flutter in my chest. All this talk of windows to the soul. "For a little while," I clarified.

She kept her eyebrow raised.

As early as it was, we didn't want to bustle around and wake up Bruce and Sharon. Audie made coffee, and I went into the basement to take care of my last chore. I'd bought a foundation repair kit and was going to fill the cracks where water was leaking in. It was a low-budget solution, just a tube of goop squeezed out of a caulking gun; a finger in the dike. I wasn't going to leave Audie and Bruce without at least plugging up what I could. We hadn't had a good rain in a while, and I'd been religiously emptying the gully, so the basement wasn't too bad. Still, there was moisture nearly all the way around where the walls met the floor. I used up all the goop; 10 tubes worth. When I ran out of small cracks, I squeezed it into the gaping crevices, not so much to solve a problem as to bandage my guilt; white scars, like the graft over my eye.

I was nearly done when I heard knocking at the back door. I was in no position to clean myself off and hurry up the steps. The knocking came again, but not so loud it would wake someone up. There was a third lighter rap, and silence. Whoever it was must've gotten the hint and gone away. Then I heard the sound of muffled voices. I wiped my hands and went upstairs. Bruce was at the back door, and Rob was on the other side of the screen.

"What's going on?"

Bruce turned to me, eyes pleading. He had thrown on the BNDRT coveralls.

"Nothing," Rob said, glancing at the lettering on Bruce's back. "Just talking to the boy. I heard he was going to be here all summer. And I told him if he was looking to make some money, I had a few jobs he might like."

"He's on vacation." I edged past Bruce to get between the two.

"Can I go?" Bruce asked me.

"Sure." I all but pushed him away.

"Nice to see you again," Rob called as Bruce disappeared. Then in a hushed voice, he said, "Really? You gave him those coveralls?"

I ignored him. "I hope you're not thinking of coming around when I'm gone."

I'd expected an argument. It was clear by the stoop of Rob's shoulders that he wasn't there to argue. "I only want to help." His voice broke.

It was hard not to feel for him. "Newf and Sharon said they'd look in. We've got it covered."

"I know."

"You know?"

"Sharon told me."

"She's not even up yet."

"She's been home since four a.m.," Rob said.

Here Audie and I had been tiptoeing around that closed bedroom door, thinking Sharon was inside. Drunk as she was the night before, I couldn't have imagined her waking before us.

"I hope she's okay," I said.

"No, she's not okay. *We're* not okay. Nowhere near."

I'd never seen Rob so distraught. "I'm sorry."

"We have to talk." He regained his composure and looked past me into the cottage. "Somewhere else."

We walked out to my backyard, the big tear drop-shaped plot Rob expunged from his diorama. In the morning light, watching him scuffle along, he looked like he'd already worked a whole day. His hair was a mess and he hadn't shaved, a rarity for him. Then there were his eyes, red and baggy, like he'd been rubbing at them.

"I need that piece of the—the tractor."

I stopped in the ruts of my old driveway. "I bet you do."

"I'm not going to hide it. I'm going to expose it."

"Why would you do that?"

He took a deep breath, then deflated as thoroughly as a man could, shoulders sagging, head pitching forward. "It's either that or lose Sharon," he murmured, barely above a whisper.

"What are you talking about?"

He managed to reinflate. His head tilted back, and his eyes got stuck looking up toward his dream resort. "She said she's going to leave me. Said she was tired of supporting me when I hurt so many people. You know about Joan. And Bruce. Sharon put it together a few days back, but we didn't have it out until this morning."

"Oh." I still didn't understand what that had to do with the metal scrap I'd hidden in the Chief.

"She gave me a choice. Turn things around. Do right by Bruce, help you with your flooding, kill the resort, or lose her forever."

I was floored. I understood about Bruce. And the health of my cottage was part of that. But kill the resort?

"A lot of old shit got dredged up," Rob confessed. "Sharon said I was like my dad, destroying Boiler Beach for my own selfish gain. She accused him of driving her dad out of business so he could get that land at the top of the hill. Said what I was doing was worse than that, that I was killing the very soul of the beach."

I'd always wondered how Rob had managed to get Sharon past what had happened between their fathers. Apparently, he hadn't. "All the way back to the store…"

"She never would've brought that up if this Joan thing hadn't come to light."

"This Joan thing? This 18-year affair?"

"I'm not here to take abuse, Tommy. I've been doing that for three hours."

"Fair enough. So, what does my souvenir have to do with it?"

"I can't lose Sharon." He was suddenly overcome with emotion. "If I lose her, I lose it all—the kids, my grandson, everything that makes me happy. The resort is just business. Sharon's my life."

I understood that much. What I still couldn't figure out was how that hunk of metal was going to help win back Sharon. "So you need that piece."

"I need a reason to stop working on the resort. And if it comes out that there never was an Aurora Quest shipwreck, that it was all a hoax, maybe that's a good enough excuse for me to reassess."

"What do you need an excuse for?"

"A lot of my investors are going to be pissed off."

I wasn't much of a businessman. One look at the Wondermat would tell you that. But the success of Mariner's Vista didn't seem to hinge on the mystique of the Aurora Quest. "How are you going to convince them that losing a side attraction is worth scrapping a multi-million-dollar resort?"

"Let me worry about that. Right now, I'm not really sure."

I went quiet. Rob watched me with sad, hopeful eyes. What the hell. What was I going to do with that rusty relic? I pointed to the road. "It's in the Chief."

When we got to the start of the path I'd worn around Rob's fencing, I turned. The entire expanse of the field was behind him. "What were you going to do with this anyway? Why was it empty on the model?"

"I was going to flood this land and the field next to it and make a little lake with a marina. Your cottage was going to be the resort's boathouse." He waved a hand over the land. "Can you imagine? All this—a quiet, serene oasis."

"Sort of like it is now?"

Rob gave a little huff, but he didn't disagree.

When I opened the Chief's door, Rob climbed in and flopped down on the flimsy couch behind the driver's seat. "Does this ever take me back." He moved his hand like a preacher blessing his congregation. "Audie painting in the corner. You, Carrie, and Newf at the kitchen table. Joan right here," he patted the couch beside him, "playing her guitar. And Grant bustling around, keeping the whole crazy circus going."

"Yeah." I followed his hand. It wasn't hard to envision.

"Sharon and I never really *were* part of this."

"You didn't want to be."

"You didn't want us here."

He was probably right about that. "Look where it got everybody," I reminded him.

Rob gave the couch where Joan had sat another tap and held his hand there. "I don't know what I was thinking," he said. "I couldn't even explain to Sharon why it started. I must've felt like I'd been missing something. Same with Joan. I bumped into her at O'Hare Airport. Then we had a few calls. Then we were getting together for a week every winter. At the Benmiller Inn."

Rob laughed at that—and I knew why before he even explained himself. "Remember how she said that's where people went to have affairs?" Well…for 15 years we played that part. Even as it was happening, I remember thinking, *what am I doing? I love Sharon. I can't keep doing this.* We only missed one winter—the year Bruce was born. You'd think that would've stopped us.

"I must've liked the danger," Rob decided. "Living on the edge, like Grant used to do. Still, I thought we were being careful. I only ever called her from that one phone. And after Joan thought she saw a beacher at Benmiller, we stopped going there altogether.

That was the year I kicked Grant out of the bunkhouse…and we just…kept…going…"

He stopped. I didn't know what to say. I patted his shoulder, like Grant might've done. Then I parted the curtains to the driving space, reached under the passenger seat, and pulled out the metal plate. When I held it out to Rob, he cocked his head from side to side, like it was some lake creature he was afraid to touch. "A lot of sleepless nights over this."

"And a couple criminal ones."

He finally took the metal scrap. "The break-in wasn't my idea."

"I was talking about draining that pond to flood me out."

"I'm sorry for that," Rob said. "It was a mistake. At least it started out that way. I was just going to drain it slowly, safely. I needed to smooth over that land for the resort. But then one of my guys accidently dropped a boulder on the pipe that came from Newf's creek. So his runoff started bypassing the pond again and going straight down the hill. I saw what it was doing to your gully, and—I don't know—I decided if I drained the pond faster, you'd see what a hopeless situation you were in."

Here it was. The truth. Finally. I should've been mad. But I couldn't muster the anger. With everything that was happening, I just didn't have it in me anymore. "So it started as an accident?"

"Yeah."

"You choked off the pipe to the pond, got Newf's creek flowing back into my gully, then just decided, screw it, might as well compound my problem?"

"Something like that," Rob said.

"Something like what Newf's and your great grandpa did when they accidently blew up a tractor in the lake."

Rob started to grin, but it quickly fell. He tapped the slab against his free hand, then ran his fingers over the *SAW* lettering. "This whole thing would've been a funny family story. Tipping over a tractor in the lake is funny. Stupid, but funny. Even claiming it was a shipwreck is funny in a pathetic sort of way. But then profiting from it. For years. That's unforgivable."

"Nothing's unforgivable," I heard myself say. Me: saying that.

"We'll find out." Rob set the relic beside him and leaned back. "All I ever wanted to do was make my father proud. He was always trying to make this beach better; building the tennis courts, dumping money into the golf course, renovating the ballfield. Some people don't see him that way. I get that. But I did. And I wanted to show him I could make this place better too." He let out a heavy sigh. "I wonder what he'd think about the resort."

"He'd love it," I told Rob. And I meant it. But that didn't mean it was a good thing.

"You're probably right. He was a numbers guy at heart, and the numbers are very big."

"Money isn't everything."

"No, it's not. And, anyway, he's not the person I need to win over anymore."

His words struck me—that recognition of the relative claims of the dead and living.

"What do you think she'd want me to do?" he asked suddenly. "After the resort is dead, I'll be stuck with all that land."

He locked his eyes onto mine and waited. He truly wanted to hear what I thought. "You know Sharon. She'd probably just want everything to go back to the way it was."

Rob's gaze drifted away. He leaned forward, put his head in his hands, and ran his fingers through his hair. "Sounds about right."

When we left the Chief, Rob held his hand out. I shook it. "I hope you don't mind," he said, "but I *would* like to come around from time to time."

"As long as Audie's okay with it."

"She looks good," he said. "Better than I thought she would. I hadn't seen her in years."

"You never visited her at the harbor?"

"I couldn't bring myself to do it," Rob conceded. "It was too painful. She's the only woman I ever felt helpless around. I could have loved her, if I wasn't so intimidated by her." It was an extraordinary admission. I assumed he stuck with Audie out of pity. I never would've fathomed that he moved on to Sharon because he was afraid to love what he couldn't understand.

Rob asked me then, "The boy—you think he's scared of me?"

"A little," I softened the truth.

"I wonder if he knows."

It was a good question. Bruce had to realize something was wrong with his parent's relationship. How much had he overheard? What had Joan told him? "I think it's best to assume he doesn't know anything. And keep it that way."

B ruce got a late start on the gully. When I looked out the window to check his progress, Bogue's wife was chewing him out. As soon as she saw me coming, she scurried away.

"Is this water polluted?" Bruce asked as I came to his side.

"Don't listen to her. All this comes from Garton land, so who's the polluter?" Bruce looked at the greenish plume snaking north along the shore. "You're not doing anything wrong. But people *will* get mad. That's why you've got to dig earlier."

The poor kid still looked rattled from the exchange. I noticed that he'd blocked up his trench. "Did she make you do that?"

Bruce nodded. "She said if she caught me emptying this out again, she'd call the police."

"What are the police going to do?" I took the shovel and freed the runoff. The kid had done it right this time. The trench angled away from the waves so it wouldn't cave in.

"I was going to tell you," Bruce said, as we watched the gully drain. "I found this on the side of the bank under those bushes." He reached into the pocket of the old power plant coveralls and held out a beat-up smartphone. I knew whose it was before I took it. Who else had a bright royal-blue paisley iPhone cover? A surge of panic coursed through me. The night he died, Grant said he was going to take pictures. Even if there wasn't one of Chloe, I'd seen him texting her. If the police got hold of this phone...

"Mr. McTavish?" I looked up. He must've been saying my name a while. "I'm not going to tell anyone."

Did he know it was Grant's phone too? I put it in my pocket. "Thanks," I mumbled, still mulling things over. "Wait. If anyone comes to talk to you about this, just say you gave it to me."

"But won't they think—" That I disappeared with evidence? That I was guilty? Exactly. "I mean, won't they…won't they…"

"Hang on…" Once the kid told them, he'd be in it up to his eyeballs. He didn't need to be worrying about this, especially now. "Maybe just—just—"

"Just what?" Bruce was leaning in, hanging on my words.

"Just do what you think is right."

The night before I was to take Chloe across the border, I woke to a clap of thunder. Rain started pummeling the roof. It was loud and distinct at first, but it settled into a steady drone. I tried to get back to sleep, but distant lightning pulsed and twitched to keep the night rumbling. Even though I had a pillow over my head, I could still see that light, throwing fragments of the cottage into my eyes—furniture tensed and hunkering, familiar ghosts of things holding their ground. These impressions came in ever-lengthening intervals, blinking then succumbing to darkness.

And when that darkness came, I'd try to let myself go with it. I needed the sleep. In the back of my mind, though, there was always that wondering: when would the next eruption of light come? What would I see? How would I react? Compress a life into one storm, and this is what you'd get; darkness punctuated by flashes of light. Some brighter. Others, no more than flickers. Some so jolting they took your breath away. Others captivating you with a long, fading glow. At some point, though, the wondering, the anticipation, would no longer be rewarded. There would be a flash. You'd wait. And nothing would come.

Then it was morning, and Audie was making coffee. Then I was out on the deck, watching the drizzle pattering on the lake. Then I was at the water's edge and my eyes were scanning the beach from the false point south near Pine River, to the waves at my feet, and all the way north across the shoreline's long curve to the tiny lighthouse in Kincardine. Somewhere near there, a lone telescope was watching. Then Bruce was digging out the gully, and I was saying goodbye, and I turned so he wouldn't see me cry. And I was thinking, this is one of those brighter flashes that burns into you and won't go away even when the darkness comes. Then I was embracing Audie and I didn't want to let go, and she kept saying, *you don't want to be late, you don't want to be late.* Then the Chief was groaning up the hill at the Eighth, and I kept looking from the bright opening between the pines at the top to the reflection in my side mirror—grey-blue water stretching, stretching, stretching to an ever-distant horizon.

Goodbye Boiler Beach.

Newf was late. We agreed on nine. Two and a half hours to the Sombra ferry, then a half hour to cross the St. Clair River to Marine City. Here it was, 9:15, and no cars were coming from Ripley. I was in the weed-infested parking lot of the abandoned Pine River store, on the corner where the Eighth met Highway 21. I texted Cam we might be late. Then I called Newf. No answer. What could've gone wrong? Was it the police? Had they started questioning Grant's youth followers?

There was a chirp behind me. I looked in my side mirror. Before I could locate a car, Wendy was rapping on the window. I rolled it down. "What are you sneaking up on me for?"

"Why are you sneaking off without saying goodbye?"

"I came to Fig. You were busy."

"I saw you leave. I thought you'd come back."

"I wasn't sure I could improve on our last goodbye."

"I should've kept driving then." Wendy offered a soft smile. "Now here we are. Pressure's on."

Finally, I spotted Newf's pickup coming from Ripley.

"Well." Wendy touched my shoulder.

"Well."

She leaned in and gave me a quick kiss. "You're missing a hell of a party."

It took a second to make the connection. The O'Shea's closing party. "I'm sure I am."

Newf was easing through the intersection now. Wendy followed my eyes. "I better be going." She stepped away.

"I'll be back," I told her. For the life of me, I don't know why.

Newf's truck pulled up beside her. She waved at him, glanced back at me, and walked out of my life. By the time I got out of the Chief, she was getting in her car, and Chloe was lugging a suitcase toward me. Wendy edged to the stop sign, then drove on for Ripley, hand out the window, fingers fluttering in the wind.

"You're late," I said as Newf came up beside his daughter.

"At the last minute, I thought you may have trouble at the border." He handed me an envelope. "An old man with a girl who isn't his daughter. An American and a Canadian. It might go easier with a letter from me." I hadn't even thought of it, but Newf was right. Now I was worried whether a letter would even do the trick.

Chloe had a suitcase and a handbag. It hardly seemed enough for as long a time as Newf hoped she'd be in the States. I wondered what exactly he'd told her and made a mental note not to raise the subject. When I opened the side door, climbed into the RV's living space, and reached down for Chloe to hand me her suitcase, she gave me this bewildered look.

"Honey..." Newf tried to jog her out of it. She stood there, unmoving. He took the suitcase from her and handed it up. "It's all a bit overwhelming this morning."

Looking at the way Chloe gaped into the Chief, though, I wondered. I got out again to say goodbye to Newf. "Here." He thrust a second envelope at me. "For the trip."

I could see as I took it there was money inside. A lot. "I don't need this much."

"Apparently, Grant never told you what shitty mileage this rattletrap gets."

I laughed. Over Newf's shoulder, Chloe flinched at Grant's name. That was the problem. She didn't know we were taking his RV. "There's no passenger door," I played dumb, as if confusion was why she hadn't gotten in. "You have to go through the living area and climb into your seat." Chloe crept toward the Chief.

"You have your passport?" Newf asked.

That snapped her out of it. "You've reminded me six times."

"Sorry." He came to her with open arms. She let him enfold her then hugged back fiercely. "Be good, Cocoa."

I walked to the driver's side. As I was getting into the RV, Newf approached me for the last time. I held out my hand. He hugged me instead. "You're a good friend. Sorry I forgot that."

We broke apart and nodded at each other. I climbed into the Chief, edged it up to 21, then waited for a gap to merge the lumbering RV into traffic. I got it up to speed, let out a deep breath, and broke the silence. "You weren't expecting to be driving this down to Florida, were you?"

"It feels like he's here," Chloe said.

"We can get an air freshener." We were passing the Point Clark turn-off. The Amberly Store was just ahead. I slowed to turn in.

"Where are you going?"

"They've got those trees that hang from the mirror."

"It doesn't matter," she insisted as I parked.

"You sure? I was going to get snacks too. We've got nearly three hours. Anything special you want?"

"Nothing." Chloe sank into the seat.

It wasn't until I was inside and saw the Beer Store sign that it struck me; that story Grant told about Chloe and her friends. How they tried to get him to buy beer, how they offered Chloe, and she laughed about it. No wonder she didn't want to stop. I grabbed a box of Smarties, two waters, and a blue cherry-scented Christmas tree, and got out of there as fast as I could.

Back on 21, I found myself struggling to break a long silence. After 10 agonizing miles, we came up on Port Albert. The road fell into a valley and spanned a high bridge that crossed the Nine Mile River. Below us, hidden among a scattering of trees, was a small cluster of mobile homes. They'd been there for years. My dad used to point them out when I was a kid.

"That's where my mom grew up," Chloe suddenly spoke.

"In Port Albert?" I seemed to recall Newf mentioning that.

"No, down there." She pointed to the mobile homes.

"You're kidding."

"What's wrong with that?"

"Nothing. It's just, what are the odds?"

"Somebody has to live there."

"True."

"She told me they used to dream of moving to Lucknow. Can you imagine? Lucknow." I looked over and smiled. She smiled back, timidly, but a smile, nonetheless.

"Not quite Vero Beach," I said.

She went back to looking out the window. Almost a breakthrough. We got to Goderich, through town, and onto the other side before either of us felt compelled to speak again.

"Do you mind if I open the Smarties?" Chloe asked.

"That's what they're there for."

She poured herself a handful of the M&M-like candies. "Sorry I've been so mean," she finally opened up. "I'm scared, that's all. I've never been to the States."

"It's not so different," I said, though I knew that wasn't true.

"Are there really as many guns as they say?"

"There are a lot of guns. You'll be in a beach town, though. That'll be fine." I had no basis for the claim. Hell, it was Florida.

"Everybody I know thinks Americans are loud and conceited."

"I guess we've earned that reputation," I said. "Americans are more arrogant; Canadians are more modest. You hear that all the time. With all the craziness going on in our country these days, you'd think we'd have a little humility."

I glanced over at Chloe. She seemed to be reading my face, like I was making some obscure point. "Maybe we need to be more sympathetic," she offered. "When you make so much out of your modesty, isn't that just another kind of arrogance?"

We were coming up to Troonorth, the golfing Eden that Carl Sinclair had built for Carrie over 50 years ago, and where he still lived. I didn't want to see it; I didn't want to know if its condition had gotten worse. But now, there was the barn, its white paint faded to grey, part of the red roof staved in. And now the driveway, the stick-made sign suspended above, the R gone so it announced "T_OONORTH." And there, the house itself, porch roof sagging, upstairs windows boarded up. And, at last, the little pond, with the gingerbread house on the island. The bridge out to it had collapsed. All the blades of the Dutch windmill had broken off.

"Why are you going so slow?"

Two cars roared past. I pulled onto the shoulder for another to pass. "I knew someone who lived there."

Chloe waited until I got back on the road. "Was it her?"

So…she knew about Carrie. Why wouldn't she? "Yes."

We were in Bayfield now, a tiny town my dad always pronounced the start (or end) of our vacation. That had more to do with the tourist traps to the south, the wait at the bridge, and the traffic in Michigan. Still, there was no denying Bayfield's charm; a picturesque marina packed with sailboats beside a winding river.

"Do you ever forget?" Chloe asked, as we rounded the bend out of town.

It hadn't occurred to me until then that she and I struggled with a similar demon. Both of us were to blame for someone we cared about being dead. My guilt was a sin of omission; letting Carrie drive. Chloe's was more direct. "No. You never do."

"That's what I'm afraid of."

"You learn to live with it." Did I even believe that? "If you have faith, it's easier," I recovered. That wasn't such bullshit.

"That's what I'm working on," she said.

We fell silent for the long stretch between Bayfield and Grand Bend, a good 20 miles. Chloe dozed off, mouth open, head pitching slowly forward, then snapping back. Working on faith…she was already way ahead of me.

Grand Bend came with little warning. One minute, farmland; the next, souvenir shops, boat rental stores, Subway, Tim Horton's, and the main intersection. I stopped there for a red light. Beside us was the Rod n' Gun bar. A crowd of tourists, bare-chested guys, bikini-clad girls, packed the patio. They raised their beers, and a cheer went up from my side of the road. More partiers were coming to join their friends. They were whooping, mugging for the traffic; drunken stragglers from a conquering army. The last of the troop saw Chloe and banged on the Chief's snub-nosed face.

"Hey babe!" He pawed at the windshield. Flat as the RV's front was, the guy came within arm's reach, and his head came up to the height of Chloe's lap. "Hey! Come party with us!"

Chloe hid her face. One of the guy's buddies tried to pull him away, but the crowd on the Rod n' Gun patio took up his call. "Come party! Come party!" they chanted.

The light turned green. The guy was still groping at the windshield. "Bring your dad, too," he shouted. The chant on the patio changed: "Bring your dad! Bring your dad!" There was honking behind me. Finally, the other stragglers dragged their friend away.

"Canadians can be A-holes too," Chloe said, as we rumbled through the intersection.

"Assholes are everywhere. That was me 35 years ago."

"Cam's not like that." I waited for her to say more, but she leaned back against the window and curled up in her seat.

We drove through a long shadowy corridor cut into forest, past The Pinery, the Provincial park where thousands came to camp. This was as far north as many American tourists came. Chloe dozed off again. She didn't stir until we were back out in open fields with the sunlight slanting into our windshield.

"Where are we?"

"Coming up on that army camp the Ojibwe took over."

Chloe sat up. "Grant said it was the other way around."

"I guess that's true."

The long stretch of wilderness that used to be Camp Ipperwash was on our right. Off in the distance, there was still a ridge of targets where soldiers had taken rifle practice. We came up on a cluster of dilapidated barracks that the Stony Point First Nation aboriginals had made their homes. Half were boarded up or smothered with creepers. Broken-down cars and garbage piles were scattered throughout the camp. Whoever was inside those barracks was likely living in squalor. But on their own terms, at least.

We turned off 21 at Kettle Point and got on Lambton 7, a quiet two-laner that hugged the coast all the way to Sarnia. We were an hour from Sombra. It was 11:00. We were going to be late.

"I'm going to give Cam a ring. We'll be closer to 12:30."

"I can text him," Chloe said. She leaned her forehead against the window, turning her shoulder from me the same way she had a handful of times already. I wondered: had she been texting Cam all along? "He's already there." Cam was never early. It wasn't on my account. He was excited to see Chloe. Did she feel the same way? I was running out of time to ask questions.

"So, how much does Cam know about…what happened with Grant?" I finally voiced what I'd been mulling over since Chloe said Cam wasn't like those partiers in Grand Bend.

Chloe seemed caught by surprise. "What do you mean?"

"I know he knows there was an accident. I just—I wondered— did he know…about you and Grant?"

Chloe caught her breath. "I haven't told him yet. Should I?"

"At lunch? No."

"Right," she said and let it drop. Something was getting left unsaid. I glanced over. Chloe was pinned against the window.

We were on the outskirts of Sarnia now. Farmland again, but more desolate than the fields around Boiler Beach. That had a lot to do with all the refineries and chemical plants in the region. This was what they called Chemical Valley, a 15-square-mile area into which 40 percent of Canada's petrochemical industry was packed. All around us, smokestacks belched out sickly clouds.

"Thank you for doing this," Chloe said, out of the blue. I didn't know what she meant at first. "I don't know that I would've gotten to America any other way."

"It's not a problem. I had to get away myself."

"What did *you* do?"

"Nothing. Just looking for a change." I couldn't help but think of the moment when I'd finally have to explain to Cam why I was in Ann Arbor.

We hit the Sombra dock almost perfectly. There was no line, we were the second to last vehicle onto the ferry, and the boat pushed off in minutes. It was a small, squarish vessel. I counted eight other cars in three rows. I'd been back and forth across the St. Clair on this ferry a dozen times, but none in the last nine years. I didn't remember it riding so low and unsteady in the water.

Chloe had other concerns. She fidgeted in her seat, started breathing hard, rifled through her handbag. "Where is it? Where *is* it?" she wailed, yanking tufts of clothing out of pocket after pocket.

Her passport. "You told your dad you packed it."

"Here it is," she cried out, waving it at me. We were halfway across the river. "What's going to happen when we get off?"

"They'll take your passport," I explained calmly. "They might ask where you live and where you were born. Then they'll want to know where you're going and for how long."

Chloe gave it some thought. Then she muttered, "Holyrood. Goderich. Florida. A year."

"Don't tell them a year!" Now I sounded panicked. "Just say— say you're going down for a month."

"And what will you say?"

"Don't worry about me." But suddenly I *was* worried. This was not going to go well; a middle-aged American man, a teenage Canadian girl, a far-fetched reason for driving to Florida. They were going to pull us over. No question. I took out the envelope Newf had given me. This would help, I thought, allowing myself a deep breath. Better read the letter so my story squared with Newf's. It was sealed. The ferry was churning into the Marine City dock. Another couple minutes and we'd be going through customs.

"Do you know what your dad wrote in this?"

"No."

"Shit."

"What's wrong?"

"Nothing. Just say what we said." I put the envelope back in my back pocket. I'd only use it as a last resort.

The ferry bumped the dock. They tied it up and dropped the gate. The cars in front of us started edging onto American soil. Just before we got off the ferry, we had to stop again. We were merging into a single lane, with traffic barricades on both sides. I looked up on the banks of the river. There, above us, was the patio deck of the Riviera, and leaning over the railing was Cam. He raised his hand and flattened his mouth. That was the extent of his excitement. He may as well have been the border guard, two cars ahead now, signaling us to stop. "There's Cam."

Chloe looked up, matched his faint grin, and gave a half wave of her own. We edged forward. The thought struck me: this may be the closest I'd come to a reunion with my son. We might not reach the Riviera. Now the woman officer in front of her partner was motioning us forward. Was it better or worse to get a woman? No time to wonder. I was rolling down my window.

"Passports," she ordered, all business. Chloe handed me hers, and I held the two out my window. She examined them, then peered up at me. "Are the two of you related?"

"No. Chloe's the daughter of a friend. I'm driving her to Florida for vacation."

The officer looked past me. "Miss?" Chloe leaned closer to me. "Do you know this man?"

"Yes," Chloe said with an edge of confusion.

"And you're with him by your own choice."

"Yes."

The officer's eyes darted from my eyes to Chloe's, mine to Chloe's. "And where did you say you're going?"

"I'm driving—"

"Not you. I want to hear her."

Chloe had that deer-in-the-headlights look of a kid who wasn't paying attention in class. "Uh…Florida?" Her answer came out with the lilt of a question.

"Where in Florida?"

"Vero Beach."

I put my hand to my mouth and let a huff of relief escape. The officer's eyes shifted to mine. We had a long stare-down. Then she retreated into her booth.

"Did I say something wrong?" Chloe whispered.

"You did fine." But now a new fear gripped me; this wasn't my vehicle. Was she checking the registration? How would I explain driving a dead man's RV? No time to think; here she came. She met me with a stern glare. I smiled. It was as flimsy as our story. She handed back the passports. I sensed a slight tug of resistance.

"Have a nice trip," she said and waved for the next car.

Just like that, we were in the U.S. I slapped my seat and burst out laughing, as giddy as I used to be when I'd smuggle joints across the border. Chloe was laughing too.

"We did it!" she roared. "I thought for sure we were dead."

"When she was going back and forth at us with those eyes, my heart was in my throat."

We turned left toward the restaurant. Both of us took deep breaths together. Then we laughed at that. Then we laughed that we were laughing together. We took another quick left into the Riviera's parking lot. I found a spot up close to the riverbank, shut off the Chief, and gave Chloe a smile. She was fidgeting again, rifling through her handbag, glancing around her seat.

"Looking for this?" I realized I'd been holding her passport.

"Oh. Almost forgot."

"What's wrong?" It wasn't the passport.

"I'm nervous, I guess. I haven't seen Cam in two years."

I understood the feeling. It had been almost that long for me, too. The last time the three of us were together was when I caught them messing around in the bedroom of my cottage. That seemed like ages ago, and hardly the scandal Newf and I made it out to be. Two young kids making out. Like we hadn't done that in our days.

"I haven't seen him, either. I hope he'll give me a chance." I started to get out of the Chief.

"Mr. McTavish?" Chloe said as I went to shut my door. She looked like she was ready to tell me something important. She probably knew exactly the sort of chance Cam would give me. She opened her mouth, moved her lips, but no words came out.

Cam was right inside the door when we walked into the Riviera. It was crowded; lunch time on Friday, the busiest day of weekend travel. Cam gave Chloe a quick hug, like they'd seen each other yesterday. Constant texting *would* beget a certain familiarity. But there was no substitute for physical immediacy. I'm sure my presence had something to do with the reserve.

"Dad," Cam said, extending his hand.

I opened my arms to him instead. He hesitated but finally suffered a quick hug. "That wasn't so bad, was it?"

Cam ignored the jab. "I got a table up by the window." He motioned us to follow. "We can watch the boats on the river."

Watching industrial activity on the St. Clair wasn't my idea of entertainment, but Cam seemed excited about it. He led us into the far corner, over by where we'd seen him on the deck. He pulled out a chair, for Chloe I assumed, but when she went to sit, he insisted it was my spot. "This is the best view." He and Chloe sat on the other side of the round top, facing into the restaurant. There was a moment of silence as we all looked at one and other.

"Well, isn't this nice?" I said to break the ice.

The waitress came seconds later. "Are we ready?"

Neither Chloe nor I had cracked the menu. Cam's was open, and his water was empty. "We need a little time," he said.

"More time," the waitress scowled. "Right." It dawned on me that Cam had been holding the table for over an hour.

"We can get drinks and appetizers. You want a beer, Cam?"

"You're not having one, are you?" He went straight to that.

"Of course not. I just like watching other people drink."

"Water's fine."

"No, it's not fine. This poor girl…" I spotted her name tag. "Meghan. She has tables to turn. You have Labatt Blue?"

"In the bottle." Meghan suddenly perked up.

"We'll take one of those. I'll have a coffee black. And Chloe?"

"A coke?" Chloe asked, looking at Cam.

"A coke," I repeated. "And two orders of fries."

Meghan left us with a little spring in her step. Cam slumped in his seat. "Were we going to get a chance?"

"We had to get the ball rolling. You can't monopolize a table during lunch rush. You've worked restaurants. You know that."

"I forgot my phone," Chloe announced suddenly.

"What do you need your phone for?"

"Jeez, Dad!"

This wasn't going the way I'd envisioned. I was being overbearing. What did I care if Chloe wanted her phone or Cam didn't want a beer? The point now was reconciling with my son, planting the seeds for reentering his life. I had an hour to do that.

I took out my keys and slid them across the table. "Sorry. I'm still a little edgy from our border drama."

Chloe hurried off. I regaled Cam with the story of our face-off with the customs agent. The drinks came. I toasted him with my coffee. He sipped his beer but didn't seem to enjoy it.

"You look good," I told him. And he did; brighter eyed, leaning forward now, jaw set, clean cut, an air of resolve.

"I feel good."

"And work? Going well?" The question seemed to stump him. "You said you were working at that fancy coffee shop."

"Oh yeah." Cam snapped out of it. "It's good. Really good."

"Full time now?"

"Yep."

"That's great to hear. Just...great." Then I couldn't think of what else to say. There had to be more. This would be the last time I'd see my son before showing up in Ann Arbor. Apologizing was a big part of it, sure, but I'd done so much apologizing over the years that it ceased to mean anything. How had I not taken the time to think this through?

"I wanted to tell you something," he spoke up, before I could figure it out. "I wanted you to know that...that I'm sorry."

"*You're* sorry?"

"For blaming you for my troubles," he said. Then: "For refusing to accept your apologies." Another pause. "For judging you when God says I condemn myself." Was he done now? "For any transgression I've committed or will commit to you."

"Okay. I think that covers it."

"Will you pray with me?"

I glanced at the tables around us. Nobody cared what we were doing. "Why not?"

Cam slid his hands across the table. When I took them, he closed his eyes, so I did too. "Dear Lord," he whispered, "Forgive us our failings, our brokenness, our faithlessness. We know that you are the way, the truth, and the life. And we pray that you give us the strength to commit ourselves to you." I went to pull my hands away. Cam squeezed them. "In Jesus's name. Amen."

Now I was able to free myself. I opened my eyes. Cam's were still closed, but they twitched like he was adjusting to some inner light. Finally, he made a circle of his mouth and blew out like he'd been holding in smoke. Then he opened his eyes with a beaming smile. "I'm glad we did that," he said, getting up from the table.

"Where are you going?"

"Gotta run to the bathroom." Cam turned to leave.

"Well, there's something I want to say, too."

He stopped a couple steps away. "Okay…"

"It can wait."

"No, go ahead."

Now he'd put me on the spot. I hadn't quite formulated what I wanted to say. What do you tell someone you've hurt so badly for so long that might start the healing? "I was just thinking. I was just—I was thinking…"

"You were thinking," Cam prompted.

"I was thinking how proud I am of you," I hurried out the words. Cam had nearly given up on me, drifting a few steps away. "And how much I love you," I remembered at the last second.

He stopped and gave me a soft smile, more sad, it seemed, than satisfied. "I love you too, Dad," he said. Then he headed off.

The fries came minutes later. Chloe still hadn't returned. I sampled a few. They were warm enough, barely. What was taking her so long? Maybe she was having trouble finding her phone. I got up and went through the door to the patio deck. I walked the length of the Riviera to the other side where the parking lot was. A partition separated me from a view of the lot, but when I leaned out past it, I could see the first row of cars along the bank. There was the front of the Chief. Now, craning my neck, the rest of it. And another car behind it, blocking in the RV. Was that Chloe in the front seat? And shutting the trunk…Cam?! Now hurrying to the driver's side. Now getting in—

I rushed back inside, around all the tables, and out the door. Cam was just coming up to Marine City's main drag. I stepped in front of his car. He hit his brakes, hard enough that Chloe pitched forward and snapped back. The bumper of the old Corolla tapped my shins. I braced myself with both hands on the hood.

"What the hell's going on?"

Cam leaned his head out. "I'm sorry, Dad. This is the only way. You would've never agreed to our being together."

"We need to talk. Just park the car and come inside."

"There's no need to talk. This is our decision." Cam looked over at Chloe. She was hiding her face in her hands.

"What am I going to tell your dad, Chloe?" She kept her face buried and shook her head. "You can't do this, Cam. You can't! Chloe's an illegal."

"It'll be fine. We're getting married. Please. Just move."

"No! You're *not* ready for this."

Cam eased off the brakes. The car pushed me into the sidewalk. I stretched my arms out against the hood. "It's going to be alright," he said. "God's in control."

Chloe pulled her hands away from her face. It was smeared with tears. Her eyes locked onto mine, wide and tender, prayerful. "Please, Mr. McTavish?"

"Come on, Dad. We love each other."

I dropped my forehead onto the hood, arms splayed out, a pathetic crucifixion. When I looked up again, Cam was wincing like a witness to my torture. "I'm moving to Ann Arbor," I told him. "I'm teaching again. I'll be there for you. I can help. Just… just… don't do this."

"We're not going to Ann Arbor," Cam said. "We're headed west. Making a new life."

"Where?"

"We'll let you know."

What could I do? Lie there and block his way forever? Why fight it? If I managed to get Chloe back and drive her to Florida, Cam would come for her sooner or later. Wouldn't it be better to give the two my blessing than to have them leave with condemnation? They didn't deserve to have my judgment hanging over their happiness. I pushed off the hood and stepped aside. Cam nosed up to the edge of the road.

"Thank you." Chloe pressed her hands together.

Cam leaned into view. "We're going to be okay," he insisted. Then he receded into shadow and turned onto the road north.

I didn't realize how many people I'd been holding up until Cam's car was gone. A group crept haltingly toward me from the other side of the parking entry, avoiding eye contact. A couple standing beside their running car looked away when I eyed them. And when I approached the crowd at the Riviera entrance, they got out of my way, like I'd infect them with a disease.

Back inside, our waitress was about to bus the table. "There you are," she said. "I thought you'd dined and dashed."

"Minus the dining."

"Same difference to me."

I reached into my pocket. There was the envelope of money Newf had given me. *Damn it all.* Cam and Chloe could've used this. It was probably more than the two had combined. And now, there was no way to get it to them. I pulled out five twenties. "Sorry for your trouble."

"That's way too much."

"Please. Take it."

She reached out slowly, as if I was ensnaring her in some sort of trap. Then she pulled the bills gently out of my hand. "Will your friends be back?"

"No."

"That beer's warm now. I can replace it. And the fries too."

"No need."

She bowed her head then hurried off. I tried my coffee; lukewarm. I ate a handful of fries; cold. Then I downed the warm beer in one big gulp.

What now? I sat in the Chief, pondering. No point in going to Ann Arbor anymore. And I couldn't go back to Boiler Beach. Too much depended on my absence: Audie's safety, Bruce's care, Chloe's freedom. And now that was more crucial than ever, with my son wedding his life to hers. I had to be gone—and stay gone. If the police concluded that Grant was killed, my disappearance would be tantamount to a confession.

Just—be—gone. What stopped me from ending this before? Blood relations. Cam. But he didn't need me; he had Chloe—and

God. Actually, he'd be better off with me gone. My whole estate, such as it was, would go him.

So how? Grant would've jumped off the harbor bridge and willed himself not to resurface. I thought of my last swim at Boiler Beach, when I panicked before finding Mammoth Rock. The instinct to live was so strong. Could I stay under? If that jack-knifed trailer had gone off the edge and taken the truck with it into the channel, could the driver have gotten out?

It would have to be late at night, so nobody saw. Then, as deep as it was in that dredged channel, no one would ever know. Five, 10 feet below the surface, the top of the Chief might be visible, looming like Mammoth Rock. But 20 feet down, with water as murky as it was, I'd be hidden forever. And wouldn't that be the right way to do this? Better to have people think I vanished, even if it was to avoid the police, than that I took my own life. How would Cam feel about that? Or Audie? Or Newf? Or Wendy?

Or God. It's a sin, they say, to take such matters into your own hands. But I wasn't killing myself so much as steering others away from danger, like Carrie had done to save me. Hers was a split-second decision; mine wasn't. But did that matter to God? Where was the line between impulse and intent that separated sacrifice from suicide?

What did it matter if I didn't have God? And even if I did, even if I could muster the faith I needed, maybe damnation was my fate regardless. I'd been doing penance for Carrie's death for 34 years; maybe I'd been building to this moment all along. Maybe this was the only way to stop suffering the anguish of being forever unforgiven. Maybe not. Maybe, like they said, asking for forgiveness was enough. If I believed. If I truly believed. If...

There was nothing left to do, nothing but to drive down that road by the harbormaster's hut, veer left before the boat ramp, and hit the water. But that couldn't happen for nine hours. Could I even get back into Canada? One thing was for sure; I couldn't take the ferry again. I'd have to get past the same agent who grilled me coming into the country. What would she think of my leaving an hour later, and without Chloe? Hell, I might not even be able to get across the bridge in Port Huron. My license plate was in the system now. Or rather, Grant's. My date of entry probably was there too, maybe even the reason for visiting. Was I trapped in the States now, until I could plausibly drive to Florida and back?

My phone rang. Audie. This wasn't the time. No time was time anymore. "I don't want you to worry," was the first thing she said.

"Then I won't."

"Rob came over and he wanted to take a look at the basement." I didn't speak. I willed myself not to. *Try not to speak. Try…*"He says the foundation needs to be replaced. He wants to do some repair work to get you through the summer. Then, this fall, he wants to lift the cottage off the foundation, and pour a completely new one…Tommy?"

"I don't know where the money's going to come from."

"Rob said he can do it for cheap."

"And where will you go when he does the work?"

"Sharon's here too. She told me I'm welcome to stay with them. You too." *Be quiet, McTavish. Stay quiet.* "Well?"

"Audie, I'm at the border now."

"You should've said so." What I should've done is not answer the call in the first place. I needed to get off before Audie told me something that made me care too much. "Rob's still here, checking the gully. He wants to know if it's okay to go ahead with repairs."

"Tell him, it's fine."

"O-kay," Audie drew it out. Then she lowered her voice. "He's got Bruce working with him."

"Well, that's good. Right?"

"Bruce seems a little…out of sorts."

There it was; the thing I didn't want to know. "He'll be fine. Rob's just trying to do something good."

"Yeah…"

"Don't worry, Audie. Everything's going to be okay."

"I know."

"I have to go now."

"Be safe, Tommy."

"I will. And don't worry so much."

She hung up. I brought up Google Maps. Ninety minutes to Ann Arbor. Six hours to Chicago. Thirty-six to Vancouver. I had to go somewhere for a couple days. Or…just take a chance and head back Canada. Two days of stewing over things and I might change my mind. I typed in "Bluewater Bridge." Half an hour away. I'd get there just after two. On a Friday, it might be a couple hours getting across. Four o'clock. Then two more hours to Kincardine. Six; way too early. I headed for Port Huron anyway. The hell with it. I might not even get across. And if I lucked out, I'd just take my time driving up the coast. There were places I'd never stopped before. Kettle Point where the Ojibwe lived. Bayfield. Goderich. I could kill six hours, easy.

On the way to Highway 94, I called Newf. "What the hell happened?" He'd already talked to Chloe.

"They had the whole thing planned. We got to the restaurant. Chloe said she forgot her phone. Cam went to the washroom. Next thing I knew, they were driving away. I tried to stop them, jumped in front of the car, but what could I do?"

"Not get out of the way," Newf answered.

"Then what? I take her to Florida. Cam shows up a day later. And it's the same story. They're going to do what they want to do, Newf. We can't stop them."

Newf huffed. "Aw, hell. We got Chloe out at least. That's the important thing. What they do now is up to them. Besides, Ann Arbor's not that far away."

Chloe hadn't told her father they were headed west. No point in my telling him either. "That's what I'm thinking."

"Just tell me Cam has a job."

"He's managing a very busy restaurant in town," I lied.

"Well, that's going to have to pay the bills." Newf said, "Chloe can't get a job in the States."

"Not until they're married."

"Married?" he boomed. "What?!"

"She didn't tell you that?"

"No." He went quiet. Then: "I guess that'll make us relatives."

"I guess it will," I agreed after a long silence.

It was worse than expected at the bridge. Traffic was backed up two miles onto the highway. I settled into line and inched along for 10 minutes before I remembered my dad's trick to avoid the gridlock. I worked my way back onto the highway, went one exit past the ramp for Canada, and rolled into downtown Port Huron. There was a duty-free store under the bridge that had its own ramp to the toll booths. You could drive through a security gate there and bypass the entire mess on the highway.

One catch: you had to buy something duty-free. No problem. A bottle of vodka would be just the cure for dead time. There was a half-gallon of Skyy on sale. No way I'd need that much. But what was the point of moderation now? I bought the bottle, wound my way up the store's ramp, and cut in line way ahead of where I would've been.

Still, we crawled over the bridge. On the Canadian side, there were 12 lanes, jammed 20, 30 deep, waiting to pass through inspection. It was already four o'clock. I veered into the far-left lane. My dad swore that was the best strategy. It didn't seem that way today. Cars were edging up to the other booths faster. It was nearly five before I stopped beside the inspection agent and handed him my passport. He tapped away on his computer, then peered up at a bank of small TVs. Cameras surrounded the Chief.

"So, Mr. McTavish, you're an American citizen?"

"Yes."

"And you're driving a Canadian vehicle. Why is that?"

"It's a friend's," I said. This was no place to lie. "I was headed down to Florida, and I couldn't take my car."

"So…he lent it to you," the agent filled in my logic, glancing at his monitor. "A Mr. Grant Rose."

Tell the truth, McTavish. "Yes, he owned it. But he passed away."

Another computer glance: "Oh? Recently?"

"A couple weeks ago."

"And you have his Winnebago."

"Yes. He didn't have any other family."

"Where are you going?"

"I'm headed to Kincardine. I own a cottage near there."

"How long were you in Florida?"

"I never went," I confessed. "When I got to Marine City this afternoon, I changed my mind, and decided to head home."

The agent's face scrunched up. "You took the Sombra ferry over this morning and now you're coming back on the bridge?"

I knew what he was thinking: why go out of my way? The truth would have to do. "I was trying to escape some problems at Boiler Beach. Now I'm deciding to face them."

"Boiler Beach?" the agent said. "My mom grew up in Pine River." I laughed. I couldn't help it. "Is that funny?" he bristled.

"There are—what?—three houses in Pine River."

"My grandpa owned the general store."

"No shit? We stopped there all the time on our way to Ripley."

"Ripley..." The agent smiled wistfully and stared off across the sea of waiting cars. Then he snapped out of it and handed back my passport. "Well, Mr. McTavish, aside from being an American driving a dead Canadian's vehicle into the U.S. one way and back out the other because you're having a hard time, is there anything else you'd like to declare?"

"Just this bottle of vodka." I showed him the duty-free receipt.

Now it was the agent's turn to laugh. "That'll make your time easier. Have a nice night. Don't miss that Boiler Beach sunset."

Just like that, I was back in Canada. By geography alone, it was a short passage. The span of a bridge. But it may as well have been admission into a gracious realm of absolution for how buoyant I suddenly felt. Hasn't Canada always been this for Americans?

I didn't crack open the Skyy until I was cruising down the long slope that led to Kettle Point. It was like Concession 8, only longer, and the cottages were small and unassuming, the way they once were on Boiler Beach. I lifted the bottle to my mouth. It was so bulky I had to use two hands and brace the steering wheel with my knees. But the road bottomed out and curved right. I set the bottle back on the passenger seat. Later...when I got to the kettles.

The road hugged a different shoreline than the sandy beach I knew. There were no cottages on the water side, just marshy fields that rolled into rock-strewn shallows extending so far into the lake the waves were breaking out near the horizon. If the boulders in the water were any indication, you could walk out a long way and still only be knee-deep. The road went on like this for a good two miles. Where were these kettles they were talking about? Were they those thousands of rocks scattered in the water? I came across two men walking back from the lake. They were indigenous. They stopped when they saw my RV and watched me pass.

Was I even allowed here? This was Ojibwe land, but I hadn't seen any "no trespassing" signs. Of course, there couldn't be, not on a provincial site, but maybe it was an unspoken rule. Further on, the road drew closer to the water. There was a wedge of mowed grass with three picnic tables and a small turn-off, rimmed with big round rocks. I pulled in and parked the Chief. I was going to take the Skyy with me on my walk, but I wasn't sure what I'd find over the rise. If this was sacred ground, I didn't want to offend anyone by drinking.

Everywhere I looked, there were boulders, huge globes, a graveyard of wrecking balls. Those *must* be the kettles. Even when I got to the water's edge and looked across the shallows, the stones were there, some bigger than the ones on land. I had my sandals on, so I could walk into the water. It was slippery, a bed of greased cannonballs. I made my way out to the nearest kettle, bent down and ran my hand over the surface. It was smooth and near-perfectly round, like it had been rolled by giant hands and placed there.

"Hey!"

I nearly fell back in the water. Three men were sloshing toward me, brandishing spears, or so I thought before I realized they were fishing poles.

"What are you doing?" asked the oldest of them, the one in the center. I recognized him immediately. It was Cecil, Grant's friend, who eulogized him.

"Looking for the kettles."

The three men came right up to within a fishing-pole length of me. "Sure you're not looking for a souvenir?" the youngest said, a long-haired wolfish teen.

"I don't even know what I'm looking for."

"You're Grant's friend." Cecil recognized me now.

"I heard you at the funeral."

Cecil turned to his comrades. "It's okay." They backed away, the teen making sure I gave his scowl due consideration.

"We get a lot of treasure hunters," Cecil explained. "The boys get a bit overeager. What brings you so far south?"

"I was driving by, and I'd never been here before. What are these kettles, anyway? Are they all the stones I see?"

"Not all." Cecil swept his hand along either side of the point. "But the round ones up and down this coast, even embedded into the shale walls down that way, they're the concretions."

"Concretions?"

"Grown-together rocks. Built up layer by layer. Quite rare."

"Why do they happen here?"

Cecil laughed. "That's a matter of scientific and spiritual debate. Which explanation do you want?"

"The spiritual one."

He grinned and motioned for me to follow. We walked back along the shoreline that I'd driven beside until we came to a gigantic kettle, nearly as tall as us. There was a crack right in the middle of it, pointing straight up at the sky and running along nearly the entire equator.

"Some call these concretions," Cecil told me. "Our ancestors called them eggs. And this one is about to hatch."

"Hatch? Hatch what?"

"Anishnaabeg legend has it that these shores are the nesting haven of thunderbirds. The kettles are their eggs."

"Big birds…"

"Flying across the sky," Cecil nodded, "Protecting us from evil spirits. They create thunderstorms with the flap of a wing, shoot lightning from their eyes. They fight serpents and heal tortured souls." He patted the crack. "And here is where they're born."

I laughed. I wasn't being disrespectful. It was a laugh of sudden wonder. A thunderbird egg, on the cusp of hatching.

"It sounds crazy. But that's what we believe."

"Do *you* believe it?"

He thought about it a moment, raised his chin, and scanned the shallows of kettles. "I believe in belief," he declared and punctuated it with a firm nod.

"And what do the scientists think?"

"Ah…" He raised a finger. Then he started sloshing through the water again. I caught up to him at the base of a ledge. The land was above our heads. The wall in front of us exposed dozens of stacked layers of shale. We rounded a bend, and there, stuck in the wall, was a kettle the size of a medicine ball. The shale swelled up and dipped down around it, unbroken, to accommodate the orb.

"This shows you what the scientists think," Cecil said. "They say the concretions are a sort of nature-made cement that formed from calcite and quartz around some nucleus—a fish tooth, a seed, an insect. That's as much of the science as I know, except that they recently discovered oil in these shale beds."

"Uh-oh." I knew what that meant: intrusion, exploitation, destruction. "You could use a thunderbird right about now." I was only half-joking.

Cecil laughed. "That's why I can't help but believe. We all need to hope against hope some time, don't we?" I mustered a noncommittal grin and looked up toward the parkland above us. "There's a shortcut back," Cecil said, sensing my urge to leave.

We climbed a pile of rocks stacked into steps and walked over the rise. When Cecil saw Grant's RV, he threw his arms out wide. "Ah…the Great Chief!" he proclaimed. "A lot of deep meditation went on in there. Treat it with care."

"I'll give it a good home," was the best I could come up with. We walked along a line of small kettles. Each had a letter spray-painted on it. "I see what you mean by vandals."

Cecil shook his head. "It's not outsiders doing that. That's First Nation. Some believe when a loved one dies, if you mark a thunderbird egg with their initial, they'll have eternal life."

I checked letters as I went along—an L, a W, an F, then a G. "Well, there's Grant's."

"I wish it were that easy. Sorry…but I forgot your name."

"Tommy." We were out at the turnoff now, facing each other in front of the Chief.

Cecil took a quick look around. "I don't see one for you."

"That's okay. Not every life should be eternal."

"What would Grant have to say about that?"

"You know Grant. He'd have a lot to say, and some of it might actually be true."

Cecil laughed and was still laughing after I got into the Chief. I left him standing by that kettle with the G on it, waving me away.

On the return ride, I kept my eye out for kettles. They were hiding everywhere in plain sight. I couldn't fathom how I missed them on the way in. And nearly every one had a letter painted on it. I was looking for one in particular. I found it about a mile down the road, where a narrow channel cut through the marsh into the shallows. There was a dented metal rowboat overturned on the bank among a handful of kettles. No one was around.

I pulled onto the shoulder and got out. The C on the egg beside the rowboat was spray-painted in red, and it had dripped into the gravel surrounding the stone. There was a crack on the lakeside of the egg. I took the Top-Flite #8 ball out of my pocket and wedged it as deeply into that crack as I could. *Go on: hatch.*

I took my first swig when I was back on 21, past the settlement at Camp Ipperwash. Then a couple more before I put the top back on the Skyy and tossed it on the passenger seat. Through the long, forested gauntlet of The Pinery, I was tempted to have another, but traffic was too heavy to take my eye off the road. Then it was gridlock in Grand Bend, lurching from one badly timed light to the next. Sneaking a swallow was out of the question. Oncoming drivers stared straight at me. Tourists streamed by on the sidewalks. And I'd already seen two OPP, one in a patrol car, the other directing traffic where that drunken partier harassed Chloe.

I didn't get through Grand Bend until eight. As I passed Tim Horton's, I realized I hadn't eaten since those cold fries at the Riviera. If it would've been on my side, I'd have gone in, but the thought of crossing two lanes of traffic to get there and back out was enough to dissuade me. Why eat anyway? Drinking, on the other hand… Clear-headed, water rising, darkness swallowing, the urge to live might overtake me. Better to dull the senses.

I grabbed the bottle and took a long draw in honor of my dad after I passed the Lake Huron Water Supply System building on the outskirts of town. When I was a boy, trusting and impressionable, he told me the building was where they made Lake Huron's water. For years, I believed it. Even after I knew the truth, he'd repeat the joke. And it came to be my joke, which I tried out on Cam when he was old enough to imagine yet young enough to believe. He bought the story for two seasons. Then, when I tried it a third time, Cam casually said, "You're full of shit, Dad."

I laughed all the way to St. Joseph thinking about that. I laughed so hard, I cried. Then I cried. How did I let my son find me out at such a young age? I was starting to feel the vodka, nothing impairing, nothing I couldn't handle. But that light, buzzing feel. That old friend, that charming demon. You'd be gone soon, too. Good riddance.

I kept the Skyy between my legs but forced myself not to take another draw until I was cruising into Bayfield. Eight-twenty now. Ah, Bayfield; where my dad finally allowed himself to be on vacation. I steered the Chief around the big bend by the village square and eased into the valley where the marina was. I opened the Skyy and took a swig. When I brought the bottle down, the Chief was heading for the bridge railing. I lurched left. A car was coming from the other way. I swerved back into my lane. Vodka splashed everywhere. I wrenched the wheel to avoid the railing again. There was scraping on the back-right side. Then I was headed straight.

I took a breath like I'd been holding it underwater, and slowed to a crawl, past the marina, up the hill, and all the way out of Bayfield. A line of cars raced past me. I pulled onto the shoulder. The bottle was still between my legs. It was half empty now, its contents spilled down my shirt and in my lap. The Chief reeked of alcohol; anyone who thinks vodka is odorless hasn't drenched themselves in it. This was no time to have a run-in with the OPP. I needed to change clothes. But not on the shoulder of 21 with all the weekend traffic. I wiped what I could off my clothes and the seat, then I capped the vodka, walked it back where I couldn't possibly reach it, and eased back on the road.

Troonorth took me by surprise. Maybe it was because that line of perfectly spaced, globed Dr. Seuss-like trees that used to mark the property's southern edge was no longer there. I was already past the pond with the gingerbread house, past the entry, and on the way to Goderich. I thought little of it at first, a fleeting curiosity for the old man, a twinge of regret that I'd never apologized. Then a voice in my head said: *why not do it now?* "Why *not* do it now?" I heard that voice argue without realizing it was coming through me.

I turned on a sideroad and drove between high cornstalks, until I was well away from 21. I parked, went to the back, and changed clothes. Wouldn't this be the last thing I ever wore? I put on some jeans and my favorite shirt, a beat-up Molson Canadian t-shirt I got for free at the Beer Store. Then I put on my jacket. Something was in the pocket. Grant's phone. I'd almost forgot. That would need to go to the bottom of the harbor with me.

By the time I drove under the broken T_OONORTH sign and parked in the weed-choked drive, it was nearly nine. The dying sun slanted through a line of birches that protected the house. Boards were missing along the floor of the wrap-around porch. I tried the doorbell. Nothing. Knocked. I stepped off the porch and went around toward the barn. Maybe there was another way in.

Just then, a raspy voice called, "Who's there?" By the time I got back around the corner, the door was shut. I knocked again. It cracked open. There was Carl Sinclair. I wouldn't have known him had I seen him anywhere else, except for those stunted arms. He was hunched so severely his face was near the doorknob. His hair was gone, and his cloudy eyes gazed out from dark, sunken sockets.

"Who are you?" he snipped at me.

"I'm Tommy McTavish."

He wobbled his head, struggling to get those foggy eyes to work. I didn't expect him to recognize my appearance, but surely the name would register. "Do I know you?"

"I knew Carrie," was as far as I took it.

Mr. Sinclair closed his eyes and worked his mouth. All that came out was the clack of him repeating the start of her name. *Cuh-Cuh-Cuh.* Finally, he shook his head. "I lose more every day."

Should I tell him that Carrie was his daughter? It didn't seem wise. Yet how else ask for forgiveness? "You knew her once," I said. "She was very dear to you."

Mr. Sinclair bobbed his head like he was looking for something at his feet. "Nurse Sarah comes in the mornings. Someone new is cleaning on Tuesday. Is it Tuesday?"

It had been a mistake to come. "Sorry to bother you. I just wanted to…to thank you for all you did for Carrie."

His dim eyes rolled around. Then, with surprising suddenness, he straightened, rising in the door's gap as tall as I remembered him. His withered fin-like hands wedged into the crack and swung the door open. He backed into the shadows.

"There *was* an angel who used to live here," he said.

I went inside. The place smelled of bad food and urine. Swirls of dust hung in the light that slanted through the front windows. "That was Carrie," I said, remembering her gravestone, where Mr. Sinclair had called her an angel.

His eyes twitched. His gnarled fingers fluttered in a kind of jumbled sign language. "I sent her away," he said, his voice rising.

"You sent her away?"

"I wanted to keep her to myself. But angels don't like that. They won't argue with you. They just leave one day."

"You didn't send her away. I took her."

"You *took* her?" He traced my outline with his milky eyes. "Will you bring her back?"

"No." I had to disappoint him. "She can't come back."

Mr. Sinclair leaned in toward me, arms retracted like a praying mantis. The sun was on his face. Suddenly, his eyes went wide, locking into focus. His mouth hung open. He recognized me.

"Are you God?" he asked.

"No," I said, stifling a laugh. He wasn't kidding.

"What did you say your name was?"

"Tommy."

"No. The other name."

"McTavish."

"That's not it," he said. "You're not a real person. I see the halo. You're an angel, like her, aren't you?"

I wasn't about to argue with a delirious old man. I came to apologize for taking Carrie. If he'd distorted that into a mad fantasy, my only chance of getting through was going along. "I am."

His eyes wandered from mine. He rolled his clawed hands together. "More powerful," he decided. "But darker."

"Not as powerful." Why I felt the need to debate the point was beyond me.

"But you said you took her…"

"It was an accident. I came here to tell you that. And to ask if you'd forgive me."

Mr. Sinclair stewed over that. I listened to the rasp of his breathing. "Do they let *you* see her anymore?"

"No."

Carl released a long wheezing sigh and wobbled toward me. "Then you're as sad as I am." He opened his crumpled arms. We hugged each other. I was stunned by how fiercely he clung to me, how strong the current of mercy was that came from him.

"Don't worry," he said after we broke away. "I'm not mad. It's a relief." A sob seized him. "To know she didn't leave because of me. To know you had to take her."

Now I was tearing up. Mr. Sinclair's hand flapped against my arm. "She was called for greater things, eh?"

"She was."

When I moved to the door, and he limped forward to see me out, the last long reach of sunlight touched his face. He closed his cloudy eyes and allowed himself to bask in the hazy beam. A kind of purifying serenity washed over him. He suddenly looked years younger, less haggard, heartier. I even saw in his expression a hint of Carrie. He opened his eyes, wide and clear, so clear it startled me. "Don't be afraid. She's at peace now."

I wasn't afraid, but I *was* rattled. I hadn't come there for comfort. I didn't expect that I'd be helping him exorcize his demons—

and he'd try to do the same for me. I'd come to accept a final punishment, to face the only living being who understood the wrath I
deserved and could weigh it against the depth of my remorse.

I came to feel right about dying.

The line of birches along 21 and the woods hiding the lake beyond looked like they were on fire. The whole sky was an
inferno of color. I didn't look back at the house until I was getting
into the Chief. And that was precisely when the front door closed.
I caught such a fleeting glimpse of Carrie's father that, if I didn't
know he was there, I would've thought my imagination had conjured him up.

Time check: 9:42. If I went straight to the harbor, I'd get there
around 10:30. Too early. I still had to wait somewhere. And it
couldn't be Kincardine; too big a risk that someone would recognize the Chief. I couldn't go anywhere near Boiler Beach, either.
Goderich was far enough away (and I was just rolling down its
main drag), but I didn't know the town well enough to pick a place
the cops didn't patrol. Fifteen miles later, I came to the old church
in Kingsbridge with its giant steeple. It hugged the road so closely
you could barely fit a car between the shoulder and the steps to its
doorway. There was an empty dirt lot beside it with a handful of
cars. Who would suspect anyone at a church? I parked facing out,
beside the end of the building where the altar was. Light filtered
through the stained-glass windows that ran the length of the chapel. Somebody was working late.

How had Carl Sinclair gotten so muddled that he couldn't even
remember his daughter's name? That he could only think of her as
an angel he chased away? Was this the fate of loved ones we lost—
that they should dissolve into no more than an idea? And what of
those who weren't loved, weren't remembered?

A man was standing at the side door, up toward the road, beside the square tower that vaulted five stories to the steeple. Had
he been there all along? He was in shadow, barely moving. Maybe
that was why I hadn't noticed him. But now that I did, it seemed
from the angle of his outline and the cock of his head, that he was

watching me. Was the chapel throwing that much light through my windshield? I looked over at the passenger seat. I could see the box of Smarties Chloe had finished off in the morning. When I looked back, the man was coming toward me. A backlit halo shone around his head, but his face wasn't getting any more visible. I couldn't tell if he was welcoming or not. I started up the Chief and drove past him with the lights off. He lifted a hand as I passed, either to wave me down or bless me on my way.

Now where? I came up on the Amberly Store. No way I could park there; I almost always saw someone I knew. I passed the store, then Concession 2 for Point Clark, then Concession 4 by the United Church. And that's when I figured out where I'd go. Concession 6 was the least travelled of the crossroads that slanted from the farmlands to Lake Huron. It was a single-lane dirt road from 21 to Lake Range, where it dropped to the dead end near Grant's old campsite; really just an access road for Ackert's fields. As kids, we used to hide away there—shoot off firecrackers, drink, get high, mess around. No one took that road at night.

I turned left off 21. The sideroad went from cracked pavement to dirt to ruts within seconds. Forty years ago, there was a cheese factory down this road. It burned to the ground, and they built the new Pine River Cheese plant out on 21. But the ghost of the original factory remained, its driveway barely passable through heaving concrete, the foundation pockmarked with weeds and surrounded by rubble. I navigated the driveway, rumbled over the concrete, and parked the Chief behind a stand of scraggly trees. When I turned the lights off, I just saw black. Then light from the slivered moon settled over everything. The fields rolled away, a single deep-blue expanse, shadows of isolated trees like hulking nomads.

I got out and walked across the factory's crumbling foundation. I had to relieve myself. Out among those eerie, outcast forms, so starkly exposed against the vast blue plain, I felt like one of them, the only one still moving, the last game piece on a landscape Audie might draw, looking for my place to rest. Off in the distance, the radio tower she had climbed kept blinking red. *Your move, McTavish. Your move.*

My last drink had come back in Bayfield, before I nearly plowed into the bridge. That and my encounter with Mr. Sinclair had scared me straight. Ten-forty…and 10 minutes from Kincardine. I could risk another snort. I was going to need it. I shuffled back to the Chief, climbed in, found the Skyy, and plopped down on the couch. It was half full. Most of what was gone had spilled out. I took a big swig and watched the night out the window. It was peaceful. Everything settled. The sky was mostly clear, but dark lonesome clouds shuffled past now and then, hiding then revealing the stars to the north, uncommonly brilliant behind the slow aerial procession.

I didn't register light bouncing inside the RV until I heard gravel kicking up on the road. A car was coming from the beach side. I wasn't worried. The Chief was tucked behind that stand of trees. They were probably just passing through to 21. But that's where I was wrong. The headlights swung across the Chief's windshield, and the car rumbled over the same cracked driveway I'd taken. I ducked down, crawled up front, and slid into the driver's seat. The car stopped in front of me, broadside and about two car lengths away. Then its lights went off.

It was my Lincoln Town Car.

A girl was in the passenger seat, her long blonde hair bright enough to glisten in the clarity of the evening. She was shaking it out, turned away from me. Then she was leaning into shadows, and two arms were enfolding her. It had to be Bruce. That sneaky little shit. *I can't drive, Mr. McTavish. I don't like to do what other kids do, Mrs. Garton.* And here he was. The girl's hair flattened against the window now. Her head tilted and wobbled. Kissing…

I took another drink. Why watch this? Bruce drove out here to be alone with this girl. *Let him be.* A kid in the throes of passion. I remember how that felt. The thrill. The mystery. I went on watching. The girl was sitting up now, turned toward the front of the car. I could see the side of her face, not distinctly, but enough to light a spark of recognition. Molly, the girl who argued so fiercely for God at Grant's youth gathering. The girl I thought was out of Bruce's league. She pulled her shirt over her head.

Jesus, what's wrong with me? This was the last thing I needed to be preoccupied with. Why were they out so late? Did Audie even know Bruce took my car? So much for having rules. How long had this been going on between him and Molly? She saved him a seat at the funeral. Now here they were, tilting back the passenger seat. A sadness overtook me. Never again would I feel that excitement, that wonder, the bloom of new love.

I turned on my brights. They could do this somewhere else. Molly gazed into the beam, eyes wide, arms across her chest. The Lincoln started up and lurched into reverse, bouncing down the fractured drive then wheeling around to aim toward the lake. The kid raced off down the narrow road, cutting a seam of light across the blue landscape. He handled my car like a champ. And now it was stopping again, turning slowly off the road, as slow as Bruce rounded the corner at Grant's hill. And now the lights were off.

Time to be done, time to take that lonely harbor road. After 11:00. Nearly all the bars in town would be closed and the streets empty. I eased the Chief back onto the dirt road. There were no headlights in either direction on 21. Everyone coming and going along the coast had gotten where they needed to be. I turned north. Within seconds, I came up to Concession 8, the road from Boiler Beach to Ripley. Full circle from the morning when Newf dropped Chloe off at the boarded-up Pine River store where my customs agent's mother had grown up. Full circle from the night I let Carrie roar down this road faster than she knew, then witnessed that split second when she decided to spare my life instead of hers. This was what I'd made of the faith she placed in me?

Too late. Concession 10, the northern border of Boiler Beach. Family Funland, where we raced go-karts. The Twelfth, heading to the RV park where I'd learned about Grant and Chloe. And now, Kincardine Avenue. I turned left and headed toward the lake. There was the town sign, with the wood-carved lighthouse in relief and the motto, "Where you're a stranger only once!"

Now I was turning onto Queen Street by the Hi-Way Variety where Carrie made a scene that day Grant and Joan tried to corrupt her on the couch right behind where I sat. The road was desolate. I puttered along, taking everything in, scouring my memory. There was the motel they used to call the Dickie Bird, which made my dad laugh so hard once, beer spouted from his nose. And that was the House of Mirrors, so named because it was covered with mirror chips embedded in the plaster. My mom never failed to point that out. I turned onto Gordon, the side street connecting Queen to Huron Terrace. Then I was on the road to the harbor, passing all the gaudy homes retirees had built along the bluff. There, just ahead, was my Wondermat. The sign still simply announced MAD TOMMY. It had stayed that way for days, as if the legion of phantom sign vandals had agreed that this was the final answer they were seeking, the last word on my life.

I turned left into the harbor and made a quick right onto that narrow dirt road that ran alongside the near row of moored boats, past the harbormaster's hut, to the channel. I was here. I parked the Chief on the road's incline, giving myself plenty of runway to launch off the three-foot drop and into the channel.

My phone rang. I glanced out of habit. No way I'd answer it.

"Wendy..."

"You answered!" she gushed. "I didn't think you would." She sounded tipsy, and there was music blaring in the background. The Tragically Hip. No surprise.

"Anybody else, and I wouldn't have."

"Where're y'now?" She was more than tipsy.

"Just driving."

"Well, you're missing one helluva party."

The O'Shea's closing party. "I figured you'd be done by now."

"Nope. Still raging. Helluva party. And you're missing it!" she moaned a drunken lament. "I wish you were here."

"I wish I was too."

"I miss you," her voice softened, barely audible over Gord Downie singing, "You are ahead by a century."

I wasn't going to say it back. Why aggravate the pain? But the truth was, I *did* miss her.

"Promise me you'll come back," Wendy said.

"I will." In a way, it was true.

"Promise."

"I promise." What harm was there in offering that hope?

"Well…it's a helluva party!" Wendy raised her voice. "Just not the same without you."

"How are you getting home tonight?"

"Don't you worry about me. Got it all figured out."

She fell silent. Gord Downie broke in again, singing something about the constellations revealing themselves a star at a time. Why was it the only other voice I could hear? I'd been in O'Shea's when it was hopping, and, small as it was, you could barely hear yourself think. How good a party could it be? "You going to be okay?"

"I'm good. I'm good!" she rallied. "It's a party!"

"Alright. I have to go. Take care of yourself, Wendy."

"You too, Tommy. You too…"

I grabbed the Skyy, got out of the Chief, and walked the route I'd drive into the channel. I could down the whole bottle now if I wanted. All I had to do was buckle in, start the RV, put it in drive, hit the gas, and go straight. Liquor would be helpful when I hit the water. Blunt that instinct to live.

When I got to the edge of the channel, I saw that I'd have to clear a strip of boulders that angled into the water. No problem with the speed I'd be going. I took a long swig. As I tilted my head back, my eyes traced up the Kincardine lighthouse. It was directly across the channel from me, on the opposite bank. The beacon swirled its red lights out past the far pier and into Lake Huron. The water in front of me shimmered with the beacon's glow, but not so brightly it would light up the Chief's splash. Or so I hoped.

Another pull on the Skyy. I wasn't quite ready yet. There was an old sidewalk off to my right that went under the bridge. I followed it, and as I came out of the shadows on the other side, the backside of town rose above me, its buildings lining the bluff, mostly dark, but lit enough that you could tell which store was which. And there was O'Shea's. I could hear music faintly playing; it had to be Wendy. Who else would be blasting out the Hip so late in this sleepy town?

I walked a little further around the bend of the Penetangore River that fed into the channel. Up on my side of the bank, I could just barely see the back of my Wondermat. Did anyone care that it was closed? MAD TOMMY. Were the rest of the letters still on the ground? What would be left? The S from TOMMYS. The WON, E, and R from WONDER. The T and that exclamation point. SWONERT! REST. REST MAD TOMMY. What else? W-O-N. REST NOW MAD TOMMY. Perfect.

The music suddenly seemed louder. Neil Young: *Now that you made yourself love me, do you think I can change it in a day?* Was Wendy all alone in her failed bar, blasting sad songs to an empty room? She didn't deserve for her dream to die this way, her success cannibalized, fame exploited, in bondage to butter tarts, of all things.

If only she could've gotten a break…a location by the harbor…a way to make as many tarts as people wanted without slaving over her oven…freedom to find out who she was…

WENDY. WENDYMART. WENDYSTART.

One more good swig, then I lobbed the Skyy bottle into the channel. Last drink forever. I walked back under the bridge and up the road to the Chief. I opened every window, buckled myself in, started up the RV and put it in drive, then twisted my wrists around the seat belt straps. I took a deep breath, let my foot off the brake, built up speed on the downslope, and punched it. The back of the Chief thumped and bounced as it bottomed out. Twenty, 25, halfway down the road, past the harbormaster's hut. Thirty. The channel in the headlights now. Closer.

Give yourself over. Give yourself. Give everything—
Wait. STOP! Please stop! PLEASE—

If I could only remember one moment of my life with absolute clarity, it would be that split second between when Wendy looked up from behind the bar and when she recognized me. The astonishment, the vulnerability, the elation. Then, instantly, tears.

"You came!" Wendy wailed. "You were gone, and then you came." She took me in like she was beholding a miracle. That was closer to the truth than she would ever know.

"I wanted to surprise you."

"You got me alright," she said, hurrying out from behind the bar. She hugged like she was never going to let go. And I hugged back, softer, like a rare gift. When we broke apart, I saw that the bar wasn't quite empty. There were two regulars at the short rail and a table of Wendy's biking friends in the back.

"Sorry I missed all the revelry."

"It was never much of a party. I just wanted you to miss me."

"It worked," I said.

She pulled out a stool. "I just gave last call. What do you want?"

"Nothing."

"That's not what it smells like."

"Yeah. It was a tough ride back. But I've had my last drink now. For good."

Wendy eyed me as she filled a pilsner from the tap. She'd heard it before. I could've told her why this time was different, but only doing it would persuade her.

"So, what happened to Florida?"

I told her about Cam taking Chloe away, being at a loss for where to go, almost not getting back across the border. I told her everything, except my aborted plans to move close to Cam...then to plunge into the harbor channel. By the time I got to the part where Cecil showed me the thunderbird eggs, the bar was empty. Wendy had made herself coffee and sobered up as she listened to me. I told my story exactly as it happened—the near-accident in Bayfield, visiting Carrie's father at Troonorth, the mystery watcher at Kingsbridge Church, the young lovers in the blue field.

"Why were you stopping so much?" I think she was offended I hadn't hurried back for her party.

"To sober up," I said. Then I changed the ending. "So, while I was sitting there at the old cheese factory, thinking how much I'd lost of Boiler Beach, of the life I thought I had, I got an idea."

"Sounds like one important one," Wendy said.

"It is."

"So?"

"So why don't I show you?"

After Wendy closed O'Shea's for good, I pointed the way up Queen, and we walked by all the dark shops to Harbour Street. Then we went down that narrow road, past the Aurora. There were still people up on the deck, their laughter echoing up from the quiet harbor. We were nearly past when Bogue's voice boomed out above us. "Aren't you the luckiest bum on the beach. I don't know how you got my brother to foot the bill for your foundation. If it were me, you'd be looking for a new home."

"Already got one," I said and hurried out of earshot. Wendy caught up with me by the lighthouse.

"What does *that* mean?"

"All part of the plan."

We crossed the bridge and came to the Wondermat. My sign still announced MAD TOMMY. I stopped in front of it, turned to Wendy, and waited.

"What?"

I took off all the letters, picked up the rest in the dirt, and started rearranging them. I put up the M's first. MMM. Then I stood back and looked at Wendy.

"Okay…"

The next line was WENDY O. That got a laugh. If Wendy could've seen the other letters, she would've gotten the ending. As I put the last word up, a letter at a time, she was still guessing. T, then A, then R. That's when she shouted out, "Tarts!"

I put up the last two letters, stepped back to her, and took in the sign. I still had an O in my hand. I saucered it to the ground. MMM WENDY O TARTS!

"*This* is your idea?"

I didn't expect her to appreciate the full meaning. "It's the perfect location, right across the harbor. You'll catch everyone before they ever set foot in town."

She smiled. But it didn't last. "It's a great place. I'll give you that. But I still can't make tarts fast enough."

"You don't have to."

"Who's going to do it?"

"Me."

Wendy leveled me with a suspicious scowl. "Why would you want to do that?"

"Because I can't think of anything I'd rather do."

"But why?"

"Because I love you, Wendy. I have for a long time."

"Tommy—"

"But for longer than that, I've lived with the belief that I'm not worthy of love. To the point where I almost didn't want to live with it." That was as close as I would come to a confession.

"Everyone's worthy of love," Wendy professed. "I've always loved you. You know that."

It was gratifying to hear, but I couldn't live just by the grace of Wendy's love. It wasn't fair to her. "What I decided," I said, "when I was on the other side of the border, wondering where to go, was that the only way I could love you was by serving. Giving everything," I recalled the offer from the serpent gatekeeper in my dream, "to get everything."

"What if that's not what I want?"

Then I was lost. That was the truth. But I couldn't put that on her. "Is there another way to give to you?"

Wendy walked out toward the road. I stood waiting. What if she said no? She came back, stopped in front of the sign, and tilted her head. "You know, if we turn the Ms over and use the other O, we could make it "Wow, mo Wendy tarts!"

"No."

"I thought you were supposed to serve me."

"That doesn't mean I have to indulge your bad ideas."

Wendy came close to me and leaned in. She found my eyes, waited, then gave me a tentative kiss. Then a longer one. Suddenly, red and blue lights were flashing. A siren yowled. An OPP patrol car fishtailed to a stop beside us. Blair burst out of the driver's side. When I turned to him, he threw his head back and groaned. "Shit! I finally catch someone screwing with your sign, and it's *you*?!"

"Sorry, Blair. We're changing the business strategy here."

Blair was doubled over, one hand up, hyperventilating. "Just a minute. Just give me a second here. You got the juices flowing."

"You going to be alright?" Wendy asked.

He straightened up and faced the sign, gathering his breath. "*The* butter tarts?"

"That's what we're thinking," I said.

"Yes," Blair nodded slowly. "Yes! So much better than old books and dirty clothes."

"Isn't it? Wendy jumped in. "He wouldn't listen to me." She gave me a sideways smirk. "But he's coming around."

"It really *is* better, Tommy." Blair said. "No offense."

"None taken."

Blair hitched up his gun belt. "Well, I don't suppose your sign troubles are going to go away. Then again, people *do* like you better, Wendy." He pinched the bill of his hat, tipped his head to her, and walked back to his car. Before he got there, he turned and said, "About that other matter, Tommy. It looks like we might have to talk to you again."

I put my hands in my jacket pockets and squeezed Grant's phone. "I'm around."

After he drove off, Wendy asked, "What other matter?"

"That's a long story."

"Should I be worried?"

I wondered that myself. Had Blair gotten to any of the youth ministry kids? Had he talked to Bruce? What did I tell him? *Do what you think is right.* Did this all depend on him now?

"Well?"

I smiled, ran my hand across her check, fingers through her hair. "You never need to worry again."

She leaned into my hand and closed her eyes. "I think I'll take you up on that ride now."

We were walking back across the harbor bridge. "I'll have to drive your car."

"Why?"

I pointed over the railing. "That's my RV stuck down there."

Wendy leaned over. The Chief was cockeyed at the end of that road where I skidded to a stop, one tire stuck in the boulders that shored up the retaining wall. The front passenger corner hung over the water.

We had been holding hands until then. Wendy let go and waited for me to face her. "What happened?"

"Another a long story."

"Now it all makes sense," she said. "You had a near-death experience and it scared you straight."

"Something like that."

Wendy looked out over the dark thicket of boat masts to the unbroken horizon of Lake Huron. The lighthouse loomed above us, whirling its red beam into the night sky. The channel ran directly below the bridge, straight out into the lake, and between the piers that Audie's giant gingerbread man once straddled. I felt like I was floating above the water. And only an hour ago, I was bracing to sink beneath it.

I thought of the gully by my cottage, and my ceaseless attempts to free that tiny stream there. Was that how this channel formed? Surely, there was someone who first tended this river and its journey to the lake—the Penetangore; Ojibwe for "river with sand on one side"; who worried when it got backed up, jumped its banks, broke out on a new course. And just as certainly, there were those who came after, the more ambitious ones, the Newfields and Gartons, with grander visions and a wealth of industry—tractors, ships, electricity, wind turbines, nuclear plants—who shaped the terrain, tamed the waters, and bent them to their will.

Of course, before all of this, there were the first people who came to these shores, those who knew this world wasn't theirs, who humbly accepted what the land and the lake and the heavens provided, and whose humble requests were made through fervent prayers to great spirits, fantastical birds, and other gods with no human form. Then, like the Ojibwe, came the Mennonites, and they had their own god, but they knew as well not to conquer the land with machinery, but to nurture it with reverence.

And today, even on the cultivated shores of a flourishing cottage community, there are those, like Grant and, in her own quiet way, Sharon, who carry on that prayer, who yearn to restore this hallowed place to the wild paradise it once was. Meanwhile, strong-er souls—the Carrie Sinclairs and Joan Duncans—rely on their own powers to escape, whether they're blessed or cursed with them. And the weakest of us? We end up raging against our lost lives, like Audie once did with her art, or surrendering to it alto-gether, like I nearly did to the channel below. Like I would've had Wendy not graced me with her love.

Grace and disgrace. Faith and faithlessness. Hope, despair. Innocence, guilt; all alive and dead, at the same time, in the same place, within the same being. I was still that little boy who sat in the sand and could fathom nothing beyond wonder; and that lost teen, convinced that he alone was to blame for ruining this para-dise; and an old man whose time had passed, waiting out a fear-some judgment; and now this blessed soul redeemed.

Hasn't it always been this way? That band of hunters all those millennia ago, who crossed that natural bridge to a new land, dreaming of abundance…was there not a moment when each of them looked at the rising water, that narrowing spit, and asked themselves, "How close is the end?" And even as that moment came, were their children not beholding those same waters, pool-ing in hidden coves, tumbling down rocky heights, and marveling at a world with infinite possibility?

And on and on, and all the way to now. And why not beyond? Why not look ahead and dream? Why not imagine a child again—Cam and Chloe's child—part-American, part-Canadian, sitting in the sand, guileless and free, even as these successions of genera-tions, living and dead, surround him, surrendering and surrendered to the gravity of this great forever falling world? Wave after wave after wave; cresting, crashing, reaching, returning, vanishing…

"You told Bogue you had a new home," Wendy finally broke the silence, as we watched the beacon swirl out into Lake Huron.

"I do."

"Where?"

I pointed down to the Chief. "Stuck in those boulders."

She laughed and nudged my shoulder. "When you get it out of there, you'll have to park it somewhere."

"Grant's campsite will do for now."

"And how are you going to get to work every day? You can't be driving that old beast back and forth to Point Clark."

"I can walk it. It's what? Three miles?"

Wendy shook her head. "Oh, no. If we're going to meet our goal of 100,000 butter tarts a year. I need you a lot closer."

"I thought it was 99,840."

"I'm a demanding master," she said. "You're going to have to park that thing in my backyard, so you can get to work early."

I straightened up and turned to Wendy. "What have I gotten myself into?"

"You have no idea." She reached out and ran her fingers across the grafted scar above my eye, that ancient mark of my shame. And then my face was in her hands, and she was kissing me. I stumbled back to the railing, put my arms around her, and kissed back properly. When we broke out of our embrace, I remembered Grant's phone. I let Wendy go on ahead, then took the phone out of my pocket, and tossed it over the railing.

Wendy turned back at just the wrong time. The royal-blue case fluttered in the swollen glow of the lighthouse beacon. Then it was swallowed up by the darkness of the channel. "Was that a bottle?"

I couldn't lie, but did I have to tell the absolute truth? "I said I was quitting drinking, and I meant it."

"And starting littering, evidently."

I held my hands out in surrender.

"At least it's glass," Wendy absolved me. "Twenty years from now, some beach glass collector will be very happy. You never find blue anymore."

I came up beside Wendy, and when we turned to go on our way, I put my arm around her, brought her close, and kissed her cheek. "True," I said. "So true."

EPILOGUE

KINCARDINE RECORD, September 3, 2018

Boy's beach discovery explodes myth of Aurora Quest

Fifteen-year-old Bruce Duncan was exploring the woods near the Aurora Quest boiler when he came across two scraps of metal that historians agree have exposed the enduring story of the famous shipwreck to be a hoax. Duncan, an American citizen from Wheaton, Illinois, spending the summer with friends at Boiler Beach, found two pieces of metal that experts have verified were removed with a blowtorch from the boiler located in the shallow waters off the shore of Lake Huron, three miles south of Kincardine. One of the pieces had lettering on it that indicated the boiler actually came from a Sawyer-Massey tractor produced between 1910 and 1915.

"It's definitely part of a Sawyer-Massey logo," said Paul Ackert, a local collector of antique tractors. "It comes from the tractor's smokebox. If a steam-powered tractor was going to explode, that's the part that would cause it."

After word of the discovery became widespread, there was another shocking revelation. Rob Garton, developer of the controversial Mariner's Vista Resort that has divided the Boiler Beach community, informed the *Kincardine Record* that his great grand-father was responsible for the tractor accident in the early days of the beach's founding. According to Garton, Bud Garton, one of the founders of Boiler Beach, was attempting to clear rocks from the lake when the tractor tipped over and exploded. The older Garton invented the story of the Aurora Quest sinking to avoid responsibility for the accident.

When asked why he hadn't come forward with the truth about the boiler's origin before, Rob Garton claimed that his great grand-father had told the story of the tractor to family members late in his life, but no one took him seriously. "My dad told us that Great Grampa Bud bragged about making up the Aurora Quest ship-wreck," said Garton. "Nobody believed him because he was losing his grip on reality at that point. Besides, he was always a question-able storyteller."

Garton, who owns the Aurora Quest restaurant with his broth-er Bo, conceded that his family has profited off the boiler hoax over the years. "I feel terrible about it," he said. "The least we can do is change the name of the restaurant. But we owe the commu-nity a lot more than that."

One major step that Garton said he plans to take is halting development of the Mariner's Vista Resort. "The more I thought about it," he said, "I just didn't feel right going forward with the project. A lot of it had to do with listening to neighbors, but I probably wouldn't have had a change of heart if this boiler situa-tion didn't come to light. My family has done a lot of good for the area, but I can't deny that we've exploited it as well.

"The lake, the beach, this land, it's all precious," Garton added. "I've spent a lot of my life making money off it. It's time to give something back."

To that point, Garton announced two initiatives he plans to undertake with local businessmen. First, the area that had been designated for the building of Mariner's Vista will be developed into a nature center, in cooperation with Holyrood farmer Gordon Newfield, who owns the land across from the property.

The second initiative Garton is pursuing has a more personal connection. "There used to be a store at the top of the hill that my wife Sharon's family owned," Garton explained. "It was a great place for kids. Every beacher my age remembers it. It's no secret that my dad encouraged Sharon's father to take some risks that didn't pan out. I thought one way of giving back is to rebuild that store, let today's kids experience a small part of what we had."

With the nature center planned for the property north of the Eighth Concession, Garton has purchased a parcel of Paul Ackert's land south of the Eighth to build the new store. Terms of the deal were not disclosed. Garton also indicated that he would devote part of the new store to selling local artwork, and has named Audie Bell as curator of the new gallery.

In another story related to the Aurora Quest, Boiler Beach Association President Larry Moore told the *Record* that the organization is launching a contest to rename the beach. "Now that we've learned that the boiler isn't in fact a boiler at all, and the origin of that wreckage on our shore is really an emblem of deceit, we have to make sure the name of our beach properly reflects what makes it so special," said Moore. "From now until the end of September, you can go to our website at boilerbeachcottagers.ca and submit a new name for the beach."

Young beacher Bruce Duncan, who discovered the metal tractor scraps, seemed bewildered by the improbable chain of events his discovery had triggered. "These last few weeks have been like a dream," Duncan said. "I can't believe this is really happening. I never thought such a small discovery would change so many lives."

AUTHOR'S NOTE

There is such a place as Boiler Beach. It's less than two miles south of the lighthouse in Kincardine, Ontario. As the cover photo shows, the boiler rests just off the shore of Lake Huron. Today, however, with the water level almost at its historic high, the boiler is nearly submerged. It's also worth clarifying that the boiler does, in fact, come from a ship. The Erie Belle exploded in 1883, attempting to free the stranded schooner J.N. Carter. The remains of the ship were dragged close to shore and disassembled, leaving the boiler about 25 feet offshore. Scavengers pulled the boiler closer to shore in an illegal attempt to salvage its metal but were thwarted.

While Boiler Beach is real, the beach community that serves as the setting for the novel is actually Bruce Beach, which is another two miles south. I have been spending summers there since 1963, when I was four years old. This year, 2020, was the first summer that I haven't been to Bruce Beach in 57 years. The COVID pandemic prevented Americans from crossing into Canada; otherwise, I would've faithfully taken my two-week rental at the beach—right next to where I envisioned Rob's glass palace.

While Boiler Beach is a work of fiction, plenty of beachers, Kincardinites, and Canadians can attest that certain people, places, and events have a basis in history. There *is* a ridge between Presque Isle, Michigan and Point Clark, Ontario that rose out of the water 9,000 years ago, effectively splitting Lake Huron in two. There *are*

Stony Point First Nation indigenous people south of Grand Bend; the Canadian Government *did* expropriate their land in 1942 to build a military training base; and there *was* a protest at the camp in 1993 where a protester was shot. There *was* a Canadian golfer named Moe Norman who Tiger Woods called the greatest ball striker ever. There *is* a Mennonite community near Holyrood, and the general store there does serve the best ice cream in the area (though it may soon be closing). There *did* used to be a bar in Kincardine called the Windsor that briefly featured strippers. Softball *is* a tradition at Bruce Beach; there *is* an annual North-South game (go North!); and there *was* a rightfielder who wouldn't budge to retrieve fly balls unless they were "cans of corn." (That would be my dad, Tom Tiernan, bless his soul.)

There is also a gully between cottages 97 and 98, and it has flooded out before, most recently days after I finished my first draft. And—I am *not* making this up—it took out the deck of cottage 98, which, ironically, is Bogue's cottage in the book, not Tommy's. This is clearly a case of life imitating art...and throwing in some karma to boot. (Apologies to the real owner of 98; I know how much trouble that drainage system has been over the years.)

Any kid who grew up at Bruce Beach also knows that the gazebo is real; I did, however, move it from its actual location on the bluff along the golf course to its deadly perch over the ravine that would flood out Tommy's cottage. Long-time beachers will recognize the name Nelson Buehlow as well. He *did* own the store at the top of the hill; he *did* have a deep, gravelly voice; and it no doubt *was* torture for him to painstakingly count out penny candy. I should also mention that the person who bought the store after Nelson Buehlow was Jack Daniels, not Jim Beam. But Jack is the reason I opted for a decidedly whisky-ish name.

One place that is *not* real is Wendy O'Shea's. I did, however, model the pub after an actual Kincardine watering hole. That would be the Hawg's Breath, which I hope will be in business after the pandemic. (I also hope, if the owner ever reads this, that she doesn't look at me funny next time I visit.) One year, after discovering the wonders of their pecan butter tarts, we did, in fact, show up at the back door before leaving for the summer and bought two dozen like we were consummating a drug deal. Their tarts are only half the inspiration for those described in the book. The other half comes from Evelyn Venner's tasty treats, which aren't as big as hockey pucks, but close. I should also thank Evelyn for her edits to ensure I got certain Canadian details right.

Only my close friends—those melded together to form the characters in the beach gang we follow through the novel—can tell you what is true and what isn't from their exploits. Yes, someone did make a legendary store run to salvage a dinner; it was David MacLennan, who tragically died in a boating accident in 1988, and was one of the big inspirations for the book. Yes, we were dumb enough to run off with Bruce Nuclear Power coveralls. And, yes, we did lie down in a field, arranged as a blossom of bodies, and marvel at the stars.

I'm sure many of those friends will see themselves in one or more of the characters. I intentionally mixed up personalities, circumstances, and relationships so I didn't cut too close to the bone. Still, I know when we're all finally able to get together again at Bruce Beach—as we did, in fact, promise to do every year back in 1976—I'll have some explaining to do. It will probably be around a bonfire. But we're a little too old now to be leaping over it.

Pete Tiernan, Bruce Beach, 1978
Photo Courtesy of Anne Bondy

Made in the USA
Monee, IL
22 May 2021